# FROM
# BUD
# TO
# BLOW

## BRIAN CONNOR

From Bud to Blow

Copyright @ 2017 by Brian Connor

Published by
Chicago Publishing
Chicago, IL

ISBN: 978-0-9984761-0-0
eISBN: 978-0-9984761-1-7

Cover and Interior Design: GKS Creative

Publisher's Cataloging-In-Publication Data
(Prepared by The Donohue Group, Inc.)

Names: Connor, Brian (Brian Patrick), 1991-
Title: From bud to blow / Brian Connor.
Description: Chicago, IL : Chicago Publishing, [2017]
Identifiers: ISBN 978-0-9984761-0-0 | ISBN 978-0-9984761-1-7 (ebook)
Subjects: LCSH: College students--Fiction. | College students--Drug use--Fiction. | Drug dealers--Fiction. | Gangs--Fiction. | Self-control--Fiction.
Classification: LCC PS3603.O566 F76 2017 (print) | LCC PS3603.O566 (ebook) | DDC 813/.6--dc23

This is for you, Mom and Dad.
Thanks for raising a middle-child that likes to make stuff up.
Ignore the bad words. You're too young for that stuff.

# ONE

**I WASN'T FOCUSED ON WHAT SHE WAS SAYING AT ALL.** Actually, I couldn't focus on what she was saying. Inside felt like a steam room, but no one else seemed to mind. I noticed myself rubbing my left elbow repeatedly. *How long have I been doing this?* I stopped rubbing my arm, but my elbow was now tingling. I could still feel the warm humid air coming from inside. *Man, I don't want to go back in there.* The music was still pretty loud outside by the pool, but I could at least hear other noises now apart from what seemed to be Swedish House Mafia on repeat. The fresh night air felt like medicine.

"Do you want to go back to the table?"

Brittney was gazing at me with this smile that seemed like it had been there for hours. Like this was the most fun she'd ever had and didn't want to waste it outside with me anymore. That constant grin with those unbelievable bluish-green eyes, I could stare at her for an entire night. She was the hottest girl in Vegas and it wasn't even close. Blonde hair, long legs, big boobs, but not obnoxious big, just, well, big boobs. She was wearing this tight blue dress that ended at her mid-thigh and had a little diamond slit showing some skin right under those big boobs. She was skinny where you want a girl to be skinny, but ultimately, she was just stunningly beautiful. I noticed my left thumb pressing down on the knuckle of my index finger really hard. I stopped doing it, but then my finger started tingling. *I can't stop moving my fingers!* I kept staring at her face trying to figure out what about her made her so beautiful. *What makes girls "good-looking"?*

It was her perfect skin, or maybe it was the fact she had no flaws. Nose was normal, eyes were symmetrical, cheeks weren't too round or too sharp. I continued to rub my hands together until my fingertips went numb. Rubbing my hands together made me feel better. I didn't know why, but I didn't care—it was helping. I really just couldn't stand still at all. I could feel my pulse in my temples. Standing there, I started to really focus on my breathing. *Is my breathing normal? What is normal breathing? Oh shit, I haven't responded to her question!*

"Oh, yeah, sure, that works," I said with as much bravado as I could muster.

I was lying straight through my teeth. I wanted nothing more in life than to sober up and not move a single inch closer to inside. *Wait, did that come out right?* "Oh, yeah, sure, that works." That works? *I never say that!*

I was so in my own head. I couldn't focus but yet felt the most focused I'd ever been. It was an internal focus. My mind was racing. It felt like my brain was overwhelmed by my senses. It wasn't like I had the spins, more like vertigo or something. There must have been about 500 people outside by the pool with us, and another 3,000 or so inside. *Does everyone out here feel woozy like this? Did all of these people take too much molly too? Is it too much molly, or is this just what rolling feels like?*

We started walking back inside. It was about two o'clock in the morning, but in Vegas time the night was still young. As we walked, I started to feel a little better. Like my brain had finally given up the fight and accepted the drugs. My senses were still heightened but not overwhelming. The music got louder the closer we got to the door, and I could feel my body start moving to the beat. My toes were squeezing down in rhythm with the song. *It has been a rough past 25 minutes, but maybe this ecstasy stuff isn't that bad.* I let out a little chuckle to myself as the bass felt heavier and heavier inside me. Brittney didn't notice the laugh, but really I wouldn't have cared. I started getting into my own little world with the EDM blaring.

"Thanks for coming outside with me, Cory. I was, well, was . . ."

"Freaking out a little bit?" I replied, reading the disappointment in her face.

"Yeah, the molly hit me like a brick wall all at once, and the dance floor was way too crowded. I felt claustrophobic for a bit."

*Wait, what?* She described exactly how I'd felt. Hit like a brick wall and claustrophobic. When I asked her if she wanted to go to the outside bar, I was saying that selfishly, but she must have thought that was me being nice and helping her out. *I can't even imagine what is going on inside her head. Hell, probably the exact same shit that's going on inside my head—a complete self-assessment of emotions, feelings, and senses.*

"No worries. The dance floor was pretty packed, and we would have had to cut around outside to get to our table anyway."

"Yeah, I guess you're right," she said in a deflated manner.

I could tell Brittney needed some reassurance. I was normally pretty good at thinking on my feet. I routinely put myself in other people's shoes as I talked to them and could tell what to say and when. In this instance, though, it wasn't too hard because I was currently in her shoes. Really, I was just thankful she was hanging out with me.

"Please, I couldn't have lasted another second in that pit. I think at one point I was physically touching 17 people."

Brittney let out a relieved laugh.

"Honestly! For a second there I don't even think my feet were touching the ground," Brittney replied.

"Besides, it's good to have a conversation with you where I'm not trying to lip-read and can actually hear you," I added with a smirk as I put my arm around her.

Brittney smiled as we walked inside.

I could see some of my friends in the VIP area. There must have been another 20 or so scattered around the club, because I only saw Joe, Cam, Kyle, and Bo talking with a group of random girls at our table.

"Excuse me, Mr. Carter, do you need anything else at your table?" the waitress said as we walked over the rope.

I scanned our three tables to see what we needed. My friends had destroyed all of the booze I'd ordered before I embarked on this dance-floor/fresh-air mission.

"Yeah, how about another six bottles of Goose . . . Oh, and can we clear off this table?" I said, pointing to the table Wolf had been standing on.

Brittney handed the waitress her credit card as she walked away.

"And one bottle of champagne." She glanced over at me and shrugged. "I owe you . . . Mr. Carter," she uttered, mocking the waitress.

Brittney started walking toward the two bouncers at the far table as I got situated next to Bo at the front table near the railing. XS was a big semicircle club. The DJ stage was at the flat part of the circle with a massive dance floor in front of it, and then elevated a couple of feet around the dance floor were the bottle-service tables, and finally the bars were around the outside. We had the three tables on the left side of the club. It was probably the best area since it was closest to the stage, elevated over the dance floor, with direct access to the outside bar/pool area.

"Casino. Bottle service. Smokeshow. Going for the hat trick, huh?" Bo shouted as I walked up to him.

He looked like a mess, but hell, when didn't he. About 6 feet tall, 250 pounds, and constantly dripping sweat. He was one of those constant hat-wearing guys who looked strange without one.

"Yeah, she's a pretty cool chick," I replied.

"Cool chick? Dude, quit being a limp dick and close already. OK?"

The lights went dim and the crowd started to cheer. Tiesto had walked up on stage. Brittney came toward me with two glasses in her left hand and the bottle of champagne in her right. It was still surreal that this girl actually liked me, or at least seemed to.

As Tiesto started his set, the molly was making a comeback. It was almost like the sounds and lights had formed some combination with the drugs inside me to jump-start my high. I started to panic that the paranoia was coming back, but this time, the feeling was different. The overwhelmed feeling from before had turned into this sensation of happiness. My head was bouncing up and down involuntarily to every minuscule beat. The whole night started to feel like some famous event that I was witnessing with thousands of other people.

The dance floor was like one mass of people jumping up and down in unison. Brittney put her arm around me and smiled. Her pupils were triple the size I remembered, but her eyes were still striking. There was no point trying to speak to each other, but I could tell she felt the exact same way I was feeling. The molly high made you feel like everyone around you felt the same way as you did. *Maybe that's not a molly feeling and just a me feeling.* Before, the club felt like there was this tension or like it was some anxiety-filled room of tweakers, but now, that sensation was sheer bliss.

Brittney looked at me, then down at the champagne bottle, then back at me. As I reached out to grab the bottle, she smirked and winked. Next thing I knew she was popping the bottle of champagne and spraying it all over the dance floor. I was never a fan of this move, especially from a chick. Whenever I saw this move in a video or at a bar, it always bothered me. Why would you buy a bottle of champagne purely to get random people soaking wet? And if you didn't even buy the bottle, then you are just wasting someone else's booze. But for some reason, in this setting, I understood it. The lights reflected off the champagne like a kaleidoscope. The club erupted in cheers as the dance floor people below raised their arms and embraced the rain of champagne. Or at least it seemed like they embraced it. Hell, I embraced it. I loved it. But I was also remarkably high on ecstasy and not getting wet, so who knows.

I grabbed Brittney and turned toward her. Without a second of hesitation, we started making out. Her lips were warmer and smoother than I had ever felt before. We were in our own little bubble as a thousand people continued to party around us. Eyes closed with the bass filling my body as I made out with the one and only untouchable, mysterious, blonde rocket of Indiana University. *I've come a long way in two and half years.*

We stopped and stared at each other, smiling. Behind Brittney, I made eye contact with Cutty and Garcia, both pointing at me and shaking their heads in disbelief. Garcia had his glass held in the air like he was giving me a toast. We both turned toward the show and kept dancing. I could tell Garcia and Cutty were still staring at me, so I glanced over and raised my glass to them. *Cheers.*

Brittney and I continued to dance at the railing for about an hour, taking in the show and the night. Our table must have gone through 20 bottles of booze, and people were standing on any elevated surface they could find. Top of the couch, seat of the couch, tables, everything.

"I'm staying at this hotel, if you want to head to my room."

It took me all of zero seconds to comprehend the comment.

"Yeah, let's get out of here," I replied.

It was about four o'clock in the morning now, but the place was still packed. I turned toward Bo, and he knew exactly what I was going to say.

"I got it. I'll see you in the morning," Bo said with a grin.

Bo and I had gotten a couple hundred bucks from our crew earlier in the night, but we knew we would practically split the whole tab between us. That was the deal when we decided to come to Vegas. Besides, we had gotten pretty good at it. Bo was normally the drunker one at the party, and I was the king at the Irish good-bye, but we always split the tab down the middle. Most of the time, I would pay the tab as I snuck out of the bar and he would pay me in the morning. Things had changed a little in the past few months, and were going to change drastically moving forward, but for now, our money was still coming from the same place anyway. He knew I would pay him in the morning.

Brittney and I walked down a couple steps and went outside.

"That was incredible," Brittney said, pulling her hair back into a ponytail.

"Couldn't agree more. Loved the setup we had," I replied.

"I don't even feel that tired either," she added with a smile.

*I'm in love with this chick.*

"Yeah, I'll probably be feeling it tomorrow, but I feel pretty great now."

We walked past the outdoor pools and cut through the casino.

"Black or red?" I asked, pointing to an open roulette wheel.

"Oh, black for sure," she said without missing a beat.

"You're on."

I pulled out two $5 chips I had saved in my pocket for this exact moment.

"Winner keeps it all," I announced as I put one chip on red and one on black.

Brittney looked at me laughing.

"You're on," she replied, mimicking me.

"If I win, I'm going to buy you a new dress that doesn't have a rip in it," I said, pointing to the diamond slit in her dress.

"Oh, OK. If I win, I'm going to buy you a cab home."

We both stood there laughing as the wheel spun around. Brittney slowly put her right hand on top of my hand on the table.

Red.

"Looks like someone gets to stay," I joked as I picked up the $10 in chips.

"The night is young—you still have time to screw it up."

"Can't wait to see you in your new $10 dress."

"But you never got to see the entire outfit," she mumbled as she displayed her body like Vanna White.

"The night is young," I replied, mimicking her.

She laughed, shaking her head as she wrapped her arms around me like she was fake-tackling me. *Holy shit, the stupid $5 chips move worked!*

We got in the elevator and went up to her room. The room at the Encore was a high-level penthouse suite overlooking the Strip. The front room had 15-foot ceilings with a staircase going up to a lofted area above. *Who the fuck is this chick?* Without wasting any time, Brittney grabbed me and we started making out as we made our way to the bedroom.

The lights from the Strip illuminated the room. Yellow, blue, and red swirling lights reflected off her tan skin and revealed what I had imagined. Her body was flawless. There were no surprises. She ran her fingers down my chest and abs and over my tattoo on my ribcage before gazing into my eyes.

———

My head was in a daze. All my troubles I came to Vegas to escape had disappeared. I had no idea what time it was. It was still dark outside, but I didn't really care. I had just banged the legendary blonde from IU. Brittney had fallen asleep already, so I got up and walked toward the window. I couldn't really comprehend the moment. Trip to Vegas with my best friends, VIP bottle service at a Tiesto show, staying in a casino suite overlooking the Strip, and ending the night by hooking up with quite literally the hottest chick I'd ever seen. And all of this just to escape from what seemed like the end of my life. It was bizarre how much shit had changed since Bo and I started dealing. I was going to miss the lifestyle, but it was a hell of a run while it lasted.

I was woken up by some voices in the main room of the suite. Brittney wasn't in bed anymore, but the voices were male voices anyway. I rolled over and looked at the hotel clock. 9:35 a.m. My best guess was that I'd slept for three and half hours, tops.

"I said I would talk to him—why the fuck would you come here?" I faintly heard Brittney yell from the other room.

*Who is she yelling at? Who did she need to talk to? Me?*

I got out of bed and found my black jeans on the floor. The hangover I had was something I had never experienced. I was surprisingly alert, like I had already had a morning coffee, but was in a brainless daze. Basically like my brain was a step slower than the rest of my body. *Must be the molly hangover.*

I put my jeans on and walked into the bathroom, not even considering what was happening outside the bedroom door to be an issue. After I pissed, I looked into the mirror. No shirt, black jeans on, hair a mess. As I glanced down at my new tattoo on my ribcage, it dawned on me. *I don't really know Brittney at all. Is that her boyfriend outside?* I hurried to grab my shirt but had already made too much noise. I opened the door into the main hotel room, and my heart dropped as I saw Bo sitting with two massive dudes standing behind him.

"Rise and shine, Mr. Carter."

*How does this dude know me?* I looked across the room from Bo to see Brittney standing next to some strange 35-year-old man in a dark grey sport coat. About 6 feet tall, 200 pounds, black hair, tan skin, pretty much your average, most likely half-Italian, male. I realized right away that the two guys behind Bo were the bouncers from the club. Or at least, the two guys I thought were bouncers. *Did Bo not pay the bill after I left? No wait, my credit card was used to hold the tables.*

"Who the fuck are you?" I said to the grey sport-coat guy.

My brain was operating at around 60 percent, so it took me a second, but then everything came back to me. *Fuck me, the cops found me!*

"I'm the guy who's going to let you keep living this life," the sport-coat man replied, pointing to the hotel suite.

I looked over at Brittney for some sort of explanation, but she was staring down ashamed, not making eye contact with anyone.

"Look, can we just cut the small talk. Are you guys the cops or something?"

The man and two bouncers started laughing.

"Bo, how about you enlighten your friend why we are here."

I couldn't really pin things together. I kept thinking of Brittney's line from earlier: "I said I would talk to him, why the fuck would you come here." *What does she mean? Am I who she is supposed to talk to?* My headache wasn't making the situation any better, but as I turned toward Bo, everything started to click. Getting the bottle-service tables so easily, getting the drugs so easily, Brittney knowing I would be at the club, paying for her own champagne bottle, talking to the two bouncer-looking dudes, this penthouse suite, knowing Bo and I worked together. I must have been so caught up in this chick that I ignored the obvious signs. *I'm such an idiot.* This was the guy. This was who Campbell was after. The real drug kingpin.

I turned toward Bo, but I already knew what he was going to say.

"Cory, they need one of us to keep dealing."

# TWO

MY MOM WAS FAKE CRYING, I COULD TELL. Third child off to college, second boy, there was no chance she was that upset. But I appreciated the effort nonetheless. My parents were both 53 but acted more like 43. They were the fun parents. Not the I'll-buy-booze-for-my-underage-kids-and-smoke-pot-with-them cool, just, well, cool parents. They punished me if I was being a dick growing up, but gave me a little benefit of the doubt in high school when they knew I was more than likely partying.

My cousin Mikey was with my dad helping me with some of my bags. All my shit was in garbage bags, so it wasn't too tough. Mike was barely working though. He was only there to get $20 or $40 from my dad for his "help." He was a junior at IU and looked a lot like me, only bigger. 6'2", 220, black hair, green eyes. He was a former defensive tackle at this powerhouse high school in Michigan, but had slimmed down substantially since then. After my uncle left a couple years ago, Mikey and my Aunt Mary moved back to Chicago, and ever since he's practically been a part of our family. *But clearly not enough of the family to be required to put in any effort helping me move.*

"Have you met your roommate yet?" Mikey asked, carrying two pillows.

"You're pathetic. But no, we talked on the phone last week. He's moving in next week."

I did a random roommate. He was a kid from NYC. Searched him up on Facebook when I found out his name; super Jewish. Not just because his name was Bennett Schwartz, or because he was from Long Island, but because his old man was wearing a yarmulke in every picture I saw. That didn't bother me at all though. I was pretty liberal when it came to people. Didn't matter if you were Jewish, Catholic, black, white, whatever—if you were an asshole, you were an asshole. I didn't want to have Max as my roommate, and the feeling was mutual. We were good friends in high school, but more we-hung-out-with-the-same-people friends rather than real friends. I wanted to do a random roommate simply for the experience.

My mom's college roommate was her best friend from high school, so she didn't count, but my dad's random roommate became his best man, and my older brother Tommy had some low-key California bro who loved smoking pot and playing golf. Granted, Tommy was six years older, so I never personally met the dude, but for all intents and purposes he seemed legit. On the other hand, my older sister had some neurotic bulimic chick who would throw up into Ziploc bags. Not even kidding—this broad would throw up into Ziploc bags then toss them in the garbage so people down the hall wouldn't hear her throwing up in the public bathrooms every day. My sis told me she would always eat a ton but also worked out a ton, so she never really thought anything of her being so skinny. Until one day she went into the bathroom and found three Ziploc bags full of throw up in the bathroom garbage can. Two weeks later, she found the same bags in her dorm garbage. Strangest part, this chick seemed cool when I went to visit Wisconsin last year, but fuck, she must have had a bunch of skeletons in her closet. But whatever. Four family members, three went random roommates, two perfect matches and then a fun girl who happened to be a lunatic. I liked my odds.

None of my other friends were going to IU with me, and honestly, I didn't really care if I was buddy-buddy with my freshman-year roommate. I knew I would be joining a house, so would be living there sophomore/junior year anyway. Most fraternities at IU had about 50 to 75 people living in, with another 50 to 100 scattered around campus. That was plenty of friends for me.

"Alright, Cory, I think that's everything."

"Thanks for your help, Pops, and thanks for dinner last night."

"You only move out of the house once, right? Well, let's hope this is the last time you move out."

"Oh, shut up Rich! Cory, you can come home whenever you want."

"Thanks Mom."

"Here, Mikey, take Cory to dinner tonight."

My dad handed Mikey a $100 bill as we gave our hugs good-bye. My family wasn't necessarily well off, but I would say we lived comfortably. Both parents worked, even when I was growing up, and certainly weren't the shell-out-100-bucks-often parents, so seeing the Benjamin took both of us by surprise. Mikey and I waved good-bye as my mom and dad got into the car and drove off.

"You know there is beyond zero chance you get any of this, right?"

"Yup. Well aware."

"Welcome to college, cuz," Mikey said as he slapped my back and walked away.

I knew the food courts were open, so wasn't too worried about dinner. I was also going over to Mikey's frat for a party that night with Max and his roommate, so couldn't really cry bully either. One hundred bucks to a college kid was like an amazing two weeks' worth of activities. We both understood that.

I walked into my dorm and looked around. It was a standard dorm room. Wood bunk beds on the right wall next to the one wood dresser, with the two wood desks in the back by the windows, with two wood closets on the left wall by the wood front door. I picked bottom bunk, because, well, bottom bunk was 1,000 times better. Top-bunk people had no logical thought process or were just insane. Climbing up and down from your bed every night and morning sounded like a legitimate punishment. Rolling out of bed in itself was tough, let alone having to jump down or climb stairs.

I took out my laptop and plugged it into the Ethernet cord at my desk. *I'll deal with Wi-Fi later.* Emily and I had planned to Skype around five o'clock, but it took me a little longer to move in.

"Hola señorita, how's the new place?"

"Hey Cor! It's really cool, actually. Ashley moved in yesterday, so the place is pretty dirty, but check it out."

Emily moved her screen so I could see behind her. Her walls were white-painted stone, and both beds were connected and lofted in the corner of the room. *Two top bunks next to each other? Miserable.* But underneath the beds were nice dressers and enough room to put a laundry basket or other college junk. She turned the screen, and on the TV side of the room were two desks and a mini-hallway with what seemed like two closets.

"Holy shit, that's like an apartment."

"We don't have a bathroom though."

"You say that like you were expecting one."

"Ugh, I know. But Ashley said she thought most dorm rooms at Vanderbilt had one. Let me see your room. Has Bennett moved in yet?"

"No, not yet, but not much to see here," I said as I moved away from the computer.

Didn't even need to show her around. You could see the entire dorm from my desk.

"Yikes. Sorry, babe, little cramped in there. What are we going to do when I come visit?"

"Cuddle up in a twin bed. You know, 'cause I'm so good at that."

"The worst."

"What's your plan tonight?"

"I think Ashley is going to bring me to her friend's apartment. It's her friend from high school who is a year older than us. But then I'm not sure."

"Oh, right. I keep forgetting she's from there."

"Yeah, her high school is 20 minutes south of Nashville. Are you still going to Mikey's tonight?"

"That's the plan. I was going to pregame in Max's dorm with his room-mate and then Jessica, Sara, and Lauren."

"Who's Sara?"

"Lauren's roommate, sorry. She went to RWN."

"Oh, OK."

Emily and I had Skyped for about 30 to 35 minutes when Max texted me asking to go to dinner. It was about seven o'clock and I was starving.

"Alright, well, I'm going to go grab some dinner with Max. Text me later and let me know your plan, OK?"

Emily started to tear up. I knew this was going to be really hard for her. Long distance was going to suck. Vanderbilt was about a four-hour drive away from Indiana, so at least not a flight distance away, but it still was going to suck. I knew she would never cheat on me. Or at least that's what I told myself. She wasn't that type of person. She was honest and too nice to do something like that. She was harmless. I was a little more deceiving than her, but that's just called being a male. Regardless, I would never cheat on her either. She may not have fully believed me, but honestly, I wasn't really a ladies' man. There was about a one-to-two-year stint in high school where I did well for myself, but besides that, I was your average hitter at the plate. When I met Em, I was more of a flirt, but when your sister is only a year older, you tend to hit on her friends growing up. *Sue me.* I was optimistic our relationship would work, but that was my perspective.

There was a knock at the door. I knew it was Max. *Dammit! Ten seconds too early.*

"OK, well, I guess you have to go. I love you. Please have your phone tonight. OK?"

"Always do, I love you too, Em. Adios."

I shut my MacBook and went to the door.

"Hello classmate," Jessica said, smiling, standing next to Sara and Lauren.

"Why hello stalkers, fancy seeing you here."

"Max told us to meet him at your room. We thought we'd tag along for dinner number one in the food court."

"Sounds wonderful, as long as you sit at your own table. Trying to pick up some freshman tail tonight. Am I right?" I said as I stuck out my fist to give Lauren a pound.

"Oh, fuck off," Lauren responded as both Sara and Jessica giggled.

Lauren played softball in high school, so we always gave her shit for being a lesbian. It wasn't mean, though, because Lauren was hot. If she were ugly, or fat, or too muscular, or well, a dike, then the joke would be mean. She also ran with the joke, which helped.

We saw Max down the hallway and walked together to the food court across the street. It had Italian, Mexican, Chinese, a salad bar with soups, and a grill that could make any sandwich or burger. It felt a lot like a mall food court, but it was free, or at least free for me, so I couldn't complain.

"Hey CC, have you met Sara yet?"

"Not really, sorry, hi, I'm Cory."

"Sara, nice to meet you," she said as we shook hands.

Shaking a girl's hand felt so weird. Always did. But there was really no other way to say hi besides the hug. I wouldn't have minded the hug in this situation though. Sara was a looker. The hottest of the three girls, which was saying something standing next to Lauren and Jessica. She looked a lot like Eva Mendes, only taller. She wasn't Latina or Filipina or anything like that. She was just a tan-skinned, brown-haired chick who was only about two inches shorter than I was.

We ate dinner and all went back to our dorms to change and get ready. My dorm room was the farthest from the shower stalls, so it would be a nice long shirtless walk for me every day. I got changed pretty quickly and walked to Max's room. His dorm was in the same quad as mine, but on the complete other side. He was listening to Kid Cudi while his roommate played *Madden 10* on Xbox. His roommate already seemed cooler than mine, even though I hadn't met mine yet. Max's roommate, Jimmy, was a guy from Chicago. When I introduced myself as being from Chicago, he immediately corrected me, saying I was from the suburbs, and he was in fact from the city of Chicago. *Didn't know Chicagoans are territorial over their city. Lesson learned.*

"What time can we go to your cousin's?" Max asked.

"He said any time after 11."

"You're going to have to introduce me to your cuz. Pi Kapps would be a dope house to join," Jimmy added.

"Yeah, for sure. Doubt he has any pull over there, but can't hurt."

"It'll help walking in with a couple of hot freshmen, huh? Are you going to sign there tonight or what?"

"Uh, no, I don't think I'm going to join my cousin's house. Kind of want to do my own thing, you know?"

"Wait, what? But Pi Kapps is an unreal house. Their parties are crazy and all the chicks love them. Do you think you'll get a bid at another top house?"

"We'll see," I said, looking over at Max rolling his eyes at Jimmy's douchebaggery.

I didn't ever think about fraternity rush that way. Jimmy was clearly panicked about it, and also a massive tool, but I guess I had been spoiled with it. A bunch of kids from my hometown went to IU. Great party school, close to Chicago but far enough to get away from the parents, really good business school, and substantially better than U of I. I knew guys in almost every top house on campus, so never thought about getting a bid or anything. But the more I did think about it, if you were from a smaller hometown, it would be intimidating to try and be cool enough at the party to get the brothers to notice you, but not too cool to the point where you're some hardo douchebag.

The three girls got to Max's dorm, and we ramped up our drinking for about an hour. Mostly shots, with the occasional beer. Mike sent a pledge to pick us up from the dorm to bring us to his fraternity for the party. The concept of free sober rides was amazing. I knew in the immediate future that would be me, but for now, I was all for the idea. The pledge dropped us off and told us to walk in the side door before speeding away.

"Who do you know here?" another pledge asked me as we walked in the door.

"My cousin Mike Carter lives here."

"He's probably up in his room if you want to go up there."

"Will do, thanks."

We walked past the dining area and toward the back staircase. I had been to my cousin's the day before to check out his room, so I knew where it was. I could hear a thumping noise coming from the basement and a variety of sounds coming from the third floor. Surprisingly, I had never partied at Pi Kapps. In high school when I came to visit, I went to a tailgate then to his buddies' apartment afterward. Never the house.

"Yo, Cory."

"Hey, Sheff, what's up?"

"Actually going up to my room now; Carter should be in there. Who are your friends?"

"Oh, sorry, yeah, this is my buddy from home Max and his roommate, Jimmy. And this is Jessica, Lauren, and Sara."

"Hello friends, I'm Nick, Carter's roommate. First time at Pi Kapps?"

"Yeah, first time, moved in today," Jessica replied.

"Well, welcome. Most of the rush party is downstairs tonight, but I know a bunch of the juniors are in my room."

We got up to the third floor and walked down the hall toward Mikey's room. The hallway was packed with guys and girls carrying red cups and handles of vodka. Each room had its own bar, and there must have been three or four rooms playing their own music because the hallway sounded like some white-noise combination of Kanye, Miley Cyrus, and Girl Talk.

"What's up little Carter?" some drunk guy shouted as I walked through the hallway.

I'd seen his face before but had no clue of his name. For some reason all of Mikey's friends called him Carter. This dated back to middle school. No one else in my family got called Carter except Mikey. It was actually a theory of mine, the name Mike. Every Mike I knew got called by his last name or a nickname. Rogo, Owens, Parker, Short, Claps, Smith, Basil, Wojo, Olson, Muy, Sully, Baker. Americans must have decided Michael and Mike weren't cool enough names to call someone, simply a filler name in order to be called something else. So Carter it was. My family was the only one who called him Mike or Mikey. For obvious reasons. Well, my family and our neighbor Mrs. Hughes, who for some reason called him by his full name, Michael Carter.

Mikey's room was at the end of the hallway. As I walked in, I noticed the room looked completely different than it had yesterday. There was no couch, no beat-up La-Z-Boy, no coffee table with ashes and chipotle-dip spit cups on it, no TV, nothing. There was just a *U*-shaped bar that backed up to the windows, and that was it.

We met up with Mikey and took a couple shots. I introduced Mikey to Jimmy, but Mikey pawned him off on Sheff. Sheff was the rush chair for Pi Kapps, so for sure the man Jimmy wanted to talk to. I didn't need to worry about Max. He knew Mikey and had a few other friends living in the house. Lauren knew a few girls at the party, too, so seemed to disappear every now and again. Max, Jessica, Sara, and I were together upstairs most of the time before Max and Jessica walked away with Mikey. The party was a free-for-all. I wasn't used to being able to have unlimited time to drink. In high school there was always a parent coming home, a curfew to make, a ride home to find, or something that would make us stop drinking. At times we went to a lake house or a concert, but that was rare. No curfew, no parents, pledges that would take me home whenever I wanted, and unlimited vodka and Keystone Light. Throw in some peer-pressure drinking for being a little cousin, and I got pretty drunk in a hurry. *Shit, Emily!*

I grabbed my phone and saw I had four texts from her.

9:14 p.m.: Hey babe, going over to Ashley's friends in a couple of minutes.

9:14 p.m.: When are you going over to your cousin's??

11:26 p.m.: I'm assuming you are already at Mikey's. Well just text me later I guess.

11:58 p.m.: Night 1 and you already don't care about me. Hope your night is worth it.

*Fuck!* I knew communication was all it would take to make the long-distance thing work, and I'd already fucked it up.

*12:05 p.m.: Hey Em I'm so sorry! Just got caught up with mile and his friends and didn't fell my phone vibrate. Yes I am at Mike's now with jessica, laura. Sara mike and jimmy.*

*12:06 p.m.: I love you and I hope up are having a fun time tonight.*

I was in such a hurry to respond as fast as possible that I didn't proofread the texts before sending. I wasn't even one-eye texting, or at least I didn't think I was. *Dammit, now I look like a complete drunken asshole.*

"Girlfriend?" Sara said, handing me a plastic shot cup filled with something clear and a plastic shot cup filled with something orange.

"Yeah. Forgot to text her a couple hours ago. Doghouse for sure."

"Cheers to long-distance relationships."

"Cheers," I said, taking the shot and the chaser.

"So you have a boyfriend?"

"Yup. Going to play baseball at U of I. Doesn't move in till next week."

"Lucky man."

Sara stared at me funny and smiled as my phone vibrated.

"I mean lucky to be playing baseball at U of I. Well, I mean you seem cool too, so I guess lucky to be dating you too?"

"Need another shot?"

"Yup. Yup I do."

12:10 a.m.: Obviously you are drunk. Be careful and text me when you get home.

*12:12 a.m.: I'm really not that drunk Em, I was in a rush to respond when I saw your texts. I love you and will text you when I get home.*

"Have you been downstairs yet?" I said as I put my phone back in my pocket.

"No, not yet, want to go?"

"Yeah, I haven't been down there yet. That's probably where the rest of our crew is."

Sara and I walked down the hallway and down the back staircase. I felt so terrible about Emily. It ruined my night. I couldn't really focus on anything except her tearing up earlier.

I knew nothing was going to happen till the morning, so tried to forget about it and move on. We got to the basement and it was nothing I was expecting. Lights were off. Black lights and strobe lights were illuminating the entire room. There was a DJ booth in the back left corner with no one inside, but music was still coming from it. The basement was about the size of half a basketball court with a hallway that led to a smaller room that had bar-type booths in it. The booth room had the lights on and led to an outdoor patio double the size of the inside. A steady flow of people walked in and out of all three areas. The place was massive and packed. White plastic shot cups and red Solo cups littered the wet, sticky floors. If upstairs was a free-for-all, downstairs was a jungle. But for some reason, it did seem more organized in the basement. Pledges were bartending and cleaning up the best they could, there was surround-sound playing only one song at a time, people in the middle of the room were dancing while people toward the outside seemed to be having more personal conversations. There was structure. Chaos, but structured chaos.

We walked to the unpainted-plywood-frat-made bar and got a couple of drinks before walking around the basement. We wanted to see if we could find our friends, but gave up quickly and walked back into the party room.

Jimmy was probably with Max and Mikey upstairs, and Jessica and Lauren easily could have left with those girls to go to another party.

"Well, Eva Mendes, I guess it's just me and you."

"I don't know why I get that all the time. I don't see it, but I guess I'll take that as a compliment?"

"One hundred percent a compliment. You could play her little sister in *Hitch 2*."

"Well, do people say you look like James Franco?"

"Um, never Eva."

"No, you do! It's when you smile. If you grew long hair, you could play his little brother in *Pineapple Express 2*."

"Or I guess Dave Franco could play his little brother."

"Oh shut up."

We stood toward the bar for a while talking and drinking. Drinking a lot, actually. There was a really weird connection between us. I think it was the fact we were both initiating long-distance relationships that night. But whatever it was, it was something. We both were flirting and laughing with each other, but there was this resistance or hesitation since neither one of us was going to do anything about it. It was almost like we were both channeling our love/frustrations from our relationships toward each other in some strange friendly/distant way.

Some guy was standing in the DJ booth with his MacBook and started playing a set list of sing-alongs and classic fire jams. "Return of the Mack," "Good Vibrations," little Hall and Oates, some Earth, Wind & Fire, "Party in the USA," just a great late-night-blacked-out-party playlist. Sara and I had stopped our conversation and were dancing like Will Smith in *The Fresh Prince of Bel-Air*, yet less coordinated and more like idiots. She was pretty hammered, but I wasn't far behind. The place had emptied a little, but the crowd still in the basement had drunken energy. Everyone was bombed. I had no idea what time it was and really didn't care. The fight I was going to have with Em was happening regardless of what time I got home, so for the time being, I was going to enjoy my first night in college.

Sara and I started dancing more together. She was as goofy a dancer as I was. Few spins, little one-leg action, lot of two-stepping. Both of us could sort of put a combination of dance moves together to make it seem like we were good at dancing, but realistically from a sober pledge's perspective, we probably looked like fools. There must have been 50 of us all dancing in the basement. I didn't recognize any of them.

Sara turned her back toward me and started leaning on my chest before turning around and continuing to dance an arm's length away. The weird hesitation was clearly still there. She wanted to dance with me, but couldn't decide if it was the right thing to do. I felt the same way. I wanted to dance with her because, A: we were having fun. And B: well, she was legitimately Eva f-ing Mendes. Then all of a sudden Sara made up her mind for the both of us. She came up close to me, pretty much chest to chest, and looked at me with this glazed-over look. I didn't know what to do. If I was sober, I would have instantly spun around and tried to get out of the situation as gracefully as possible, but in the moment, that seemed unnecessary. Sara backed up against me again, and I put my arms around her waist. We were full-blown grinding.

A few times it seemed like we were going to make out, but neither of us had it in us. I would never cheat on Emily in a million years. I felt bad enough dancing with Sara, but at the end of the day, it was harmless. Cheating was such a cowardly and downright mean thing to do to someone. And I loved Emily, so that too. But man, did I want to. At one point we were forehead to forehead, but we both looked at each other and kept dancing.

Neither one of us said a word to each other the remainder of the night. All we did was dance, sexually, for a long, long time. The lights in the basement turned on, and I instantly realized how blacked out Sara was. Her hair wasn't up like it was earlier in the night and the makeup around her eyes was smeared from sweat. We walked upstairs to find pledge rides waiting for us. We both got into a car and headed back to the dorms.

"Wait! We have to wait for Jess and La."

*La? Yikes, it's bedtime.*

"I think they left a while ago. Did they text you when they left?"

"I didn't text them."

"No did *they* text *you* saying they left?"

Sara grabbed her phone.

"It's three a.m. College! Going to be so much fun. We had a lot of fun, right?" Sara said as she put her right hand on my knee.

I looked up and saw the pledge laughing. There was no chance Sara would remember the car ride in the morning, so I ignored being polite and took her hand off my knee and grabbed her phone.

12:31 a.m.: Hey Sars! We are down on the second floor with Jess's sister's friend. Come drink!!

1:43 a.m.: Jess and I are leaving now! CC's cousin said you were with him. Don't do anything I wouldn't do ;)

"Jess and Lauren left a couple of hours ago. No need . . ."

I stopped talking as I noticed Sara was passed out. Head against the window, arms together, knees together. Snoozing.

"Hey, man, can you drive us around to the back of McNutt? I'll walk her up to her room."

"Uhh, sure thing bro."

The pledge stared at me with a puzzled look on his face. It took me a second to realize why.

"No, I'm not sleeping with her. Just making sure she gets up to her room. Unless you want to walk Sleeping Beauty upstairs?"

The pledge didn't respond. We got to the back of the dorm and I woke up Sara. She was a zombie. Eyes open but brain off. We walked together to the back door and up to her room on the third floor. I grabbed her keys out of her purse and opened the door to find Lauren sleeping. Without saying a word, Sara stumbled over to her bed and fell asleep. I left Sara's phone and keys on the desk next to her door. Before I left, I grabbed a picture of Lauren in her softball outfit off some collage taped on the wall. *Framing this. Such a lesbian.*

As I walked down the stairs to my room, all I could do was think about the night. "Night 1 and you already don't care about me." Emily was right. The only times I thought about her all night were when I forgot to text her and when I was forehead to forehead with another girl. I knew I didn't cheat on her, so whatever, but the part that kept bothering me was the fact that I had a fucking blast with Sara all night. I enjoyed flirting with her. I enjoyed the similarities we shared. I enjoyed dancing. I enjoyed night one of college. *Maybe I really don't care about Emily as much as I think I do. Maybe everyone is right, long-distance relationships are impossible.*

First night in a long-distance relationship and I was already questioning it. First night in college and I already found a girl I had a connection with. At least I knew Emily would never find out about Sara. *Ignorance is bliss, I guess.*

# THREE

**THE KNOCK AT THE DOOR WOKE ME UP.** *What time is it?* I leaned over and checked my phone to see a text from Bennett.

11:25 a.m.: Hey Cory!! I am going to move in with my mom and dad in about 30. R u in the room?

*Oh shit, Bennett!* I jumped up out of bed and threw on my jeans and short-sleeve button-down from the night before. I could hear the key to the room going in as I hurried to get dressed. I saw a reflection of myself in the full-sized mirror behind the door before it opened. *Considering the circumstances, cleaned up nicely. Attaboy Cory.*

"Anyone home?"

"Hey Bennett, nice to formally meet you. Sorry I didn't see your text till now."

"Were you still sleeping?" Mrs. Schwartz blurted out bitchily as she gave me the up and down.

*Well, guess I'm not that put together.*

"More or less lying in bed. Getting the Wi-Fi set up. I'm Cory, nice to meet you, Mr. and Mrs. Schwartz," I replied as I shook their hands.

Bennett was about my height, but his parents were tiny. Well, tiny as in height. Dad couldn't have been taller than 5'6", and the mom was a 4'9" bowling ball. Right off the bat I could tell the mom was a bitch and the dad was a complete pushover. He just looked like one. Short, skinny, glasses, yarmulke, sweater, and his handshake felt like an eight-year-old's.

"So you have, like, been here all week?" Mrs. Schwartz said with disgust.

"Uh, yeah, I moved in on Tuesday with my parents."

"I don't understand why the school lets these kids move in a week early to party. School starts Monday, so kids should move in Saturday and Sunday. What have you even been doing?"

*Jesus Christ, nice to meet you too. My brain can't take your bitchiness right now. Five straight days of partying and the tailgate yesterday. I need water, not an interrogation on morals.*

"My cousin is a junior here, so I hung out with him a little and he showed me around campus."

"And from the looks of this place, quite a bit of socializing too. I don't get it."

I looked at the dad and Bennett for backup, but neither one of them was reacting to the comments. This must have been normal dinner conversation at the Schwartz household. Shut up and let mom rant.

I asked the Schwartzes if they needed help moving in boxes, and thankfully they said no. I needed water, food, and a shower. In that order. I hit up Max and we went to the food court before I came back to shower and get to know Bennett.

He was a nice kid, just weird. I say kid because he seemed like a kid. High voice, very soft-spoken, nerdy, but not hipster nerdy, more I-don't-drink-or-go-out-much-because-I'm-too-focused-on-my-academics nerdy. Every question I asked he didn't really seem to know how to answer. Just awkward all around. Exactly what I thought he was from the Facebook creeping a few weeks back. Now it was obvious where his personality came from. For the two minutes I met his dad, they seemed identical; both under complete control by the Grinch. I didn't mind having this kid as a roommate. Actually kind of liked the idea of a polar-opposite roommate. I knew he would never stumble in drunk a night before I have a test and wake me up, wouldn't steal my shit, wasn't going to nag me about hanging out, and wasn't going to be an asshole. He was a quiet and polite bookworm here to graduate with honors in only four years and move on.

Me on the other hand, I was already texting a guy I met at the tailgate about a rush party. The dude was in ATO, a house similar to Pi Kapps. Mostly former athletes in high school who liked partying, but not degenerate partying. More like I-have-no-tests-coming-up-so-let's-booze partying.

Not I-have-a-test-Thursday-but-I-can-pull-an-all-nighter-tomorrow-so-let's-booze partying. That was Acacia. Who, not surprisingly, Jimmy was talking to.

Mikey and Sheff were telling me stories at the tailgate about Jimmy from our first night. I guess he was talking about high school sports the entire time to everyone he met, girls and guys. Don't get me wrong, I was as big a sports fan as there is, but supposedly he was bragging about how good he was at football, trying to bet on Colts vs. Bears with complete strangers, and at one point he challenged a senior to a wrestling match. Jimmy was a cartoon character. Like if Johnny Drama was an 18-year-old frat guy.

The ATO rush event was a *Monday Night Football* watch party where there would be drinks and food. Not a massive party or anything, more a chance to meet the brothers and check out the house. Max and I were planning on going after class. He had already gotten an informal bid at Sigma Chi, but couldn't turn down free beer and wings to watch football. A friend of Max's family was the president of Sigma Chi, and we all knew Max was going to end up there. If Pi Kapps and ATO were 70/30 party-to-school ratio and Acacia was 90/10, Sigma Chi was probably 50/50. They were a top frat with an amazing house, but every guy seemed the same. A smart, wealthy, white male from a suburb studying marketing, finance, accounting, economics, or some sort of management degree, who happened to have a Sigma Chi alum for a relative. Not saying there was anything wrong with that type of person—I mean, I was a white finance major with a relative in Pi Kapps. But what I meant was, the entire house was that way. Everyone. Zero diversity. Individually, most of the Sigma Chi guys were pretty normal, but all together, that's exactly what they were. Normal. A party there was like hanging out with 100 people from the same family. Max bought into it in high school, and I couldn't blame him. It's not like he was joining some lower-tier house that couldn't find sororities to pair with, or some academic fraternity or something. *Whatever the fuck academic fraternities are.*

I spent the remainder of Sunday watching the Bears and the Sunday NFL slate in my room. Bennett was in and out all day, but didn't seem to care much about the games anyway. Em and I were texting back and forth the whole Bears' game and Skyped during the 4:00 p.m. games. Our conversation was short. She was still mad at me, but also as hungover as I was from the past week. An overall body hangover. Not as much stomachache or headache, but total exhaustion. Classes started tomorrow for both of us too. Emily wanted to be a nurse, and for some reason her classes were at absurd hours. She had 8:00 a.m. classes Monday to Friday, then a 7:00 p.m. lab every Tuesday and Thursday. I was more on the 10:00 a.m. to 3:00 p.m. timetable, and even that sounded terrible. We both called it early and went to bed. I told Bennett he didn't need to shut off the lights or turn off the TV, but of course he did anyway.

As expected, the first few classes were a joke. No teacher took attendance because the first week you could shuffle around your schedule and switch classes without punishment. Every teacher did the same exact thing. Said their pregame pump-up speech, handed out the syllabus, and expected us to read something by Wednesday. The only reason for going was to figure out where the actual classroom was on campus and get a copy of the syllabus. I got a text from Max during my final class saying he was out on the ATO rush party and was going over to Sigma Chi instead. Didn't matter to me, though, I wasn't going solely to hang out with Max anyway. I had met a few guys from the tailgate, around the dorms, and at other fraternity parties that were going to the event, so I wasn't going to be a loner.

I took the bus to the ATO house around seven o'clock, and there were about 50 freshmen and 75 or so brothers there. The basement was arranged so some Beer Pong was being played on the pool table while the game was on in the background. Upstairs was slightly different to Mikey's place. No big, cold dorms. Every two to four guys had their own rooms with mini-bunk bed rooms, or "sleepers," connected. Each room had the game on with food and beer. I hung out in Alex's room most of the time. He was from Riverwood North, which is where Sara went. It was our rival high school too, so we had a few friends in common.

The room was mostly brothers because the freshmen tended to stay in the basement, but there were two other freshmen, Bo and Cam, in the room with me. Max and I had met Bo at Pi Kapps and hung out again at Acacia last week. He was also from RWN. We were both captains of our football teams in high school, so while we didn't know each other personally, we knew of each other. Cam was from Cincinnati. Tall and skinny black guy who looked like John Salmons from the Bulls. Spitting image. The dude even had that Greg-Oden-look-40-in-your-20s gene like Salmons did.

"Moss dude, holy shit he's still got it," Alex blurted out as we watched the game.

"He's not *that* old bro," Bo responded.

"He is for a guy who doesn't give a shit. You think Straight Cash Moss is hitting the gym hard at age 32 up in New England?"

"Speaking of old," I added as the cameraman cut to Terrell Owens on the Bills sidelines.

"Better career, TO or Moss?" Alex proposed as we continued watching.

"TO," I responded without hesitation.

"Stop it Cory. Moss by a billion," Alex said as he sat up on the couch.

"Moss had Chris Carter and now Wes Welker not allowing double teams. QBs were Culpepper and Brady. He went to Oakland for two years and became irrelevant till Brady was throwing him bombs again."

"TO had Jerry Rice on the other side and Steve Young throwing. What the hell are you talking about?"

"He had Young and Rice for what, two years? Besides, TO never became irrelevant. Not with Jeff Garcia, a shitty Romo, or McNabb, and none of those guys are Culpepper or Brady. I mean, he's still putting up numbers with Trent f-ing Edwards."

In my heart I really didn't even believe TO was better than Randy Moss. I just enjoyed a good debate. Once I picked a side, I felt obligated to stay on that side of the argument.

"But Moss! He's a stud."

Terrible timing, as Moss catches a 31-yard pass from Brady for the first down. It was a week one Bills–Patriots game, so for a Bears fan it was meaningless, and the new second *Monday Night Football* game ESPN had was Chargers–Raiders. So another meaningless game for fantasy football and my Chicago fandom, but I loved football and really all sports. I knew a bizarre amount about the NFL, NBA, NCAAF, NCAAB, MLB, NHL, and soccer. Probably in that order too. I wasn't a fanatic or anything, but if someone got me going, I could argue with the best of them. The rest of the night had conversations like that. A lot of picking on Indianapolis sports, telling funny stories, some gambling, it was a good time. I knew deep down this was going to be the house for me, but I still wanted to see what a night party was like. Nevertheless, ATO was slowly checking each box. Top fraternity, cool dudes, cool house, 70/30 ratio, good location, and good sorority connections.

We ended up staying into the second game and smoking in Alex's room. He invited Bo, Cam, and myself to their party Thursday night. Us three talked during our pledge ride home and all planned on going to the party together. I had already told my cousin I was going to go to Pi Kapps Thursday night, but he wasn't going to care when I told him I wasn't coming. Honestly probably would prefer if his little cousin didn't come to his party. I still needed to talk with Mikey about not joining his house. I think he already knew I wasn't going to follow in his footsteps, but Sheff was probably on his ass, being the house rush chair.

Tuesday and Wednesday I stayed in. First real non-drunk or hungover night sleeps of college. Em and I talked on the phone both nights. I hated Skype. To me, the ability to see her didn't outweigh the frustrations of choppy video. I also couldn't tell if it was my Wi-Fi or hers that was the problem. It seemed like hers, because mine ran perfectly fine doing anything else, but she claimed the same. Bennett seemed to always be in the room. He had classes from 8:00 to 9:30 a.m., then came home to study, then classes from 10:30 a.m. to 4:00 p.m., then came home to study more, and eventually he'd stay in for the rest of the night. So when I woke up and came back from class, he was home studying, and at night, he never went out, so was still in the room. I asked if my talking to Em bothered him, and he said he never really noticed. The kid was unbelievably polite. A pushover, but polite.

On Thursday I went over to Max's and Jimmy's room to pregame the night. Jessica, Lauren, Sara, and Jessica's roommate, Carolyn, were all in there. Max was planning on going to Sigma Chi, Jimmy to Acacia, and I was going to ATO.

"How's the Jew?" Jimmy said as I walked in.

"Um, he's a nice kid, but incredibly shy. He also doesn't go out much."

"You should bring him out one night!" Jessica added.

"No, sorry, I mean he doesn't go out at all. Like he doesn't drink or smoke or anything. I think he's trying to graduate early."

"What a pussy," Jimmy mumbled under his breath.

"Whoa, yeah, that's a little strange for IU. Well, if he does want to drink, tell him we would love to have him."

"Will do Jess."

I looked over and made eye contact with Sara. We had hung out about three or four times since the first night, but hadn't talked much to each other. It was like the first night never happened. Judging by the way she had acted the past week or so, I think she remembered enough of the night, but neither one of us ever brought it up.

"So tell me again, why won't you guys come to Pi Kapps tonight?"

Max looked at me wondering who should answer the question. He poured a few shots and handed them out to everyone.

"Because today is the first official day of fraternity rush, so this is the night freshmen can officially start signing their bids. I'm going to sign at Sigma Chi, Jimmy wants to go with Acacia, and Cory already got a Pi Kapps bid, so wants to check out ATO."

"Have you girls been to ATO yet?" Sara said from the corner.

"Why, Sars, you want to go?" Lauren asked.

*Yeah, Sara, why you asking?*

"Yeah. I mean, I've never been. And Jess, didn't you say Allison is going there tonight?"

"Yeah, she's going there, but Carolyn wanted to meet up with a couple of friends at Pi Kapps."

"Oh, don't worry about me. I don't need to meet up with my friends," Carolyn responded boldly.

"You sure?" Jess asked.

"Yeah, I have like five or so friends going there, but they go there almost every night 'cause three of them are dating Pi Kapps guys. I haven't seen ATO either and heard it's awesome."

"Fun, let's do ATO then! Sara, I'll text Allison," Jess announced with a smile.

I glanced at Sara as she started talking with Max with a smirk on her face. *The fuck just happened? She's making this so much harder?* The timing of the comment and the awkward eye contact before made it seem like she wanted to go to ATO because of me, but a part of me didn't want to believe it. I didn't want to confuse things any more than they were, and had finally gotten over that shameful feeling of how quickly I caved to another girl the first night. Neither one of us wanted it, neither one of us would do anything about it, it was just one big tease. But at the same time, there was a part of me that was thrilled. I wanted them to come. I wanted her to come. I wanted to talk to Sara again. I had a blast at Pi Kapps with her, so why not do the same thing at ATO? It was the strangest battle of emotions I was fighting.

We weren't drinking as aggressively in Max's dorm. First because Max's RA came over on Friday and gave us a warning, but also 'cause Max and I didn't want to get hammered before going over to the parties. That would become inevitable if we signed our bids. Jimmy didn't give a shit how drunk he was. Neither did Acacia for that matter. We drank for another hour or so then went our separate ways. Max walked to Sigma Chi with some other freshmen, and the rest of us hopped in an ATO pledge ride. Jimmy got out with us at ATO before walking next door to Acacia.

ATO had an insanely old house. Not run-down old or like-your-grand-ma's-country-club old, just old school. The first floor had all red carpet with old paintings and composites on the wall with a piano, a fireplace, and leather couches with tables for studying. The party setup was identical to Pi Kapps. Bigger bar/club-type party in the basement with more individual high school style parties upstairs in brothers' rooms. Their basement had a pool table and darts room that connected through a hallway to an open area dance floor room like the one Sara and I danced in. ATO didn't have an outdoor patio, though. The front of the house did have a wraparound porch that connected to a basketball court on the side, but for party purposes, it was all inside. Except for the parking lot area, but that seemed like it was strictly for drunks to bum cigarettes off pledges.

I ran into Alex right away, and the girls found Allison, so we separated. Alex introduced me to a few of the guys, some of whom I met on Monday, but no chance I would have remembered their names. I wanted to get better with names in college. I was always terrible at it, and trying to learn names in college was like learning how to swim by getting thrown in the ocean. You learned like 30 new names a day, it was impossible to remember them all. *Alex, Brandon, Bates, Duffy. There's always a Duffy. Alex, Brandon, Bates, Duffy. Alright I got it.* I didn't talk to them long because the party was packed, and they clearly didn't care about rush. To them, this was the time of year where random dudes partied at their house. The concept did sound pretty awful for fraternities.

Alex and I started walking to the basement when we ran into a couple freshmen I had met on Monday. The basement must have been 10 degrees warmer than anywhere else in the house. There was this gradual warmth you felt, like each step down the stairs was another degree. No one seemed to mind, and really, I didn't care either. Almost every house was like that except for Beta. For some bizarre reason their basement was an icebox. It was the strangest thing. Like, "Hey guys, how 'bout you turn down the air a little bit." Just a thought.

I ran into Sara and the girls in the basement and we all took a bunch of shots together. It was hard not to drink a lot with these girls. They had this weird thing where individually or two at a time they would ask you to take a shot or get a beer with them, but never all together. So I would take a shot with Jess, five minutes later with Sara and Lauren, and then 10 minutes later grab another beer with Jess and Carolyn. I guess I could have said no, but whatever, the plastic shot cups were tiny. Consequently, the effects took a while to hit me. It must have been doing enough for Cam, though, as he stumbled over to us and put his arm around me.

"A-T-BLOW! You fucking gon sign yo bid tonight C?"

"Don't know yet. Wait, you think this place blows?"

"Nah, you idiot, I mean A-T-Blow. Like blow, snow, coke brotha."

"Yeah, what do you mean by it, though?"

"Man you slow, boy. ATO does a lot of blow. Sooo, A-T-Blow."

Cam took his arm off my shoulder and grabbed a drink.

"What house doesn't, though?" I said to avoid the awkwardness.

"Aight. You right, you right," Cam said as he looked around for someone.

I was pretending to be as cool as possible as Cam and I grabbed a couple of beers. I had no idea what he was talking about. *Is this common knowledge or just Cam being drunk?* I pretty much prided myself on knowing a lot about every house. I had heard my cousin and his buddies talk shit about all the houses a hundred times. I knew every negative stereotype for each house whether it was true or not. Pi Kapps was a bunch of cool guys but were obsessed with IU basketball and let athletes and whoever they wanted come over whenever. Acacia was the frat from Old School before Dean Pritchard came sniffing around, who threw great parties, but you weren't quite sure if the brothers were actually enrolled in classes. Sigma Chi was a bunch of white suburban legacies. Beta was Sigma Chi on steroids. Fiji was a cult who only hung out with Fiji. Sigma Nu was the high school wrestler who thinks basketball is a pussy sport, but 16-inch softball is a man's game. Delts were all from Indianapolis and were the guys in high school who painted their bodies during home football games. Phi Delts were the second-string athletes in high school whose names you knew, but had no clue who they hung out with off the field. Phi Sig was Phi Delts who did drugs. ZBT was all rich legacy Jews, Skulls was poorer nonlegacy Jews, and APES was NYC club-scene Jews. I could go on and on. But the more I thought about it, the more I didn't know ATO's negative stereotype. I only thought of them like my group of friends in high school. Mostly good at sports, the ones who weren't good still played, all outgoing, and relatively smart, but no honor students. All positive things—I didn't know a single negative thing about ATO, and that made me uneasy.

Alex grabbed me and we started walking upstairs. I was with Alex, Joe, Bo, and two other kids I had never met. Everyone was laughing and smiling. The one kid put Joe in a mini-headlock out of excitement as we walked up the back stairs to the third floor. I knew I was walking to get a bid, but couldn't stop thinking about what Cam said. *A-T-Blow. Is that ATO's negative stereotype? Closet cokeheads? It can't be true, because Mikey would have 100 percent told me. Right?* I knew I should have been excited to get my first bid that wasn't just Sheff texting me, but now I was nervous and didn't know what to do.

We sat on this black leather couch in some dark, candlelit room on the third floor. There were six shot glasses filled with some dark liquor next to five index-sized cards and pens. There were about 20 ATO guys in the room all staring down at us. Alex shut the door as this tall dude started talking. I immediately got chills. I had never seen him before, but he started this Al Pacino–like pump-up speech.

"I know none of you know who I am, and that's fine. I'm a senior at Alpha Tau Omega. In front of you is a bid to the best house on campus. I'm not saying that in a douchebag way or like I'm some meathead who thinks ATO is better than life itself. I'm saying it the only way I can. ATO is the best house on campus. Tradition? Been here since 1915, and the house was built for the military after the Civil War. We started Little 500 and are still the last fraternity to win it. Academics? Currently in the house is the president of the I-banking workshop, multiple IFC members, an ethics board member, business majors, econ majors, journalism majors, chemistry, biology, sports management, Spanish, and whatever the fuck Sweeny is doing with music . . ."

Everyone laughed noticeably hard at the Sweeny joke. It must have been an inside joke, but us freshmen laughed anyway. As this senior spoke, all I was hearing were the positives I had already known. Tradition, academics, top house. I already knew that. But I also knew he wasn't going to just say, "Oh, and we all do cocaine constantly," but that thought still lingered and was making me second guess. I wanted an answer to it.

". . . Parties? Our parties here at the house are legendary. Our Ménage party, we all bring two dates who are only wearing lingerie. Playboy named it the number-one college party in America. We have theme parties, regular parties, day parties, weekday parties, tailgate parties, you name it. We also have the best off-campus houses to throw bangers. Women? We pair with the top sororities on campus. We are down the block from three of them and have hooked up with all of them. Guys at Alpha Tau Omega are not the creepy guys who hit on drunken girls. Not the losers who can't talk to women sober. Not the disrespectful meatsticks. We are the gentlemen who don't need to force anything with girls. We are the guys girls want to sleep with, want to date, and want to party with. When I say best house on campus, I mean tradition, school, parties, and girls. What more can you ask for? So, gentlemen, raise up those shot glasses in front of you, and let me be the first to introduce you to ATO. Let's do this together, boys. Congratulations, and sign that bid to the best house on campus, ATO."

I realized this was not the time to ask questions, so as everyone in the room erupted in applause, I picked up my shot glass from the glass table and raised it into the center. The energy in the room was electric after the speech. Even the ATO guys were clapping and seemed jacked up. I guess that rah-rah stuff didn't get me as fired up as the rest of the guys. Don't get me wrong, it was a solid speech, and the whole process was a lot more organized than I expected a frat-house bid speech at midnight during a party to be, but maybe the speech didn't pump me up because of the cocaine thought stuck in my head. I didn't want to join a drug house. I mean I smoked probably two to four times a week and had no problem with people doing shrooms once or whatever. I just wasn't OK with all the hard drugs. I didn't have any friends in high school who did cocaine, ecstasy, or anything harder. Not that I looked down on people for doing party drugs, but it was a culture I didn't want to be a part of. To me, people get peer pressured easily into coke and ecstasy. If you don't smoke, seeing me smoke and eat a lot of pizza isn't going to change your mind. But if you don't do blow, seeing me do blow and have some incredible night may possibly change your mind. So if Cam was right, and ATO was a hard-drug house, it would be a deciding factor against them.

As I took the shot of Jäger, I saw everyone on the couches grabbing their bids. I looked down at mine and froze. I'd been positive I would sign with ATO just 10 minutes prior, but somehow a drunken Cam had made me skeptical. A lot of the ATO guys started clapping louder as I realized the two unknown freshmen were already signing their bids. *How have I never seen these two random dudes before? I've been to ATO's tailgate and the* Monday Night Football *party, and have been here for the past two hours or so and not only haven't met these guys, but have never even seen them before. Not even at other fraternities' rush parties. I should know these guys!* Then it all hit me. *I should know!* I had been to three ATO functions in the past week. Two were big parties, too, involving sororities, day and night parties, and not one time did I see any hint of drugs. All the other negative stereotypes I had overheard from my cousin or around campus were validated the second I met the brothers from that house. Acacia's party was out of control, guys at Sigma Chi were wearing oxford shoes and pressed shirts, I saw Sigma Nu at the tailgate shotgunning beers. Each fraternity. Validated the second you met them. I mean, they were all so obvious. If drugs were ATO's negative stereotype, I would have known about it by now. And if it was, it was a stretch at best, especially because I would have heard it from my cousin. Even if they were hiding it, it clearly wasn't ATO's culture. It easily could have been their reputation back in the day, but I mean, the Bears' reputation was the "Monsters of the Midway" but had been a league average defense since 2006. *A-T-Blow is definitely not ATO's current reputation.*

I grabbed the pen next to the bid card and looked over at Bo. He looked equally as skeptical but had the pen in his hand too. We both started smiling as we opened our bid cards.

"Fuck it, let's do it." Bo said.

*Fuck it, let's do it.*

# FOUR

**I DIDN'T HAVE CLASS ON FRIDAY.** Sophomores, juniors, and seniors not having Friday class was normal, but rare for a freshman. I had one second semester, but till then, I was going to enjoy Fridays off.

Bennett and I walked to the food court together when he got back from class. It was essentially the first time we had done something together. Well, really, we just happened to have been leaving our room at the same time and both walking to the food court. I had asked him to grab food a couple times before, but he was always busy with something or had microwaved his own meal. I hated going to the food court alone. Not that I cared about what other people thought about me, because everyone ate alone eventually, but it was really awkward sitting at a table by yourself eating and not doing anything else. As I made a beeline for the Mexican buffet, I could feel Bennett opening up a little bit. He wasn't as shy as the first week.

"So tell me how the hell you will graduate in three years. That going to be pretty tough?" I said as I grabbed a tray.

"Not as hard as you would think. I already planned it out with my advisor. I came in with 17 credits, so that's one semester right there. Then I would need to stay this summer in Bloomington to catch up."

"Seventeen? Jesus, I came in with zero and am taking 15 credits now."

"Yeah, I have 12 credits in French alone. I'm going to double major in accounting and French, since I'm already fluent."

"That makes sense, shouldn't be too hard. Not sure what I'm even talking about, I have zero clue how hard it will be."

"But yeah, French is mostly verbal, with a few history classes."

"Was that what you had this morning?"

"Yeah, I had business writing at 9:00 and a French discussion at 10:15."

"How was business writing?" I said, throwing a couple tacos on my tray.

"It was good. The professor spoke most of the time about the process of how he grades and what to expect all year."

"The first week or two is so stupid. I have business writing next semester. I think my advisor said it's only Friday mornings. Not thrilled about it."

"Yeah, sorry if I woke you up this afternoon."

"If you have to say afternoon, you should never be sorry about waking someone up."

"But you didn't get home till really late last night."

"Oh shit, did I wake you up?"

"Oh no! It was the light from the hallway, you were quiet. I went right back to sleep."

"What have you got there?"

"A turkey sandwich. What about you?"

"Al pastor tacos. Stomach needs a little grease this morning."

"Why is that?"

"Uh, had a little too much to drink last night. The fraternity Alpha Tau Omega had a rush party for freshmen and I actually ended up joining the fraternity last night."

"Wow that's awesome! Congratulations man! Now is that your cousin's fraternity?"

"No, he's in Pi Kappa Phi, which is up on Jordan Street near the basketball and football stadiums. ATO's down on Third Street across from Swain."

"Sorry, I don't know much about the Greek system here, but that's awesome. Is your cousin OK with you not joining his fraternity?"

"Yeah, he won't care. I told him a couple of days ago that I wasn't going to join him. I didn't want to be known as his little cousin to everyone older than me in the house."

"That's a very logical reason."

"Thank you. That's what I thought too. Sorry, I have a pulsing headache and need these tacos."

"Oh wow, that bad of a hangover?"

"No, not that bad. This is one of those manageable ones. Throw some greasy food, about a gallon of water, and maybe a Sprite in the ol' stomach and I'll be alright."

"What is an unmanageable hangover?"

"Well, throwing up is the obvious answer, but sometimes you can't get out of bed. Water, food, and even just fresh air would fix it, but the hangover controls you so much you won't even get out of bed to get water. You're really just a piece of shit for a full day, or until you muster up the energy to leave your room."

"Wow, that sounds terrible. Sorry, I don't know a lot about hangovers."

"Have you ever gotten one?"

"No, I've never drank before. I mean, I've had sips of wine with my parents, but never, like, drank."

"Excuse my ignorance, but is that a religious thing or a personal preference?"

"Oh, personal preference. I don't know, I mean I had friends in high school that would drink, but even then, my parents would never have allowed it. I think my mom would send me to jail if she heard I was drinking."

"Did your mom know your friends drank?"

"My mom assumed everyone in high school drinks at some point, even though we are technically still underage . . ."

*Um, I thought everyone drank in high school too.*

". . . She would tell me to stop hanging out with some of my friends because they were 'bad influences,' but those were mostly empty threats. As long as she knew I wasn't drinking or getting into trouble, she didn't care if my friends went to a party."

"Did she care if you went to the parties?"

"My friends never really had parties. They would drink when their parents were on vacation or something. But if they went to a party, I would go back home. My mom would be able to smell the alcohol on me if I went to a party, and since I wasn't going to drink, the parties didn't sound that fun."

"Yeah, I guess you have to drink at a high school party."

"Are college parties much different?"

"No, I guess in the most general sense, no, not really. They are a lot bigger and have a lot louder music. And the houses are built for the party, not just using your parents' basement to party. But not everyone at the house is partying, though. Like at the fraternity houses, there are always people not going out."

"Really?"

"Yeah, it's not like all 75 people living in the house or whatever go to the party every night. All the houses are big enough where you'll always find a room where a guy and his girlfriend are watching a movie, or a couple of guys playing Xbox or something."

"That would be me during every party."

"Do you think you'll drink once you turn 21?"

"Yeah, I think so. More on occasions, not all the time. I don't know, I've never really thought about it. Not drinking in high school was just something I did for my parents and the police. So I guess neither of those would be an issue at 21."

"Neither are really issues now. As long as you're not drunk in public."

"Yeah, I guess. I don't know."

"Well, if you ever do drink, I'd love to be there."

"I'll keep that in mind."

"Hey, really off topic, but I was curious, the yarmulke your dad wears. Is that all the time? And what's the significance of it?"

"Of his or in general?"

"In general."

"It's to show respect to God, who is above you."

"Oh. For some reason I thought there was going to be a lot longer explanation."

"Well, it was originally only worn during prayer and eating, then some Jews starting wearing them to differentiate themselves from the non-Jews. And it has kind of stuck ever since. But that's why I don't wear one. Doesn't make complete sense to me to wear it all of the time."

12:31 p.m.: Hey Cor I'm back at my dorm now, want to chat?

*12:31 p.m.: Leaving the food court now. I'll call you in a minute.*

"Very logical explanation, if you ask me."

"I thought so too."

"How do you like NYC?"

"I like it. I live up on Long Island so I rarely go into the city, but when I do it's awesome."

"Are you thinking of moving there after school?"

"Well, this summer I'm going to stay in Bloomington."

"Oh, right, forgot about that."

"But then after sophomore year, I hope to get an internship so I can be on pace to get a job after I graduate junior year."

"Here, I'll take your tray," I said, standing up so I could call Em soon.

"Oh, thanks."

"You going back to the room?"

"No, I have to go to the bookstore to get supplies for my discussion class. I'll see you later."

"OK, sounds good. Adios Bennett."

"See you later Cory."

"Hello?" Em answered as I walked out the door.

"Hey Em, walking back from the food court now. What's shaking?"

"Eh, nothing. Ashley was out till like two o'clock last night and woke me up, so a little tired."

"Yeah, Bennett said I woke him up too."

"Cory!"

"Whoa whoa whoa. As a matter of fact, he said I was quiet and that the hallway light woke him up."

"That's him being polite. You woke him up."

"Dammit. You're probably right. He for sure was just being polite. How was class?"

"It was fine. I like my teacher a lot, so that'll be fun. Hard but fun."

"Well good."

"So Mr. Frat Star, how you feeling this morning?"

"I don't know, I feel pretty good."

"Don't sound too excited."

"Sorry, I'm tired."

"You slept till like noon."

"I know, I was talking to Bennett about that earlier."

"You guys like best friends now?"

"Pretty much. I got a lot of information out of him, actually. Sounds like his mom is the sole reason he doesn't go out. She sounds like Mrs. Temple, or no, worse, Ally Reynold's mom."

"Yikes. Does he drink?"

"No, he doesn't, and when I asked why, he said he never really thought about it. Didn't do it because his mom would kill him."

"Well, his mom isn't at college."

"That's exactly what I said. In a nicer way. His friends would drink, though. I don't think he was that popular 'cause he said his friends rarely went to parties, and even when they did, he wouldn't go."

"So is he going to drink in college?"

"Not till he's 21. Actually, I don't know. He might. He said it was nothing to do with religion or anything. And really, it was almost like he had never thought about why he doesn't drink."

"Well, if he doesn't want to, don't force him, Cory."

"You think I'm a bad influence?"

"You can be very persuasive."

"That doesn't mean I'm going to persuade the kid to be an alcoholic."

"Wait, so tell me about last night."

"It was fun, I went with Sara, Lauren, Jess, and her roommate Carolyn to ATO, then . . ."

"Hanging out with those chicks a lot, huh?"

"Um, kind of. I mean, besides Lauren and Jess, it's really only Sara and Carolyn who are their roommates. Why do you ask?"

"I talked with Heather. She said she hated that Sara chick."

"Who the hell is Heather?"

"One of Ashley's friends. Said Sara's a social climber, really fake, and doesn't have any real friends."

"She has a boyfriend, according to her, at least."

"Yeah, the baseball guy. That's how Heather knows Sara. She was friends with him. Think he goes to Illinois."

"You seem to know a lot about her."

"All from Heather, who said there is no chance Sara doesn't cheat on him, so be careful around her, OK Cor?"

"I'll make sure I cover up my cups at parties."

"Cory, I'm serious."

"I know, ya tweak. I was kidding, but can I finish with my night now?"

"Ugh. Yes please."

*Yeesh. Thank God.*

"So we all went to ATO, and I met up with that Alex kid I was telling you about from ATO. Then after about an hour of drinking and hanging out, I got pulled upstairs with a couple of kids. One of them was that Bo kid I was telling you about. And we all went into a room and some ATO guy gave us a little speech about the history of the house and stuff, then we signed our bids and went back downstairs to keep drinking."

"*We* signed?"

12:45 p.m.: Fifa?

"Yeah, me, Bo, a kid on my floor Joe, then these two kids I had never met."

"Bo signed with you?"

"Yeah, why?"

"Just wondering. Heather likes him. They live near each other but didn't hang out much, but she said he was funny."

12:46 p.m.: Cory. Get the fuck over here before I have to make Jimmy play.

"Glad I have this Heather chick's approval."

"What about Max?"

"Max signed Sigma Chi and his roommate Jimmy is unsure yet. Max texted me last night saying Jimmy didn't get a bid at Acacia."

"I thought you said he was already in Acacia?"

"That's what we thought too, but Jimmy must have been lying saying how much they loved him. On second thought, of course Jimmy lied about that."

"When does all of this nonsense start?"

"Should start pledging in about a week or so. Don't know much more besides that, though."

"OK."

"You don't sound too thrilled."

"I am happy for you Cor, sorry, I'm just worried. Pledging sounds terrible and I worry a lot, you know that."

"I know. I love you."

"I love you too. What time did you get home last night?"

"Whenever I texted you. So around 2:30 or so."

"Oh, right, I forgot about that. So what's your plan this weekend?"

"I don't know, I'll probably head over to Max's room later and hang out for a little. Probably going to ATO tonight—we might end up going to a real random fraternity house for shits and giggles."

"Alright, well, let me know."

"What's your plan?"

"I don't know, really. I think I'm going to go out with Michelle and her friends tonight. I'll let you know though. Text me later, OK?"

*Who the shit is Michelle?*

"Will do."

"I love you."

"Love you too, Em, adios."

*12:48 p.m.: 20 bucks. You're on.*

# FIVE

I KNEW PLEDGING WAS GOING TO SUCK. It sucked for every house. I heard rumors that ATO's pledgeship was harder than most, but I always took those with a grain of salt. Mikey didn't talk much about his pledgeship. He was always pretty short when talking about it. Sheff would tell funny stories from pledgeship, but neither really talked about the hazing or anything like that. I also never asked. I was pretty oblivious about it, really. Like, I understood fraternities still hazed, but I had no idea what that even meant. Pledge rides, a study hall, clean the house, be a bartender, I knew all of the job-type aspects of pledging, but was that it? What was the actual hazing stuff? I saw shit in movies, but didn't know if those were based off real instances or just overdramatic film scripts. I didn't know, but I was going to find out soon.

We were supposed to meet at ATO at 10 o'clock. I met up with a couple of guys in Joe's room to walk to the house around 9:45 p.m. The other guys seemed a lot more nervous than I was. I mean, I was nervous too, but more doing-a-new-thing-with-people-I-don't-know nervous and not I'm-going-to-get-killed-tonight nervous. I didn't even know what the worst-case scenario could be, so was more interested than nervous.

As we were walking, we saw 10 other guys waiting at the bus stop. I had met most of them, but didn't know all of their names. Mostly everyone seemed nervous except Bo and this kid Kyle. Kyle had an older brother in the house, and Bo was high school buddies with Alex, so both probably knew what was coming. Looking at those two solidified my anti-nervous feelings. *It can't be that bad.*

We got to the back of the house, and there were already about 15 guys there. I looked around but only recognized half of the people and really only knew a handful of their names. Joe, Bo, Kyle, the two kids from signing night, and Cutty. Cutty was a kid Kyle hung around all the time. He was from Wisconsin, and I had originally met him at Sigma Chi with Max, which is where I would have thought he would end up. *Where's Cam?*

"Yo, Bo, where's Cam?"

"Acacia."

"Wait, what?"

"Yeah, I know, told me Thursday night. Didn't really have a reason."

*Damn, that's shitty.*

The back door opened and some tall guy started walking up to us. Everyone outside stopped talking. We could hear "Requiem for a Dream" playing in the basement. As the door shut behind him, everything went quiet again. Hearing that song instantly gave me the goosebumps. I knew it was a scare tactic, but it definitely worked. We all knew from the song that we were going to be in the basement, and sure as hell not for a party. The tall guy stood facing us and lit up a cigarette. We all faced him, waiting for him to say something. He started counting how many of us were there. I couldn't tell what the number was.

"Give me all your phones," the guy said as he held out a baseball hat.

We all put our phones in his hat. He counted the phones then took a puff of the cig and walked back toward the door. As he opened the door, he looked back and waved us inside. We all followed him as he continued to smoke inside. As soon as the door shut behind us, the place erupted in yelling. There must have been 25 to 30 guys in all black yelling at us to take off our shirts and blindfold ourselves with them. As the yelling continued, we blindfolded ourselves and walked in a single-file line down the stairs into the basement. There must have been three times as many people waiting in the basement, because the yelling got progressively louder to the point that I started to shake. Random comments about weight, height, fashion, a few personal jabs here and there, pretty much anything they could think of. I heard one guy ripping into Bo pretty badly, but it was probably just Alex and his buddies. One kid was yelling at me to go join Pi Kapps. With a blindfold on, all the shouting eventually sounded like white noise. Not many people were yelling directly at me, probably because I didn't know many people. Clearly some people knew my cousin, but nothing specific about me. The single-file line stopped somewhere in the basement. I was a little turned around, but pretty positive we were in the main party room. I felt someone behind me pushing me to the right, so I shuffled over, then the guy pushed my shoulders down, insinuating that I should sit down. The yelling stopped as we sat down. Thirty guys sitting on a frat basement floor, shirtless and blindfolded. *Well, here we go.*

"Turn and face me!" a voice yelled above the rest from behind us.

"We will be your pledgemasters!" another voice belted out.

"So remember our three voices well, because you will not make eye contact with us for the remainder of your pledgeship!"

"If one of you pieces of shit does happen to make eye contact with one of us, you will be in bows and toes for the rest of the night. Understood?"

*The fuck is a bow and toe?*

The three pledgemasters continued to yell at us for a while. Saying we were going to do this and do that. It was in essence just a lot of random yelling on top of "Requiem for a Dream" playing on a loop. Two of the three guys had voices that sounded identical. Both real intimidating loud yelling voices. They would go on and on about how terrible our lives will be, without stuttering or missing a single beat. I couldn't tell the two apart, but could tell there were two 'cause sometimes they would yell on top of each other. But one of the three guys was not the yelling type. Every time he would start talking, it almost killed the mood. Not that I wanted the mood to stay the way it was, it was fucking terrible sitting shirtless and blindfolded in a frat basement getting yelled at, but I found a little joy hearing the third guy try and scream "fuck you" but sounding like a soft-spoken stoner. Almost like if your head football coach was giving you a pump-up speech, but your chemistry teacher chimed in every now and then. Didn't really matter what he said, the flow and energy of the speech was sucked right out of the room every time he chimed in.

"Now stand up and take off your pants!"

*Whoa! What the fuck?*

"We'll see if you want to be ATOs badly enough or wish you had joined Sigma Chi, you pussies!"

I heard belts hitting the ground as people apparently started to take off their pants. My body and mind froze. Sort of like that blacked-out feeling graduation night in high school when you know you're walking across the stage but everything feels like a blur. I could feel my body moving to take off my pants, but I did it involuntarily. It sort of just happened. I didn't know what else to do. I also couldn't see what everyone else was doing, so just went with it and took off my pants but kept them around my ankles.

"ATO is a house of brothers. All of us. Now, how do you become brothers? Well, it isn't only the partying, the chicks, smoking together, getting drunk together, and it sure as hell ain't because you share a fucking business class together. You will have to become one. Have to earn it. You guys think you can come to our parties, drink our booze, walk all over our house the past two weeks like you already fucking live here? You're not a fucking brother yet! These brothers, all of us in this room, had to sacrifice together for months being pledges. Sleepless nights cleaning the house, bows and toes till 4:00 a.m., wall-sits and push-ups all night. You develop a bond with your pledge class. You scrawny little shits will learn to rely on each other, to help each other, and so one day you can grow a little hair on your balls and call each other brothers."

"And you know what, guys? That sacrifice, those sleepless nights, all that starts tonight, you little fragile teenagers."

"So stand up, and sit the fuck back down in rows of four facing us."

"NOW!"

*This is going to be living hell.*

My entire vision of pledgeship had changed. I didn't understand how Bo and Kyle were acting like this was going to be fine. As the brothers started yelling louder, we tried to figure out how to sit in rows of four blindfolded. It was impossible. Eventually they started arranging us so we were in position. I had no clue what was about to happen.

*If there is any gay shit, I'm leaving. I don't give a fuck how much they would yell at me as I left, or how much Pi Kapps would rip on me for quitting ATO after one night. I'm not about to grab another dude's dick. Period. I will do whatever fitness shit they want to throw at me. So be it. But I'm not going to be used as a puppet for no fucking reason.*

I had finally realized what worst-case scenario was. I heard the brothers shuffling around and shushing each other. A few guys in the background started laughing as the pledgemasters started talking again. *Fuck this.*

"You will be ours, all three of ours. Us pledgemasters will control you for the next eight months or however long it takes you. So for the remainder of the night, everyone else in this room gets to call the shots."

Everyone in the background exploded. The noise made me flinch sitting on the ground. There was still a lot of shuffling of furniture and footsteps moving around in front of us. I had no idea what was going on, but from the sounds of the movement, there was going to be an arena type of thing happening, or some sort of activity that required space.

"Alright boys, this is your one night with these faggots. Make sure they clean everything up when they're done."

"Six o'clock p.m.! Tomorrow! Out back again!"

The pledgemasters were intimidating, but they at least seemed organized; from all the yelling, the brothers sounded like a pack of wild beasts. All the brothers started shushing each other again as one guy started talking.

"My name is Jordan Phillips, and I'm the president of ATO. Pledgeship is going to suck. Your body will hurt, you won't sleep much, you'll have to do some shitty stuff, but there is a light at the end of the tunnel. The light that you probably experienced one-tenth of the past couple weeks partying here. So, for the rest of tonight, I want to remind you of that light, and what you really have to look forward to. So gentlemen, take off your blindfolds and enjoy."

As we took off the blindfolds, the song "I'm in Love with a Stripper" came on, and we were all facing the stage with two girls in bikinis standing on separate mattresses. One blonde, one brunette, both with unbelievable bodies. The blonde was hotter but older; the brunette had the better body, but looked really young. Not like underage young, but in her low twenties young. Brothers started cheering and handing out beers as the strippers pulled two freshmen on stage to lie on the mattresses. *Wait, how long have these girls been in this basement?*

I was still shaken up. Was not expecting this kind of night, but I grabbed a beer and opened it. I made eye contact with Alex, who was holding a beer to the left of the stage. He lifted his drink to cheers me and was laughing. I forced a mini-smile and started drinking. *Now I know why Bo and Kyle weren't worried.* The whole night was to scare the shit out of us before eventually congratulating us and reminding us that at the end of the day, this whole fraternity thing was going to be a good time. The concept of the night made all of us start laughing uncontrollably. Thirty freshmen, no phones, blindfolding ourselves, getting half naked, sitting in rows of four, all in preparation for strippers. It was like a stripper assembly line. Shirts already off, pants already off, ready for a lap dance.

The brothers were throwing around singles like it was a game, but that didn't faze the strippers. They kept giving lap dances to the two freshmen lying down on the mattresses. Each lap dance lasted about five minutes, then the next two would go up. As the dances went on, the strippers started getting a little more erotic. Started with bikinis on, but after a couple dances the top came off, few more the bottom came off, few more and they would start spanking or getting dirtier with their dances. Brothers started pushing other brothers to rotate in with the freshmen. Some of the brothers were rearranging the rest of us freshmen to make a few of us get dances before the strippers eventually left. Alex and Bates moved Bo, Kyle, and me toward the front row. *If they went from clothed to spanking after a few dances, what is going to happen to us?*

There must have been 300 singles up on the stage, and the money kept coming, but hell, the strippers were earning it at least. They were both sweating from dancing for what must have been an hour already. They were pounding champagne between dances too. Add in the brothers hooting and hollering in the background, and these two chicks were getting wild. The brothers had already decided that Kyle and Bo were going to be the last group and I was going to be in the second-to-last group. I was lined up to where I would have the blonde chick, which I originally wanted because she had a better body, but she had started doing a lot more with her dances than the brunette. She made it a game to give the guys a boner, and if they got one, she had started using belts to whip them. She would turn the guy over, lower his boxers, and the brothers would count down from three before she spanked him with the belt. It left an insanely big welt on this one junior's ass. The brunette was doing a lot more giggling and shoving her tits in guy's faces. Pretty much standard lap dances from her, but the blonde had turned into drunken theatre. She was doing the splits, licking chests, riding guys backward. It was damn porno on that beat-up mattress.

Cutty was the guy right before me and had grabbed her boobs while she was doing the splits over him. It seemed completely customary given the circumstances, but for some reason the blonde took offense to it. She lowered her head down to his boxers and bit his boxers, ripping the top left side. To the brothers' applause, she continued to rip his boxers off. Not completely off, just ripped them into the shape of a thong. It was mildly impressive how she could do that so easily, but after everything I'd seen, this was not even close to her first time. And by the brothers knowledgeably applauding throughout, doubt it was even her first time at ATO either. She continued to grind on Cutty while his balls were pretty much showing. It was as close to sex as Cutty could possibly have without actually being inside her.

"Cory, all you, bro!"

My legs started to quiver like it was freezing in the basement, but it was about 100 degrees. I went to chug the rest of my beer but realized it was empty. I really didn't want to get spanked by this chick, and I sure as hell didn't want my boxers shoved into my ass like a thong. I didn't know what could possibly happen, but hell, at the end of the day it was still a lap dance. I made eye contact with the brunette chick as she grabbed the champagne bottle.

"Oh, Jen, you got a cute one. Here, want some?"

She held out the bottle of champagne. It was a really bizarre sight, seeing a completely nude chick handing you a bottle of champagne. Without really having a choice, I grabbed the bottle and took a sip. Well, I more or less poured it into my mouth rather than taking a sip. I didn't know where these chicks had been before, and really didn't want to find out.

"Oh, you think you can have some of my champagne, do ya?"

*Oh shit.*

The blonde grabbed the champagne bottle out of my hand and pushed me down onto the mattress. She started pouring the bottle of champagne into her mouth like I was doing before, but she kept going. She sat on my lap and let the champagne spill all over both of us until we were soaking wet. She was already sweating, but now both of us had about three-quarters of a bottle of champagne on us. She started dancing on top of me and licking the alcohol off my chest. *This girl is an absolute lunatic!*

I couldn't help but think of Emily while this was going on. It was an insanely nonmanly thing, to get a lap dance from a chick while thinking of your girlfriend, but I couldn't help it. I felt guilty all over again. We had put a lot of effort into this long-distance bullshit, and day one of pledging I had a hot blonde licking champagne off my chest. Not to mention dancing with Sara day one of college, but that was an afterthought now.

After a few tricks, I was really hoping the champagne move was her one big variation before the strippers ended with the Bo/Kyle finale.

"Not having a good time?" the blonde stripper whispered into my ear.

"Who can complain about this?" I replied, trying to act confident.

"Well, it doesn't feel like you're having a good time," she said while bouncing up and down.

I didn't know what to say, so I just shrugged. The music was really loud, so no one could hear our conversation. The blonde stared into my eyes like she was envisioning something. Her hair was soaking wet, makeup all messed up, smiling with this grinding-of-her-teeth smirk, and had a sensual stare with these massive brown eyes. Actually these weren't brown eyes, they were legit black eyes, gazing into mine with this drunken-tired stare.

"Well, I'm going to fix this, then."

She sat up and scooted toward me so she was sitting on my chest. She flipped over so her knees were by my ears and was now lying on top of me. She lowered her head right over my boxers and started exhaling. I could feel the long warm breaths, one after another. The brothers were laughing as she continued to blow warm air into my boxers. It was getting pretty difficult to keep my composure, but with pure determination to give me a boner, she started motorboating my dick. I had held strong for as long as I could, but now it was genetically impossible to avoid the inevitable. I felt my boxers start to move, and next thing I knew, the blonde stripper flipped me over and grabbed my boxers with both hands. She ripped my boxers all the way off and threw them off the stage. The brunette walked over, and they both grabbed belts as the brothers counted down from three. I knew what was coming, so I clenched as the first two belts hit me.

I was naked, soaking wet, on a stage in front of 100 people I met a week ago, getting whipped by two Indiana strippers. The belts hurt way more than I would have thought too. After the second wave of belts hit me, I lay on the mattress in agonizing pain. One of the strippers had missed and hit my lower back. The whole situation had gotten out of control, but I knew there was no turning back. Pledgeship was going to be miserable. I realized earlier in the night that I was going to have to lie to Emily about most of pledgeship, but being facedown on some random wet mattress made it official—I was going to have to lie about pretty much everything. Shooting pains went up my spine as the third wave of belts hit me. My ass was numb. *The lying is going to have to start tonight. Well, I guess it started night one, but fuck, now it's actual lying.*

If tonight was supposed to emulate this light at the end of the tunnel as life after pledgeship, then me lying to Em wasn't going anywhere. I always believed that ignorance was bliss, but it would be impossible to hide your entire college experience. Breaking up with Em was the only thing I could think of. *We will never make it all four years.* The cycle of lies would be too much to control. I knew the pain from the belts would go away sooner or later, and the guilt of the night would wash over eventually, but struggling to keep all of college a secret would be unbearable. *I'm going to have to break up with her.* It was unfair for her, and fucking dreadful for me. A surprising fourth wave of belts hit me as I started to get up. The blonde put her hand on my ass and started to squeeze. It felt like one of those Indian burns you got in fifth grade. My entire naked body collapsed on the mattress. The brothers were roaring in applause as the brunette grabbed my boxers from the ground. Still squeezing my ass, the blonde leaned into my ear and handed my boxers to me.

"Welcome to ATO."

# SIX

"HOW WAS IT, COR?"

"It was fine. Didn't really do much. Pretty much just sat and listened while they tried scaring us?"

"What do you mean?"

"We got there and went into the basement, and sat down and got introduced to most of the brothers. Then they gave us a bunch of rules we have to follow, like no walking up the front stairs or using the front door. Stupid shit like that. And like what our normal days will be like with study tables and cleaning the house and stuff."

"But I mean, how did they scare you? By telling you not to use the front door?"

"Yup, exactly. But no, by yelling. That's pretty much it. By yelling and looking pissed. I mean, I'll pretty much be their bitch for a couple of months, but not physically or anything, just go pick up their food, clean the house, that dumb shit."

"Did they haze you?

"No, not at all. We literally sat in the same spot all night."

"I don't get fraternities."

"Frats are pretty easy to understand. Pledges do brother's chores for a semester while they party, then become brothers and have new pledges do their chores while they party. It's an enjoyable little cycle. Now sororities, I have no fucking clue."

"So you are going to be someone's slave so you can have a slave and party next year?"

"I was joking, but apart from the whole making friends, living together, and socializing parts, yeah, ultimately pledgeship is slavery."

"It's not funny, Cory—it's so fucking dumb."

"Em, I was kidding."

"Ashley is going to join a sorority, I think."

"Which one?"

"Don't remember the name. I met a couple of the girls, they seem really fake."

"All are."

"Oh, that makes me feel better. You're going to be partying with 'fake' girls every week."

"You took that comment way too literally."

"I just don't like it, Cory. I don't understand why you want to be a part of that shit. Like does ATO haze you guys at all?"

"Not that I know of. I would know if they did, I think."

"How would you know?"

"From Mikey or from one of the other guys."

"Like how can you be someone's slave for a semester while they hit you with a paddle?"

"Em, come on. The paddles aren't for hitting us; it's like a trophy type of thing."

"OK. Whatever. You'd better not lie to me about this."

"I won't, Em, have nothing to hide."

"Now you don't, but like if they hit you, you have to tell me."

"I won't let anyone touch me, Em, I promise you."

"I hope so."

# SEVEN

**STUDY TABLES WAS THE FIRST THING WE HAD TO DO.** Joe and I walked from class together and met the rest of the guys at the computer lab across from ATO. Our three pledgemasters were by the front door, so we all had to look down when we walked in. We had the whole place to ourselves. Four rows of desktop computers, about eight computers per row, the place was pretty big. Two of the pledgemasters left, and the other one shut the door and stood in front of us.

"Alright dipshits, this is study tables. We have this room reserved every Monday to Thursday from 6:00 to 9:00 p.m. If you can't do your school-work in that amount of time, then you're a fucking idiot. No one has an excuse for bad grades. Here's the sign-in sheet. Looks like two of you already quit after last night . . ."

*Who quit?* I looked around but only knew half the people anyway, so it was pointless.

". . . Every time you leave, you have to sign out. Only two people can be out at a time, and can't be gone longer than 20 minutes without having an excuse. Trust me, we will be checking in on you. Be at the house at nine o'clock. Got it?"

No one responded apart from a few head nods.

"Did I hear a *yes sir*?"

"Yes sir!" we all shouted.

The pledgemaster left. We had the place to ourselves but didn't know what to do. School had barely even started yet. On top of the fact I only knew about six out of the 30 guys in the room. Bo and I were in the corner reading ESPN articles and talking football. Our conversation led to an entire study table's debate over NFL teams. Handful of Colts fans, Rams fans, Giants fans, and then majority Bears fans. There was also a Lions fan, a Steelers fan, a Buccaneers fan, a Packers fan, a Jets fan, and a Texans fan.

"Like, you're not a true Texans fan, right?" Bo said to a kid from Houston named Garcia.

"What are you talking about?"

"You can't be a born and raised Texans fan. Like, what were you before the Texans?"

"Rooted for the Cowboys—that's all there was in Texas."

"So you're a Cowboys fan."

"No, I was never a fan. I only rooted for them when they were on. I was young."

"So then the Texans come to town, and you just jumped on the bandwagon?"

"Dude, the Texans have been a team since when we were in fifth grade. That's plenty of time to become a fan. My dad was a Houston Oilers fan."

"So is your dad a Titans fan now?"

"No, he's a Texans fan."

"So if you were in your twenties when the Texans became a team, would you still be a fan?"

"Dude, I have no fucking idea."

"So right. Everyone is like a fake fan. Like, more convenient than real tradition."

Garcia sat there shaking his head. Everyone around was laughing watching the two idiots argue. That's how most of our conversations went. Dumb, meaningless, and about nothing. Bo was aggressively persuasive, which was a perfect fit for me because I was very argumentative. Not in an asshole way; I just enjoyed debating different sides of things. Any sports-related conversation, we hopped right in. It was nice to share common fandom with Bo because he was a ruthless arguer.

Time went by quickly, and none of the pledgemasters returned, so that was a plus. We walked back to the house around 8:45 p.m. Everyone stopped talking the instant we could see the house. It was a very demoralizing feeling, knowing you are walking into a shitty night. There was a lot of hesitation in our walk. Looking up the hill at the house, we all realized study tables would be a break from pledging, but the inevitable shittiness lingered the entire time, so it wouldn't feel like a break. Almost as if a prisoner got to leave every day but had to walk back to jail by nine o'clock.

We got inside and were told to go into the basement and sit in rows of four again. The basement had three chairs on the stage facing outward. The brothers were in the basement again, but this time not nearly as many. Only about 10 to 15. Once we sat down, the three pledgemasters came in like clockwork. We all sat there with our heads down, staring into our laps.

"Every day, 9:00 p.m. sharp, you will sit like this. In this exact spot. After our meeting, you will clean the house till 10, then you will hold security positions around the house and be available for jobs. Whether we have a party or not, you will be in position every night. That means rides, bartenders, front door, back door, front stairs, back stairs, second floor, third floor, all of it. You will be prepared for a party every single night. Then we will have a final meeting down here at either midnight or three in the morning or whenever the fuck we tell you, got it?"

"Yes sir!" we shouted in unison.

*Bartending while there is no party?* The more I thought about it, the funnier it seemed. Especially for the older brothers. Come home from the bar on a Tuesday night or something and bring a small group of people back to the house and *boom*. Music playing and a bartender waiting for you. Dangerous concept in reality. Having the option to party without any planning.

"Weekends are a different story. We'll play those week by week!" the soft stoner barked out, attempting to sound intimidating.

His voice was still the only one I could recognize out of the three. I hadn't seen any of their faces. Based on a brief second walking by them in the computer lab, they were all big guys. Sitting there, I wondered who would want to become a pledgemaster. The power trip you felt had to be crazy. For an entire semester or however long pledgeship was, you have 30 people afraid of you, looking down when you walk by, and doing anything you ask them to do. They must have that retired-police-officer syndrome.

Is that even a thing, or did I make that up? Like how a police officer can boss people around and tell people what they can and can't do for 35 years, always being the one with the bigger dick in any confrontation. But when they retire and lose all their power, they can't adapt to society and get arrested for battery or assault or something. I definitely didn't make that up, has to be a thing. Needless to say, I knew I was going to avoid the pledgemasters at all times.

When the pledgemasters finished talking, we walked around the house cleaning. The place was a mess. No one had cleaned our party from the night before. If you wanted to call that a party. Bo, Kyle, Cutty, and I walked up to the third floor to start cleaning. Those were the juniors, and in our eyes, the cooler grade. Maybe because they didn't care as much about pledgeship so were generally nicer, or I just knew more of them. Nevertheless, one of the pledgemasters walked by and assigned us the third-floor cleanup crew, so I was going to get to know them even more.

I walked around with Bo from room to room cleaning up. Clothes, shoes, dip cups, ashes, pizza boxes, dirty napkins, you name it. The rooms were everything you would imagine a frat room to look like, but once we finished cleaning a room, the whole fraternity was a lot nicer than expected. I was pleasantly surprised and excited I would be able to live in an objectively nice room. *As long as pledges clean it.*

"Yo bro, can you come in here," some lumberjack-looking junior said, poking his head out into the hallway.

Bo and I looked at each other, confused who he was talking to. The guy must have been 6'5" with a massive jet-black beard. He looked like he was a 35-year-old retired hockey player who had never shaved his playoff beard. We both followed him into his room and were astonished how clean it was. The cleanest room we had seen, and none of the pledges had cleaned it yet. He had music posters all over the wall. Bob Marley, Lil Wayne, Kid Cudi, and Snoop Dog, and a framed picture of the Rat Pack around a pool table. He had a black leather L-couch and what must have been a 60-inch TV mounted on the wall with two big speakers on either side and a subwoofer on the ground. This dude's setup was dope.

"What's good, boys? I'm JR," the retired hockey player said as we walked in.

"Hey man, what's up, I'm Cory and this is Bo. You need your room cleaned?"

"Nah, I keep this place pretty fresh, but I will eventually. I do need one of you to do me a favor. You guys got a car?"

"I have my cousin's car in the parking lot," I replied.

"Cool cool. Well, my buddy left his backpack here this afternoon. I want one of you guys to drop it off to him. He lives over in Smallwood. That cool?"

Smallwood was the biggest apartment complex on campus. It was also known as little New York City. Every non-Greek student from NYC or New Jersey lived there. I couldn't confirm this stereotype 'cause I'd never been, but I always heard Mikey joke about it.

"Yeah, that's fine, we can—you want us to now?"

"Yeah, I'll text him now to come outside in five minutes. Thanks, boys."

"No problem."

"Wait, here's my number too. Call me just in case."

Bo and I took the bag and got into Mikey's car. Another break from the house felt nice, even if it was merely a five-minute drive to Smallwood. The guy was waiting out front when we pulled up. Wasn't dripping NYC like Mikey had hyped it up to be, but I guess he was wearing a white V-neck and had that accent that made you sound like you were a Newsie, so maybe the stereotype was true. Hell, if the fraternities' stereotypes were true, why would apartment complexes be any different? We dropped off the bag and started driving back to the house.

"Cory, you gamble?"

"As in poker?"

"No, well that too, but I meant sports betting."

"I mean, yeah, I make bets with people individually, but not like with Vegas or at the casino if that's what you mean."

"Yeah, I'm not talking about betting the ponies on a Wednesday afternoon at the OTB, but like, betting NFL spreads or college games on the weekends."

"OTB handicapping on Wednesday afternoons sounds electric."

"We should go, has to be some bumblefuck casino in Indiana. But anyway, I was thinking of starting a sportsbook."

"Like for our pledge class?"

"For whoever will bet. Like just go off the Vegas spreads posted online."

"Go for it dude. Or wait, are you asking me to book with you or bet with you."

"Well either one, really. Was more or less verbalizing my idea."

"Oh, for sure. Yeah, I mean I would for sure bet with you. Take your money like I do in FIFA."

"Literally everyone knows you play twos in FIFA and NHL. One on one is child's play. But my buddy booked in high school and made a killing. Vegas wins every time."

"I would love to make the spreads in Vegas. That job would be dope."

"It's not just the spreads that get people. They take 10 percent on top of all wins. That's what people don't realize, you have to be better than 50 percent to break even, and the more you bet, the more Vegas wins 'cause of the 10 percent juice."

"I'd never really thought about that. I only bet with my buddies and do $20 straight up, or like $5 on a game of *Madden*. So stop me if I'm wrong. Someone bets 10 times and wins half of them, then he's down money? Five wins of let's say $10 bets, five losses of $10 bets. Throw in 10 percent fee per win, which means he lost $50 and won, what, $45?"

"Right."

"Damn, legit, never thought about that. I feel like this isn't public knowledge. I knew Vegas was rigged! Well damn, how much money would you need to start it?" I said, now more intrigued.

"Shit, my buddy only had a G at first that quickly tripled before going up and down. So to be safe, though, I would want around $3,000. I got about $2,000 I can play around with now."

"Oh yeah? The Riverwood kid playing around with two Gs."

"Yeah yeah yeah, not play around, but I have that much to fluctuate at first, yeah. But like I said, eventually the book wins. You just have to be prepared to take a hit at first. In fact, taking a hit early on is better because then people start betting more. And when people start losing, that's when they throw in the parlays and teasers. It's the ones who lose at first that might stop gambling."

"The fuck is a teaser?"

"Hard to explain. But it's like a parlay, where you bundle a bunch of bets together and they all have to win in order for you to win. But the difference between a parlay and a teaser is you don't win more money like you do with a parlay—instead, you get to tease the spreads down. So like, if you pick Alabama, Ohio State, and Notre Dame to all win their games by 10, if you do a teaser, then you can change the spreads to have them win by only three. It's complicated, but that complication is where people fuck up."

"Because Alabama winning by three sounds better than winning by 10."

"Exactly! Like, people think favorites will always win, but like, won't bet on Notre Dame because they think they might only win by seven instead of 10. But if you can tease that number to three or even one, then people will take all three teams, without thinking that they are now betting on three teams to win, not just one."

"And that's how Vegas makes their money."

The more I listened, the more I thought how nice it would be to be on the other side of sports betting.

"For the bad gamblers, yeah. But it's like you said. OK, I'm going to sound like a salesman, but when you bet, being better than 50 percent against the spread is hard in itself, but over time, decent gamblers would eventually get to 50/50, thus down 5 percent because of the 10 percent on the wins. Bad bettors get simply murdered. Get caught by tricks and traps of Vegas, like betting heavy on favorites, play a couple of NFL Sunday parlays, three-team teasers. Could easily be a 40 percent bettor, so ultimately like a 35 percent bettor or worse."

"If it's as easy as you say it is, I mean, I have a couple bucks in my own personal checking account. I can chip in on this."

"Hell yeah, dude! That makes things so much easier."

"But it would be easier to go 50/50, right?"

"Yeah, I mean if you have $2,000 we would start with a safe 4K and split it down the middle."

"I could find 2K. Let me rob a RWN garage then I'll be good."

"Great. But for real, you in?"

"Yeah, honestly I do have money in my savings from umpiring over the years. Only if your 2K gets eaten up first."

"I'm fine with that."

"Dude fuck it, I'm serious. If you're fine sacrificing your money first, I'm in. So how do you want to do it?"

"Well, actually, my buddy took the 10 percent on the losses and not the wins. Said people bitched more when someone thought they won $100 and you give them $90. Sounds dumb, but said it was easier asking someone who lost $100 for an extra $10. But essentially, we'll have people text us their name, the game, the spread, time, and amount. Then we'll respond with 'OK' or something to make the bet official."

"Damn. There's no online site?"

"No, not that I know of."

"Alright, well what if we don't text back?"

"My buddy would still accept it, unless it was within five minutes of game time. The site he got his spreads from has up-to-date spread histories. So if someone texted like, Bo, Bulls v Celtics, Bulls -3.5, 5:04 p.m., $20, then he would go to the site and look up what the spread was at 5:04 p.m. for Bulls–Celtics and accept the $20 bet if the spreads matched. And iPhones show the times of the texts, so not like anyone can lie about that."

"So, you really don't even need the confirmation text."

"No. That's just for the other person. Like, if you don't respond, they may think it doesn't count, so if they lose, they really won't think it should count. The 'OK' finalizes the bet."

"Gotcha."

"So, you in? I want to start as soon as possible while NFL and NCAA football are going on."

"How are you so confident you won't go broke?"

"Dude, Vegas sportsbooks exist for a reason. My buddy ended up making like 10 grand for two years of booking. I can assure you, after at least three months, you will have more money than you started with."

"And you don't feel bad taking our friends' money?"

"No one will go broke on this. Besides, there will be some people who will make a lot of money off us. But in the end, you make a small amount from everyone, and the more people you have, the more you make. Think of it as our friends paying for entertainment."

I couldn't tell if it was just Bo's persuasiveness or general reassuring tone, but a blanket 10 percent fee for essentially receiving text messages sounded too good to be true. The whole texting thing still felt sketchy, but avoiding the Internet paper trail sounded better anyway. I always had my laptop at class and my phone when I was hanging out, so it would be easy to check the spreads and send the confirmation text.

I knew Em would not approve of this. I could explain the 10 percent rule and throw statistics and facts in her face, but she wouldn't get it. It would still be gambling to her. Not that she was opposed to sports betting or anything, we had gone to a casino a couple of times, but it would be the gambling on this scale that I was positive she would be against. And I wouldn't blame her. I was still contemplating the breakup anyway. Not that being a bookie would push the breakup over the edge, but it would be another issue to deal with. I really didn't want to break up with Em, though. There was something about her that made me comfortable and laugh all the time. I loved it. At first I thought the lying would be too much, but the more I thought about it, the more I thought it would be totally doable. I wasn't going to be some professional bookie or go to strip clubs regularly or hook up with other chicks or anything. In the grand scheme of it, the only things I was going to have to lie about were some pledging stuff, *easy*, being a bookie, *little harder but still pretty easy*, and some long party nights like welcome week, *already did it, and it was easy*. I was still going to be the same Cory Carter from high school. A good loyal boyfriend. *I mean, it's college; I can handle a few white lies to my long-distance girlfriend.*

Bo and I talked logistics a little more as we pulled back up to the house. The rest of the night we really didn't do much. There was no party, so our security, for all intents and purposes, was to be accessible for the brothers.

If a brother needed something, there was someone in every hallway or bathroom, or in the basement. That's pretty much how it was the next couple of days. Study tables, get yelled at, clean the house, sit in security, do random jobs, get yelled at again, go home. Lather, rinse, repeat.

I understood it was going to get harder down the road, but I wasn't as worried or intimidated by the verbal abuse like some of my pledge brothers. I don't know if it was because I was more self-aware than the rest of my pledge class, but it was clear what ATO was trying to get out of pledging. Apart from being a slave for stoned/drunk brothers to do jobs for them, pledgeship was supposed to be a repetitive, monotonous, shitty experience that you did as a team. Just a drawn out shitty roller-coaster ride you did together. I knew other houses at some other schools that got brutally hazed and lived in hell for eight weeks straight. Like, slept on brothers' floors and missed classes, but then after eight weeks they were done. Two months, then brothers. ATO's and really most of IU's pledgeships were three times longer than that, but not as chaotic. A slow and painful death rather than a sudden gun to the face.

I actually sided with the slow and painful route. I didn't understand the eight-weeks-of-hell pledgeship. For starters, that meant brothers only got to use pledges to clean and do shit for two months, then the remainder of the year they got nothing. But more importantly, I didn't think the pledge class itself could become good friends in two months. Hearing from Mikey and Sheff, pledgeship was the time you became good friends with your pledge class, then living in was the time you became good friends with everyone else in the house. If you spend all day every day with your pledge class, you eventually will learn to like or at least understand and respect everyone. If you draw out the pledgeship for a long time, the pledge class has no other choice but to get along, joke around, and become good friends while everyone goes through the same shittiness together. That was exactly what we were doing in the first week, and it was already obvious this was going to be a long and repetitive next couple of months.

Bo and I opened up our sportsbook and let whoever wanted to bet, bet with us. To be honest, it was apparent real quickly that gambling was bringing us closer together. It was a distraction from the awfulness of scrubbing toilets and mopping the basement floor after a long night. It was also hilarious. Just shocking to me how people would persuade each other to all make a bet together. Study tables became the time where our pledge class would try and "take down the book." Guys instantly became NFL insiders or college-football experts with comments like:

"Dude, Saints on the road in Buffalo, fade them! Heavy on the Bills or at least the under."

"*Always* ride Urban at home. Tebow will not lose in the Swamp."

"It's the Bears' first time against Seattle since the NFC Champ game. Take the Seahawks first half. The crowd is going to be nuts."

"Yo bro, we *have* to go Chris Johnson's under 93 rushing yards, right? Rex is going to be blitzing all night."

"You know what, I really like the Longhorns this year. They are 8-1 odds to win the BCS Champ. Let's put a hundo on it."

"Boise will go undefeated again. I don't care the spread, just bet the money line every single game."

The shit they came up with was something you couldn't make up. I had Max and Jimmy betting with me too, and Bo had Cam and a few from other houses. All together we probably had 20 to 25 people betting. Mostly $10 to $50 bets. Nothing major, but it brought everyone together. It gave everyone something to talk about after a long night or when we sat in security. Looking up spreads and researching NFL or Vegas trends.

Cutty was the best about it. Or worst about it. Couldn't really tell whether he was the best or worst yet. Either way, he was the funniest for sure. He would come up with these obscure parlays that he would convince himself were good.

7:27 p.m.: Cutty, 5-team parlay, Vikings first quarter under/second half over/Peterson rush yards over 89/Favre under interceptions 1.5/49ers cover +7.5, 7:27 p.m., $20 to win $326.

*7:30 p.m.: OK. Might as well give me the $22 now.*

7:33 p.m.: Vikings always start slow. LOCK, yo

First four nights he made a combined 10 bets. He lost 8 of those 10, but hit two obscure parlays, not the Vikings one, thankfully, and so was close to even, besides the juice, Bo and I were pocketing that. It all felt like fake money. We would win $200 one night, then lose $350 the next. Even though the wins and losses were fluctuating, the adrenaline of betting was constant. I thought I would eventually get used to it and not care about the bets anymore, but when an NFL kicker is lining up for a 45-yarder in the fourth quarter of a blowout, and you have $400 on the line, it's a feeling I don't think you ever get used to. The thrill of victory or agony of defeat was not something I was planning for when I told Bo I would book with him. I did it as a business decision. An additional 10 percent on every lost bet. A 5 percent bonus if everyone is 50/50. Bo's money gets used first. Plain and simple. I mean, yes, I knew there would be some jitters or nerves risking my money, but having no control over the bets and watching your money either double or disappear based on your friends' decisions was unlike any emotion I'd ever had. It was intoxicating, actually. Like skydiving. You knew in the end you would most likely be safe, but the adrenaline rush throughout was addicting. I had been sucked in, and I loved it.

# EIGHT

**I MADE AN EXCEL SHEET TO TRACK ALL OF THE BETS AND DID MOST OF THE DOUBLE-CHECKING OF THE SPREADS.** Everyone realized quickly that Bo was terrible at responding to texts, so would text me instead. Bo was more of the money collector and distributor anyway, which I was completely fine with. He could deal with the actual exchanging of money, I could deal with the actual bets. I was more organized than he was, but he was more straightforward and, well, an asshole, so he did the asshole things. We remarkably made a solid team.

It had only been about a month or so, but things were running pretty smoothly. One of Cam's buddies in Acacia was up about $1,100, but he bet daily and was starting to get cocky with his bets, so that number was bound to change. Our pledge class was down a combined $955, so that $1,100 number didn't seem too terrible.

Brothers in the house had started betting too, including two of the pledgemasters. It was really strange to text back "Yes sir," but it surprisingly made life easier. It was a way to break the ice in the pledgemaster-pledge relationship. One of the pledgemasters, Hahn, had started coming to me for everything he needed. He would text or call me at any point in the day and ask for someone to do something for him. Get food, pick him up, pick up his girl, clean his room, grab a blunt, etc. Most times I just did it myself, but I would forward the text to my whole pledge class if I was in class or didn't want to go get him a blunt at three in the morning. It was annoying as shit at first, but being the pledgemaster's right-hand pledge had its perks. It was almost like a respect thing between us. If I did whatever he wanted, he wouldn't treat me like a pledge. He would let me get away with some things that most pledges couldn't do. Like smoking during security or bartending every big party instead of sweeping pubes off toilet seats. He even let me have a couple drinks while I bartended, which didn't sound like much, but in the moment of being sober at a massive party, having a couple drinks felt heavenly.

The one thing that sucked about running the sportsbook was dealing with friends owing you money. Granted, that was mostly Bo's job, but after a mere five weeks, Cutty had already been cut off after he couldn't pay back-to-back weeks. He wasn't down big, but he would get into this hole, then keep doubling down until he hit. Matter of fact, Cutty was turning into a mess in general. He had overslept a Sunday morning meeting, missed a study table, and did a shitty job cleaning our pledgemaster's room the second or third week of pledgeship. The line between big, jolly kid and kicked out of ATO was starting to be drawn. It was annoying to deal with too, but we all loved him, so never got too mad.

It was Saturday and we had to work a day party with Tri Delt at three o'clock, so I walked to Pi Kapps to grab my cousin's car. It was a 2001 black Jeep Grand Cherokee. The most stereotypical family car imaginable. Pledgemaster Hahn wanted me to bartend the day party because his girlfriend and her friends were coming over. I had driven his girlfriend Stephanie around about 20 times over the past month, so she loved me. Steph was pretty cute, but her friends were absolute rockets. They were all sophomores. Day parties consisted of loud music, a lot of drinking, and a revolving door of people to and from sororities, to and from the bars, to and from live-outs, it was just insanely busy. I knew I was going to bartend, but still wanted Mikey's car to help with the rides.

The house was in decent shape. We cleaned late the night before, so there wasn't really that much time for it to get out of shape. But it was a different type of cleaning they needed. Make sure speakers were working, laptop in the basement, enough booze behind the bars, etc. We never went to get the booze, though—ATO didn't want anyone to get pinched for a fake ID. Not for the pledges' sake, God forbid they cared about us, but for ATO as a whole. They would get put on social probation if one of us got busted buying them beer.

I walked down into the basement and ran into Cutty sitting on the couch, fake cleaning. I handed him the keys and made him responsible for driving Mikey's car all day. He still owed us about $200, so driving was the least he could do. It was 1:15 p.m. and our pledge class was slowly trickling in. There was no meeting before the party. We just had to have the house cleaned, rides ready, bars stocked, bartenders in place, and be in security by 2:00 p.m.

I followed a bunch of the brothers down into the basement so I could start bartending for them. "Bartending" was a loose word. It was ultimately just filling shot glasses and handing out beers. The dean had made a rule that no hard-alcohol bottles could be floating around the party; they had to stay behind the bar at all times. We were supposed to be making sure that was happening, but a pledge telling a brother to hand him the bottle of booze was like telling a dog to give back a treat he had eaten. It was pointless.

The girls started arriving in waves, all by grade. Steph and her friends walked right up to where I was standing and gave me a hug. Their friends called me "C" because Steph had forgotten my name one of the first nights I drove them. Drunken sorority girls yelling "pledge C" did get annoying, but they were all really hot, so it almost didn't count. There was like a hot/annoying chart with me, and "pledge C" was nowhere near the threshold.

The girls kept telling me to drink, but I couldn't unless one of the pledgemasters said so. Joe came down to help bartend once the party got bigger. Day parties were always the bigger parties. Night parties were more organized, but day parties were an open invite from three o'clock till whenever for any girl who wanted to drink. There were about 50 to 60 people in the basement. Pledgemaster Mueller came up to the bar and started fucking with Joe and me by making us look down as we bartended. He was a prick and the meanest by far. Throw in being the best at yelling, and he was the most intimidating of the three pledgemasters. A loose-cannon cocksucker, plain and simple. He got his dick hard by making us as uncomfortable as possible, and flexed his pledgemaster muscles around other people any chance he got. *He'll have retired-police-officer syndrome, I'm positive.*

About an hour went by with more and more people coming in and

Joe and I constantly filling up shot glasses. The music was blaring, and everyone was wearing day-partying outfits. Guys were wearing T-shirts, jerseys, or tank tops, and the chicks were all in brightly colored tank tops and jeans shorts, or wearing some cheap Tri Delt jersey with short shorts and high white socks.

"Six shots."

"Yes sir."

"And two beers for me and Steph."

"Yes sir."

"Hey C!" Steph said standing next to pledgemaster Hahn.

"Quit looking like a weirdo and look up. Just don't make eye contact with me, you shit," Pledgemaster Hahn shouted over the music.

I looked up and smiled at Stephanie but avoided pledgemaster Hahn. She smiled back as her friends were drunk giggling.

"Now pour those shots into that cup."

I discreetly followed his eyes to a red Solo cup sitting at the bar. ATO's president told us to only use the white plastic shot glasses for hard alcohol. But I didn't give a shit, and wasn't going to say no to pledgemaster Hahn. We had our respect deal, and I wanted that to keep going.

"Yes sir."

"Drink it."

"Excuse me?"

"What did you say?"

"Excuse me, sir."

"That's for you . . . *Ceee* . . . Now fucking drink it."

Pledgemaster Hahn had let me drink before, but not peer-pressure drinking and definitely not six shots of vodka.

"I . . ."

He took his hands and grabbed my jaw and moved my face so I was looking right at him.

"Just drink the fucking cup, Carter," he said in a whisper-yell so only I could hear.

I looked into his eyes for a couple seconds before realizing he wasn't fucking around. His grip on my jaw was that of drunk muscles. He wasn't letting go until I grabbed the cup. I took the cup and tried not to think too much, so took a big inhale before chugging the vodka. There was a lot of liquid in the cup. I mean, six shots was nine ounces. Luckily this came from the pussy white plastic shot glasses, so it was probably closer to six ounces. But fuck, that's still half a beer amount of liquid. I took the first gulp and it seemed surprisingly fine, but as soon as I swallowed, I let out an exhale through my nose and into the cup, and the air from my exhale bounced off the vodka and created this reflective smell coming from the cup. The warm vodka smell hit my face like a tidal wave. A tiny gag/cough came out as I continued to drink. The vodka was room temperature, and with each passing gulp, I could feel my stomach turning. I finished the third and final gulp and my eyes were watering as I looked up at pledgemaster Hahn, who was holding another red Solo cup. This time, it was filled with orange soda. Without asking, I grabbed the drink and chugged it. It was a vodka-and-orange-soda mixed drink. My stomach was already full, but my mouth was watering and needed to replace the vodka taste immediately. As I drank it, streams of the drink went down the sides of my cheeks and down my neck. I smelled the vodka from the mixed drink and felt a throw up coming on. I put the cup down and Steph grabbed her two beers, shaking her head at pledgemaster Hahn, and walked away.

*What the hell is going on?*

I had that feeling right before you throw up where it seemed like someone was squeezing your stomach and your mouth was watering. I looked over at Joe, but he wasn't watching. He was on the other side of the U-shaped bar. A burp came up of warm vodka and orange soda. I turned to the garbage as swiftly as possible, but it was a false alarm. My stomach was in a knot and I had goosebumps that were out of control. I poured myself some generic version of Sprite into an empty cup and casually drank it to try and help both the taste in my mouth and the knot in my stomach, but it was useless.

After another two hours of bartending, the party showed no signs of slowing down. The shock from the booze had left, but I had a solid buzz going when I saw pledgemaster Hahn walking back again.

*Goddamnit!*

"Two beers."

*Here it comes . . .*

"Yes sir."

I glanced at Stephanie, and we made eye contact until she quickly looked away. *What the hell did I do?*

"Quit being a stiff, bro. Be normal."

*What?*

I turned around to see if I was missing something. I had no response, so got the two beers and handed them to him.

"Pour 'em into cups, por favor," Pledgemaster Hahn said, slurring his words.

I knew what was coming, so without thinking, I stared right into his eyes. He was grinning back at me.

"Last one to finish it has to shotgun a beer. 3, 2, 1 . . ."

Without hesitation I took the cup and started to chug. I could feel the beer spilling off pledgemaster Hahn's chest as he poured the whole cup onto himself without drinking a single drop. After two seconds, he put his cup down with still a half a cup of beer in mine. It was a lose/lose to even attempt to challenge him, so I took another beer and began to carve out a hole with my dorm keys. Trying to be as incognito as possible, I shotgunned the beer behind the bar. I didn't want my pledge brothers and the other brothers to see me drinking while I was pledging. It was more an unwritten code that pledgemasters could allow you to drink, but they weren't supposed to. Or at least, we were supposed to say no. Besides, I didn't want to make it seem like I had special privileges as a pledge. But in all honesty, it was not like I was enjoying chugging six shots of vodka and two beers.

It was about 7:15 p.m. and the party was dying down. The juniors and seniors were at the bars, and the sophomores were still going strong, but were more dispersed throughout the house rather than packed sweaty-shoulder-to-sweaty-shoulder in the basement. My movements had slowed a little, but pledgemaster Hahn wouldn't let me sub out with another pledge. He made me keep bartending. He was practically sleepwalking at this point. Could barely stand up and was completely incoherent. He was eyeing me like I did something to him, and Stephanie had stopped coming over to talk to me. After about five minutes of just looking at me, he walked up to the bar and made me take another shot. This time just one shot, so I didn't argue and took it. Minutes later he came back and made me take another. But by the way he said it, it genuinely seemed like he didn't even remember making me take the first shot. I looked around for backup, but no one was around to help.

"What the fuck are you doing? I said *beer*," Pledgemaster Hahn said as I took the second shot.

"You said shot, sir."

"I know what I fucking said . . . *Ceeeee*."

*There's that fucking C again.*

I didn't know what I'd done to that motherfucker, but all the perks of longer study tables before tests, casual beers during parties, and smoking on weekday nights that he had given me all seemed irrelevant. It was pointless to put up a fight, though. A blacked-out pledgemaster was not someone you wanted to fuck with, especially when the juniors were at the bars. Way too much control and power with no one sober enough to monitor it.

"Sorry, sir."

I grabbed the beer and handed it to him.

"Well, drink the fucking beer."

I took the beer and poured it into a cup. I chugged the beer as he laughed and threw an empty red Solo cup at my head before walking upstairs. Once pledgemaster Hahn left the house, I switched out bartending with Ray and went upstairs to fake clean the third floor. I was pretty drunk at this point. My stomach consisted of eight shots and three beers with no food since noon. Joe and I half-assed cleaned for another hour trying to avoid all the drunken brothers and stressed-out pledges. All the brothers were hammered and stumbling around the house. Majority of our pledge class was driving all over campus, but the rest of us were cleaning and doing security positions in case IFC or the cops came.

9:47 p.m.: Anyone who is not driving or has someone to drive has to go to Seventh and Dunn in 15 minutes. Pledgemaster Mueller approved.

Kyle had a droid, so no one could tell who was in his group texts, but I assumed it was our whole pledge class. Seventh and Dunn was the senior live-out. It was almost an extension of the house and was really the only live-out we had to consistently clean and bartend. The brothers who lived in Seventh and Dunn were ex-pledgemasters and the ex-president of the house, so they got a little preferential live-out treatment. Most of the other live-out houses got a once-a-week cleaning if any at all. It was a dope house though. All wood inside with no doors separating the rooms, and the second floor had a lofted balcony wrapped around overlooking the first-floor living room.

The house was only about a half mile away, so Joe, Kyle, Bo, Ray, KT, Wolf, and I met on the porch and walked over. Barr and Russ stayed at the house for security. Normally if it was just a few of us who had to go there, it would be to clean up or bartend a pregame, but asking for every nondriver was a new request.

There was pretty much an open-door policy at Seventh and Dunn, so we walked in, but no one was home. There were empty plastic shot glasses and cups all over the place. We instinctively started cleaning up. I looked at Bo, and he was signaling for me to come over. I walked over and followed his eyes down and saw white powder residue on the glass table. It almost looked like a dusty glass table, but we both knew what it was. I had never seen cocaine before, and from Bo's face, he hadn't either. We didn't know if we should clean it up or if that was like throwing away their drugs, so we just left it. Seconds later a car pulled in the driveway. I looked outside and saw Garcia walking in the house with his head down followed by four seniors. I didn't know any of the seniors, but one looked like if JR had shaved his playoff beard and lost 20 pounds during his hockey retirement.

"Get in the fucking basement, all of you!" some tall, lanky senior barked out.

*Shit.*

We all ran into the unfinished basement and instantly were getting yelled at by the four brothers.

"Can someone explain why we didn't get a ride!"

"Heads down, you fucking pieces of shit!" another senior screamed.

*There is no way a ride home makes them this pissed, right?*

"Sir, I'm Kyle, the pledge class president. Did you text someone for a ride?"

"Hi, Kyle pledge class president, do you think I would be fucking yelling at you if I never asked for a ride? Jesus, how fucking stupid are you guys?"

"Well, sir . . ."

"Don't 'well, sir' me, you fucking retarded long-faced piece of shit. Get in bows and toes, all of you!"

We all looked around at each other and sluggishly started lying on our stomachs.

"What the fuck is this candy-ass bullshit? You haven't done bows and toes yet? Jesus Christ, no wonder you're a bunch of pasty, no-face, soft twats. What the fuck does it sound like, elbows and toes, you fucking morons. Balance on your fucking elbows and fucking toes!"

We all got into a plank position, but instead of having our forearms and toes touching the ground, it was elbows and toes.

"I know the car that was supposed to get us, so we can do this all day until that person speaks up."

Every text message we got for rides we would forward to Kyle, who would then coordinate the ride. Kyle knew where every car was at all times and knew who needed rides next. He would get the text, see who the closest driver was, then copy and paste that text to that driver. But we didn't know if the seniors originally texted one of us or Kyle directly.

My elbows were on fire and felt like they were digging into the ground. My whole body was shaking trying not to put a lot of weight on my elbows, but it was impossible. Bo had already fallen down and was really struggling to hold the position. I was trying to recall if I got any texts for rides, but couldn't remember anything.

"What . . . was the phone number . . . sir?" Kyle said as he struggled to hold his plank.

"Dude, shut the fuck up! I asked your pledgemaster for a ride and he said he got out of a black Cherokee and it would turn around and be there in five minutes."

*Fuck!* That was Mikey's car that Cutty was driving. Cutty wasn't in the room, so I didn't know what happened or what to do. Everyone in the basement knew I had the black Cherokee. I knew everyone was thinking it was my fault. *Fuck you, Cutty!*

"The Cherokee is my cousin's car, sir."

"Why the fuck does that matter to me? Who said that?"

"I did, sir . . . in the blue shirt . . . my name is Cory," I said, trying to stay upright.

"Why the fuck didn't you pick us up then?"

"I was bartending in the basement."

"Well, then who was driving?" another senior chimed in from the back.

I hesitated. I didn't want to rat out Cutty. He was already the worst pledge, and it wasn't even close. We all knew another slip-up and he could get kicked out of the house.

"I don't know . . . sir."

"You don't know who drove your fucking car?"

"No sir."

"I'm going to pretend like I didn't hear that. Does anyone here know who was driving this clown's cousin's car tonight?" the tall, lanky senior shouted.

No one said anything. There was a lot of huffing and puffing at this point, and KT and Bo were pretty much lying on their stomachs trying to muster up the strength for just 10 seconds of planks.

"Bows and toes make you break. You cocksuckers will learn soon enough," the tall, lanky senior said, walking over to us.

My elbows felt like I was putting all my weight on a bruise, but my elbows weren't even the worst of it anymore—my abs were exhausted from the sheer plank workout. I felt like I was going to pass out or throw up or both.

"Well, someone is fucking lying to me!"

This guy wasn't joking around. His yelling wasn't a forced yell, he was furious. I glanced around and saw Kyle, Bo, Wolf, Garcia, and Joe. I was positive none of them would say a word because they were all boys with Cutty. KT and Ray were tricky, though. Both good dudes, but KT was shy, so I couldn't really get a read on him.

"Get the fuck up, you pathetic, unathletic fat-asses!"

I saw Bo and KT lying on the ground trying to balance on their elbows while the tall, lanky senior was leaning over screaming at them. I knew it was a matter of time until KT broke.

"Well, blue-shirt Cory? You going to say something?" the senior said as he turned toward me.

My whole body was still shaking, and I could feel the pain in my elbow radiating to my fingers. My back was practically completely bent as I tried to stay off my stomach.

"I honestly don't know, sir."

"Is that fucking alcohol on your breath? Wait. Are you fucking kidding me?"

*Oh fuck.*

# NINE

"EVERYONE BUT THIS MOTHERFUCKER GET THE FUCK OUT OF MY FUCKING BASE-MENT RIGHT NOW! GO!"

I collapsed onto the floor and lay there as the other pledges left the basement. Kyle, Wolf, and KT gave me a look of confusion as they walked out. Clearly they hadn't known pledgemaster Hahn was force-feeding me booze.

I lay on the ground catching my breath and resting my elbows and abs as I waited for the inevitable. At this point, it was only the one angry senior and two other seniors I didn't recognize standing over me, and then the skinnier nonbearded JR sitting on the stairs. My whole body hurt, I was light-headed, but still tried to figure out what to say. *If I say it's Cutty, he will be gone, I'm positive of that. If I say I was drinking, I don't know what they will do to me since pledges can't drink. But two of them used to be pledge-masters, so they know how it works. Right?*

"Did I tell you to get off of bows and toes? Here, you piece of shit, rest your elbows on these."

I got off my stomach as the tall, lanky senior tossed two beer-bottle caps at me. I was in shock. The senior was already positioning the bottle caps for me as I put my left elbow into the first bottle cap. The bottle caps lightly touching my now raw elbows felt like bee stings. I tried to find my balance on them but physically couldn't. My elbows were throbbing so severely, my mind almost wouldn't let me put my weight on them again. The booze was really affecting me now. I was sweating straight through my shirt. I finally was able to dig the open part of the bottle caps into my elbows and got up into the plank position.

"Are you drunk?"

"Yes sir. Pledgemaster Hahn let me drink."

"Hahn *let* you drink?"

"Yes . . . sir, well . . . made me drink."

The bottle caps dug deeper into my skin. The seniors stood over me for about a minute as I struggled to keep my balance.

"Well, then who the fuck had your car?"

"I don't know, sir."

I tried to keep my butt in the air, but it was impossible. I tried bending my arms down so I was more on the forearm side of my elbows, but any movement made it worse. The pain was growing exponentially. It felt like the edges of the bottle caps were slowly sawing my elbow bone in half.

"We know you know—why the fuck are you protecting some deadbeat cocksucker that fucked up? No one just puts their keys on a table and walks away to go get drunk bartending a basement party."

"I . . . don't know what to say . . . sir."

"Well, we'll wait till you know what to say."

I didn't know how this was going to end, but it had to end. The pain created a light-headedness that I wasn't going to overcome. Eight shots, two beers, no food, an intolerable elbow pain, and an impromptu ab workout. I was stunned they cared so much about not getting a ride. *Oh fuck me, the cocaine!* I knew I could keep saying I didn't know, but they would just stand there until I broke. Every five seconds to a bunch of coked up ex-pledgemasters felt like five minutes to me in bows and toes. I was going to lose this battle. I had to say something.

"I'm not . . . going to tell you . . . who it is, sir," I said as I tried to steady my breathing.

"What the fuck did you just say?"

"Who was driving my car . . . I'm not going to . . . rat him out?"

"Jesus Christ, you're fucking kidding, right? Who the hell is this kid you're protecting?"

I didn't respond. I was really hoping the whole having-a-backbone thing would work. It was my last chance.

"Dude, who the fuck are you? Like just fucking tell me who it was!"

I didn't respond again. My mouth was watering as I collapsed to the ground. The bottle caps were stuck in my elbows as I lay on the ground wheezing for air. I tried to regain my balance onto my elbows, but couldn't gather up the ab or elbow strength. My left elbow was bleeding pretty badly, and the stream of blood ran all the way to my fingers. I pulled the bottle caps off my elbows and attempted to put them on the ground more in front of me so I was on more of my triceps, but my arms slipped on the blood and I fell again.

"Get out of bows and toes and lie on your back."

I was delirious at this point, but I recognized the voice. The JR look-alike was for sure JR's brother. The tall, lanky senior looked at JR's brother as I lay on my back taking inconsistent deep breaths. I heard him mumble something to the tall, lanky senior, but I couldn't tell what. I was broken.

"Get up, I'm driving you home," JR's brother said.

My shirt already had blood on it, so I wiped my elbow off with my shirt. There was a bottle cap–shaped cut on my left elbow and a red outline on my right. The mix of blood and sweat made it look way worse, but none-theless, it didn't look good.

I didn't say anything to JR's brother as we walked upstairs. I stopped by the kitchen sink to splash water on my face and wipe off my arm. We both walked out the side door toward his car. He had a black Audi with tinted black windows.

"What's your name?"

"Cory Carter."

"Yeah, I thought I recognized you, you're Carter's cousin. Wait, you're the bookie, right?"

"Yes sir."

"No need to *sir* me. I'm Jason."

"Yeah, I know JR. Cleaned his . . . his room."

"That must have been an easy job. Kid's a neat freak. So who was this kid you were protecting? I don't give a shit about pledging, by the way—trust me, kid, you'll lose interest too after like first semester junior year."

*You'll lose interest? You just sat there while I was being tortured to speak for the past 20 minutes! What the fuck are you talking about?* We pulled out of the driveway and sped off. The inside of the car was all black leather with completely unnecessarily loud speakers built inside.

"Some pledge who would get kicked out of the house if he fucks up again."

"Damn. Holy shit I respect that, I really do. We had two boys get kicked out of the house in the first couple weeks of pledging. Cool dudes, but didn't give a shit about pledging. One transferred, not sure what the other is doing now. I could tell you weren't going to say shit, that's why I ended the bows and toes."

"Appreciate it."

"No need. Shawny is literally crazy. One of my best friends, but a legitimate psychopath. He would have stayed all night."

I had heard stories about Shawny because he was Bates's and Alex's pledgemaster, but I didn't know what he looked like. Jason and I sat in silence for a couple blocks.

"Tell me about the handicapping? Your cousin was telling me about it a couple weeks ago."

I wasn't down for small talk. I was exhausted, in agony, and downright miserable.

"It's fine. As long as people can pay you."

"I don't sports gamble, really. How many people betting with you?"

"Around 40 to 50."

"You guys got a website and shit?"

I looked over at Jason but his eyes stayed on the road. *Well, I guess we are small talking.*

"Um, nah. Guys text me or my buddy Bo the game, spread, and all that information. Then we just look online at the spreads to double-check they were correct."

"How you doing with it?"

*Seriously? Just stop talking, bro.*

"As in money? Up a couple hundred per person. Nothing major. Some guys only bet once or twice total, others daily. But once NBA and college hoops get going the same time as bowl season and NFL playoffs, well, the longer betting people the more money we make."

I could feel myself not making much sense, but felt woozy so didn't care to correct myself. Jason caught the hint. He gave me a double take as I put my head in my hands to rub my eyes.

"So listen, this probably isn't the best time, but I've been looking for someone to help out me and JR once I graduate. I'm not sure what you've heard from your cousin or pledge brothers, but JR and I deal some bud to our house and a few other people around campus. Like you said, nothing major, but I'm graduating this spring and JR is studying abroad in Barcelona next fall. So the house will need a go-to guy."

"Why you asking me?"

"Look, I have real respect for your cousin—we were in a bunch of classes together my sophomore, his freshman year. He's a good dude. But really I have a lot of respect for what you did tonight. It takes a real man to stand up to a senior for your boy. I feel that. Clearly older guys respect you if they are betting with you, and you obviously can handle the money part."

"I don't know. My buddy Bo is the one who started it. So I'm not sure if I'm looking to start selling weed too. But thanks for the offer."

"It honestly sounds worse than it is. I used to deal when I lived in the house, but now JR does most of it. Really, you just buy from this dude who's been selling to ATO for years, then hand out the bud around the house. I mean shit, I'm not pressuring you to start selling, bro—it's an opportunity to make a little extra cash if you want it. You and your buddy, Bo, is it? Can do it together. You can say no if you want, thought I'd come to you first."

"Is there a reason it's going from senior to junior to freshman?"

"JR said the sophomores are mostly pieces of shit, and it's always been a dude living in the house 'cause that's easiest. So another junior wouldn't make sense because that would be for one semester."

We turned into the parking lot behind the dorm. Everything was still hazy. I was nauseated, if my elbows touched anything I would get a shooting pain down my arm, and on top of it all, I was starving. As Jason turned down the music, I noticed how loud the music had been and how nice the car was. All black everything. Then it dawned on me. *JR's dope TV, overall setup at the house, and Jason's blacked-out Audi? Either these kids are loaded or ATO's weed dealer makes more than "a little extra cash."*

"I'll think about it and get back to you. Been kinda a long day."

"No worries, bro, let me know. Don't want you to feel pressured from a former pledgemaster. Oh, speaking of, for pledging tonight, don't worry about it. I'll talk to your pledgemasters. It's Mueller, Gilbert and . . ."

"Hahn."

"That's pledgemaster Hahn to you." Jason said sarcastically.

I forced a laugh and thanked him for the ride as I got out of the car. Pledging the rest of the night hadn't even crossed my mind. After what I went through, I felt like I deserved the rest of the week off, let alone the night. *Cutty should have to pledge for me for a week, that piece of shit.*

I walked into my room to find Bennett passed out. It was only 11 o'clock on a Saturday night, and he was sleeping. His innocence was baffling to me. I knew he didn't drink, but I had seen him walking around with friends, so it's not like he was a loner. I turned off the TV and opened up the mini-fridge. Pizza rolls, two meatball Hot Pockets, and Bennett's leftover dinner. The food court was closed, and no chance I was walking to the late-night food court, so I grabbed the Hot Pockets and put them in the microwave. I was going to shower but didn't want the microwave to go off while Bennett was sleeping, so I waited.

I grabbed my phone and saw I had 37 text messages. Most were group texts among my pledge class, a few angry texts from Em, and then the rest were college football bets. I went through and texted "OK" to every bet without checking the spreads. Most of the bets had already finished, so it didn't even matter.

*11:34 p.m.: Hey Em, sorry about tonight. I had to walk over to this senior's house to clean up and left my phone at the house. I'm back in my dorm now. I love you and text me when you get back tonight.*

As I sat there, the whole night flashed through my head like a replay. Almost like I had been blacked-out drunk and was now rehashing the night in the morning.

*Why the fuck did I keep drinking? Why didn't I just say it was Cutty and then explain everything standing and not in bows and toes?*

While I replayed the night, the idea of JR being the house dealer while I cleaned his room kept popping into my head.

*I am in his room every single day cleaning. Granted he let me smoke with him a bunch of times, but I have never seen a mass amount of weed, or a scale, or cash lying around. None of it! Hell, I've never even seen anyone come into his room asking for a gram. If anyone at Indiana University were to find out, it would be the guy cleaning his room every day.*

I took off my bloody shirt and stared at it as Jason's proposal reentered my head.

*Jason and JR both seem like good guys, but they do sell drugs. If I get caught as a bookie, it wouldn't be that bad, but getting caught selling drugs to an entire house would be a felony. Not to mention dealing with Em. Hiding being a bookie is hard enough with all the texting, but selling pot from my room would be downright impossible. I would have to live a double life.*

My Hot Pockets were about to be done, so I stopped the microwave with two seconds left and took them out. I sat on my futon burning the shit out of the roof of my mouth one bite at a time, thinking.

*Would have to live a double life? Here I am, already home at 11:00 p.m. on a Saturday night, eating two Hot Pockets as I try not to wake up my already asleep roommate, while I apologize to my long-distance girlfriend for not texting her back soon enough. On the flip side, I have a pulsing headache from being drunk from alcohol hazing, bleeding from physical hazing, and I'm a bookie who was just asked to start selling weed. I'm already living a double life.*

I looked up at Bennett as he slept on the top bunk. The thought of a double life continued to circle my still-unhinged brain.

*Is a double life even a bad thing? Bennett's sound asleep, dead sober, and probably going to wake up in the morning feeling great and rested. He's either been too sheltered his whole life, which has made him naïve and oblivious to his surroundings, or he has been sober long enough to see the negative effects of drinking and drugs firsthand and so he has chosen to never do them. But whichever it is, Bennett is Bennett. There is no double life with him. No multitasking, no vices, nothing. He's a cardboard cutout of an 18-year-old that parents created in a lab. Whereas I've been drinking and smoking longer than he has been able to drive a car. Yet here we are. We both ended up in the same place, at the same university, with the same major, living in the same dorm room, both in on a Saturday night. Sure, he'll get better grades than me and graduate before me, but once he gets to the real world, what is going to be the difference between us? Grades won't matter after our first job. No one is putting their GPA on their résumé at age 30. At this rate, Bennett will still be socially awkward during meetings or even at a happy hour with coworkers. Where he may have me in book smarts, I will have him in social experiences and approachability. Tailgates, pledging, fraternity parties, bars, spring-break trips, skipping class and binge-studying for finals. Things normal college students share in common, and things everyone will probably have in common with their managers, their manager's manager, and so on. Hell,* Animal House *and* Old School *are the same movie, just across different generations, so it's not like times have changed a lot. His business job will be better than mine at first, but five years down the road, we'll be roughly in the same position. All of the partying, pledging, and things I've seen and done haven't been a double life—it's just me. It's molding me into a more self-aware, outgoing person.*

I finished eating and chugged my water bottle before getting into bed. I sat there staring up at Bennett's bed.

*JR and Jason are both nice guys who happen to sell weed. It isn't a double life they live; it's who they are. It's not like they are selling heroin and getting ATO hooked on it or something. They're the bridge between smokers and a drug that'll be legal eventually.*

I was so in my own head. I couldn't tell if the night had caused me to think so carefree or what, but being the house drug dealer and house bookie made too much sense. Bo and I would live together, and all the money from our house would go in and out of our hands. Wouldn't be hard to hide things from others, clearly JR had the recipe for that. The only thing I would have to worry about would be the "dude who has been selling to ATO for years."

That line stuck in my head. Some random guy sold to ATO for years, with a revolving door of new customers eager to buy. But the thing that stuck with me was that this guy probably had no need to worry about getting caught because college kids cared way more about protecting their image than he probably did. So this dude just had to make sure JR and Jason found a new guy every two years, and everyone could keep the relationship running smoothly. Not to mention that two years as the fraternity's pot dealer wasn't even enough time to get in any real trouble. It was a cycle. It was a flawless plan.

*A plan that won't be living a double life; it will just be another experience that will continue to shape me as person. It won't change me. I'll still be me, and I'll never lose sight of that. It's a harmless cycle. I'll just be in control of it . . . I'm going to do it.*

# TEN

**I WOKE UP IN THE MORNING ASHAMED OF MYSELF.** I had been brainwashed to do things I never thought I would do, and that gave me this sense of defeat. It was a feeling of being broken down and stripped to my core. I had done nothing wrong—better yet, I had done everything right—but was tortured like a terrorist. It was such a mindfuck. There was no other way to describe it. I had let them control me, and that really, really bothered me.

Pledging felt different after that night. I guess the executive board yelled at both Hahn for getting me drunk and the seniors for hazing me without their permission or supervision. We weren't a part of those meetings, but according to Alex, the house was pissed because all hazing was supposed to be done in the basement of the house. The worst part about it was Cutty claimed pledgemaster Mueller never told him anything about picking up the seniors. Or at least that's the story Cutty was going with. But regardless of whether the house was on my side or not, my mentality on pledging and on just myself had changed.

I didn't know how to get a hold of Jason, but I talked to JR briefly the next day. He told me he would introduce me to his hookup sometime after winter break, and I could make my decision then.

The final month of the year went by slowly, as the parties had started to die down before finals. Bo and I made sure to collect and distribute money to everyone before winter break and promised everyone we would keep the book open during the break. After collecting from everyone, we were up a total of $2,135. Cam's buddy had lost all of the $1,100 and then some. Our pledge class had bounced back to close to even, but the house as a whole was down a good $1,800. Which seemed like a lot, but with about 50 to 75 people, that was only equivalent to everyone losing a single $25 bet.

Winter break went by quickly. Bo and Kyle came over to my parent's house a couple times, but really I just drank with my high school friends and hung out with Em every day. It was reassuring to hear pledging stories from my high school friends, but to them the stories were more a joke they could laugh about. To me, it still didn't sit well. My buddies Steve and Ricky both had similar, yet a lot tamer, hazing stories with bows and toes, but Steve's pledgeship had already ended. His was one of those eight-weeks-of-hell pledgeships that consisted of no sleep and being on call 24/7 for eight weeks. Ricky did have a great story about driving two brothers home from the bar and getting pulled over. The brothers were underage, so as soon as the car stopped, they ran. The cop chased them but never caught them. Ricky said he didn't drive away because clearly the cop had his license plate. Once the cop came back he started yelling at Ricky, but Ricky said he was a pledge in SAE and those guys he was driving were from a different house. The cop was an SAE alumnus, so he laughed and told Ricky, "I'll let you off with a warning, but tell your SAE brothers not to leave the pledges out to dry like that again. By the way, no pledge drives other frat guys home, so find a new excuse, because that one is horseshit."

When I got back to school, the intensity of pledging ramped up another notch. Old rules everyone had ignored over time were now enforced. Rules like calling brothers by their last name, not looking at our pledgemasters in the eyes, only one person could be gone from study tables at a time, staying until at least 1:00 a.m. every night, etc. Also, physical hazing got formally introduced. Pretty much everyone in our pledge class had been physically hazed already, especially Bo, Kyle, Wolf, Garcia, Joe, KT, Ray, and I, but now any screwup led to hazing in the basement. Before, it was just staying late and getting yelled at, but now it was you forget to vacuum a room, you do wall-sits; you're late picking up a pledgemaster, you do push-ups. Simply any mess-up led to physical activity. But in most cases, the brothers would just make up reasons for us to get hazed. For example, we had to give pledgemaster Mueller our class schedules in alphabetical order, and so I went and printed out everyone's schedules while everyone else cleaned the house. I put them in alphabetical order, but then pledge-master Mueller made us do bows and toes because they were out of order. It was one of those things that everyone in the room knew was dog shit because, well, I have a brain and know how to alphabetize names. But the pledgemasters needed predetermined ways of making us get hazed, and that was the part that fucked with everyone's head. There was no way around it. I wanted nothing more in my life than to have the lack-of-self-control feeling to be over with.

Weeknights were longer, weekends were close to 24 hours, with every night ending in some sort of physical hazing. It was hell, but it was already almost over, so I wasn't going to quit. People would purposely wear layers of clothes so if the night called for push-ups or wall-sits, we would take off the sweatshirts, and if bows and toes were on the agenda, we had a little more cushion at the elbows. My brain had tried to compartmentalize real life with frat life, but the longer nights and physical hazing started to blur those lines.

The nights got progressively worse too. On the first Friday of February, Russ and Wolf had to drink a bottle of hot sauce and Joe had to eat a raw onion because they all forgot to clean the house. The next night we got called into the basement around midnight. It started with push-ups, moved to wall-sits, then bows and toes, then just sitting. It was a dark steam room of sweat. My legs were dead, ass was numb, elbows burning, neck throbbing. The yelling had turned into a dull hum in my ear. I was so exhausted I couldn't really depict individual voices. Everyone sounded the same, everyone was yelling, and all I could focus on was my throbbing legs.

I heard shuffling around, so I assumed we had to do wall-sits again. Everyone got up and walked over to the wall and squatted down. A blacked-out sophomore who no one really liked ordered us to have the first person in the wall-sit line walk across everyone's thighs then reestablish wall-sit position at the end. Everyone had to shift over and do that until we had all walked across everyone's thighs. Wolf went first and started walking, but by the time he was halfway across and standing on KT's legs, the douchebag sophomore chucked a bucket of ice water at KT. KT's legs slipped out from under him and Wolf and KT went falling to the floor. The water- and ice-throwing shenanigans continued for the remainder of the night. Our legs were Jell-O, so even leaning on the wall was painful, let alone trying to squat while getting pelted with ice cubes.

Bo was the last to go, and the one we were most nervous about. It wasn't necessarily Bo's weight that was the problem; it was close to an hour of wall-sits on top of five hours of being in the basement doing a cross-fit-like workout. We realized after five minutes of constant failure that Bo had to lie across everyone and crawl—this way, not all his weight was on one person's leg but rather spread across three people. He got past the first few people, but his sweatpants started getting pulled off as he crawled over everyone's thighs. His hands were in front of him doing an army crawl, so he couldn't shift over to adjust his pants or else he would fall off. By the time he got to me, his pants were already off. I looked to my right at the beginning of the line, and everyone was standing up, laughing out of hysteria. We were all so drunk off exhaustion at this point that the sight of Bo crawling on top of our legs with his pants at his ankles was one of the funniest things we had all ever seen. No one was thinking about the physical pain of wall-sits or the mental pain of being awake at what must have been four in the morning, everyone was brainwashed to laugh at Bo.

After about five more pairs of legs, Bo's boxers started to get pulled off as he slid his fat, wet, butt-ass naked body across everyone. At this point, we were howling at Bo to finish as his dick just dragged across each person's wet lap. Once Bo got to the end, he and Cutty both fell down. We all started cheering as Bo put his pants back on. The brothers in the room were crying laughing as well, and we all circled up and yelled the creed of ATO together before finally leaving the basement. In some weird, deranged way, it was my first time feeling like a part of the house and not exclusively a pledge.

The moment we got upstairs and walked outside, we all snapped back into reality. That mindfuck feeling I had experienced the bottle caps night had taken control of everyone. I never believed in the concept of hypnotizing people, but after doing an extreme Olympian workout from midnight to six a.m., a damn magician could have snapped his fingers and we could have been convinced to do anything.

We had this type of physically demanding hell pledgeship for another three days, but after that six-hour-hazing night, nothing was going to phase us anymore. That night was bizarre and just insanely shitty, but it felt like a fitting and perfect metaphor for the end of pledgeship: just dragging your dick across the finish line.

When it was all over, the amount of free time I had was silly. I would go to class for an average of an hour or two a day, maybe. Then I would be done. That was it. No cleaning, no study tables, nothing. Just sleep, school, then free time. Garcia's roommate had transferred to a small college in Colorado, so Cutty had pretty much moved into his dorm room. That dorm room turned into the gambling den. *FIFA, Madden, NHL, NBA 2K, Call of Duty,* on top of sports betting with Bo and me. We recruited Cam to gather the money from Acacia, since he was officially done with pledgeship as well. We would throw him $50 or $100 here and there for helping us out. It seemed like everyone in Acacia was losing bets daily. Like, nobody over there was winning. We felt bad, but no one was losing that much either. Just every bet they sent in seemed to be wrong. It was impressive, actually, to lose that much. Bo and I would always joke that people in ATO should bet the complete opposite of whatever Acacia was betting every week, but that was essentially what we were doing anyway.

JR had set up a time for me and him to go meet his hookup. I was nervous to meet JR's weed dude 'cause I still didn't know if I wanted to do it or not. I couldn't really pinpoint exactly the image I thought he would look like, either. Part of me imagined a washed-up college student who grew pot in his house and just lived off his drug dealing money. Another part of me pictured some sadistic businessman with ties to the police and shit. Regardless of the image, I was nervous.

On Thursday, I left Garcia's place and headed over to meet JR at ATO. Em was coming to visit over the weekend, so I was glad I was getting this drug dealer visit out of the way beforehand.

"What's good Cory," JR said as I walked up to him in the parking lot.

"Hey JR, what's up," I replied as I gave JR the slap-hand-then-pound handshake.

JR was the only person I knew who still did that slap-hand-then-pound handshake outside of everyone from 1996 to 2006.

"Does he prefer us walking or driving?" I said, motioning to JR's car.

"Mike? No. He doesn't give a shit," JR responded as if it were a dumb question.

*Well, there goes my theory that everyone named Mike goes by a different name.*

"I just text him when I'm coming, then call him when I'm in the driveway and walk in on the phone like it's my apartment. When I text him I'm coming, he unlocks the front door."

We jumped in his car and drove about four or five blocks and pulled into a driveway on the right side of the house. There was a long alley in the back that was parallel with the entire street. The house had stone stairs leading up to a tan front porch. The second floor of the house was a beat-up brown color, almost like he decided to paint the house but ran out of paint before finishing the top. The house wasn't secluded at all either; it was in a neighborhood surrounded by other college houses.

"Yup, in the driveway, walking in now with my buddy," JR said on the phone as we got out of the car.

I followed JR through the door and walked into the house. The whole house smelled like weed, but not fresh burning weed. Just that smell a sweatshirt gets after you smoke in it a couple times without washing it. Or when you smoke on the way to the movies and forget to crack open the windows. It was that smell when you get back in the car.

Before we reached the dining room, JR turned through the open doorway into the family room on the right.

"'Sup amigo?"

"What's good Mike? This is my buddy Cory," JR said as he did his signature slap-and-pound handshake to this Mike guy.

"'Sup Cory? You can call me Mike."

*Hey Mike, that's a filler name, right? You go by another name, don't you? I bet you do.*

"Hey, nice to meet you."

"So you're going to be taking over for the Norris brothers, huh?"

I didn't know what to say. I looked at JR hoping for a save, but he wasn't even looking at me. I realized there was no downside to saying yes now, so just kept up with the flow.

"That's the plan, yeah. Next year."

"Oh, right, you're going to like Europe or some shit next semester, right?" Mike said, looking over at JR.

"Yeah, Barcelona, and when I come back I won't be living in the house. I'll be graduating next May."

"Damn, you graduating? Fuck man, time flies when you're having fun, am I right?" Mike joked, playfully nudging JR.

Mike was the former in those images I'd created in my head. He was in his late thirties, maybe a rough early thirties. He was wearing a grungy green String Cheese Incident sweatshirt with baggy jeans and wasn't wearing shoes. His place was nothing special, just a normal college-town house. It was obvious he was living here alone, but the place was relatively clean. Apart from the post-hotbox-after-the-movies smell.

"So Cory, you a freshman?"

"Yeah, just got done pledging."

"Oh shit, hell yeah. Well, next year we can work out our own plan. The Norris bros did things differently than each other. Jason liked buying a lot at one time and then coming every other week or once a month or something. JR likes coming often and only buys an O or something."

"'Cause then it gives me an excuse to only sell grams to the brothers, instead of eighths or even quads. And I don't really like having more than an ounce of pot at the house. I'd rather swing by here and pick up some more."

"I'll always have more here," Mike said as he slapped the side of the couch.

"OK, sounds good," I replied, trying to keep it simple.

"You staying the summer?" Mike asked me, looking down at a stain on his sweatshirt.

"No, I'll be moving into the house at the beginning of August."

"Yeah, Mike, I'll still be here for the first part of the summer, so I'll probably be stopping by, but not the normal weekly ounce or anything. Not that many brothers still on campus. You know?"

"Right, right. Cool, man. Well, do you guys want anything to drink or something?"

"No, I think we're good, just wanted you to meet Cory."

"Well, the deed is done, my friend. Now for the real matters. Your herbs and spices."

Mike reached to the side of the couch with a big grin on his face and grabbed a big army-green fabric backpack and flipped open the top. I couldn't see inside, but Mike pulled out a Ziploc bag of weed. It was roughly the size of a normal lunch-sized Ziploc. It was the most bud I had ever seen in person. Each nug was about the size of a golf ball, and there must have been at least 30 of them.

"So prices stay the same, Cory. $175 for the halfer, $300 for the O, $500 for 2, then $750 for the QP."

*Seven hundred and fifty dollars' worth of weed! Jesus Christ.*

"Sounds good," I responded confidently, but he could have been speaking Swahili and I would have had the same response.

"It's some good shit too, the guy I get it from grows it. If you ever want mids for like edibles or some shit let me know. I could probably get my hands on some of that cheap shit too."

I roughly knew how much large amounts of pot were, but Mike could have swayed $100 on each one and I would have nodded my head and smiled. JR's logic of buying smaller amounts made sense to me, but from doing some quick mental math, it seemed as if it was a better deal to buy in bulk.

JR handed him $300, and we left out the front door again. The whole operation was effortless. JR dropped me off at the dorms, and I started walking back to Garcia's room. As I walked, I could feel actual excitement. It was a feeling I wasn't expecting. A feeling that was missing from my life. It was the first time in over five months I felt like I had control. I felt like I was my own person again, getting to call my own shots. Even though I hadn't told JR I was going to do it yet, I knew deep down I was going to say yes. I was tired of going through the motions and doing what others told me to do. The pledgeship-brainwash had really fucked with my head, but that broken and defeated feeling was over with. Whether it was pledge masters, ATO guys, or even Emily, I wasn't going to let anyone tell me what I could or couldn't do ever again. The excitement of doing something for myself was real. It was my turn to live my life the way I wanted to live it, and that felt somewhat thrilling. I had control back, and I wasn't going to give it up again.

# ELEVEN

"COR!"

"Hey Em, how was the drive?"

"Ugh, it was terrible. Glad I'm here though."

"Where's Ashley?"

"I dropped her off at her friend's place and took her car. Just us now!"

We walked from the parking lot into my dorm room. Bennett wasn't in the room, not sure where he was exactly, but I was going to take advantage of the moment. Em and I hung out over winter break, so we were able to "hang out" quite a bit, which was nice. But it had been a long two months since then, and a man has his needs.

It was already 8:00 p.m., so after we had a quick bang session, unfortunate emphasis on quick, we showered together in one of the stalls down the hall. We were planning on going to the ATO house that night for a party, then hopefully to a live-out Saturday for a day party. It was about 43 degrees, but on Saturday it was supposed to get to around 55 and sunny. In southern Indiana in the spring, all you needed was sun in order for it to be perfect day-partying weather.

I threw on some dark jeans and a blue flannel button-down, tossed a little gel in the hair to mess it up a bit, and was ready to go. I turned around and saw Em still in her towel, another wrapped around her hair, sorting through her bag.

"Em, didn't you pack what you were going to wear?"

"I packed different options, now I have to pick one. What is the party going to be like?"

"Em, come on! You'll look great regardless, just pick something, and let's go meet up with my friends to pregame."

"Will Jessica be there?"

"Pregame no, party yes."

"Will there be any girls at the pregame?"

"Solid question, going with a solid no."

"Cory . . ."

"Would you rather me be pregaming with all girls or all guys?"

"Oh, shut up. I'll text Jessica."

I always forgot how long it took girls to get ready. Once she knew what she was going to wear, she contemplated the outfit for about five minutes, then blow-dried her hair for about 10, straightened her hair for another 10, makeup was about 20, then trying on the outfit took about five. Most of the time she didn't love the outfit, so would try on another just in case, ultimately realizing she liked the first one better, so that added another 10 minutes there, then the finishing touches, which *always* took an additional five minutes. No clue what "finishing touches" were, but whenever she said she was ready and looked ready, there were always five more minutes of something. Always. So from out of the shower to out the door it always took over an hour.

The spring pledges had started, but there were only about 15 of them, so not enough to run the house and give rides at the same time. We decided to take Ashley's car and leave it at Barr's overnight. We got to his place to pregame around 9:30 p.m., and most of my pledge class was already there. Emily had texted Jessica and confirmed that she was going over to the house around 11, so that was going to be our plan as well. I introduced Emily to some of the guys: Barr, Kyle, Joe, Cutty, Garcia, Wolf, and Russ.

"Where's Bo at?" I said as I got a couple drinks from the fridge.

"Not sure, thought you would know," Joe responded.

Em had met Bo and Kyle over winter break, and I wanted some common faces she could hang out with. Em was mingling with everyone the best she could, but I never realized how bro-y my friends were until I threw my girlfriend in the mix. Barr loved EDM and insisted on being the DJ at every party. By DJ, I mean use his phone for music. We let the kid do his thing while we all chilled around the bar in his family room area and watched the Michigan/Michigan State basketball game. Em was a pseudo sports fan and could keep up in conversations pretty well, but wouldn't argue about sports like my bro-y friends. More just talk about them.

We kept drinking at Barr's for another hour. It was good to spend time with Em. She made me happy when I was around her. Her smile was contagious. There was something about her I naturally loved. To be honest, I didn't really know what it was I loved so much. She had this way of making you feel like everything was going to be OK no matter the situation. Our eyes would lock, and I would feel this sense of pride to call her my girlfriend.

"Yo Cor, who's the money on tonight?" Russ said, turning around toward me.

I felt anxiety coming on as I tried to defuse the situation. I wasn't super close with Russ, and he never bet, so the word must not have gotten to him about not bringing it up in front of Em. I could see Kyle and Joe shaking their heads at Russ as Em faced the other way.

"Got to be on Michigan State, right? Izzo at home? I don't know. What do you think the spread is?"

"Uhh, I don't know. Three?"

"I would take that in a heartbeat," Kyle responded quickly to detour the conversation away from me.

I took a sip from my cup and finished the beer. Em didn't even react to the conversation. There were times I could tell she was tuning out the sports conversations, and this was luckily one of them. I walked toward the fridge to grab another beer as I fake nut-tapped Russ.

"Idiot," I whispered as I walked by.

*Crisis adverted.*

It was about 10:45 when we left to head to ATO. I wasn't quite sure who-all was going to be at the house, but I knew Jessica would be there. Em and Jess were friendly in high school, sort of like Max and me. Good friends, but not best friends. Em and I weren't even in the same group of friends in high school. As a matter of fact, she was more in Max's group of friends than mine, and Jessica was more in my group than Emily's. When we started dating we would tag along to each other's friend's parties. Emily and Jessica had become better friends because of that.

It took us about 15 minutes to walk to the house. The party was already in fifth gear by the time we arrived. The juniors had a bar crawl, which must have gotten things going early. Girls and guys flooded the first floor and the music from the basement was blaring. It was madness. Our pledge class took to the basement, where two pledges behind the bar were furiously trying to pour enough shots. It was a weird sight, seeing other pledges bartending a basement party. It was like watching a movie about myself.

Em and I took a shot together and grabbed a couple drinks before I realized she had never seen the house before. We walked upstairs and I gave her a little tour. I felt proud to walk her around. I was proud of the house in general. We got to the second floor, but most of the doors were shut, and the whole floor smelled like weed.

"Can I see the room you're going to be living in next year?"

"Yeah, sure, it's at the end of the hall. Bo and I got first choice out of the soon-to-be sophomore class thanks to our superb pledge rank. Not even worth asking what that means."

"Yeah, don't really care or want to know."

*Yeah, you probably don't.*

Our room was a two-man facing the street at the end of the hall. The door was shut, and I could hear Gorilla Zoe thumping from inside. I knocked and slowly opened the door. If it were just me I would have barged in, but with Em, I didn't really know protocol. As I opened the door, I could see a couple of seniors sitting on the leather couch with a few sophomores.

"Cory, what up? How's it like to be done?" one of the sophomores said over the music.

"Pretty great. Hey, just wanted to show my girlfriend Emily my room next year. That cool?"

"Hi, girlfriend Emily!" one of the seniors announced awkwardly loudly as he signaled to another senior on the couch.

I followed his eyes and saw a vanity mirror lying on the wood table with a rolled up $20 bill, a credit card, and white and blue powder on it.

*Oh fuck.*

"Thanks guys. So over here is where Bo and I will sleep," I said to Em, trying to get her to walk into the sleeper on the left.

I couldn't tell if it was all chopped up Adderall or the blue was Adderall and the white was cocaine, but regardless, I didn't want Emily to see. As I moved toward the sleeper, Emily walked right by me to say hi to the guys in the room. I saw her eyes go straight to the table as a senior unsuccessfully tried to move a case of beer to block the view of the powder.

"Hi boys," Em said with a fake smile.

I could see her face getting red as she quickly looked around the room and walked out. I let her out first and turned around to look at the guys. One of the seniors pointed down at the table and raised his eyebrows, gesturing if I would like any of the colored powder on the mirror. I shook my head out of disbelief and shut the door on my way out.

"What the fuck was that?" Em blurted, pissed off.

"Those were the seniors in the house snorting some Adderall."

"Don't be an idiot Cory."

"What?"

"That was fucking cocaine!"

"I don't think so. I thought it was Adderall."

"Don't try and cover up for your friends!"

I decided not to respond. I was thinking of emphasizing that it was the seniors in the room, but there were sophomores in there too, and Em probably knew that. Emily walked in front of me, visibly upset, as we made our way back to the basement. Luckily, Jessica and Lauren had shown up, so I pawned Emily off on them for a little.

Em took Adderall to study for tests, as did every college student, but I had to agree with her, it wasn't a pretty picture. A bunch of dudes blasting ghetto rap, blowing lines in my soon-to-be bedroom. On top of that, it was the first room she saw at ATO. The very first room. A-T-Blow stereotype really held strong, but the ironic part was I rarely saw coke or Adderall blown openly during pledgeship. Only a handful of times. But I guess the door was closed, so it wasn't openly. About four hours into Em's visit and already gambling had been brought up and swept under the rug, and she had walked into a coke pregame. *Rough start.*

I met up with Kyle in the basement, and we took shots with Jess and Em. Em was doing a good job shaking off her uneasiness, but we had been dating for long enough where I could see right through it. Jess and Em walked over to Jess's friends at the other side of the bar. Sorority rush was last week, so the freshman girls were insanely clingy with each other. I walked to the open area where Kyle and Joe were.

"Ceeeeee!"

"Hey Steph, what up?" I said as I gave her a hug.

"You know my friends Nicki and Megan, right?"

"Yes I do. Hey girls, how's it going?" I said as I gave each of them a hug.

"What are you guys doing away from the bar? Come on!" Megan interjected.

"Being losers," Kyle replied.

"Hey Steph, you got to meet . . ."

"Let's get a shot!" Megan interrupted again.

"Uhh, yeah. Yeah, alright, let's go," I uttered back.

I led the group toward the bar area and walked by Em to grab her. Steph was a year older in the same sorority as Jess, so I was hoping they could become a sorority Em could be friends with when she visited. The music was loud where Em was standing, so I tapped her arm. Jess and Em turned around right as everyone was walking by.

"Hey girls, this is my girlfriend Emily."

Both Nicki and Megan didn't even flinch and kept walking. Steph stopped for a second and threw up the fakest smile imaginable.

"Hiiii! So nice to meet you!" she said as she kept walking toward the bar.

*What the fuck was that?*

Em stared at the girls as they walked away then looked at Jess then back at me. Clearly Jess had seen the same thing, because she shrugged her shoulders and started walking over to Steph and Kyle at the bar.

"Which one was that Stephanie girl?"

"The Mean Girl in the black who faked the 'nice to meet you!'" I said, mimicking Steph.

"You mean the black bikini?" Em said before finishing the rest of her drink.

I was confused why they all dismissed Emily. Steph and her friends were always super nice to me. Even flirty over-the-top nice at times. I thought at least Steph would stop and talk to Em for a little. *Sorority girls are the worst.*

We both walked over to where they were standing and waited for the pledges to pour the shots. It went Nicki, Megan, Joe, Jess, Steph, Kyle, Em, then me at the bar. Kyle put his arm around Em as she walked up.

"Whisky or vodka?" Kyle asked Em.

"Vodka, please." Em responded with a genuine smile.

"Good, 'cause that's all we got," Kyle said as he shook Em in his arms.

All night I had noticed Kyle being nice to Em, and I think it was really helping her. He was doing a fantastic job of neutralizing any awkward situations, being a great third wheel, and saving her from murdering me. Not sure where he learned the third-wheel moves, but they were much appreciated.

The pledge had removed the safety stopper on the handle to attempt to pour faster, but he was filling up the shots one at a time by picking up the shot cup with one hand and pouring with the other. As soon as the pledge had poured five of the shots, Megan turned to everyone.

"Cheeeers to ATO and Pi Phi!"

"Uh . . ." I blurted out to try and stop Megan, but it was too late.

Nicki, Megan, Joe, Jess, and Steph had taken the shots as Kyle grabbed his shot and took it as well. All six of them threw their shot cups back on the bar as the pledge poured the last shots. Em grabbed the shot cups and turned toward me.

"Cheeeeers to ATO and Pi Phi!" Em said sarcastically.

I laughed and put my left arm around her as we bumped cups and took the shot.

"I'm going to go to the bathroom."

"Alright, it's over there in the corner, I'll grab us some beers and meet you by the bathroom."

Em gave me a thumbs-up and held it as she walked away. Her uneasiness had turned into frustration, and I didn't know what to do. I wanted the first night to go smoothly for her sake, but then also selfishly for my own sake. Em deserved a good night because she was a good person, but also, if she had a good first night, then she would feel more comfortable about me at IU and the long-distance thing. That first impression would also ultimately make things easier for me to lie about the gambling and selling. So again, selfishly, I wanted things to start off smoothly, but that didn't happen.

I grabbed a couple beers and went to meet Em outside the bathroom. Megan stepped in front of me while I was walking over.

"You're not leaving, are you?" Megan said, putting her hand on my chest.

"Uh, no, going to give a beer to Emily."

Megan didn't say anything; she just stared into my eyes with her hand on my chest, biting her lower lip. I looked over her shoulder at the bathroom and didn't see Em. I smiled a nervous smile and slowly walked away to the bathroom and waited about a minute or two. I knew Megan, but not well enough for her to be worried if I was leaving or not. *Sorority sluts, my lord.*

"I talked to Ashley. She wants us to meet up with her," Em said, walking out of the bathroom.

"Do they want to come here?"

"No, I think I'd rather go to her friend's house party."

I caught the hint. Em was done with the party. From the all-bro pregame, to the senior coke den, to the Pi Phi chicks snubbing her, she'd had enough. I never noticed the girls at IU being so bitchy before, but it was probably because I never was around a situation where I would notice girl-on-girl crime. Whatever it was, it was stupid and catty, and I felt bad for Em.

We went outside and opted to walk to Ashley's party. It was only about six blocks away, so right between the drive/walk threshold, but neither of us wanted to wait for a pledge ride.

"Em, I'm sorry about the party. With the seniors and then Steph and her friends. It was a shitty introduction to IU."

"Yeah, it was."

"I know, I'm sorry."

"I'm just really worried, Cory. You're surrounded by slutty girls and druggies. I don't want you living around that!"

"I don't know what to tell you. Girls at every school are like that. And as for the drugs, I honestly do think it was Adderall, but even if it was harder drugs, none of my friends do that, only the seniors, so I won't be around it next year."

"Cory, what can't you see? This fraternity life is a pattern of shittiness. That's all it is! They bring in naïve high school boys and surround them with slutty bitches, alcohol, and drugs. Over time, people will just start caving in. It's what happened with Jack."

Jack was her older brother. She was blowing things out of proportion, but her brother did go to Miami of Ohio on a soccer scholarship and ended up getting kicked off the team and losing the scholarship. He wasn't a drug addict or anything, but the few times I hung around him, he and his friends did have some pretty aggressive drinking habits, so I never knew what to think.

"I'm not most people Em. I'm not going to cheat on you with slutty girls or become an alcoholic or druggy."

"That's not the point Cory! I don't want you around it! I don't want to come visit and feel uncomfortable every time. I fucking hate this!"

I didn't know how to respond. She had her mind made up that she was going to be angry and hammer home the "live around it" point. The rest of the night was pretty shitty. We went to some weirdass GDI house party where they had the music coming from the TV in the living room. Em clung to Ashley the rest of the night. It was like she needed to ease the tension and avoid me. There was nothing I could say to her. All of her fears about me at school she had seen firsthand. *Imagine if she saw the whole thing? The amount of money I virtually toss around every college basketball game or what the next month is going to be like with March Madness. Or how about when I start buying $300 worth of pot every week.*

Surprisingly, we had been at a pretty good point in our relationship since pledgeship ended, but I never thought it was going to last. I really loved Emily as a person and wanted things to work, but we had two completely different lifestyles, and they were pulling us further apart. Which fucking sucked. At first, it was like taking two steps forward every time we saw each other, then two steps back every time we are away. But with taking a step back while we were together, the writing was on the wall. As the night went on, I did my best to fit in with everyone, but the guys and girls at the party couldn't be more different than me or my friends. Not in a bad way, just, I don't know, just different. They seemed more immature than me even though they were my age. I wanted to leave, but I knew there was no point in battling Em. Her mind was made up, and so was mine. My argumentative leash was shortening with each passing fight, and I could feel myself closer and closer to waving the white flag on everything. If it came down to it, I knew college life was going to win the battle sooner or later; I just didn't want it to.

# TWELVE

**FRESHMAN YEAR SUMMER BREAK WAS A STRANGE TIME.** Of my group of eight or so close high school friends, five of them were back in Chicago for the whole summer. One buddy was a point guard at Michigan and another was a right guard at Northern Illinois, so both had summer camps throughout the summer. Another buddy wasn't doing too hot school-wise freshman year at Kansas and so enrolled in both summer-school sessions. But of the five guys home for the summer, two of them became super strange during freshman year. Both of them were GDIs and for some reason had gotten very outspoken against the Greek system, among other societal topics. I couldn't tell if they'd gotten denied from frats at their schools, DePauw and Eastern Illinois, and so were bitter or what, but they seemed to look down on us for being in a house, as if they were more mature for not joining one. It was a really uncomfortable feeling hanging out with them.

We were all drinking in Ricky's backyard one night, and this kid Garrett went on this rant about how Obama had fucked over our community and how our socialist government was going to ruin America, then stopped and said, "You guys wouldn't understand." Ricky, Steve, and I just sat there stoned, drinking Miller Lites, staring at the kid as he continued his rant. We had no clue who "you guys" were in his sentence, as we were all from the same high school, but weren't remotely offended either. Both newly developed dickheads were just big wet blankets and brought nothing to the table. Neither really cared about sports or smoking pot, they weren't fun drunks, were super vulgar and borderline sexist toward women, and mainly just not friendly people. The more I thought about it, it didn't even make sense that we were friends in the first place. We all became friends in like sixth grade and had never really thought about it since. It was really hard to stop being friends with someone all of a sudden. They would sort of just hang around and were always at parties. The worst part about the summer was that the two kids didn't realize they were way different than we were, so they still called and texted us almost every day. I mean it was obvious our friendship was headed for a divorce, but they continued to act like nothing had changed.

My brother said this was normal, and every summer he had a few friends who would fall off the map. But it wasn't the falling off the map that was the problem; it was that these two had mentally gone awry but were still trying to cling on and be friends.

I was working for the suburb I grew up in making nine dollars an hour. Trimming bushes, unloading public garbage cans, wood chipping, cleaning out street sewer drains during storms, cutting down trees, you name it. Realistically I drove around in a pickup truck for two hours every morning, then got a break, did about an hour of work, got a lunch break, drove around for another two hours, then did a little work before 3:30 p.m., when I had to clock out. So it still was a shitty and low-paying job, but a union job, so it was a joke. I was hungover most days, which sucked, but still a joke.

Em and I had been fighting a bunch back home. We drunkenly broke up one night in early July, and it had been uncomfortable since. The next morning she almost pretended like we didn't break up, but we both knew it was going to stick. It was impossible to go back to college, go out, be surrounded by guys/girls partying every weekend, and not let jealousy or frustrations get the best of us. She came over to my house one night when no one was home and we had a long two-hour talk. We both cried, and she just ended it for good. I tried to salvage the situation and be friendly, but that made it worse. I didn't know how to break up with someone, but in hindsight, it probably would have been easier to say "I'm done" and start running away than do the whole stay-friends song and dance. Leaving hope for the future meant we would wait out the partying/college storm, and that was unfair for both of us.

So I was officially single for the first time in about a year and half. It was bittersweet. I knew it would make sophomore year more fun and carefree, but I really, really did love Em. She was the most down-to-earth girl I'd ever met. I was going to miss her.

ATO got to move into the house on August 11, but classes didn't start till the 16th. I got a text from Hippy Mike saying anytime I wanted to start picking up, that he had a "fat stash man." My cousin and I were planning on driving down to IU together on the 11th, so I told Hippy Mike I'd be over then. I didn't know how much to start off with, but my guess was to go a full ounce on the first week, since no one in the house had any bud yet. I was starting from ground zero. Regardless, it wasn't really a big deal because if I ever ran out, I would just text Mr. String Cheese Incident and grab some more. I hadn't really worked out how I was going to loop Bo into the mix. The kid was super unorganized unless he took Adderall, in which case he was a persistent and determined dude. He also smoked practically all day long. So giving him 28 grams once a week was not the greatest idea, but there was no way to avoid it.

I was thinking I would buy the bud and when I get to the house, one of us would take all 28 or so grams, weigh them, and split them up into individual gram/10-sack baggies. That way, whenever someone wanted to buy some, we would toss him a baggie and get the money, or tell him to grab a baggie and leave money in our sleeper. The alternative would be having to weigh out a gram every time someone wanted some, or worse, have the house weigh out their own grams and leave the money.

Regardless, I knew I needed to get a safe or something to lock the baggies in. I stopped at Target as Mikey was going to pick up Sheff before we left for school. My mom gave me some money to do some light sophomore-year shopping, but really I just wanted to grab a safe and find those little Ziploc baggies that were about two inches tall and an inch wide. I looked around Target, avoiding asking, "Hey, excuse me, where are the little cocaine Ziploc baggies," but I gave up caring about a Target employee judging me after about five minutes and asked one of the ladies in the store. Apparently they are called "jewelry bags" and were in the women's jewelry section of the store. I literally would never, ever, have found them.

The drive to IU was pretty quick and easy, about three and a half hours. Mike and Sheff told sophomore-year stories the whole time, trying to lift my now single spirits. Their stories were hilarious. Welcome week, then getting pledges, then winter break, then sorority bid week, followed by spring break, then little 5, boats, and finally summer school. Sheff was saying everyone in their pledge class except like two or three kids stayed at school the summer after sophomore year. He kept repeating himself by saying summer-session sophomore year was the best time of his life. From what I gathered, somehow the business school, journalism school, econ, and a bunch of liberal arts schools simultaneously ramped up their classes between sophomore and junior years, and if you got behind or didn't take at least 16 to 17 credits a semester, you'd be screwed. So advisors recommended staying the summer so junior year you could have a lighter load of 14 to 15 credits. That way, you could focus on your résumé, interviewing, and finding an internship instead of having to stay the summer junior year and missing out on an internship opportunity. I hadn't thought that far out, but "best time of my life" was all I needed. I was sold on summer school. I think I had overstayed my welcome as the constantly hungover 19-year-old public works employee anyway.

The house was as clean as you could possibly imagine. The second- and third-floor carpets were cleaned, walls were repainted, kitchen was polished. The whole place looked incredible. Bo had gotten there a couple hours before me, so he had moved in the couch and his mattress already. He took bottom bunk, which was devastating, but I didn't want to fight him on it because Bo's sweaty body climbing over me every night and morning would wake me up every single time. There was no chance that 250-pound, pizza-loving ass would be quiet putting those boards he called feet on the edge of my bed and struggling to leap up into his bed. I would have rather taken top bunk than deal with that every day anyway.

Our room was a corner room on the second floor. When you walked into the room, the door to our sleeper was directly on the left. Most rooms had three guys in them, but with our pledge class having an uneven number, Bo and I got lucky with only two of us in the room. On top of that, the guys before us left their manmade bar. It was an L-shaped wooden bar painted all black in the corner of the room. On the front of it, there were light-blue painted wood *A-T-O* letters with yellow trim. Next to the bar, along the windows overlooking the front porch, was a black leather L couch Bo had taken from his parents' basement. On the other side of the couch we put the TV. Bo had a decently sized flat screen, and I had taken my grandma's old TV stand from her garage. Now that it was all set up, our room surprisingly matched. The TV stand, the bar, the couch. It was all black. We had no plans of having a well-decorated room, but it somehow seemed that way.

"When you heading over to buy the herb?" Bo said as he sat down on the couch.

"Probably an hour or so."

"Well, demand is pretty fucking high. I would love some."

"Oh, you want some free weed, do ya Bo?"

"Best kind of weed. I only said I would help you sell so I can smoke for free. Making a couple grand a year on the book is all I need."

"Well, I'll gladly keep all the money if you smoking for free is enough."

"Fuck off."

"Well then, I think you might be making more than a couple grand."

"How much you buying?" Bo said, looking for the TV remote.

"Probably an ounce today."

"How much?"

"You deaf?"

"No, how much money you cunt."

"Well, I wanted to chat with you about this. I don't want to be real open with everyone about how much we buy and how much it costs. Don't want people bitching about 'making money off your friends.' But it's a half ounce for $175, ounce is $300, two ounces is $500, and then a QP is $750."

"You planning on buying QPs?"

"Had that exact same reaction."

"But no, I agree on not saying shit. I'm not even going to tell people I'm doing this with you. I'll just pretend like I'm a good roommate."

"So if the cops catch us, you're all squared away?"

"Exactly."

"Smart plan. So speaking of being a good roommate, I'm going to take your car to the dude's house. I don't want to walk there every day, and my cousin's car is like five blocks away."

"Yeah, you can take the keys, I never use my car."

*5:45 p.m.: I'm going to leave here in about 5. Be there in 10.*

"I'm just going to go grab it now. When I get back, I'm going to weigh it all and put the gram baggies in the safe."

"I'll help you, I got my scale somewhere in my bag."

*5:46 p.m.: Call me and walk in my man!!*

"Sounds good, I'll be back in a little."

I grabbed his keys and walked out. I wasn't that nervous or anxious talking about it to Bo, but as soon as I walked out of the room, I felt the excitement and adrenaline building again.

I got to Hippy Mike's place and called him. He answered but didn't say anything. I didn't know what to do, so I didn't say anything either and just walked in his house. He was sitting in the same spot on the family room couch with the green fabric backpack under him watching *South Park*. I told him I was going to start with an ounce, and he joked that I would be back soon.

I handed him 15 $20 bills, took the bag, and left. It was as simple as simple could be. Walked in, handed some 35-year-old hippy money, he handed me a Ziploc bag, I walked right out the door, and was home in five minutes. The simplicity of it didn't change the fact that giving a man $300 in exchange for drugs was terrifying. My heart was pounding the entire time. I got back to the house and walked directly upstairs. I must have looked like such an introvert as I walked by some of the now juniors hanging out on the first floor.

Bo and I zeroed the scale with a plastic cup and dumped all the pot into it. 29.6 grams. Hippy Mike gave us an extra 1.6 grams. We couldn't tell yet if it was him being nice the first time, or he just didn't give a shit and eyeballed 28 grams.

"Well, I'm smoking 1.6 grams tonight," Bo said. He immediately grabbed some of the bud and started packing a one-hitter.

"Oh, by the way, we're going 1.0 grams or over in every baggie. No .9s. Don't want some fuck yelling at us 'cause he weighed his sack and got sold .8 or .9," I said as Bo was already lighting the one-hitter in our room.

"Agreed. Don't want to deal with that. Just 0.1 or 0.3 is not going to make a difference in the long run."

I used the same excuse with my pledge class that Jason and JR used with theirs in order to sell exclusively grams. People could buy more than a gram, but it would be $20 per gram. There was no discount for buying more like the Phish-loving Mike was giving me.

*6:30 p.m.: Yo Boys I got some bud for whoever wants some. $10 and $20 sacks. Didn't get enough to be selling eighths right now.*

*6:31 p.m.: Yo Bates, tell your boys I got some bud if they need it. $10 and $20 sacks. Didn't get enough to be selling eighths right now.*

*6:31 p.m.: Yo Duff, tell your boys I got some bud, if they need it. $10 and $20 sacks. Didn't get enough to be selling eighths right now.*

The house went from clean to a mess in a span of two hours. Everyone moving shit in, boxes and garbage bags all over the place, some guys trying to build bars in their rooms and leaving the spare wood in the hallway. There wasn't going to be a party the first night, so most of ATO would just smoke and have beers in each other's rooms.

Of course, Garcia and Cutty were the first ones in my room asking for baggies. Both handed me $10 and each wanted his own personal 10-sack.

I went into the sleeper, opened the safe, and grabbed two 10-sacks. The safe had two shelves, which made it easy to split up 10-sacks and 20s. After Garcia and Cutty walked out, there was a revolving door of people for the next hour. Russ, Joe, Bates, Brandon, a couple more juniors, and a senior I didn't know well. It was weird referring to the old juniors as seniors and the sophomores as juniors. But it was even weirder thinking I was a sophomore.

By about 10 o'clock, I had already sold five 10-sacks and 14 grams. I knew tonight would be an initial rush, but didn't think 16.5 grams would be sold in one night! I knew tomorrow would be more chill because everyone already had their bud, but they were all rolling gram blunts and smoking in their rooms the first night, so I had no clue.

Three hundred and thirty dollars. I only spent $300 on pot, sold about 60 percent of it, and had already gotten $330. So the next 11.5 grams would be all profit. Not including the 1.6 grams of free pot Bo had already smoked. It was almost too good to be true. It wasn't like the sportsbook. The book felt like I fought and clawed for that money, struggled through tough losses and close wins in order to make only 10 percent on all losses. Not with this. This, I was buying 28 grams for $300, so close to $10 a gram, then turning around and selling for $20 a gram. Making $10 on everything I sold. The more I bought, the cheaper it would be, and thus the more I would make. There was no chance of losing money like the book. There was no slow and uneasy income; this was a constant stream of money.

I sat in Cutty's room with Bo, Kyle, Joe, Garcia, and Wolf while we smoked a blunt, just amazed at the position I was in. *I just made $30 and have another $230 coming in the next couple of days for doing essentially nothing. And I get to do this every week!* I laughed to myself as I grabbed the blunt from Joe. I understood I was splitting the money with Bo, but about $150 a week for a college student was way more than I needed. I could live like a king as a college student with $150 a week. Hell, drinks were legitimately two dollars at some bars. Throw in about $1,000 a semester of gambling wins, and sophomore year was shaping up to be a pretty good time.

# THIRTEEN

**6:23 P.M.: YOU WERE RIGHT, GOING TO NEED MORE.** *Can I stop by and pick some up?*

6:25 p.m.: LMFAO! Told ya my man!! I'm home call me when you're here and walk in.

About 24 hours was all it took to sell 28 grams. Bo had sold Cam a couple grams and Mikey and Sheff had stopped by to check out the new spot, and so I gave them a gram as well. We told both Cam and Mikey/Sheff that we got the pot from a kid in our house. Didn't want other houses thinking we were dealing.

It was surprising how many people bought from us. There were 78 guys living in the house and another 80 or so sprinkled around campus. It seemed like everyone in the house wanted some to stash away. Like a just-in-case weed reserve. Maybe bring a girl back, want to watch a movie, want a joint after binge-studying on Adderall, whatever the reason, everyone kept getting an extra 10-sack every time they stopped by. Even three roommates in the same room would all buy some separately. It was a lovely little wrinkle for Bo and me.

I went over to Hippy Mike's house and asked for two ounces this time. While it was remarkably laid-back, I still didn't like going to and from his house to ATO with drugs in the car, so I wanted to have enough for a couple weeks. I was also too lazy and hated going five blocks to do anything apart from getting Qdoba breakfast burritos or wings from BuffaLouie's. So $500 for 56 grams. About $9 per gram this time. *This is too easy.*

I was still getting the majority of the texts from as the bookie, which wasn't a lot because football hadn't started yet, but I didn't mind it. Now that I wasn't dating Em anymore, I realized it was crazy how much I used to use my phone. Every 5 to 10 minutes I would be texting her. I was accustomed to being on my phone all the time, so a handful of texts a day didn't bother me.

I was doing a shit ton more work than Bo. I understood that, both on the book side and the dealing, but having Bo collect money was still the most crucial part. That was the one thing out of all of this I didn't want to do, especially when we had started booking for Acacia and Pi Kapps too. Bo would collect money from Cam for Acacia and collect from Sheff's good buddy from high school Adam for Pi Kapps, and I would deal with the texts from everyone. Dealing was the same way. Bo was in the room 90 percent of the day, so he collected the money from everyone and passed out the baggies.

I never wanted to tell the house how much I had at any given time. I wanted to make it seem like I had just enough for however much they wanted. No one seemed to wonder where I was getting all of it from. People understood I'd taken over for JR and was now the guy who had weed, but that was it. Kyle, Joe, Cutty, Garcia, even the juniors like Duffy, Brandon, or Hahn never asked where I got it from. No junior ever asked, either, why he wasn't the one to replace JR. I think no one knew there was a replacement system. To everyone, it just kinda happened. Someone in the house had bud to sell, but no one knew or cared to know the details.

It was apparently great shit too. Hippy Mike had said the guy he got it from grew it, so my guess was the dude was growing medical marijuana and selling it to Hippy Mike. I never knew how you even start growing medical marijuana. Like, who was the first conversation to? A doctor? The government? Do you just start growing in hopes that no one will question you? I had no fucking clue. I'd looked online and had seen people talk about prices of weed, and it seemed like Hippy Mike's prices were closer to the expensive side, but not dramatically. But, at the same time, some of the websites I was looking at were talking about "Shake from Bama" or "Mids from Texas," so these great hybrid nugs I was buying were at least visibly above average, aka, above average prices. I understood supply and demand too. Forty thousand 18-to-22-year-olds living in a small town in Indiana. It was pretty obvious that demand was going to always be there.

Our house was setting up for a party on Thursday. The pledges from last semester had a couple more weeks left, but this time they were cleaning my room. Bo's Subway wrapper, Wolf's dip spit, vacuuming the room, it was fantastic. The party was going to be up on the second floor because the basement bar had been knocked down by the house manager.

We were paired with Sara's sorority. I'd seen her quite a bit toward the end of freshman year, but hadn't really talked to her since. Hahn came into our room earlier in the day and said Steph and her friends were coming over too, so my guess was it was going to be a free-for-all type of party. I hopped in the communal showers around nine o'clock and got ready. A few of Sara's sorority sisters came early to pregame in Kyle's room before everyone came over. I didn't know the girls well, but Kyle was like best friends with the sorority. It was AChiO. They had plenty of talent, and their IU stereotype was that God had made yoga pants because of AChiO, but their house was far from ATO, so we rarely paired. I always had fun hanging out with them, though, and always had fun with Sara, so I was excited.

"Hey Cory!" a group of girls said as I walked down the second-floor hallway.

"Hola señoritas," I replied, not knowing a single one of their names.

I noticed when I was dating Em that I was especially terrible with girls' names. Maybe I didn't care to know them because I knew I would never do anything with them, but whatever it was, I was atrocious.

I changed into some grey jeans and a light-green V-neck and went into Kyle's room. I had only been living in the house for a couple of days, and already the dorms seemed like a prison. Couldn't drink, couldn't smoke, didn't know your roommate or neighbors, had an older guy living on the floor to monitor you, it sucked.

It felt weird mingling with girls without dating Em. I'd always been open and friendly with all girls because, again, I knew it wasn't going anywhere, but now that it could go somewhere, I felt myself overana-lyzing conversations and wondering if I had a chance with every girl I talked to. Whether I wanted to or not was irrelevant. I started talking to one girl who wasn't even that good-looking, but her eyes were piercing blue, and the first thought that went through my head was, "Yeah, I could bang her." I don't know why or when my subconscious brain decided to go full savage mode and view girls as either yeses or nos, but luckily that Stifler-like mentality didn't last long. Part of me still wanted to be respectful toward Em and not do anything for a couple days or weeks, but the other part of me knew it didn't matter in the long run.

Sara and the rest of her sorority came about an hour later. Four rooms on the second floor were being used: mine, Kyle's, Garcia's, and Russ's, with spillover in the hallway between the rooms. I saw Sara and gave her a hug when she walked in. That connection we had freshman year was gone. We were both friendly toward each other, but our conversation was a quick hello. Probably because I was single now. That flirty barrier knowing neither one of us would do anything was gone.

My barbaric-yes-or-no mind had vanished, but the feeling of not being smooth or good at talking to girls stayed most of the night. I don't know if the fact that I was wifed-up had lost its luster, but it seemed like girls I had sort-of bonded with before didn't give a shit now.

"Ceeeeeee!"

*Except for Pi Phi.*

"Hey Megan, Steph, what's up?"

"I heard the news!" Steph said to me as she nudged me with her elbow.

"Which is . . .?" I responded, knowing what she meant but not wanting to sound arrogant.

"You're a free man now?" Steph said, smiling with both fists clenched in excitement.

"Yeah, Emily and I broke up a couple weeks ago."

"Well, she sucked anyway, come on, let's grab a drink," Steph said, grabbing my arm.

*She what?*

I made eye contact with Megan, but she immediately looked forward and walked to the bar. Steph saying Em sucked rubbed me the wrong way. She met her for two minutes total and was a complete bitch the whole time. I tried not to care, but it bothered me. I went with Megan and Steph to take a shot, but said I had to take a piss and left to go into Kyle's room. Only a couple minutes later, Megan walked in. I did a quick glance around and realized that none of her sorority sisters or even grade were in the room with her.

"Sorry to hear about your girlfriend."

"Oh, you are?"

"Well, in a respectful, polite way, yeah. I mean, I could tell you liked her."

*Zero chance you could tell that, but OK.*

"Well, thank you, in a respectful, polite way."

We both awkwardly laughed and went to grab a drink. Kyle's room had practically no furniture in it, so there was plenty of space to walk around. Megan and I talked at the makeshift bar for a couple minutes while we took a shot and had a drink. She was way nicer than I remembered, and a lot better-looking too. She was short, with blondish-brown hair, brown eyes, and really clear, smooth skin. It may sound weird to describe a girl that way, but it was noticeable. Her skin didn't have like a single mark or blemish on it. Could have been a dickload of makeup, but whatever, still noticeable.

Standing at the bar, she apologized for the night Em came to visit. She claimed she was hammered and didn't remember ignoring her. I was about to ask how she knew she ignored her if she didn't remember ignoring her, but she seemed sincere, so I let it slide. I was skeptical, but appreciated the apology nonetheless. I caught myself feeling standoffish at times during the conversation, but had no ultimatum or agenda anymore. Maybe it was out of admiration for Em, but regardless, I was a free man and could talk to whomever I wanted to at any time.

Everyone drank aggressively all night. It was one of the first true nights back at school, so people were getting rowdy. After hours and hours of boozing heavily, Wolf was standing up on the couch with his shirt off, and Bo was blacked out and had everyone chanting his name as he danced to "Cooler Than Me" by Mike Posner. Kyle was passed out in my room sitting up on the couch while some of the AChiOs were taking pictures. The rest of the night was like this. People slowly started filing out around three o'clock or so. Actually, I wasn't exactly sure what time it was. Garcia, Ray, and Joe had brought girls back into their sleepers. Joe and Garcia shared a room together with Cutty, so it was funny they were both having sex on bunk beds together. A couple of the girls stayed super late, Sara being one of them, and Cutty, Bo, Barr, and I smoked with them. And technically Kyle too, since he was passed out on the couch next to us. It was obvious some of the girls wanted to spend the night, but looking around, it was clear it was with either me or Barr. Cutty and Bo were way too focused on smoking and getting the pledges to get food. I sat next to Sara and this girl Jenna as we smoked. Jenna was being outrageously flirty with Barr, to the point where Bo eventually blurted out, "Yo, go suck his dick, Jenna, Jesus Christ."

Everyone laughed, more at Bo because he was drunkenly swearing, still sweating from dancing earlier, eating pizza, and smoking a bowl. It was Bo in his truest form, especially knowing it was free pot for him.

I had a couple of juniors stumble down while we were smoking, asking for bud. There was one guy I didn't really know asking for five grams. It was a strange number, but it didn't matter to me. Drunk or not, I wasn't going to say no to people, so I sold it to him for $100. I think he was some chick's boyfriend from another house, but I didn't give a shit. A hundred bucks was a hundred bucks to me, didn't matter who it was from.

Eventually I shut off the music, as Kyle and Sara were both passed out on the couch. Not together, but on opposite ends. Bo had climbed into bed as I dealt out some late-night herb. Before I passed out, I walked into the bathroom to take a piss. Walking down the hall, I saw Wolf passed out on his couch with a fatty packed in his lip and a half-full spitter opened in his hand. I walked into the room, grabbed the spitter, put it on the coffee table in front of him, and walked out. *Good job Cory,* I said patting myself on the back.

I could hear noises coming from the first floor, so I walked down the first set of stairs and leaned down to see what was going on. The pledges had made a circle, and two drunken juniors were wrestling shirtless on the first-floor carpet. I saw Jenna standing next to the pledges watching the juniors wrestle. *Desperate for the dick.* I laughed and walked back upstairs. I wanted no business with the testosterone wrestling, so I walked into my room to pass out. I opened the door and remembered Sara was still in there. I debated waking her up and getting her a pledge ride home, but she seemed pretty comfy on the couch. Also didn't want her waking up out of a blackout to me shaking her. Besides, she knew Kyle real well, so it was fine. Either one of us would just drive her home in the morning. She had laid down flat on the couch, whereas Kyle was still sitting up straight. I grabbed Bo's extra blanket from the floor of our sleeper, shook it to get the Bo off of it, and put it on Sara. I walked into my sleeper and hopped up into my bed. I lay on my back waiting for my too-stoned, scattered brain to recalibrate, praying it didn't turn into the spins.

It was a successful first night, and even though the thought of Em saying IU was going to change me as a person circled my now close-to-spinning brain, in some irrational way, picking up Wolf's dip spit and giving Sara the blanket made me feel content with myself. *I know I will never change, regardless of circumstances.*

I had a sense of pride as I fell asleep.

# FOURTEEN

PARTIES WERE LIKE THAT FOR THE ENTIRE FIRST TWO AND A HALF WEEKS. A whole sorority would come over, both houses would cram into a couple of rooms, and then a random assortment of girls would make their way in and out till about three or four in the morning.

Bo and I had already sold about six ounces. I talked with Alex and Bates and they were telling me that JR would sell only to guys living in the house and that Jason would still sell to the seniors. So the fact that it was just me and Bo meant we sold to the seniors too. I made a couple of deliveries to Alex and Bates, but for the most part, nothing changed. Everyone walked into our room or texted us when they wanted some.

Sheff was the only outsider I was selling to. Well, and Cam, but he wasn't a true outsider. He was over at our place every day. He and Bo were inseparable, so he knew Bo and I were dealing even before most ATOs. Bo was selling him like four grams every other day because Acacia's guy got the shittiest weed. Eventually we decided to let Cam buy half O's for $220. Expensive, but Bo and I still wanted to make money on it. Not going to just give Acacia our weed guy at no cost. We figured $220 for 14-plus grams still came out to a little under $16 a gram, so Cam was still making like $60 every half O he cleared.

Bo and I sat in our room watching *SportsCenter*. It was syllabus week again, so class had become a suggestion rather than a requirement at this point.

"Bro, selling this shit could be the greatest thing ever. People hand me money for weed, and then feel obligated to ask me if I want to smoke with them," Bo said as he handed me a blunt.

"Yeah, I don't get why people feel inclined to smoke us out. Like you don't owe me anything, that's what the money is for."

"That's the same shit as people buying the bartender a shot. Motherfucker, I would never buy a bartender a shot. Dude can get them for free."

"You don't buy shots, period," I said, coughing from the blunt.

"I will now. I tell you Adam's dude Mark or Marcus or whatever is finally going to pay up? Dude was down $950 betting on the MLB. Adam cut him off—I was going to let that penis keep burying his own grave."

"No shit! Fuck, I haven't checked the book in a while. Adam's actually on his way over with my cousin's roommate Sheff now."

"For what?"

"Buy some pot."

"We selling to Pi Kapps now?"

"No, just to Sheff slash my cousin."

"And Adam."

"Well, yeah, I guess after today, Adam too."

"So we sell to Pi Kapps now."

"Would saying yes make you feel better?"

"Yeah, a little. For real though, we should just give Adam or Sheff or whoever the same deal we gave Cam. I mean shit, they do the same jobs for the book anyway. Why not loop them in with the weed."

"But they don't know I deal, they think I just have weed."

"That's retarded."

"Don't want everyone knowing I'm a dealer."

"No, I mean it makes sense. Retarded but makes sense. Well, you can keep it that way and make it seem like ATO will supply the weed, not you personally. I mean fuck, that's technically what I do. I get handed bud and ask to pass it around the house. You do all the work."

"You bring up a good point, I do do all the work."

"Besides, you're still making the easiest money on Cam. $220 a half O is obscene. You buy a full O for 300."

"I know, but I need to make money on Acacia somehow. Why would I sell Cam at the same amount?"

"No, that's not what I mean, fuck it, sell the half O for $300, I don't give a shit. I'm saying, it's easier money than selling just grams. Like, that shit takes time. Just simple math, we buy half Os for around $150, sell them for $220. That's 70 bucks in one swift move. Why not do that with Pi Kapps too?"

Bo and I had been selling close to two ounces a week to ATO sophomores, juniors, seniors, and then Cam. Adding another half or full ounce a week would be a lot for me to buy. This was the same with selling to the seniors—it wasn't the fact that I was uncomfortable selling to Cam or Adam, because it didn't really affect me, but I was worried about Hippy Mike getting suspicious or pissed off selling more than two ounces every week.

Sheff and Adam walked in a couple minutes later. I always felt nervous talking about dealing because I didn't want Sheff telling my cousin I was ATO's weed guy. Luckily, bigmouthed Bo ran the show. Apparently the reason Sheff and my cousin had been buying from me the past two weeks was that Pi Kapps didn't have a steady dealer yet. Adam said they probably had 10 guys at the house buying eighths and selling a gram here and there, but that was just guys like Adam picking up a couple grams once in a while from a dude in another house. No one ever had enough for the entire house.

"Yeah, ATO has the same thing, just a lot more volume. There must be like, what Cory, seven? Seven guys in ATO who constantly have a quad or something?" Bo said looking over at me.

"Damn, seven guys like that? Pi Kapps needs one of those guys—do you think I could talk with them?" Adam replied, still standing.

"No need, I can get you the quad or half O anytime," Bo responded quickly without even acknowledging me.

"I'm in dude, how much?" Adam said looking over at me.

"Well, I think the guys in the house like selling small amounts, 'cause they . . ."

"But . . . I'm sure they would be able to sell like half Os if you gave them a heads-up," Bo blurted out, interrupting me.

I turned toward Bo but his eyes stayed on Adam.

"I'm in. Think I could grab a half O now?"

"Come back tomorrow—I'll get some from someone, but then we can work something out. I mean fuck, I see your ugly mug every week collecting degenerates' money anyway, shouldn't be a problem," Bo said from the couch.

"Thanks Bo. Cory, I'll take a gram now then and stop by tomorrow."

"Yeah, I'll take a couple grams too, Cory, if you got some," Sheff added.

"Yeah, I grabbed five grams from down the hall before you walked in. That work for you guys?"

"I'll take four if you want the one, Adam?"

"Sounds good. Here's $20."

"And here's $80."

"And oh, Bo, I got the money from Marcus, I'll give it to you when you come over."

"Thanks brotha."

I went and got five grams from the safe as Bo grabbed the money. I waited for Adam and Sheff to walk completely out before I said anything.

"So much for talking about it—dude, what the fuck?" I said to Bo on the couch.

"Quit being a pussy Cory. You're the one who said this hippy fuck told you, 'I'll always have more here.' The guy he gets it from fucking grows the damn stuff, like literally, weed grows on trees. There is always more."

"He did say that. But damn, that's a lot, though, dude. I'll talk with the hippy and see what he says."

"No need to even bring it up. Just say there is no senior dealer so you'll be buying shit for everyone. Tell him the house got bigger, you think a difference of a couple of ounces matters to this bum. You think you are his only buyer?" Bo said, grabbing the blunt.

It never really dawned on me how many houses this guy probably sold to, but maybe Bo had a point. *I wonder how much he actually has.*

"Do you think most houses have their own dealer like we do, or like a bunch of guys getting quads or something and just have a few guys that 'have pot'?" I said, sitting down next to Bo.

"Well, out of the two houses we're close with, both don't have a true dealer. And out of all houses, Acacia and Pi Kapps you'd think would."

"I never noticed my cuz not having any."

"I mean they probably always have some, but it's more difficult. I mean houses like APES and Phi Si for sure have their own dealers. 'Cause their dealers are for sure the coke and ecstasy guys too."

"Right."

There was a silence for a second. I think we were thinking the same thing. Bo re-sparked up the blunt and turned Kid Cudi's *Man on the Moon* back on. We both sat there smoking for a little without talking. I knew he was right, but hated the thought of being an actual guy who sold weed, not just the ATO pot guy. If that differentiation even made sense.

"Dude, I get this shit is up to you, but we should sell to more houses," Bo said, breaking the silence.

"Like not grams, but sell to people like Cam and Adam?"

"Yeah, I'm not talking the whole f-ing school, but Cam, Adam, you can ask your buddy Max at Sigma Chi, or that doorknob at Delts."

"Jimmy? He actually might do it, but no chance Max would."

"No, not them specifically, just ask them who their dealer is."

"Oh, gotcha. I don't know, dude—I'm not looking to be some legit drug guy here. The more people knowing, the sketchier it gets. Right?"

"It's fraternities bro. Our entire life is secrecy. Hell, you won't even tell your cousin's best friend that you sell. We'll be fine."

Bo had a good point. Frats were a system of silence. No one knew anything of substance about each house. There were stereotypes of the people inside the house, but as for tradition, hazing, drugs, or stuff inside the house, no one really knew shit. Each house was a steel trap.

"So would you ask Max who . . . ?" Bo said as he let out a vicious cough.

Bo's coughs were like a smoker's lungs. They were this low-pitched, bass-filled roar that sounded like he was clearing everything within both lungs at the same time.

"Jesus, you alright? Um, would I ask who Max's dealer is? I mean, if I did it, I would just ask for a gram or something. And whoever he introduces me to, I'll ask that guy if he wants more."

"That works too. We would be like a sales team. 'Excuse me, sir, I was wondering if you had a chance to evaluate your inventory recently. We at

ATO are offering a remarkable one-time deal.'" Bo said, impersonating a sales guy.

"This deal would include some of the highest-rated marijuana on the market. And wait, there's more! If you say yes now, I can throw in free shipping," I joked with a stoned chuckle, passing the blunt to Bo.

"Wait, you would deliver the pot to the houses?" Bo asked as he continued to smoke the blunt despite the cough.

His perseverance to overcome his coughs was award-winning.

"I was rolling with the infomercial. But it wouldn't be a bad idea."

"Why?"

"Because I wouldn't want random dudes walking in and out of ATO all the time. Everyone in the house would know what was going on."

The more I talked about it, the more realistic it sounded. When I first said I would deal, I was nervous about the buying aspect the most, but that part had actually been the easiest. If I was already buying ounces of pot, it wouldn't be a big deal to buy more ounces. Like, once you buy two ounces, having an additional two ounces makes no difference besides carrying a more packed backpack.

"You going to ask Max and Jimmy?"

"Yeah, fuck it, I'll text Max now, then go from there. Delts sucks, and so does Jimmy, so we'll try to avoid them at all costs."

*3:20 p.m.: Yo Max do you or anyone at Sigma Chi have any bud? ATO is dry right now.*

"Alright dude, sounds good. Want any more?" Bo said, offering out the millimeter blunt that was still in his hand.

"No, you fiend. You can keep it."

"With pleasure."

3:25 p.m.: ATO dry? Didn't think I'd hear that. Yeah Tommy should have some.

*3:25 p.m.: Cool think I could stop by and grab some from Tommy?*

3:26 p.m.: Do you have his number? Just text him and ask, I'm in class.

I was in a couple classes with this Tommy character, so I knew him, but not well enough to text him. He was one of those kids I said *what's up* to in the hallways, but had never had more than a 10-second conversation with before. We both knew of each other, but that was about it. I decided to text him anyway. Tommy texted back that Max gave him a heads-up and to come over to Sig Chi and pick up whenever. I had a four o'clock lecture, but was planning on skipping that anyway, so I grabbed Bo's keys and walked outside. As soon as I stepped outside, I realized how stoned I was. It was a residual effect. Like the weed was waiting for me to stand up before kicking in.

I drove to Sig Chi and it was like a Vineyard Vine's catalog. I'm not exaggerating. Everyone looked the goddamn same. It was crazy. Button-down, short shorts that were most likely pastel colored, and Sperrys. *Everyone* wore fucking Sperrys. *Like it's Tuesday, why the fuck do you have your white PFG shirt tucked into your light-pink, whale-printed shorts?*

Tommy had told me where his room was, so I walked up the front stairs in that direction. People stared at me like I was a black person in the 1960s because I walked in with flip-flops, black athletic shorts, and a faded red Chicago Blackhawks shirt. Shameless staring too. *Such cocksuckers.*

"Hey Cory, what up man, come in."

"Hey Tommy, what's good."

"So ATO went dry? How is that possible?"

*Alright enough ATO drug jokes. You're the one about to sell me drugs, big guy.*

"I know that's what Max was saying too."

"So how much you want?"

"Uh, two grams would work."

"Yeah, for sure, $40."

Tommy brought out a scale and about a little more than a quad of bud to weigh out the two grams. I was more ripped than I wanted to be, so didn't really know how to bring up my proposition. If he had a scale and a quad of pot, my guess was he dealt to his pledge class or maybe even the whole house.

"You get some good herb?" I asked as I sat on the edge of the TV stand.

*You get good herb? Who the fuck am I?*

"Gets the job done. How about ATO?"

"Yeah, actually really good stuff. It's medical, so there are a bunch of different kinds or strains or whatever. That shit means nothing to me, I just know I get really stoned smoking it."

"Oh, for sure I bet. Yeah, that shit doesn't mean anything to me either."

"If you ever wanted some, I know a few guys in the house pick up every Wednesday or some shit."

"Nah I should be good, I get mine from this GDI a couple blocks away."

"Oh, for sure. Yeah, the big plus is the guy delivers the bud. Which is amazing. Pot delivery should be the future."

"Wait, the guy drops it off at ATO?"

*There it is.*

"Yeah, well not to me, I've never seen him. But yeah, he drops it off."

"How much is it, do you know? Cause I'll fuck over this GDI guy if I can get pot delivered here."

"I'm not sure, I'd have to ask, but doubt it's much different than normal. Don't think he charges a surcharge or anything."

"Actually can you ask? 'Cause this GDI is real hit or miss, and kinda sketchy. So a delivery guy would be pretty sweet."

"No doubt, I'll let you know."

"Cool, thanks man. Not going to F202?"

"No fucking chance," I replied laughing

"Alright, let me know what that guy says."

"Will do."

*Boom!*

Delivery was the kicker. I couldn't believe I didn't think of that earlier. I mean, I did think of it, but not his reaction or in the true sense of how convenient weed delivery would be. The worst part about selling weed was buying it. Finding a guy who isn't sketchy, who's reliable and easy, who you can hand a shit ton of money to in return for drugs. I got super lucky that Hippy Mike lived close, always answered his phone, let me come over anytime and buy however much I wanted, and was a real laid-back dude. There couldn't be any relatively big dealer on campus who was easier to deal with.

I drove back to ATO to find Bo watching *The Dark Knight* in our room with smoke coming from the one-hitter on the table.

*And you wonder why your cough sounds like bronchitis.*

"How'd it go?"

"At first he said no, he was good, but then I said the guy ATO gets it from delivers."

"The hippy delivers?"

"No. Like what we joked about. I don't know, it was the first thing I thought of. But then he said if ATO's dude delivers, he would buy it and bail on the GDI guy he buys it from."

"So would you deliver, or ask the hippy?"

"Oh, it would have to be me. I wouldn't even tell the hippy. I would just pick it up from the hippy and drive it right to Sigma Chi."

"How much he want?"

"I told him I'd get back to him. After I talked to our guy. Just like you said to Adam."

"Dude, this is it. This is how we sell to more houses. The delivery was like the deciding factor for this prep school fag, right?" Bo said, sitting up on the couch.

"Right."

"Well then, we'll tell people we'll deliver. If the prices were relatively the same, would you say 'F off' to the hippy and say yes to weed delivery? Of course you would! I have to guess most frat dealers would do the same."

"So you want to start a weed delivery service?"

"Not like grams, but yeah. Let's sell to one guy in like every house, once a week. You know how easy that would be?"

"I was thinking that on the ride home. The hippy makes life so much easier, so if we delivered to houses, that would be the kicker for most frat dealers who don't have a laid-back stoner they buy from. Acacia, Pi Kapps, Sig Chi, and Delts. Like anywhere from a quad to a half O or whatever per week."

"I know a couple guys in Fiji, Kappa Sig. Phi Delt."

"The Jews in ZBT and APES. Just have to do the same thing, offer the same delivery, and then we'll tell them that you or I will deliver it because the ATO delivery guy didn't want to go all over campus."

"Do you understand how easy the money would be? Buy in more bulk from the hippy, how much did he say like a quarter pound would be?"

"Jesus."

"He gave you a price for it, right? How much?"

"Yeah, said $750."

"So . . . uh," Bo said as he typed into his calculator on his iPhone.

"That's $6.69 per gram. And we sell half O's for what? $220?"

"Probably have to lower it if we're going to sell to actual dealers and not Cam, but yeah, let's say $200."

"Well, $200 divided by 14 grams is $14.28. So we buy for $6.69 grams, sell for $14.28. They will buy for $14.28 and sell for $20. So then that's what? 14.28 minus 6.69 is 7.59. So we would make $7.59 per gram we delivered. Right? Meaning, 14 x $7.59 would be $106.26 per half ounce."

"Make $106.26 per delivery? For a half ounce?" I said looking for Bo's calculator confirmation.

"Yeah, and if these houses smoke as much as we do, that number easily could go to a full ounce, so like $200 per delivery."

"Per delivery."

"Per week."

"Dude."

"I know, and we already have two houses on board too! I'm texting my buddy Dieters in Fiji now."

"You have a buddy in Fiji?"

"No Cory. But I'll call him my buddy if he makes me $200 a week."

"Fine, I'll text Jimmy too, but let's not get overboard here. We still have to hope the hippy checks off on giving us double or triple the amount of herb he's used to."

"When you picking up next?"

"I'll go tomorrow, text Adam, and let him know we're good to go."

# FIFTEEN

HIPPY MIKE DIDN'T SAY A THING WHEN I PICKED UP FOUR MORE OUNCES. He was even more baked than usual, so maybe he had picked up himself and did the famous Bo Special: buy pot, smoke pot, sell pot. But really the Bo Special was: have Cory buy pot, hand Bo free pot, Bo smokes free pot, gives Cory the rest of the free pot, let Cory sell that pot, and give Bo half the money. Truthfully, Bo wasn't all useless. He talked with his buddy Dieters in Fiji, Kelly in Kappa Sig, and Matsui in Phi Delt. However, hearing Bo talk about those conversations, I don't think they were friends. Not even like me-and-Jimmy, just like, friendly. But regardless, Bo's persuasive nature must have worked.

Dieters said Fiji didn't have a guy, but was interested in buying a little at first to see how it went. Which made complete sense because Fiji only hung out with Fiji, so of course they didn't have an outside hookup. Matsui said the same thing, but Bo persuaded him to get a half ounce to start, whereas Dieters was getting only a quad. Finally, his buddy Kelly's pledgemaster in the house was Kappa Sig's dealer but was going to have Bo talk to him.

I got Jimmy on board. To be specific, he said, "I don't care who sells pot in this house—I will outsell them." The kid was such a try-hard, but was the perfect man for the job.

Bo and I had told each person he could arrange his own order every week, ranging from none to an ounce. I had to make a separate Excel tab in my bookie spreadsheet in order to keep everything straight:

| Pot | Grams |
|---|---|
| ATO | 35 |
| Acacia | 14 |
| Pi Kapps | 14 |
| Sigma Chi | 14 |
| Fiji | 7 |
| Delts | 14 |
| Phil Delt | 14 |
| Kappa Sig | ? |
| **Total** | **112** |

The only part that sucked was that the selling pitch in all of these meetings was the delivery. Bo agreed to deliver to Dieters in Fiji, Adam in Pi Kapps, and Matsui in Phi Delt. That left me with Tommy in Sigma Chi, Jimmy in Delts, and then Cam, but Cam was easy. He came and picked it up whenever he wanted.

We still wanted to keep it a secret that Bo and I were the gram-level ATO drug dealers, which was the best part about all of this. Each frat dealer thinking Bo and I were just doing the deliveries as a favor in exchange for free weed from the actual dealer in ATO. So the middleman's middleman. Which is exactly where we wanted to be and where we wanted to stay.

I told Tommy and Jimmy the guy came on Wednesdays, but really it was because I had this bullshit 10:00 a.m. class that was across the street from ATO, then a break till my next class completely across campus at 1:00 p.m. So I would drive after class to Delts and Sigma Chi, then keep the car and drive to my 1:00 p.m. class, then drive home. Bo told the other three guys Tuesdays for similar reasons, but Bo went to even fewer classes than I did, so really only said Tuesdays because his car would be available.

The first week went smoothly. The nugs I got had some purple tint to it, which Tommy and Cam specifically loved. Jimmy and I didn't give a shit, but I also threw in an extra gram per person, which must have given the same first impression Hippy Mike gave us. I sold the half O to Jimmy and Cam for $220 then Tommy for $200. Adam' was $200, Matsui's $200,

Dieters's quad was $100, then the Kappa Sig guy told Bo he would do it for $190, which we said OK to. We were still buying less than $7 grams, and $190 would be $13.5 a gram. So still doubling every gram. The final tally was six half-ounces and a quad, sold for a grand total of $1,330. Bo and I bought a QP, or 112 grams, for $750, sold 91 of those grams in a span of two days to seven other people, for $1,330, so a profit of $580. On top of having 21 extra grams to sell to ATO for ultimately $20 a piece, thus sitting on another $420. The delivery-middleman system was a joke. All cash, easy transactions, with fraternities that were built for and founded on secrecy. It was more chill than I had even imagined.

Bo and I sat in our room with the door locked with all of the cash and leftover baggies laid out on the table: $1,330 plus the $950 Bo had picked up from Adam for that Marcus kid's gambling debts. It was an otherworldly feeling. I must have counted it five times: 112 $20 bills and four $10 bills. With an extra fucking $420 worth of weed in the safe! Despite that random kid Marcus's gambling debts, it was all honest money. At least in my eyes. Everyone in the world knew it was a matter of time until weed was legal and Marlboro was selling Marlboro Greens, or there were pot-type liquor stores where you walk in, show ID, buy a couple joints and some brownies, and walk out. So it felt like clean money.

"Dude," Bo said looking down at the money.

"Brooo," I responded also staring down at the money.

"Duuuuuude!"

"This is half as much as I made all summer trimming bushes!"

"I mean, this pays for my schoolbooks, social fee, gas to and from home, everything."

"And it's all cash," I said as I lifted up the stack of twenties.

"And no one fucking knows we have this!" Bo said, punching me out of excitement.

"Pretty nice gig."

"We could do this to the whole fucking Greek system."

"I mean, no need to go overboard."

"Cory, I weighed out 14 grams a couple times, drove a combined 20 minutes, and got paid $690. Plus the $950 for accepting a couple text messages from some degenerate I don't even know. This is too easy! Why would we limit it?"

"Oh, I don't know. Maybe the whole illegal part?"

"But it's not like it would get any harder! This is as hard as it gets. We would just have to repeat it more. Like come on, you have to see how easy this is."

"I know, I was shocked how easy it felt. I left the car running at Delts, Jimmy got in my car, and I dropped him off at the economics building."

"Exactly! Like pretty much picking up $200 on the way to class."

"Literally."

"How much extra pot we got?" Bo said gathering up the money.

"I weighed it out, we got about 20 grams here, then there's another 15 or so still in the safe from the last pickup."

"Honestly dude, I'm going to see if some of my other buddies in different houses want to get in on the action. I know a kid a year older than me from R-Dub. There are kids in Beta, Sig Nu, I think Cam has a few buddies sprinkled around the Jewish houses."

"A black dude from Cincinnati has New York Jewish friends?" I asked as I handed Bo a shoebox to put the money in.

"Yeah, couple from his floor freshman year. I think that Cane kid is ZBT, and the super fucking huge dude in APES."

"Ooo right. I mean, ask Cam what he thinks. We could always give Cam a little more responsibility, you know what I mean?"

"Agreed, have Cam drop off to the Jews. Sell a bunch to him at a lower price, then he can deliver them or sell them."

"Sounds good to me. Talk to Cam."

"I'll talk to anyone who will listen. You?"

"Alright, pump the brakes. But honestly, yeah, I can talk to a few kids from my football team in high school. There are some in Pi Kapps and Beta, which I guess we'll have covered. There are two super strange kids, ones in Phi Sig and another in Lambda Chi."

"Lambda Chi? You know someone in Lambda Chi?"

"Yeah, this like fifth-string linebacker on our football team. Went to elementary school with the kid. Not friends at all, but friendly enough where I could ask him for a gram and do the same thing I did with Max."

"Lambda Chi it is. What's next? DU, Delta Chi, Skulls?"

We both sat there cleaning up the cash and putting it in the shoebox. We were both in great moods and cracked open a couple beers to celebrate. This great mood kept getting better over the next couple weeks. Bo added Beta instantly with another half ounce for $200 and Dieters decided to up from the quad to the half ounce. So now we were at seven half-ounces a week to seven houses, with Cam being the eighth house, but he picked up his half ounce every four to five days so was close to an ounce a week. Bo was doing the heavy lifting on the deliveries, with Pi Kapps, Fiji, Kappa Sig, Phi Delt, and Beta. Whereas I only had Sig Chi, Delts, and then Cam. Bo tried to stick with his one-time Tuesday deliveries, but the Beta guy had class, so he had to make that a separate delivery later in the day. I stuck with the Wednesday afternoons.

About a month later Cam convinced ZBT and APES to ditch their weed guys for the delivery man and buy full ounces. Cam settled on $375 by bringing up how convenient delivery was and how good the bud was. Cam made that agreement without talking to us, but it didn't matter. The more bulk we bought, the cheaper it was anyway. Cam told me he could try to deliver it but didn't have a car. I knew the two guys he was talking to in both ZBT and APES, so I told them I would do it for him. At the end of the day, that would put Bo at five houses and me at five houses, so I was fine with it. Only problem was I didn't have enough weed to sell.

Hippy Mike didn't seem to give a shit I was buying the quarter pounds. At least I didn't think so. The third week in a row he did make a comment like, "You trying to run me dry or something, or you teaming up with another frat now?"

I just told him he actually nailed it, and I was giving my best friend in Acacia one of the ounces. He seemed skeptical, but ultimately didn't seem to mind. I was walking in his door handing him $750 every week. The more I bought from him, the more I thought he himself grew the weed. He seemed to have an endless supply. Or at least I hoped he did, because he hadn't given me prices past a QP when we first met, and I was going to have to ask to double that.

It was Friday and I had enough to get through the weekend, but had to add the two ounces for the Jews on Monday, so again, decided it was time to text Hippy Mike. I left a little after five o'clock to make sure he would be there. As I pulled up, I noticed his car was in the driveway, so I walked in.

"Hey Mike, you home?"

"In here," he said from his usual family room.

"What's up man, how's it going?"

"You know, I'm not sure. You here to clean me out again?"

"Yeah, was actually going to talk to you about that. So you know how I was telling you about my best friend I was giving an ounce too. Well . . ."

Before I could finish I could see Hippy Mike's eyes close slowly as he looked down and took a deep inhale. He knew what was coming.

" . . . Um, I got another buddy that wanted some too."

"Does your buddy happen to be in ZBT, by chance?"

I didn't know how to respond. Guessing the right frat with the inhale and eye-close wasn't a coincidence. I immediately felt uncomfortable. I always felt relaxed at his place because he was such a chill guy, but at the end of the day, he was still selling me drugs, and clearly was not in a good mood.

"No. My one buddy is in Acacia and the other is my cousin in Pi Kapps. He's a senior and I guess Pi Kapps doesn't have a guy anymore."

I felt uneasy saying Acacia and Pi Kapps. I would never snitch on people, but it almost seemed like a drug dealing code where you could tell the guy above you who you sold down to, but never tell the guy below you who you bought from. So it was like a hierarchy of dealers, and the knowledge of where the drugs came from went only as far as the person above you. So Cam knew me, I knew Hippy Mike. That was it. I didn't know Hippy Mike's guy, and Cam didn't know Hippy Mike.

"Oh well, so I was selling to this guy in ZBT and he told me a couple days ago he was done buying from me and was getting some pot delivery service. So that's not you?"

*How do you know people? You're like 35!*

"No, not me. Pot delivery service? Like, Jimmy John's or something?" I joked to try and diffuse any tension.

"I don't know, but it was just a coincidence that ZBT bailed on me after a bunch of years, while you're asking for like four or five times the amount as JR or Jason did."

"No, that's not me. I'm not delivering shit. Yeah, there are no seniors this year dealing, so it's only me at ATO. So throw in Pi Kapps and Acacia with the seniors and that's where mine is going."

"Cool cool. Yeah man, that's fine with me. I mean hell, lose ZBT gain more of you. Whatever, that's fine by me. How much you need?"

*Gulp.*

I wanted to say the smallest amount I could possibly get away with, but with me selling three half O's, two O's, and ATO guys, then Bo doing another five half Os, that was seven ounces right there. Plus Cam always leaned on more than a half O each week, so round up to eight, and eight was exactly a half pound.

"Was actually thinking like eight ounces this week. Just to play it safe."

"Christ! You want a half P? Didn't you pick up a Q last week?"

"It was two weeks ago, but yeah, I got three ounces two weeks ago. I just want to be sure, you know."

"No I think it was a QP, and for sure last week," Hippy Mike replied in a direct tone I hadn't heard from him before.

"Yeah, I'm not sure. I know with the Acacia and Pi Kapps guys, there will be more of a need than a couple ounces."

"Hey man, I'm trying to be straight with you. I appreciate you and ATO buying from me, I really do. But if you're going to be asking for a half pound every week, then I don't really know what to say. You feel me."

I didn't know what to say either, so I just sat there nodding my head.

"'Cause man, I got a nice little setup here. Selling to you guys, I was selling to ZBT, and there are a couple of older guys I know. Nothing big, real simple. Not trying to start a cartel or anything—just trying to make a little extra cash and stay under the radar, you feel me?"

"Yeah, I totally understand. Just trying to give my cousin and my buddy the same bud I get. None of them know who you are or where I get it from. All they know is I get really good bud."

"Yeah man, I mean, without ZBT I do have more herbs now, so could give you the half elbow, but wanted to let you know that I don't want to be adding any more customers."

*The fuck is a half elbow?*

"Understand, man, neither do I. Appreciate it."

"So for the half, let's go with 13 . . . 1350. Sound good?"

"Yeah, works for me."

I pulled out a stack of twenties and started counting. I wished I had $100 bills, but wasn't going to go to the bank with all that cash each week. So twenties it was. I counted to 67, then didn't have a 10, so I gave him $1,360.

"Here's $1,360. You can keep the $10."

"Damn right I will."

"Hey thanks Mike. I'll hit you up next week, OK?"

"Next week?"

*Shit.*

"I mean, whenever I run low."

"Alright man. Peace."

I knew Hippy Mike could see right through me, but there was nothing I could really say. I didn't know what to do but try not to be awkward and leave his house. He was giving me a warning, but if I didn't add any more people and only bought the half pound every week, then I think everything would be fine.

*Buy just the half pound every week? Jesus, things have escalated quickly!*

I thought that amount of weed would make me nervous or afraid to get caught or whatever, but really it didn't feel any different than buying a half ounce the first time. If anything, it was more exciting. The only thing different was the size of the bags. Hippy Mike gave me two of those big gallon, slide-shut, Ziploc bags, both filled to the top with nugs. I mean, a half-pound was 224 grams, but it didn't feel any different. It felt the same as the QP, only difference was now I had to carry two of the Ziploc bags instead of one.

I got back to the house and weighed out the baggies for ATO: 20 gram bags, 16 10-sacks. 28 grams total. I always started with ATO, because to me, that was still the most important part. I was buying $6 grams and selling to ATO for $20. But more importantly, that's why I was the middleman in the first place, to deal to ATO. So I never wanted to screw with that. Next I weighed out the half ounces and ounces for all the other frats. APES and ZBT got ounces. Pi Kapps, Fiji, Sigma Chi, Kappa Sig, Phi Delt, Beta, and Delts got half ounces. Anything left over was for Acacia and ATO, but I weighed out two half ounces and put them in separate bags for whenever Cam wanted them. The whole weighing process took me about an hour, but I locked the door and listened to the *No Ceilings* album the whole time. Weighing out weed and counting the money. It was surprisingly enjoyable. Maybe not surprising that counting money was enjoyable, but it was like an adrenaline rush. It wasn't necessarily addicting, but knowing how much money I was going to make was something I knew I could get used to.

I finished up and shoved everything in the safe to wait for Monday. After I closed the safe I grabbed my phone and went over the numbers of everything.

*So $1,360 for what came out to be 232 grams, sell 6.5 ounces or 182 grams for $2,560. Leaving me 50 grams for ATO to sell $20 apiece. That's a total of $3,560 from selling. Minus the $1,350 I paid for it, and that comes out to . .* . I stopped and looked down at my phone and was startled at the number looking back at me. I was speechless. *$2,210 in profit. A week!*

# SIXTEEN

**NEXT COUPLE WEEKS FLEW BY.** All I did in class was fool around with my Excel sheet, seeing how much money we were making per week. I was obsessive over being careful and diligent. I couldn't tell exactly how much money we'd made, since the cash I got would go directly to Hippy Mike the following week, but mathematically, Bo and I were each profiting around $1,100 a week.

I got back to the house around 4:30 p.m. and cracked open a beer with Kyle, Joe, Wolf, and Cutty. A couple of the seniors were going to pregame at this bar called Bears. It was down the street and home to the famous Hairy Bear drink. It was about six to eight shots in one drink, with a shit ton of sugary soda mixer in it. Surprisingly, it tasted great—like passion fruit or if you mixed orange juice with grapefruit juice and then mixed in some Sprite and a couple lemons and limes. Then of course if you added in some tequila, rum, vodka, and gin. Somehow that tasted fantastic, which made it dangerous. I had my cousin's ID so had been there before. Kyle had his brother's ID, and Wolf and Joe had good fakes too, so we all decided to join the seniors for some drinks. I wanted to celebrate with Bo, but he was too much of a chicken to go to the bars with his shitty fake.

The seniors came to the house to pregame around eight o'clock. Which ultimately was another pregame before going to Bears, which was the pregame before going to the bars. A pregame had turned into an expression for getting a little drunk before going to the next place, but ATO was only blocks from Bears, so it made more sense to walk from there anyway. We went into Wolf's room and had a couple drinks.

"Wolf, you mind?" one of the seniors motioned to Wolf.

"No, go for it."

"Want some?" the senior motioned again.

"Yeah, I'll take some," Wolf said, walking over to the couch.

I stood there talking to Kyle, not really paying attention to the seniors in the room. The whole selling pot thing had made me a little spacey. I tried not to think about it too much, but it was always on my mind. *How much bud do we have in the safe? Should I let Bo talk to Sigma Nu? Should I let Cam or other houses sell to GDIs? How about selling grams to other houses? What would Hippy Mike do if I attempted to ask for more?* It filled my head all day long. I mean fuck, it was like $1,000 a week. I'd feel guilty not thinking about it.

I noticed a couple of the seniors sitting on the couch start rearranging stuff on the coffee table. I looked over and saw a couple dudes leaning forward with a bunch of white lines spread across the table. *How long has this been going on?* With the music going, talking to Kyle, daydreaming about dealing, I must have been oblivious to the door being shut and people snorting lines in the room. I made eye contact with one of the seniors emptying out a baggie.

"Carter, Kyle, you guys want some?"

"Adderall or blow?" Kyle responded.

"Blow, but I got a couple addies if you want that."

"Yeah, I'd rip an Adderall. Cory?"

I had never snorted anything before and didn't think Kyle had either, so was a little rattled when he asked. My mind didn't really have time to think, and ultimately wasn't against Adderall.

"Uh, yeah sure, I'll split the addie with you."

The senior handed Kyle the Adderall. It was in a capsule, so Kyle spilled out the little orange beads onto the table. He took out his credit card and placed it on top of the beads. With a quarter, he started to crush the beads by sliding the quarter across the credit card until the beads turned into powder. He split up a couple lines using his credit card and rolled up a $20 bill. I knew the difference between taking it and snorting it was that snorting it made the Adderall hit you faster, since it went directly into your bloodstream, but that's all I really knew. And honestly never googled that before. Heard it once and never questioned it.

After Kyle went, I grabbed the $20 from him and bent down. I had seen the senior check which nostril was most clear, so I did that too. *Left.* I put the $20 bill in my left nostril and snorted up the line. Instantly I had the urge to grab my nose and squeeze both nostrils shut. I let go and took another aggressive inhale through the left nostril to get whatever felt stuck in there out. It felt like my nose was stuffy or I had an itch in there or something. I coughed as I wiped my nose a couple more times. I looked over and saw Kyle going for another one. It really wasn't that bad, but I was also doing Adderall and not cocaine so didn't know the difference. Once Kyle finished I did one more line, up the right nostril, and then we headed out.

All 15 or so of us left the house to walk over together. There was a big bouncer at the door named Al. Rumor was if you slipped him a $10 bill, he would let you in underage. But another rumor was that undercover cops hung out at Bears all the time because apparently word got out about the Big Al handoffs going on. Luckily we all had IDs, so got in without paying. We grabbed a booth near a group of girls sitting in the back. They must have been seniors, because all the guys we were with went up and hugged them hello. I recognized a few of them from bartending some of their parties, but, yet again, didn't know any of them by name.

I kept having the urge to wipe my nose like I had a runny nose, but when I looked around, I noticed a couple of the other seniors were doing it too, so I resisted. *Do people who snort shit rub their noses all the time?*

"You're Carter's little cousin, right?"

"Yeah. Hi, I'm Cory."

"Hi Cory, I'm Kayla. And this is Mia and Shannon," Kayla said as she shook my hand.

*Dammit, she went hand first. It will never not be weird, shaking a girl's hand.*

"Hey everyone, nice to meet you."

"You're identical to your cousin," one of the girls said.

*Are you Mia or Sharon? Sharon or Shannon? Shit!*

"Yeah, I'm using his ID, so I hope so."

"Want a Hairy Bear, we have a few extras?" the girl responded.

"Yeah, I'll take one. Thanks."

I took a couple sips from the straw. Exactly how I remembered. Grapefruit juice, Sprite, orange juice, and then mostly tequila and rum.

"Sorry, what house are you all in?"

"Zeta," Kayla responded with a smile.

"Oh, cool cool. Honestly don't know many girls my age in Zeta. Actually wait no, two girls. I know two girls. Carolyn and . . . can't think of the other name. She's Carolyn's roommate in the house I think."

"Liz?"

"Yeah, Liz. Thank you."

"Oh my God! Carolyn's the best. How do you know her?"

"We hung out a bunch welcome week and freshman year really. She was my friend from high school's freshman-year roommate. Yeah, she's pretty great. Honestly haven't seen her in a while."

I took another sip from my drink and noticed it was almost half gone. *Wow, must have been thirsty.*

We sat there talking for a while. Once I finished my drink I went up and bought another round. I still felt timid buying a round of drinks, since I wasn't used to spending money. Even though I had made a ridiculous amount of money, it still felt like I didn't have that much.

We moved to the back part of the bar, which had more standing room. Kyle, Wolf, and I were all finishing up our second Hairy Bears at this point. My mind was going a million miles an hour. At one point I was talking with Kyle about going to class or not going to class and which made more sense, then I was talking to a random senior about whether baseball or soccer would be a bigger sport in the USA in 2020. It was hilarious. I could feel the Adderall arguments coming on instantly. My conversations consisted of a lot of long-winded responses and getting cotton mouth while I spoke.

Everyone was already pretty drunk. We had probably only been there 45 minutes to an hour or so, but a bunch of people looked hammered. I glanced down at my drink while Wolf was saying something to me. *I've had two Hairy Bears and I'm fine. How many have they had?*

I turned toward Kyle standing by the bar with an empty cup.

"Want to split one more?" Kyle asked.

"That is exactly what I want to do," I responded, handing him my cup.

We hung around the bar for another hour or so then hopped on the bus that drove by, heading toward the main strip of bars on Kirkwood. We walked into Kilroy's and went straight to the back patio area. I had only been to Kilroy's one other time with my parents because I didn't want to lose my ID there, but I didn't even think about it this time until I was already inside. I saw one of the girls, either Mia or Shannon, and their friends at the back left table near the outdoor bar, so I walked over to them.

"Want a drink?" I said as I got up to Mia or Shannon.

"Yes, I would love one."

I saw Joe walking up, so knew if I introduced him to the girl, she would say her name.

"Hey sorry, this is my friend Joe."

"Hi Joe. I'm Mia."

*Mia! Trick works every time.*

"So what do you want?" I said to Mia, leaning against the bar.

"Shots or drink?"

"Both."

"I'll take a vodka soda and then . . . How about a tequila shot?"

"Tequila? Alrighty then, three shots of tequila coming up."

I got Joe a whisky coke and myself a whisky ginger on top of our tequila shots. Drinks were all three dollars on Thursdays at Kilroy's, so buying rounds of drinks to celebrate making over $1,000 a week was a little anticlimactic, but I wasn't complaining. I stood outside bouncing around from conversation to conversation. I knew more people there than I was expecting. Some of Mikey's buddies, the seniors, some of the juniors in ATO showed up. It was a good time. A bunch of juniors bought me some shots because I rarely went out to the bars. I wasn't going to insist on paying, but I had a weird feeling like I should. I just looked at every ATO and saw dollar amounts. *You gave me $150 last week because of the 49ers, you buy* *like a gram a week, and you bought a 10-sack from me then proceeded to get drunk and leave it in my room.*

"Cor, you good?"

I turned around and Sheff was grabbing my shoulder.

"Yeah, pussy, what's up?

"Bro, you're hammered! I love it. Fuck, I wish Carter was coming out tonight."

*Hammered?* I honestly didn't feel that drunk at all. I mean I wasn't sober, but I was still talking to everyone and bouncing around the bar just fine.

"Oh fuck off, want a shot?"

"Hell yeah, J-Mo?"

"J-Mo it is."

We took a shot of Jameson as Mia and her friends walked by. We chatted for a little then took another shot, this time tequila. I didn't have a go-to shot so went with the flow of the night. Then the strangest thing happened.

My eyes jolted open and it was pitch-black in the room. I looked to my left to see Mia sleeping next to me, facing the opposite way in the bottom bunk of a cold dorm. *What the fuck?*

I rubbed my eyes a couple times. *Nope, this is real.* I heard a rustling noise above me and looked around to see a bunch of girls sleeping in bunk beds everywhere. My jeans and belt were still on, but my long-sleeved black V-neck shirt was on the floor next to me, along with my wallet and Bo's car keys. I reached into my pocket and felt my phone. *Thank God.*

I heard the rustling noise above me again and then saw two massive legs draped over me. The dude hopped down and whisper-yelled, "Fuck!" as his feet slammed on the floor.

"Gilbert?"

"Cory? What the fuck? Let's fucking roll," he whispered at me.

Gilbert was the stoner pledgemaster who didn't really give a shit about the process. As I leaned forward to get up, it felt like all the blood in my body rushed to my head. I sat up in the bed and grabbed my face with both hands and kept my eyes closed as I waited for my body to recalibrate. Quietly, I rolled out of bed and grabbed my shit off the floor and followed Gilbert out. A couple of girls rolled over as we walked out, but none really saw us leaving. We walked down the stairs and out the side door toward the parking lot. It was well past sunrise. I looked down at my watch. *9:03 a.m.*

"That your girlfriend?"

"Huh? No. Sorry. No, met that chick last night?"

"And she brought you back? You barbarian, you."

"Fuck, I don't remember shit. Did I come with you?"

"No, I was at Kilroy's and went back with my girlfriend to smoke and she made me stay over."

"No, I was at Kilroy's too."

"So this chick picked you up at the bar?"

"I guess so," I said rubbing the back of my head.

We were all the way across campus so started walking. I didn't feel the hangover yet, but I could feel my eyes not all the way open and my head dizzy. *I'm still drunk.*

I tried to recall the night, but only bits and pieces came to mind. I remembered taking shots with Sheff and Mia. Then vaguely remembered talking with the big dude Mo I sold to in APES for a while. There was something in my head about walking down a street with Mo, or maybe it was a group of people, but I couldn't tell if that happened or was just a dream or what. I didn't remember leaving, didn't remember if I banged Mia, nothing. I just, kind of, woke up.

I was one of those guys who got debilitating stomach hangovers and could feel one brewing, on top of a startlingly awful pulsing headache. I had a theory that hangovers all depended on the type of drunk you were, as in the type of hangover had to relate to blacking out or not. From being around hundreds of people who aggressively drank every week, I started noticing that people who blacked out all the time had iron stomachs and so got head hangovers, while people who you almost couldn't tell if they were drunk and never blacked out were the ones who threw up in the morning. I never cared enough to actually do the research, but my guess was that it had to do with your body accepting or fighting the booze. For instance, if you drank the same as everyone but didn't black out, your body was fighting the alcohol and thus working in overdrive to digest the booze and battling to stay coherent and not act like a bumbling, hammered fool. So in the morning, your stomach struggled from fighting all night. Like, that battle was the sickness. Instead of the flip side, when your body accepts the booze and lets it do its thing. So when your body accepts it and you black out, your stomach wasn't exhausted in the morning because there was no fight—it surrendered and digested the alcohol normally. But instead of the nausea, your head killed, since, well, you blacked out.

None of this mattered, though, since I had taken Adderall. My body fought the booze like always, but I blacked out from drinking gallons and gallons of booze. So fighting to stay sober + eventual body surrender blackout = head and stomach hangover. But at the moment I was still drunk, so all of this was still to come.

I got to my place and went straight into my sleeper to pass out. Couldn't be longer than five minutes later Bo's alarm went off. He had Friday morning classes so always had his alarm set for them, but he never went to class. It was the most annoying shit Bo did. Every Friday, I lay in bed waiting for him to realize he wasn't going to class, turn off his alarm, then go back to sleep. But today I was not in the mood.

"Oh shit, Cory my bad," Bo said, scrambling for his phone.

"Fuck off."

"What time you get back?"

"Right now. Now fuck off."

"Wait, what? Where did you sleep?"

"Zeta."

"Zeta? What the fuck? With who?"

"Some senior I met last night."

"And you slept there!"

"Well aware of the weirdness of it. Now realize you aren't going to class and fuck off."

"Attaboy Cory. Give me some knucks, brotha. First since Emily?"

"First since Em, now please, fuck off quietly," I said as I gave Bo a fist-bump.

"I'll be grabbing breakfast downstairs big bad Cory. And oh, we need more bud. Cam picked up another ounce last night. We're down to the ATO bags."

*Fuck.*

"I'll talk to Hippy Mike later."

"His name is Mike? Never knew that," Bo said as he walked out of the room.

I never realized I had never called him Mike in front of anyone before. I called him "the hippy" to Cam and Bo. But I really didn't care right now. I was starting to feel the hangover coming on strong. My stomach was in a knot, and I felt like I was going to throw up. I grabbed my phone and saw I had a text from a 513 number.

2:11 a.m.: Mia Edwards

And then two missed texts from Mo.

2:57 a.m.: Cool bro thanks. Yeah ask your boy next time you go and let me know

2:57 a.m.: And how much it would be

*My boy? Ask "my boy" for what? What the fuck happened last night?*

I scrolled up on my phone to see a conversation between Mo and me around three in the morning.

2:37 a.m.: Yo bro it's Mo. I'm serious about talking to your guy about the snow.

*2:51 a.m.: For sure dude Illl ask him next time I go.*

2:52 a.m.: When you going next?

*2:55 a.m.: I go like once a week . I'll ask him.*

# SEVENTEEN

"WHAT'S GOOD A-T-BLOWS."

"What up Cam."

"Man, you look like shit C. You get smacked last night?"

"Apparently."

"Hey did you talk to Mo at all?"

"Uh . . . yeah, I was with him last night. Why?"

"That boy was telling me he might start getting coke from some dude, wanted to know if I wanted any for Akak."

*Some dude? Fuck.*

"Yeah, I don't remember much of our convo from last night, but I think I told him I'd ask the hippy."

"Wait. What about dealing coke?" Bo said as he started paying attention to the conversation.

"No. I mean, I blacked out told Mo I would ask the hippy if he sold any. Then I would only get it for Mo."

"No, I got that. But like, are you actually gonna ask for coke?"

"Don't plan on it. I texted him a couple hours ago for some more bud. He said to come on Monday, so I have till then, I guess."

"Oh, aight, well if you do ask your hookup let me know. I know my house would take some. Same kid with the shitty bud now has shitty coke," Cam said as I could see Bo still staring at me.

"I've never even done coke before. Trust me, if I start selling it, you and Bo will be the first ones I tell."

I wasn't going to ask Hippy Mike for blow. First, I didn't want to even risk him saying he was done selling to me, and secondly, well, I wasn't going to be selling cocaine, so that was that. My hangover was unbearable, so I stayed in all weekend smoking and following the bets we had for college football and the NFL Sunday slate of games. Neither Mia nor Mo texted me all weekend, which was nice. I didn't want to deal with either of them. Especially Mia. I barely knew who she was, so that fling was just going to drift away and get logged as a funny memory.

Monday came and nothing changed with Hippy Mike. He seemed upset I was still buying so much, but I didn't bring up "the snow," so it was business as usual. It was like that for a couple months. There was no more small talk with him anymore. I would walk in, he would have the two bags of bud on the table, I would hand him $1,350, he would say, "Thanks man. See you later," we would do the JR and Hippy Mike signature slap-and-pound handshake, and I would walk out.

The new crop of pledges added 35 freshmen to our list of guys Bo and I were selling $20 grams to, so we were racking in a solid three grand a week all the way up to winter break. Bo was closing the book over break, so the week before he went around and closed everyone's tab. Adding in the additional $2,120 from bookieing, the money was quickly stacking up in the shoebox in our safe. Bo and I locked the door, turned on some Kid Cudi, rolled up a blunt, and decided to count it all up.

It wasn't like what you saw in the movies, with nice crisp $20 bills, all stacked in rows of 500, spread out on the desk neatly. Nope. The money was all in two shoeboxes locked away in Bo's safe, mostly wrinkled, a lot of five-dollar bills, bunch of singles, it was a mess. I emptied the boxes out on the table, and we started separating the singles, fives, tens, twenties, fifties, and hundreds. It took us quite a while, but like, it was money. So it was pretty fucking cool to have it take a while.

"I got 513 $20 bills over here," Bo said from the floor.

"I got 218 over here," I said, plugging in the numbers on my computer. "You writing this down?"

"Yeah, got the Excel sheet open. That's 731 twenties, so, $14,620."

"Holy fuck," Bo gasped.

"Uh . . . Alright . . . I got 29 hundreds," Bo stuttered now sounding in a hurry.

"None over here."

"Alright . . . There's . . . 34, 35, 36, 37. So 37 fifties."

"OK, 29 hundreds and 37 fifties. That's 29 hundred aaaand what, 18 hundred? So 47 hundred more."

"Holy fucking fuck!" Bo said again, this time louder.

"You count the tens?"

"Yeah, got a shit ton of them down here. I wrote it down but I'm pretty stoned, so might want to recount it."

"Dude, who cares at this point, what did you get?"

"It's 562."

"I have 236 more over here. So what's that, 7. . . 98? 798?"

"You have the Excel sheet, I don't fucking know."

"Ha! Yeah, 798, so $7,980."

"Then I got 165 fives and 37 singles."

"So another 862," I said, reading the Excel sheet.

"What are we at?"

I grabbed my laptop and plugged in the rest of the numbers. It was easier for us to count the actual bills than the amounts, so I had it all sorted by singles, fives, tens, etc. I plugged in a few calculations and summed all the numbers at the bottom. My heart dropped. I couldn't believe the number. Bo and I had been taking money from the stash to pay for stuff too. Like food, booze, shopping, etc., but it seemed as if that didn't even make a dent. I glanced down at the table that had the money spread out everywhere and looked back at the number.

"Dude, what's the fucking number?"

"Bro," I said looking up at Bo.

"That good?"

"Bro, it's $28,212."

We were both speechless for a second. We had made $14,106 each, in one semester.

"Twenty-eight thousand fucking dollars? For dropping off a couple Ziploc bags every week?"

"The fucking delivery man!" I yelled as I stood up.

"Everyone loves the delivery man!" Bo screamed as we both gave each other a big bear hug.

We split the money in half, and Bo put his share into his shoebox and then into his own smaller safe he had from freshman year. His parents had access to his checking and savings accounts, so he didn't want to put it into his bank account. My rents had the ability to see my accounts, but never did. Also, I don't even know if they knew how to, so I took half of my share and put the rest into my safe. The half I left out was going to be deposited into my savings account. *Half of my half is $7,000!*

Winter break came and went, even more low-key than freshman year. Freshman year winter and summer break, everyone was excited to see each other, tell stories, even brag about their schools. After sophomore year, people took winter break as it was meant to be, a break. Break from partying, finals, shitty night sleeps, just college in general. For the first time in my life, I was pumped for some home-cooked meals. Ricky, Steve, and I stopped hanging around Garrett and Drew all together, and they had stopped reaching out to us too, which was nice. I avoided Em at all costs too. We were at the same house parties a few times, but we would just make awkward eye contact from opposite sides of the room. My guy friends stuck more to hanging with Jess's friends and slowly stopped hanging around with Max's or Em's friends. Not because of me, though. I just don't think anyone wanted to combine all four friend groups at one party that often anymore.

I didn't tell anyone about selling. With my IU friends, it felt natural to be the drug middleman and the bookie. Someone was going to have to supply it, so the fact that I was that someone didn't faze me. But for some reason I felt guilty selling bud around my high school friends, or even them knowing that I was running a sportsbook or selling bud. I had brought a couple grams, but passed them out instead of selling them. I didn't know where the shameful feeling came from or why it didn't exist at school, but I wanted to keep my IU life separate from my high school life.

I drove to school a couple days early. It was Mike's last semester, so he wanted nothing to do with the suburbs. Class started on the 10th of

January, but the house opened on the 8th, so I was fine with going back early. The start of the semester was going to be like the start of the year. At ground zero, aka no one had any weed. I didn't want to get more than a half P, so I was just going to get a half then go back a day or two earlier, if need be, in order to make up for some houses probably wanting full ounces. Bo wasn't in town yet, so I walked over to Hippy Mike's with my backpack on. It was cold as fuck but sunny, so at least was manageable. I turned onto his street and saw a car in the driveway. It was a black Mercedes. I wasn't a car guy so couldn't tell the difference between an S-class, E-class, Z-class, whatever, a Mercedes was a Mercedes. All I could tell was that it looked newer, and sure as hell not a Hippy Mike car.

I was hesitant to go inside, but I was walking, so couldn't just drive around the block. I took out my phone and called Hippy Mike to double-check everything was alright. He answered, but didn't say anything then hung up like usual.

I walked up the front steps, through the front door, and turned right into his family room but walked into an empty room.

"In here," I heard Hippy Mike say from the back of the house.

I walked past the family room and into the kitchen/dining room where Hippy Mike was sitting at the table with another guy. The other guy was about 6'1", with brown hair slicked back and a reddish-brown beard. Must have been in his late twenties. Actually he was identical to Chris Pine, but with a thicker beard. I looked at him and then over at Hippy Mike. The new guy was wearing acid-wash jeans, a black quarter-button sweater, and a slim-fit leather jacket. Hippy Mike was wearing black sweatpants and a ripped-up dark red IU hoodie with the sleeves rolled up. *How the fuck do these two know each other?*

"Hey Mike, what's up."

"Mike? What?" the Chris Pine–looking guy said to Hippy Mike.

"Yeah, that's the name I tell the college kids."

"That's amazing," Chris Pine replied, laughing.

*Well, I guess my "no one goes by the name Mike" theory is still accurate.*

"Hey, sorry, I'm Cory."

"Yeah, Cory, heard a lot about you, I'm Eric."

*Heard a lot about me?*

"And you are?" I said jokingly to Hippy Mike.

"Nothing against you man, I always tell people *Mike*. You know, to be safe. So hey Cory, yeah, so this is Eric, he's the guy I get my nugs from."

"Oh, the grower, yeah, what's up man."

"So Cory, I know I was talking to you a couple weeks ago. But, well, with the amount of pot you're getting, um, I don't think I can keep up, or, better yet, we, don't think I should keep up. I don't like getting involved with that much, man, you get it right?" Hippy Mike said as he kept looking over to a nodding Eric.

"Uh, yeah, I understand."

"Yeah, Cory, so Phil was telling me, or shit, Mike. My bad Phil," Eric said, slapping Hippy Mike's back.

"It's fine."

*Of course he's a Phil.*

"So Phil started buying more from me, which I was completely fine with, but then he told me that all of it was going to you. And, well, we decided I could just sell directly to you, since Phil feels a little uncomfortable moving that much."

"Oh, so I'm going to start buying from you? You sure you're OK with that?" I said to Hippy Mike.

"Yeah man. I liked having my little gig with ATO and ZBT. Selling an ounce, maybe two at the most. And knowing exactly where that is going. Now I don't know where the eight ounces I give you are going each week. And, well, like Eric said, I just feel uncomfortable."

I knew it wasn't worth lying to him on where the bud was going. He knew three houses couldn't blow through eight ounces every week. I nodded my head and let them keep talking.

"So yeah, Cory, don't feel bad, dude. I'm getting too old for this shit anyway," Hippy Mike added as he awkwardly laughed.

"Yeah, Cory, nothing will change for you. Only thing is, you'll have to drive to my house to come pick up instead of here. But we can talk more about that later. We both wanted to make sure this was OK with you."

"Um, yeah, I don't see why not," I replied confidently.

"Yeah, Cory, I can vouch for Eric. I've been buying from him for years."

"Good enough for me."

"You drive here today?"

"No, actually walked."

"In this weather? Well, that's perfect. We can drive to my place. That OK with you?"

"Uh, yeah, that's fine."

"Well, hey Cory, it's been fun getting to know you man," Hippy Mike said sheepishly.

"Yeah man, you too."

I gave the hippy one last slap and pound before I walked out. I liked Hippy Mike, or Phil, or whoever he was. He was low-key, he liked being low-key, and he wasn't in it for a lot of money, just to make an extra buck. I actually felt bad I was undercutting him and going straight to his dealer, but ultimately it was his decision. He could have kept going, or at least, that's what he said. On second thought, Chris Pine easily could have forced him out, which made it worse. Chris Pine looked more like one of the movie drug dealers. Rich, good-looking, drove a Mercedes, leather jacket. He had the image down pat, which made me nervous, but whatever, I wasn't being the middleman delivery guy to make some hippy more money.

I followed Eric out the side door and into his car. For some reason, as I got in the car, I finally felt like an actual drug dealer. Like I had taken the next step up, even though the amounts weren't changing. It was a terrible uneasy feeling.

"So Phil said you had pretty much plateaued at a half pound a week?"

"Yeah, pretty much."

"So I got some good news for you. First off, my shit's cheaper, 'cause you're cutting out a dealer . . ."

*OK. Starting to like this.*

" . . . and secondly, there really is no limit for me. So if you plateaued because Phil was uneasy or apprehensive or whatnot, don't worry, you can get as much as you want."

"Yeah, right now I probably only need a half pound. Maybe a

three-quarter pound or so for the first buy because we are just getting back to school. You know what I mean?"

"Yeah, I get it. Hey man, I used to be in your shoes, I understand it."

*Used to be? What, an IU drug dealer? Seems like you still are, buddy.*

We drove for about five more minutes, driving past College Mall and into a more secluded area off campus. I didn't like being this far off campus, but truth be told, it was only about two to three miles down Third Street. It wasn't that far; I just couldn't walk to pick up anymore.

Eric pulled into the straight part of a U driveway and pulled into the two-car garage connected to the house. His house was sweet. It was a brick house with white stone. The front door had a vaulted arch above it. Easily could have been a four- or five-bedroom house. As we were pulling up, I saw what seemed to be a pretty big backyard, but couldn't tell. Honestly looked like he was raising a family of four in a nice suburb of Bloomington, IN.

"Welcome to my house. Shit, I probably should have had you follow me here, did you pay attention on how to get here?"

"Yeah, I should be able to find my way, I can plug in the address if not."

We walked through the garage and into his house. It was the definition of a bachelor pad. It was all hardwood from floor to floor, no carpets. The kitchen opened up into the family room which opened up into the front room toward the front door. Everything was so clean and there was a shit ton of empty open space. The entire back wall was floor-to-ceiling windows that faced the backyard, which, yup you guessed it, had a pool.

"You want a drink?"

"No, I'm alright thanks," I said, scratching the back of my head.

*Do I scratch the back of my head when I'm nervous?*

I stopped scratching and tried to act normal as I walked into the main room. *Or whatever you call this giant area.*

"So yeah, this is my place. I doubt you want a tour or whatnot, so we can get right to it."

He walked behind the bar and plugged numbers into a safe. He pulled out a couple massive black duffel bags, put them on the bar, opened up the duffel bags, and pulled out two airtight bags of weed. I couldn't tell how much was there because it was all compressed, but it was like a literal brick of weed.

"So I go 1100 for the half, 2K for the pound, then 3.5 for two and 5 for four. Sound good?"

*Five for four pounds? Jesus Christ!*

"Uh, yeah . . . Sounds good to me, I'll take the half for now."

"Oh, right, you said you wanted three-quarters. Well, how about you take the pound because it's already weighed out, and that way you don't have to come pick more up in a couple days, sound good? Did you bring enough?"

"Uh, no, sorry, only have the $1350 and maybe a couple twenties in my wallet."

"That's fine. Get me back next time. That work?"

Something didn't feel right. The guy was super nonchalant about money, but super organized with his airtight Saran-wrapped pounds of pot in two gigantic black duffel bags. It made me nervous how easy it felt. I had met the guy 20 minutes ago, and he was already going to front me $650 worth of weed? I also didn't know if this was common dealing practice, since I was just used to dealing with a hippy on his couch.

"Yeah, I mean, if you're OK with it. I have, I have an extra . . . $100 in my wallet. So that'll be $1450. So I owe you $550 next time."

"Locked in the old memory. Five hundred and fifty for next time," he said, twisting his finger against his head like he was physically storing the memory.

I stood awkwardly for a second before Eric remembered he had to drive me home. I took the pound and put it into my backpack. It was surprisingly a lot easier to carry than the half pounds I was getting from the hippy. It was tightly wrapped and sealed, so slid right in. Plus it didn't smell at all. We got into his car in the garage and started driving back.

"So do you want me to text you and let you know when I need more?"

"Oh shit, yeah, exchanging phone numbers would help, wouldn't it? I got your number from Phil, so take my phone and send yourself a text."

*You already have my number?*

"How much time do you need for a heads-up? Like, when I'll be coming over."

"Yeah, I'm up in Indy a lot these days so it could be a couple days' notice, it could be five minutes. It all depends. So I would say, to err on the side of caution, give me one day, and I'll let you know my schedule later. Unless, do you have any days that work best for you?"

Eric was so much more intimidating than the hippy that I wanted to say Tuesday but had this urge to say "it didn't matter." I didn't know why I felt like impressing him, but I did.

"It really doesn't matter; I was going midmorning on Tuesdays but can come anytime."

"Yeah, Tuesdays should be fine. Especially morning. Thursday through Sunday I'm pretty much always in Indy, so those days are tough."

I didn't even want to ask him why he was in Indy on the weekends, so I let that comment go.

"Alright well I'll let you know; with this pound I should be good for a while."

"Sounds good, my man."

As we pulled into the parking lot of ATO, Eric stopped short, almost behind Acacia. I looked ahead and didn't see any reason for him to be stopped.

"So I know I don't have to say this, but to be sure. You don't know me, I don't know you. Got it?" Eric said, keeping his eyes forward.

"Of course. Yeah, no one knows who I get this from anyway," I said as I jiggled my backpack.

"And we both want to keep it that way. If you're ever in some shit, hearing rumors, or feel some heat, call me, alright? Don't want to get any other people involved."

*Some heat?*

"Yup I agree. I guess if you're in some shit, just call me too?" I joked, laughing to cut the mini-tension forming.

"Will do," Eric said with a smirk.

"And hey Cory, if you ever need anything else besides the greens, let me know. I can get my hands on pretty much anything if you give me enough time."

I raised my arm to start scratching my head, but caught myself, so gracelessly rubbed my chin instead.

"Yeah dude, sounds good, I'll let you know."

"I know a bunch of people in this town, and I had never heard of you. So you must be doing something right. Keep it up, alright?" Eric said as he stuck out his hand for a handshake.

"Will do," I said as I shook his hand firmly.

# EIGHTEEN

I TOLD BO THAT HIPPY MIKE WAS OK WITH BUYING MORE, so he finally got to add his buddy in Sigma Nu to the half-ounce delivery club for $200, and I let Cam deal to his buddy in Phi Sig for a full ounce for $350. I didn't tell Cam or Bo about the little second semester change from a Phish-loving hippy to a Mercedes-driving bachelor. I wanted to give it some time to see how smoothly everything went before figuring out how to bring it up to them. I knew he and Cam would push to get Xanax, Adderall, or blow from Eric. Especially if they knew he told me he could "get his hands on anything."

I wasn't necessarily opposed to doing coke. I knew in my mind I would eventually try it, just didn't really want to sell it. To me, that was a legit drug. Pot was pot. It was in its own category between alcohol and cocaine. I sure as hell wasn't going to do Xanax. Knew a kid in high school who did a shit ton of Xanax bars and then proceeded to steal a bunch of shit from our school and get expelled. I fully recognize the innocence of a bar or half bar before watching Sunday night HBO, but seeing this kid's eyes in high school as he left study tables and broke into a teacher's classroom and yanked out her credit cards from her purse was something I'd never forget. His eyes were soulless. Just a dark pit of nothing. Didn't want to be involved with that.

Without Bo or Cam knowing about Eric, everything stayed roughly the same. Months went by with each passing week seeming easier and easier. I actually liked the drive to Eric's place. The whole ordeal felt more professional, and safer, honestly. The more times I went, the more I thought about how lackadaisical it was to text some hippy off campus I was coming over, walk in his front door to him stoned on his couch watching the Palladia channel, grab a half pound of weed, and drive someone else's car around campus dropping off bags of weed. It was careless. But I guess I was still driving someone else's car and still driving around campus dropping off bags of weed, but whatever, it felt more professional. Felt like Eric had my back, or better yet, like he genuinely cared about me not getting caught. Like he was on my team.

Second semester sophomore year was a shit show. Freshman year, you pledge and get introduced to IU and have aspirations and ideas flowing and everything feels amazing because, for the first time, you aren't living with your parents. But sophomore year, no one cared about their careers or grades because no company would hire a sophomore anyway. It was straight partying, which led right into spring break in early March. My whole pledge class and Cam's pledge class went with a bunch of sororities down to Puerto Vallarta. It was madness. That was the first time Bo and I actually started spending our money. Bottle service, booze cruise, you name it. People knew we made some money dealing grams and with the sportsbook, but no one had a clue to the extent we were dealing, and I didn't want to be throwing around thousands of dollars at the bars and have people asking questions. So everything we did with our friends, Bo and I would pay for half and everyone else had to come up with the other half. I tried to plan most of the events so no one knew exactly how expensive everything was. I told everyone the booze cruise was $50 a person when it was $100. Bottle service was $200 to $500 a bottle, but I said it was buy one get one free.

We had this ridiculously lavish penthouse suite that slept about 10 of us. Bo and I both got bedrooms and everyone else crashed on the couches and floor. Spring break was when Cam and his buddies formally introduced drugs to my pledge class, and it wasn't a soft introduction either. Guys in my pledge class had done blow before, but nothing like this. This was every night. About 20 of us would meet up in our suite, listen to some music, and then some of the guys would go into Bo's room and rip a couple lines before inviting the girls over to pregame. Just a bunch of geeked-out 20-year-olds partying and fucking in Mexico. And then me, paying for half the geeked-out 20-year-olds to party and fuck in Mexico.

After spring break there was only one thing on everyone's mind: Little 500. Little 500 was a yearly bike race on the third Saturday in April. It's a 200-lap race around a quarter-mile track. It was supposed to be like the Indy 500, hence the Little 500 title, but there were about 30 teams, 20 of them frats then about 10 or so GDIs who trained year round for the race. The movie *Breaking Away* was about the most GDI of GDI teams.

In 1997, Lance Armstrong said, "I've attended Super Bowls, World Series and the Monaco Grand Prix, but the coolest event I ever attended was the Little 500." Obama showed up in '08 to the women's race, whatever, it's pretty cool. More importantly, each frat paired up with a sorority like homecoming and partied for a long, long time together. The qualifier for the race was in the end of March, and each house treated it like the biggest tailgate of the year: wakeups at 4:00 to 5:00 a.m., day partying all day at the frat, stumbling over to the bars late afternoon, just reckless. Then the actual Little 5 week was a week straight of parties. The Saturday beforehand a bunch of sororities had semiformals that kicked off the week, and then there was some big show or party every night from Monday to Friday.

The shows were going to be Mac Miller and Wiz Khalifa in ZBT's parking lot on Wednesday, Rick Ross/Nicki Minaj/Lil Wayne at Assembly Hall on Thursday, then Pretty Lights in some field on Friday. School was pretty much optional all week too. Teachers gave out extra credit for showing up to class or bullshit pop-quizzes that consisted of writing your name on a sheet of paper, who you want to win Little 500, and a fun fact about yourself. The sole purpose of the quizzes was to give credit to anyone who showed up to class. Which was normally 25 percent of people.

I went on Monday to show my face, well, and because I needed that extra credit, but I skipped out on Tuesday, Wednesday, and Thursday. On Thursday we had a big sophomore/senior pregame at Bates's place before the Lil Wayne show at Assembly Hall. It was the seniors' last Little 5 and our pledge class was tight with the seniors, so we all fed off each other's energy all week. The scene at the pregame was unlike anything I could describe. There were people standing on every surface their two feet could fit on. Couches, coffee tables, bars, the countertop, stairs, the stove, window ledges, bar stools—it was just layers and layers of people partying. Handles floating around, viking chugging beers, smoking blunts in the house. The age gap from seniors to sophomores went unnoticed at this party, and no one would guess it was a pregame for a Lil Wayne show. That is, apart from upstairs in Bates's room. That was the powder room. A rotating group of three to five people would walk in, do some blow, and walk out. Sophomores, seniors, guys, girls, it was mayhem. Every time someone walked down the stairs, you knew they had done a couple lines, but no one was judging because almost everyone was walking down the stairs eventually. The speakers at Bates were also excessively loud, so everyone blended in, and no one seemed to notice anything.

I felt like the pussy at the party because I was only having beers, but I was so pumped up for Lil Wayne that I didn't need any uppers to get me going. I did have two Cam-rolled blunts in my back pocket for the show, which I was positive the powder-room customers were going to love later on.

The concert was unreal. We missed Travis Barker open up the show, but Ross and Wayne killed it. Nicki was OK. Going from Rick Ross to Nicki Minaj was tough for the stoned/geeked/drunk crowd. Afterward we carried the momentum and had a party in the basement of the house.

Friday morning I woke on our couch to Cutty and Garcia playing *NBA 2K*.

"Morning, you want next?" Cutty said.

"What time is it?" I asked, sitting up.

"Noonish."

"Why are you in here?"

"Need some herb, 10-sack."

"Just go get it yourself."

"There was none in the sleeper."

"Where's Bo?" I said, rubbing my eyes.

"Sleeping."

"In our sleeper?"

"I don't know, I didn't check."

"What?"

"What are you whating bro?" Cutty said, focusing on the game.

"How do you know there was no pot in the sleeper if you didn't check the sleeper?"

"Because Bo was sleeping, so I didn't ask."

Cutty was too dumb to handle. I slowly got up and walked over to our sleeper and grabbed a gram.

"Here ya' go. Pack up the bowl and then take the rest. Your boy needs some right now," I said as I handed Cutty the gram.

"Yeah, last night was crazy. You going to Pretty Lights tonight?"

"Ugh fuck. Yeah, I have a ticket, but I feel like dick."

"Oh suck it up. We're rolling tonight," Garcia responded.

*Huh?*

"You talk to Wolf?" Cutty added.

"About what?" I said, still confused about Garcia's statement.

"He bought a shit ton of molly for Pretty Lights and now wants to find enough people to do it with him."

"Bought a shit ton of molly? The fuck? From who?"

"You know that Mo guy in APES?" Garcia replied.

"Yeah, big Mo."

"From him. He's got a buddy in town from Wisconsin who brought like a boatload. So Wolf got a couple grams from him."

I didn't know measurements or prices of anything but weed. Didn't know if a couple grams was "a shit ton" of molly or enough for one or two people. I actually thought molly came in pills, so was pretty confused altogether.

The rise of ecstasy and molly came with the rise of EDM. I remember seeing people taking ecstasy in the movie *Bad Boys 2* and like *XXX* with Vin Diesel, and even that was only grimy Russians. In high school I knew people who smoked, only knew of a few people who did blow, and no one did ecstasy or molly. In college it progressed to everyone smoked, I knew people who did blow, and only knew of people who did molly. It was almost like molly wasn't mainstream yet, but clearly, there was an emphasis on the word *yet*. It was like shrooms; everyone would talk and say they would do it eventually, but no one ever actively pursued it.

"No, I'm not going to roll. You guys are?"

"Yeah, we both are," Garcia said.

"Have you ever?" I replied curiously.

"Nope. Pumped though," Cutty answered.

I grabbed a pair of shorts from the ground and walked downstairs to get food. Everyone at the house was beat up and it was only Friday morning. Saturday was the actual Little 5 day, but no one ever thought about pacing themselves during Little 5 week. It was one speed, and you carried that speed and rode the peer pressure from Sunday to Saturday. Just bigger and bigger parties every day until you couldn't do it anymore.

"You hear Mo sold molly to Wolf?" I said to Bo as he joined me at one of the kitchen tables.

"Yeah, talked to him last night."

"Talked to who?"

"Well, I talked to Cam who talked to Mo."

"And?"

"Told Cam I didn't want to sell any, so then Wolf went up to Cam and asked if he could buy some. You going to roll?" Bo said as he stacked his plate with what must have been seven eggs' worth of scrambled eggs.

"No, you?"

"Hell fucking yeah. Just didn't want to be in charge of all of it. Why aren't you?"

"Haven't thought about it, really, but shit's not for me. I think I would tweak. I don't trust my brain enough to roll."

"Real philosophical of you. Jesus, it's ecstasy, not acid. It's not like it makes you trip."

"Eh, I'm alright. I'll live."

We finished up the leftover scrambled eggs that had been sitting out for hours. Surprisingly the shitty eggs made me feel better, but not enough to start my day. I went into my sleeper and passed out for another hour or so. When I woke up I could hear music blasting down the hall. People were already pregaming for the show. The show was relatively early, around six or seven or so, but still, it was only two o'clock.

I showered and threw on some clothes and walked to Wolf's room. Most of my pledge class was already in there, and a handful of Alpha Phi girls were as well. Those girls loved drugs, so I wasn't surprised they were hanging around before the show.

I went to the bar and grabbed a Keystone Light from the case. The outfits everyone was wearing were hilarious. Tank tops, shorts, headbands, lot of neon, few of the guys had CamelBaks—people were prepping for a full-on rave. Honestly, I wasn't any better. It was about 100 degrees outside so I was rocking one of those dark-grey tank tops that was more like a basketball jersey, jorts, and white midcalf socks with my ever-so-fancy black PF Flyers. Embarrassingly, I threw the outfit on before I saw everyone was preparing for an ecstasy-driven-20-hour-Russian-nightclub rave.

Not everyone was drinking a lot. About 10 to 15 of the people there were just sipping on beers. Since most of the people were rolling, they didn't want to get drunk as well.

"You rolling tonight?" Kyle said as he handed me a shot of Jameson.

"No, are you?" I said as I grabbed the glass.

"Nope. Looks like you and I will be babysitting these kids tonight," Kyle said as we clinked cups and took the shot.

We stayed and drank for a little longer before we all started leaving for the show. Pledge rides were on their game. Granted, it was 5:30 p.m., so I really hoped the pledges weren't busy, but there must have been 10 cars waiting in the parking lot. I jumped in a car with Kyle, Joe, Cutty, and Garcia.

When we got to the show, we all planned on meeting at the front left of the stage. Security was volunteer college students, so Kyle and I had brought in a bottle of Jameson and a couple Keystone Lights in a backpack. We were all set. Little 5 was all about your frat partying with your sorority pair and your pair only. Both frats and sororities tried sticking to that, so in the future, when houses picked who they wanted to pair with, a house wouldn't get the stigma of being the house that bailed on their pair to go to other parties. But at concerts, it was way different. Everything was a free-for-all. Mostly everyone followed the directions as our crew met up with Bo, Barr, Ray, Cam and some of his friends, and then a random assortment of girls.

The place really started filling in right before the show started. I looked over at Joe and Wolf, and both were sweating profusely. It was hot outside, but the sun was going down, so it wasn't that hot. The show started and everyone went crazy. The bass was so intense it felt like a subwoofer was inside of you. Pretty Lights was one of the artists that you knew like two or three songs, but then the rest all sounded the same. He opened with one of the songs I knew, but I also understood that the majority of the show was going to end up being purely some sort of bass/synth remix of other pop songs.

About five minutes into the show, Wolf belligerently walked past me and started to walk through the crowd and toward the fence on the far left side. I looked back to see if I could see where he went, but he was gone. As I turned around, Cutty grabbed my arm and pulled me toward him.

"Yo bro, I don't feel good at all."

His pupils were the size of his entire eyes. I didn't know what his original eye color was, but I was positive it wasn't full pupil.

"Here, have some water."

I grabbed a water bottle from one of the Alpha Phi girls to my right and handed it to Cutty. As I grabbed the bottle I noticed Cam's buddy to my right staring at his hands, squeezing them as hard as he could.

"Dude, I think everyone rolling is freaking out," Kyle leaned in and yelled into my ear over the music.

"You noticing this too?" I yelled back.

"Yeah, I think Wolf and Bo already left."

"Jesus. Yo check out Cam's buddy," I said, leaning out of the way so Kyle could see the guy still squeezing his hands together.

"I mean, I've never done molly, but didn't think it made you freak out," Kyle said as we stared at Cam's buddy playing with his hands.

I didn't know what was going on, but it completely killed the mood of the show. It was clear who had taken molly and who hadn't. The drunk people were jumping up and down as Pretty Lights did a Notorious B.I.G. remix, and the rolling people were rocking back and forth like zombies nodding to the beat. I was shocked how many people were rolling, especially my friends. I mean it was Cutty, Joe, Garcia, Wolf, KT, Barr, Russ, Cam, and practically all of Acacia, a bunch of the Alpha Phis, Tri Delts, Pi Phis, some Pi Kapps kids behind us, it was outrageous. *Clearly Wolf did have a "shit ton of molly."*

I noticed Cutty and Garcia were no longer there. I made eye contact with Kyle, and we both shrugged. I had never really been around people who were too fucked up on drugs, so it was the only thing I could think about.

I kept looking around making sure no one was passed out or throwing up or whatever you do when you tweak on drugs. It seemed like our section was the only section of the crowd not having the time of their lives. After about 25 minutes of sulking in the tweaking section, Kyle and I eventually realized that while everyone was abnormally high, they could still function and take care of themselves, so we just left everyone and walked up about 30 feet closer to enjoy the show. Periodically I would turn around, but after another 20 to 25 minutes, most of the people in that section of the crowd had left. Kyle and I were riding solo with our bag of booze.

The show was pretty wild. He played for more than two hours, mixing in a lot of cool rap songs I loved. After the last song, Kyle called the pledge-class president, and we walked about a half mile before our pledge ride showed up. When we got to the house, there wasn't much of a party going on at all. Most of the freshmen and sophomores had gone to the concert, and the juniors and seniors were already at the bars or at a live-out. Kyle and I walked upstairs and saw my room was shut and locked. We rarely ever locked it, but the door was never really locked anyway. All you needed to do was throw your shoulder against it and it would open. I opened the door and walked into a cloud of smoke, and at the same time, Bo, Wolf, Garcia, Cutty, Barr, Barr's friend from Kansas, and Joe slowly turned their heads to look at me. The TV was off, no music playing, just seven dudes sitting on the couch smoking pot, simultaneously turning their heads to look at me. I made eye contact with Bo, but it was like he couldn't see me. It was the eeriest room I had ever walked into.

"Jesus Christ," Kyle said as he walked in behind me.

We stood there for about two seconds when we realized no one was going to say anything.

"Big Gulps, huh? Well, see ya' later," Kyle joked as we both walked out of the room laughing.

"My lord they look like robots," I said as we walked into Kyle's room.

"Those eyes. Yesh. So what, the party tonight is canceled?"

"Yeah, Jess texted me saying a bunch of their friends are tweaking too."

"There is no way everyone took molly."

"No, I saw Wolf dish it out earlier."

11:16 p.m.: Yo CC you need to talk to your boy man. This shit can't happen again!

*11:16 p.m.: What do you mean?*

"No, I mean there is no way what they thought was molly was actually molly. I've been with my bro and Bates and Duff and them when they have rolled. Did it before Quals couple weeks ago. I'm positive the shit tonight was laced."

"Damn, didn't even think about that, must have been big Mo's buddy who brought it all down."

"I saw one of the APES kids when we were walking out, that tall dude I was talking to. He seemed fine, that's what's strange," Kyle said as he handed me a beer.

11:18 p.m.: Talk to your boy about getting more shit man. I ain't takin shit like this again, some of my boys here be tripping out.

*11:18 p.m.: Yeah, same over here, we aren't having a party anymore.*

"Sketchy APES kids and their drugs. Here check this out, Cam just texted me saying Acacia is tweaking too. You must be right," I said, handing Kyle my phone.

"See man, I'm telling you. That's a crack den in your room. Those aren't people rolling on molly."

11:19 p.m.: Damn for real? Well we still got a party down in the basement. Come down.

We finished our beers and decided against hanging out with more crack-tweakers at Acacia and so went to go meet up with the seniors at the bars. As we walked there, I couldn't help but think how crazy it was that Cam was even thinking about getting more molly while he was tweaking on it. Like when people are hungover, the last thing on their minds was getting more alcohol. I couldn't imagine being uncontrollably high off some drug, and thinking about buying more of it. Honestly, it showed how much of a desire there was for it. Granted it was Acacia, but still, Cam could differentiate his current state to that of the real side effects of molly, and could chalk tonight up as an outlier that he wanted fixed.

We got to Kilroy's and found the seniors in the corner out on the patio. I grabbed a Long Island from the bar and walked over to them. As I stood there, all I could think about was Cam's text. *Talk to your boy about getting more, this can't happen again.* Thinking about drugs the way Cam did was bizarre to me. Not as an addiction or a disease or anything like that—my brain was too small to wrap my mind around that concept. But no, I'm talking about thinking of party drugs as a normal part of life. Like bud, booze, cigs, or dip. Just something people did to be more social with others.

I saw Hahn walk in but didn't think twice about saying hello. I was in my own head thinking about Cam's text.

*But is Cam's thinking bizarre? The demand for drugs will always be a thing as long as partying is still a thing, and with the rise of EDM, the demand for party drugs is only going to be greater. Eventually, molly will become a household thing. In a span of two years, EDM has become pop music. Kiss FM is already playing Calvin Harris and Avicii on the radio. There is a category of the Grammys for best dance song and album. And not one of those, oh-and-by-the-way-we-gave-out-30-awards-before-the-show-started awards; it was an actual-presenter-presents-the-award-on-live-TV award. It was obvious how many people were rolling during the show, and honestly, the show was only Pretty Lights. It wasn't Tiesto, or Avicii, or Swedish House Mafia, or even Steve Aoki or Afrojack. It was Pretty Lights. A B-list DJ in a college town, yet still, Kyle and I must have seen 40 people we were near who were rolling. The trend toward party drugs is growing whether I'm going to sell them or not. Even Kyle said the seniors rolled before a day party a couple weeks ago. Not a concert, not an event—a day party in March in Indiana! The demand for harder drugs is getting too strong to overlook.*

I partied at the bar the rest of the night, but my mind had already been made up. *Maybe Cam is right, maybe I should talk to Eric.*

# NINETEEN

**"SHIT WAS LACED WITH SPEED, DUDE."**

"I heard the molly was cut with oxy and heroin."

"We all took ecstasy but there was crack and acid in there. I was hallucinating."

"It was meth."

Anyone you talked to who tweaked had a different combination of drugs they were positive it was laced with. Everyone was walking around saying nonsense. It was not like Mo's buddy from Wisconsin cut it himself. It was just bad drugs. Period. I don't even think a doctor could tell. Like, if you went to the hospital, the doctor could see you have a bunch of amphetamines or some other medical term in your blood. Not like the doctor could be like, "Well, son, you took a powder that was 20 percent molly, 40 percent crack, and 40 percent meth." That would be like going in for alcohol poisoning and the doctor saying, "Yup, she had five margaritas and seven Rumple Minze shots in a two-hour span." I could be 1,000 percent wrong, but regardless, no one went to the hospital, so no one knew what those drugs were.

As it turned out, Mo's buddy got two different batches from two different guys up in Madison, Wisconsin. He and his friends took the first batch and the second was sold to Cam and Wolf. That's why Mo and them weren't tweaking, but Acacia and ATO were.

After the dust of the weekend settled, ATO had our elections for who was going to be president and shit like that. We were supposed to have them months prior, but I think everyone honestly just forgot. I was voted to be the risk manager, ironically. Instantly I was going to say hell no, but after hearing the junior who previously held the role say it was something bullshit that looked nice on your résumé, I said I would do it. One of the reasons I also wanted to do it was because the risk manager got to have an annual meeting with the dean and go to monthly meetings with every fraternity. Sounded like a pain in the ass at first, but since I was dealing to a lot of the fraternities, it sounded like it would be beneficial for me to show my face to the dean and be in the know with issues around the school. I was always curious what was going on in other houses and with the Greek system anyway, so getting to talk to the dean and ask him face-to-face questions, to me, would be somewhat cool.

On Tuesday I finally talked with Bo and Cam about Eric. I told them the switch happened a couple weeks ago, even though it was coming up on four months, but neither of them really cared. Everything had stayed the same in those four months, or I guess those couple weeks in Cam's and Bo's eyes, so nothing for them to really worry about.

Cam was pushing for me to get harder drugs from Eric, especially because no one trusted Mo anymore, so everyone had to look elsewhere. Bo and a few others were still a little shaken up about the Pretty Lights incident, but I knew they would get over it soon. Finals were next week, so the dull time would be enough for everyone to compose themselves before summer session. Finals week was always a big smoking week.

On Tuesday I told Eric I was going to stop by and pick up. I was planning on asking him about prices and information about coke and molly, but didn't really know how much to ask for or what to expect.

I drove to his house and he let me in through the garage door. He seemed to be in a hurry, so he already had the brick sitting out on the kitchen counter. It looked real odd walking into a suburban home and seeing a brick of weed on the counter.

"So Cory we all good?"

"Yeah, all good. Hey I know you said you could get your hands on some things, that still true?"

Eric stopped what he was doing and started walking toward me.

"Yeah, pretty much, what are you thinking?"

"Well, since I'm staying the summer, wanted to see if I could get some coke and maybe some molly if you had any."

"Anyone ask you to get this?"

"What? What do you mean?"

"I mean is this for you or for someone else?"

"Oh. Little of both. I want it for dealing to some friends and for myself. During Little 5, a bunch of my buddies took bad stuff and kinda freaked out a little bit."

"Wait, what do you mean bad stuff?"

Eric's demeanor was so straightforward. I couldn't tell if I liked it or not, but I guess he was very diligent about this whole dealing thing, so I couldn't complain.

"Bad molly. Or at least, that's what they thought."

"Who did they get it from?"

*Why do you care so much?*

"Some kid's buddy visiting from Wisconsin brought it down."

"Ooo OK. Yeah, I got some of both, how much you want?"

"Not sure, honestly. Finals are next week, so really wouldn't need it till the following week."

"Sounds good. I'll make sure I have a couple grams, maybe an ounce or so of each. Let me know exactly how much next week, alright? Hey I got to run, sorry, we cool?"

"Yeah, sounds good. Thanks, I'll text you next week."

*Well, that was easy.*

I got back to my room and sorted out all the bud. After Little 5 we were bone dry, so it was good to have some again. Finals went by quickly. A group of us had a routine each semester where we would learn four months of material in five classes in four days. It consisted of taking a bunch of Adderall, studying for four hours straight, then smoking cigarettes outside the computer lab and having Adderall arguments about the dumbest shit, taking a deep breath, and then going back to studying for another four hours straight. None of us smoked cigarettes, but somehow that became our routine once or twice a semester. We weren't in full business-school mode yet, and were still knocking out gen-ed classes, so it was read-the-textbook-on-Adderall studying instead of the have-to-understand-the concept-and-apply-the-material studying. Which helped.

People started to move out on Wednesday, and I was getting texts from everyone asking for a little more weed to bring home for the summer. Random people too, like Duffy and couple Acacia kids. I hated everyone texting me directly for gram-level stuff, but really couldn't complain with the money we were making. With Acacia, Pi Kapps, Delts, and Kappa Sig upping to a full ounce a week, and the addition of Cam's buddy in Phi Sig and Bo's in Sigma Nu, we were selling a little less than 11 ounces a week for about $4,300, and then at least two of the frats were asking for a full ounce a week or every other week, so it was more like 12.5 ounces a week. So closer to 350 grams for around $4,800, and I was buying a pound from Eric, so 448 grams, for only $2,000. So after the week and a half it took to go through the full pound, it came out to a little over four grand profit to split between Bo and me.

When summer session started, I moved into a live-out on Seventh Street about a block or two from the main bars. Since mostly everyone had been living in fraternity houses, it was kind of a free-for-all for summer live-outs, so Bo and I went with Cam and Kyle. The place was actually a six-bedroom that a couple of the Acacia kids had lived in senior year, but when they graduated, we were the only ones who would sublease for the summer, so we got the whole place.

Everything Sheff and Mike said about summer session was accurate. It was foolish. I had one class every Monday and Wednesday from 1:00 to 2:30 p.m. That was it, and even that started week two. The weather was 85 and sunny every day, so we constantly day partied. *If Bennett's mom was upset about welcome week, wait till she finds out about summer school.* In the beginning of summer session, some of my friends were buying coke from a couple GDIs living in Smallwood, but would bitch about it constantly. On the first Tuesday of summer session, I went to Eric's to pick up the harder drugs. Cam had nailed it. It really was the perfect time to start selling it.

I didn't know much about coke, so I let Cam pretty much run that part. It almost felt like it was turning into a company where everyone specialized in one area. Bo had the sportsbook and helped out with the distribution,

Cam ran the coke division, and I was the CEO who watched over everything and dealt with supply and our business relationships. I didn't hand over the coke to Cam like I did Bo and the book. I still wanted to know what was going on, because at the end of the day, I was positive Cam wasn't as good or careful as I was about all this shit. From talking to Cam and hearing my friends talk about it, it seemed like a half gram was enough for one person for a good night out and a gram was for one guy to share key bumps with others and have a great night out. I had picked up an ounce from Eric for $1,200, but Cam said an 8-ball, or an eighth, would sell for like $200 and a gram for $60 to $80 depending on quality. Molly was going to be completely different. It was going to be sporadic, whereas weed I would sell consistently and coke would be relatively consistent. I knew I was going to sell no molly one week, then sell a shit ton in one day, i.e., Pretty Lights. Knowing that, Eric floated me a couple grams of molly but asked for a couple days' notice if I wanted to buy more in bulk.

The molly sat in my safe for the first week, while the coke was being sold faster than I expected. I first thought it had to be because fraternity guys felt better buying from other fraternity guys because, for some reason, they thought it was safer. But when I talked to Cam, he told me it was because of the quality. He admitted he wasn't an expert in coke tasting, but when he stuck his finger in the bag and tasted it, his entire mouth went numb. Tongue, gums, everything. And it wasn't just Cam saying that either. Mo told me at Kilroy's one night that he wanted to buy in bulk because his friends wanted Eric's coke instead of the Smallwood GDI kid's.

During summer session, there were no fraternity pairs. Whoever was in town partied together. ATO, Acacia, Pi Kapps, and APES had pretty much become one fraternity of about 60 guys. Sororities were still weird and kept to themselves, but at every party there was Tri Delt, Alpha Phi, Pi Phi, Zeta, Kappa, and AchiO.

One Saturday we rented out a bunch of double-decker pontoon boats from 1:00 to 6:00 p.m. on Lake Monroe. We tied them together and created a line of about 10 boats. Each boat legally held 30 people and had slides on the back and a bar on the first level. We had cases of beer, vodka, whisky, and a couple of TapCo speakers on every other boat blasting music. Everyone seemed to congregate on a couple boats, so at one point there must have been close to 100 people on one boat. It was full-fledged pandemonium with 300 people partying out on a couple of boats.

After boats, everyone in our summer fraternity of ATO, Acacia, Pi Kapps, and APES went to our house to rally before going to the bar Sports. And what do IU sophomores do when they need to rally? Blow. It was unreal. Our house turned into a coke den for about an hour. No one changed clothes, everyone still had on their boat gear. Everyone packed into Bo's room to do a couple lines off the mirror that he had laid on his bed.

"Cory, you in?" Wolf yelled out over Avicii's "Levels," which was on for what felt like the 200th time.

"Wait, you've never done it, right?" Kyle said before I could respond.

"No, only blown Adderall a couple of times," I said.

"Want to try?"

"Um, not sure honestly. Might have a taste."

I had seen a bunch of my friends do a numby before. Essentially it was licking your finger and putting it in the leftover coke, then rubbing your gums and letting the coke absorb that way instead of snorting it. It was the drug equivalent of taking one shot of alcohol, whereas blowing lines was a full night's worth of drinking.

Wolf had turned toward the bed and ignored my not answering. Kyle walked over to me so only he and I could hear our conversation.

"So my brother's boy from home told me this before I did blow the first time, and I totally agree with it. So, do you have an addictive personality?"

"Are you asking me?" I responded.

"Yeah, sorry. This is what he said to me, but I'll say it to you. Do you?"

"Have an addictive personality? No, not all at."

"Then I would suggest you do blow at least one time in your life. It's an incredible time, you will have an absolute blast, and then, if you don't have an addictive personality, you will have the self-control to just not do it again."

I hesitated for a second. I was planning on doing coke once in my life at some point anyway, honestly for sheer curiosity, like getting a tattoo. I looked around the room as the house music blasted from the TapCo outside

Bo's room. *I'm at a pregame for a night out in a controlled environment with all of my friends, and no one really cares if I do it or not. The external factors are perfect for doing blow for the first time, and internally, I'm pretty tired from being in the sun all day, so would enjoy a little kick in the ass.*

"Fuck it, I'm in," I said as Kyle handed me a rolled-up $20 bill.

"Hey hey!" Cam yelled out as I walked across the room to the mirror.

Everyone started clapping really loudly and then kept clapping in unison and starting hooting and hollering jokingly like it was fourth down of a close game. I leaned over the mirror and put the bill in my right nostril and snorted the line. My initial reaction was that the feeling in my nose wasn't as sharp as the Adderall—it was actually a lot smoother, but I could taste it more in the back of my throat. It was bitter and almost sour, but after 15 seconds, my nose and throat started to feel numb. The numbness made it feel like I had a runny nose and almost a sinus infection, like that postnasal drip feeling in the back of my throat. I grabbed a beer and had a couple sips, but unlike with the postnasal drip, drinking didn't help it go away. The numbness was still there. I didn't want to completely black out like I had the last time I snorted Adderall, so I wanted to make a conscious effort to not drink a lot and not wake up in Zeta's cold dorm.

After about another 30 to 45 minutes we walked to the bar. Everyone who went on boats had the same idea as we did; no one changed outfits. Girls wearing bikinis, only some of them with cover-ups on, guys in bathing suits and T-shirts. It was only about eight o'clock, so we took over the bar. It looked like a beach-themed bar crawl.

I was noticing the effects of the blow right away. It was identical to snorting Adderall, but was more a smooth focus as opposed to a jittery one. My brain just felt awake and alert, but not in an intolerable concentrating way, more or less just energetic. However, the numbness feeling was lasting a lot longer than I wanted. My tongue, roof of my mouth, back of my throat, it was like I had taken Novocain shots.

Sports had three main rooms and then an upstairs. The upstairs was more a dance club area with bottle service and whatnot, with the downstairs area being your normal sports bar. Hence the name, Sports. The middle had a massive circle bar in the center. Cam had drunkenly ordered 50 shots of Jameson, so the bartenders basically started handing them out to anyone in a bathing suit. We pretty much had the bar to ourselves for the first two hours. I was talking to Cutty and Garcia about the NBA finals when I heard someone behind me saying my name. I turned around and was stunned when I saw Bennett.

"Hey Cory, how's it going?"

"Bennett, what's up dude? I'm good, how you been?" I said as we gave each other the slap-and-hold handshake.

Bennett was wearing a black-and-white, short-sleeved checkered button-down with skinny jeans. He had about three bracelets and a watch on his left wrist and a rubber band around his right. Since the last time I'd seen him about a year ago, he had transformed to a full-blown skinny hipster who apparently drank and went to bars. *The fuck happened?*

"Good man, been good. You go on boats today?" Bennett said, looking down at my sandals.

"Yeah, it's been a long day."

"Yeah, honestly was confused when I walked in seeing all you guys. Hey Cory, this is my roommate, Dave. Dave, this was my freshman-year roommate, Cory."

I felt almost like a proud father as I shook Dave's hand. He was your standard college student. Red polo with khaki shorts, holding an Amstel Light, and a tattoo around both biceps that you could see a half inch of underneath the polo. *Bennett has a friend with a tattoo who drinks beer!*

"Where you living right now?"

"In Smallwood. Living there next year, but they let us move in this summer."

"Wow look at you," I said as I slapped his shoulder.

"Yeah, I know. You were right about drinking, I was going to do it eventually."

"Everyone always does," I stated as we both laughed.

"Want to get a drink?"

"Yes I do. Shots on me," I offered as we walked to the bar.

I bought a couple shots of Jameson for the three of us. I stayed at the bar talking with Bennett for a while. He was telling me about how his mom had wanted him to get a job while at school and how she went psycho when he told her he was going to South Padre for spring break. I had always thought that his helicopter mom was going to eventually drive him insane, or at least drive him away, but it was good to hear confidence in his voice. He had a personality now. He'd felt almost robotic when I lived with him. Like his actions were scripted all the time. Now he seemed natural.

We eventually separated from each other in that drinking-in-a-bar kind of way where you're talking to someone and then there is a break in conversation and next thing you know, the other person is gone. As the night went on, people slowly started to filter upstairs. I went upstairs with Kyle and Cutty and joined Cam and Mo at their table. The bottle service on the second floor of Sports wasn't so much a "service" but more just an area where you could put your drinks down. I don't even know if there were waitresses or servers. If you bought a bottle, I think someone would just come over and hand it to you. That was about it. Oh, and if you wanted a drink, you had to go up to the bar and order one yourself.

I walked up to Mo pointing at me and doing his little fat-man jig. I laughed at his 375-pound frame dancing, but then noticed this group of girls I had never seen before at the table next to him. I took a step up and saw Kyle and Wolf trying to talk to the girls, but most of them were way out of their league. There was this one girl, though, who stood out the most. She was this absolutely stunning blonde chick with these bluish-green eyes that glowed in the dark-lit room. *Who the fuck are these chicks?* I wasn't some big player or anything or like the coolest guy at the school, but I did pride myself on having a decent memory when it came to facial recognition. I was record-setting bad with names, but remembered faces. I mean, IU was a massive university, but when it came to the bar scene, it was a pretty tight-knit group. So it was shocking to see a group of such beautiful girls that I had never seen before. That feeling must have been shared by every male at the bar, because throughout the night, dozens of guys went up to them and started talking or trying to dance with them. But for some reason, no one would ever talk to the eye-poppingly gorgeous blonde chick for that long. *Who is this perfect woman?*

I didn't know if it was the coke in me or what, but I couldn't stop thinking about the table of girls. It was so weird that these girls, who clearly weren't in a sorority and looked roughly our age, were at one of the three bars we went to all the time, but no one knew who they were.

"Hey Cory, right?" Bennett's roommate yelled into my ear over the loud music playing in the background.

"Yeah, what's up?"

"You're in ATO, right?" he yelled.

"Yeah, are you in a house?"

"No. GDI unfortunately."

Dave paused and took another sip out of what looked like a Long Island. He was acting very paranoid and strange, but I also didn't know the kid, so could just be who he was.

"Hey so, would you or anyone at ATO you know of have any blow I could buy off?"

*Excuse me?*

"Uhh, I'm not sure really, I can ask."

"Oh, alright, cool. Yeah, Bennett left, so I don't have any more."

*Why would Bennett leaving matter? Does Bennett have this kid's blow?*

"Oh, do you want some right now?"

"Yeah, sorry, I meant like to buy tonight. Would love to do a few bumps . . ."

*Jesus! Kid's a fiend.*

" . . . Also for some like, later. It's hard to find some good stuff in the summer, you know?"

"Yeah, I don't think any of my friends have any tonight."

"Damn, alright man, well can I get your number and you can let me know if you have any?"

Dave handed me his phone before I could even say no. I knew Bennett had my number and so Dave could get it anyway if he really wanted to, so I grabbed the phone and typed my number in. I was sort of in shock finding out Bennett not only drank, but might possibly have had his roommate's cocaine. More shocking though was the fact that Dave would ask me of all people for more cocaine. Granted, I did have more cocaine, a lot, actually, but still, he didn't know that. At least I didn't think he knew that.

*"It's been hard to find some good stuff"? You're living in Smallwood, home of the coke dealers my friends were buying from as recently as last week. Unless he means good stuff like better quality.* I did coke for the first time, and it did seem like pretty good stuff. My energy was high, I was outgoing, having a good time. I could now vouch that Eric did have good stuff, but also had nothing to compare it to. Clearly Dave was a big coke guy if he was asking a dude he met a couple hours ago for a few bumps. To me, when it came to weed, unless it was dog shit, all weed was relatively the same. With coke, it seemed like the quality really made a difference. Obviously same with molly. *I must be sitting on a gold mine. I wonder if he heard there was better coke at IU now.*

It must have been just past midnight. I was coming down from the high and getting exponentially tired by the minute, so decided to Irish good-bye and walk the couple blocks home. On the way home, I walked by the apartment building Garcia and Cutty had moved into and heard loud music. I decided to keep walking and ignore the after party that must have been going on at Cutty's. I kept walking and couldn't help but notice so many different apartment buildings I had never really seen before. Above Subway, the Omegas apartments—it was never ending the entire walk home. *Who the fuck lives in these?* I started thinking about all the apartment complexes at school. There must have been 10 to 15 major complexes that combined held thousands of students, not to mention the hundreds of live-out houses and smaller condo-type places. *IU is a fucking massive school, and I am sitting on a gold mine of drugs. A gold mine only shared with 15 or so fraternities. If the delivery system works with frats, why wouldn't it work for apartment complexes too?*

When I started selling to ATO, I did it because of the Hippy Mike relationship and the fact that ATO was built around secrecy. I had never even heard of Hippy Mike, and the fact he had been selling to ATO for years assured me that the secret partnership was working. Then I expanded to other houses because the Greek system had a culture of concealment and keeping things internally. Even with that confidentiality embedded within the Greek system, I sold only to one person and let that one person sell to his house, which, in turn, created separation between the drugs and me. I understood I would be naïve to think only one person in each house knew I was selling to them, but it didn't matter, because what made it all work was distributing the risk of getting caught to other people. Purposely having Bo and Cam sell to some houses, always selling to only one person, never talking about how much I bought or sold to anyone, never selling more than an ounce to a house, and letting Bo run the book and Cam handle the hard drugs. It wasn't being a middleman anymore—it had turned into a legitimate business, and deep down, I'd be lying if I said I didn't love running it. I was good at it. Really, really good actually. There aren't words in the English language to describe the feeling of getting thousands and thousands of dollars handed to you without doing any real work.

When I got home I crashed onto my bed. My body had shut down, but my mind was still going. I just lay in bed thinking. *I know I can sell to GDIs too, especially in the summer when everyone hangs out together. Adding apartment complexes could honestly double the money I'm making. Smallwood, the Villas, it's the perfect time; I know I can do it. Hell, I want to do it. It's just too easy.*

# TWENTY

SUMMER MADE EVERYONE COME TOGETHER. All fraternities, sororities, GDIs, it was just whoever was in town went to the bars every night. It was easier to build relationships in the summer, before tens of thousands of students returned in the fall. I still wanted Cam to do the coke selling so I put him in touch with Bennett's roommate Dave, which felt insanely odd, and then I sold directly to Mo. Mo knew a bunch of GDIs and was already selling a bunch to them. It must have been because APES wasn't like an actual fraternity. They had been kicked off campus years ago but were still rushing and acting like a fraternity. When it came time to officially pair for Little 500 or homecoming, they had to find another alternative. Enter Mo's GDI connections. That and selling cocaine. People forgave Mo for the Pretty Lights thing. Everyone understood it wasn't his fault, and he was a big, jolly kid, so it was hard to stay pissed at the guy.

With Cam selling to Dave and a random assortment of frat guys, and Mo selling to a bunch of GDIs, I felt like I was turning back into the middleman, but this time I was higher up the food chain. Cam and Mo took my place, and I took Hippy Mike's place. I knew letting Cam and Mo sell to others directly was cutting into the money I was going to make, but honestly, it wasn't by much. I wasn't letting Cam and Mo buy large quantities. The numbers for coke came out to $80 a gram when buying only a gram, $57 a gram for an 8-ball, $54 a gram when buying a half O, $43 a gram for an O, $32 a gram for a 62, and $30 a gram for a Big 8. A *62* was 62 grams, and *Big 8* was slang for a big 8-ball or an eighth of a kilo. For some reason, coke weights were different than pot because they stayed in kilograms instead of converting to pounds. Nevertheless, Cam and Mo were buying in half-ounce quantities. They were still selling grams or 8-balls for $80 or $64 a gram when it only cost them $54, so I didn't feel bad that I was still making $11 per gram sold on those half ounces. It was a win-win for everyone. The money I lost not selling at the gram level was not enough to force me to want to stop by Smallwood to drop off bags of cocaine to GDIs.

The rest of summer session was the same as it began. Perfect weather, day parties, boats, and a lot of testosterone-filled-coke-den rallying before going out at night. It wasn't real life. I don't think I could have told you a single news story that was going on anywhere in the world apart from the NBA going into a lockout. The class I was in was pretty hard, but I never went to it, which probably didn't help. I missed a couple quizzes to start, which made it a tough uphill battle to get to a B- in the class.

School was starting back up August 22, but I was moving in the 18th. Since Mikey had graduated and didn't need it anymore, my aunt let me take her car down to school, which I was pumped about. Bo's car had pretty much become my car, but it was still nice to have my own. At one point during the summer I'd been thinking about buying one, but there was no need. It would have looked sketchy to buy a new car anyway.

I was still living with Bo, but we were moving directly up one floor. Same room, same layout, but now on the third floor. That way, we could keep all our money and drugs in our brand new three foot safe. We were each making about $2K a week for 15 weeks second semester, plus the $14K we made first semester; we split $8K in bud money in the summer and another $3K from bookieing. Then, adding in about $11K I made from selling coke and molly in the summer, I had saved up close to $61,000 already. After moving in, I immediately started getting blown up by the different fraternities for their deliveries. Mo was the only one of them asking for coke and molly. He must have texted me six times in a row. Bo and I had officially moved in and were sitting on the couch when I finally started to respond to the texts.

1:19 p.m.: Yo I'm setting up a concert first couple weeks of school. It'll be in a field like 10 min off campus. Going to need a truckload of molly. Cool?

*3:32 p.m.: What concert?*

3:33 p.m.: Don't tell anyone yet, but Deadmau5 is confirmed for the 26th and I think Porter Robinson will open.

*Well, damn. Wait, how much is a truckload?*

The molly that sat in the safe was in powder form. Eric gave me one bag of a couple grams, but if I was getting a truckload of molly for Mo, then I didn't want to have a shit ton of powder that I had to separate into little baggies. I didn't know how Cam weighed out the blow— all I did was hand him a big bag and he paid me—but I didn't want to have to separate the various weights for everyone. I also didn't want to just give Mo all the molly and let him make all the money.

This was a little confusing, but Eric told me the guy he got the MDMA from didn't do large doses. Because of that, Eric had to sell me half-ounce quantities to make it worth it for him. So if I bought three ounces, I would really be buying six half-ounce bags. So exactly like what I was doing for Cam and Mo with blow, but molly wasn't like coke in the sense of wholesale pricing or buying in bulk made it cheaper. It was more a lateral pricing until you got down into the single-dose amounts. So the profit margin pretty much stayed the same until you sold to individual people. Unlike coke, where I bought a 62 for $32 per gram and sold the half ounce for $54 per gram, molly stayed around $29 per gram from ounces down to eighths. And Mo knew that.

Single doses were different. If I bought a half ounce of molly from Eric for $400, sure I could up the price to $600 and sell it to Mo and make $200, but if Mo broke down the powder into individual doses, he could sell them to each individual for $20 a dose. A single dose of good molly, and according to Eric it was pure molly, only needed to be about 150 milligrams, or .15 grams. So selling 150-milligram pills or capsules for $20 is the equivalent of selling at $133 per gram. There are 14,000 milligrams in a half ounce, so that's 93 150-milligram capsules in one half ounce. Meaning, if I did lie and upped the price of the half ounce from $400 to $600, sure I would make $200 on the deal, but Mo would then turn around and sell individual dosages for a total of $1,860.

I needed to figure out how to take 14 grams of white powder and break it up into 93 150-millagram dosages. I texted Eric letting him know I was going to pick up a lot of everything on Friday. I was dry and had a massive order for pot, coke, and now molly. My Excel sheet was really coming in handy now.

| Pot | Grams | $ | Selling |
| --- | --- | --- | --- |
| ATO | 35 | $700 | Me |
| Acacia | 28 | $350 | Cam |
| Pi Kapps | 28 | $400 | Bo |
| Fiji | 14 | $200 | Bo |
| Sigma Chi | 28 | $400 | Me |
| ZBT | 28 | $375 | Mo |
| Kappa Sig | 28 | $375 | Bo |
| Phi Sig | 28 | $350 | Cam |
| Phi Delt | 14 | $200 | Bo |
| Beta | 14 | $200 | Bo |
| Sigma Nu | 14 | $200 | Bo |
| Delts | 28 | $400 | Me |
| Apes | 28 | $375 | Mo |
| Total | 315 | $4,525 | |
| Paid | 448 | $2,000 | |
| Leftover | 133 | | |
| Profit | | $2,525 | |

| Coke | Grams | $ |
| --- | --- | --- |
| Cam | 48 | $2,592 |
| Mo | 62 | $3,348 |
| Total | 110 | $5,940 |
| Paid | 125 | $3,800 |
| Leftover | 15 | |
| Profit | | $2,140 |

| Molly | Grams | $ |
| --- | --- | --- |
| In Safe | 28 | $ 800 |
| Paid | 28 | $800 |
| Leftover | 44 | |
| Profit | | $0 |

I needed a pound of weed, a Big 8 of blow, and two half Os of molly. That was $2,000, $3,800, and $800 respectively. I went to Eric's on Friday and picked everything up. He gave me some beginning-of-the-year speech about being careful and making sure I didn't get in over my head, shit like that. He said, "This powder stuff is a different animal. The money you'll make off it seems fake, but cops crack down hard on it, so cross your Ts on everyone you sell to, alright?" Bo wasn't in town yet, so I went back to the house and locked the door to my room and broke out the bud into the ounce, half-ounce, gram, and 10-sack bags, then separated the coke into four half-ounce bags to sell to Cam and Mo. Then, there was the molly.

Eric had given me empty capsules that the guy he got the molly from had given him a while ago. There must have been 500 of them in the Ziploc bag; empty, clear, digestible capsules. My scale wasn't perfectly accurate when it came down to milligrams, but a quick incognito Google search told me to put the amount on a dime, and that would be a rough way to get a dose. After Googling different methods and attempting to weigh everything out, I learned I could pour the dime of molly into the long half of the capsule and that would be roughly .15 grams or 150 milligrams. So that's what I did. I took my IU student ID, scooped up the powder, shook it into the half capsule, and shut the capsule. Over and over and over again. In the beginning I was very careful to fill the half capsule all the way, but after about 20 of them I said fuck it and did one scoop and if it was close enough, it was good enough. The molly was pure MDMA, nothing cut in it, so no one was going to notice a .05 let alone a .01 difference. I was getting a little light-headed after about 30 minutes of handling the molly, but I was pretty positive it was just in my head. I hadn't touched my fingers to anything but the capsules and student ID.

One hundred and eighty-two. That's how many capsules it filled up. One hundred and eighty-two. My scale had said I had 30.54 grams of molly, so 182 capsules would be 168-milligram dosages, give or take about 20 milligrams per dose. They were a little bit on the strong side. The good thing about the capsules, though, was that they were just that, capsules. A group of friends could buy five of them, empty out the capsules into their own Ziploc bags, and then take dips the whole time instead of taking the pill all at one time.

I went to the bathroom to wash my hands and face before texting Mo.

5:54 p.m.: *Got your truckload . . . All in capsules, $20 a pop.*

5:57 p.m.: My man! Thanks bro. How much in each capsule.

5:58 p.m.: *About 170 milligrams. 90 capsules per half ounce.*

6:00 p.m.: Yup, I'll buy 100. Cool?

*Shit, what am I going to do with the leftover 82 pills of molly?*

I knew I was going to have to ask the sophomores if they wanted any. It felt strange again calling the now sophomores *sophomores*. I still viewed them as pledges, but that was just the progression of school. I viewed everyone above me as what they were when I was pledging and everyone below me as freshmen.

Once Bo moved in on Saturday morning, business was back to normal. I delivered the ounce or half-ounce bags on Monday this time, Bo went on Tuesday, and then I let Cam buy a QP for $1,000, since he was now selling to Acacia, his buddy in Phi Sig, his buddies from Cincinnati, and then to some kid in the Villas. The dude from the Villas was on the football team, but Cam never told me his name. That didn't matter to me. The guys he was selling to didn't even know I existed, so there was no need to worry about him. I didn't know what to do with the 82 pills of molly, though.

The next couple of days, Mo added another two buddies he wanted to sell bud to, and Adam at Pi Kapps wanted to sell to his freshman-year room-mate living up in 10th and College. Each time someone asked, I seemed hesitant to his face, like I wasn't going to be able to, but I knew I easily could. Especially if it was someone else making the delivery. I had finally made commitments to the point where I had to buy over a pound of weed a week, which, granted, fluctuated about one to five ounces every week. But I now had to ask Eric for two pounds every other week to keep up.

After I picked up on Tuesday, Kyle and I decided to walk to Chipotle to grab a burrito. On the way we ran into Sara and a couple of her girlfriends.

"Hey long time no see," Sara said as she raised her arms out for a hug.

"Hey Sara, what's up," I said, returning the hug.

"You guys hear about the concert Labor Day weekend!" she blurted out looking at Kyle.

*Guess it's official.*

"Yeah, the Deadmau5 show?" Kyle responded.

"How nuts! Just a random welcome-week concert," Sara's friend added.

"Tommy Miller in Sigma Chi said it was going to be in some field?" Sara asked as we all started walking together.

"Yeah. Was talking to some guy I'm in IUDM with and he was saying they will have buses going to and from there. It's like 15 minutes away," Kyle answered.

"That's going to be amazing. Hopefully it'll be better than Pretty Lights," Sara's friend said as she jokingly nudged Sara.

"Oh, were you a part of the freak-out crew?" Kyle replied, shaking Sara's shoulders.

"No, I was not, but played mom to a few of the girls in our pledge class."

"Yeah, Kyle and I did too," I said as we walked into Chipotle.

"Are you guys going to roll for this one?" Sara asked, looking at me.

"I'm . . . ," I started to say before being cut off by both Kyle and Sara's friend.

"Yeah, I'm going to."

"Me too."

Sara kept her eyes on me with her eyebrows raised like she was waiting for a respond.

"No, probably not."

"Well, do you, or Kyle, do you know where we could get some? I think most of my pledge class is going to, and then I'm positive the sophomores will want some."

*Alright Cory, play this right.*

"Funny you say that, last night I was talking to some kid on my floor freshman year and he told me he was selling rolls for the show," I told the group, trying to act casual.

"What, who?" Kyle replied.

*Dammit Kyle.*

"Uh, guy who lived next to Joe. Brett was his name."

*Standard white guy name. They'll never question it.*

"You trust him? Don't want another mishap like last time."

"I mean, as much as I trust anyone with drugs. He's not an out-of-towner or someone random. Yeah, he's a good dude, I trust him. How many do you want?"

"I want one!" Sara's friend said, raising her arm quickly and looking at Sara.

"Yeah, me too, but I'll ask my house and get back to you."

"Alright sounds good, I'll text him now."

"Aw shucks Cory, you're such a good friend!" Sara said as she put her arm around me.

I put my arm around her as we waited in line. Instead of ordering to go we decided to eat there. We sat and talked about welcome week and funny stories about living in sorority and fraternity houses. As I listened to Sara's friend go on and on about some IU-themed rave they had at Sigma Chi, and how some dude named Matt was going to get them molly but never did, it dawned on me.

When I first started selling I wanted to keep it just my friends, but now that I had pretty much become the main supplier, I had to view things differently, and I had missed a crucial part. I couldn't tell if more people were doing drugs, or I was just noticing it more because I was the one supplying it, but it was crazy. It was like every house had a weed guy and a coke guy, and everyone wanted to roll for concerts or big parties. Or whatever the fuck an IU-themed rave was. I was dealing bud to almost every fraternity and a couple of the apartment buildings, then relatively speaking was dealing coke to about half of the fraternities and a couple apartments, and now supplying molly on an occasion-by-occasion basis. When it came to keeping a low profile, I had clearly done that if Sara and even Kyle didn't know I had molly or, better yet, were surprised when I said I even knew someone with it. I had kept my innocence while I continued to expand, and it felt the more I expanded, the safer I was. Everyone assumed Cam and Mo had the drugs; no one knew it was because of me. Didn't matter if I sold to one guy in a fraternity or to one guy in an apartment building, it was all the same system, and all through me.

I had done my part, and done it well, but there was still one part of selling that I had no control over. The final piece to the puzzle. The puzzle piece that was the least trustworthy, talked and gossiped the most, and was the hardest to contain. Sororities.

The whole time selling, I had ignored sororities. For sheer fear of getting in trouble, but half the population at IU was women, and the chicks at IU partied as hard if not harder than most of the guys. I mean, yeah, when you go to the bars they get the majority of their drinks paid for by guys, but when it came to drugs, I had never heard of a guy being polite and buying chicks' drugs. It wasn't a chivalrous thing to do like buying a girl a drink. Sororities were always going to buy their own drugs and, more importantly, were always going to talk about them. Talk about how they were, who they got them from, how their night was with them, all the late-night food they regretfully ate, and so how fat they were, etc. Sorority girls acted like they were invincible and were so carefree when it came to what they said. Sara's friend was throwing around names of guys she bought drugs from like she had a plea deal with the cops. It was baffling how nonchalant she was snitching on essentially drug dealers.

Sororities were the most risky part of any college, and it wasn't even close. Ignoring them in fear of getting in trouble seemed right in the beginning, but the more I sat and listened to Sara and her friend gossip, I knew it was only a matter of time until my name was brought up. I couldn't ignore them anymore. I knew I had to start paying attention to them and being more careful. Instead of just not selling to them and running the risk of them gossiping over how they got their drugs, I had to be proactive. Get ahead of the rumors and make sure I controlled exactly what the girls gossiped about. Either by distancing myself further and further from the drugs or selling directly to one of them I trusted and letting them do the rest.

On the walk back from Chipotle, all I could think about was how to deal with sororities. I figured the solution was to involve every fraternity possible. Spread it out to as many people as I could, muddy the waters and continue to separate myself from the person taking the drugs. If it went Eric, Me, Mo, chick, then that chick would say she got it from Mo and everything would come crumbling down. But if I could sell as much as possible to a lot of people, then it could go Eric, Me, Mo, frat guy, frat guy's friend, his girlfriend, and at that point, I'd be golden.

# TWENTY-ONE

**THREE DEGREES OF SEPARATION FROM WHOEVER TOOK THE DRUG,** especially chicks. That was the goal. Besides my friends—I sold directly to them. But when it came to molly, holy shit did I underestimate the market. Almost my whole pledge class asked for a capsule, and the sophomores bought 30 as soon as the show was announced. Thirty! I ended up having to text Eric and pick up more of everything. Mo and his 100 pills had APES and Acacia under control, as well as ZBT, Sammies, Phi Sig, and then the apartment buildings. Sara asked for 10 directly. I gave it to her this one time, but I trusted her. Besides her, I kept my ear to the ground and listened to what all the girls were rumoring about to see if I ever needed to stop selling to someone.

I had my first risk manager meeting with all the other risk managers from each house. It was the beginning-of-school pep talk from the dean and IFC. The concert was next Friday, so everyone knew what the main agenda was going to be, but really no one seemed to have a clue about anything else going on within other frats. It was good to shake a couple hands and meet the dean face-to-face, but besides that, nothing important came out of the meeting. The dean seemed completely out of touch with what the actual issues were that he should be worried about in 2011. Almost like he had watched some nineties movie and assumed that was present day. He kept talking about not having a main source of liquor, like punch bowls or a keg, and not to play drinking games like beer pong because that could get people drunk faster, and to register with IFC if you had any event like a band playing or a party paired with a sorority. *Hey buddy, no one is playing beer pong or has punch bowls while a band plays. I just sold about 200 pills of molly for an EDM concert—get out of 1998.*

The dean stressed having every person write his or her name down before entering your house for a party and checking school IDs, but no one was going to do that, and even he seemed to know that, so it was a big waste of time.

The summer partying didn't fade away once the new school year started up. Weather was still perfect, bars still packed, drugs still everywhere, but this time it was all of IU, not exclusively the summer crowd. It was funny being at the bars with everyone because whenever we saw someone from the summer crowd, it felt like seeing a longtime friend. KT was giving us shit for hugging "every Jew in here." Which honestly might be true, but whatever, there were a lot of Jews at IU and a lot who stayed the summer, and we had created a mini-fraternity.

The Deadmau5 concert was on Friday, August 26. Cam got blown up in the morning by Bennett's roommate for some molly and I hadn't really looped Cam into the whole molly thing yet, but luckily I had gone and gotten some more from Eric earlier in the week. I had lost count, but I think it was now closer to 325 pills sold. Filling up 325 capsules with molly was downright excruciating. It was the most barbaric thing I had ever done, but I didn't have a better way to create single doses, so just kept doing it. I also didn't want to tell anyone, because it was almost embarrassing. But whatever, overall I sold 100 to Mo, about 50 to ATO, 50 to Cam, 15 to Sig Chi, 12 to Pi Kapps, 10 to Sara, then a handful to Beta, Delts, Phi Delt, and Sigma Nu. Mo told me that he and his buddies had sold about 8,550 tickets for the show. This thing was going to be massive. The 325 pills of molly all of a sudden seemed tiny, but still $6,500 for me.

Bo and I were in our room watching *SportsCenter* when Mo texted me.

3:36 p.m.: What you doing before the show?

*3:37 p.m.: Just drinking at the house, then pledges driving us over.*

3:39 p.m.: Dude fuck that, come over! Deadmau5 and Porter Robinson are meeting at my place now.

Bo and I didn't even blink twice before saying we were in. We both went over to Mo's around 4:15 p.m. I had become a big Deadmau5 fan in the past year and was a fan of a couple Porter Robinson songs, but mostly because other DJs would play his shit.

Mo lived in the penthouse of the apartment building on 10th Street, but really, that meant he had the top floor. There was nothing penthouse about it. Bo and I walked past a massive black bus out front and went up the elevator to the sixth floor. We walked into the room, and it was surprising how normal it all looked. I recognized Deadmau5 immediately, but really everyone was just sitting down drinking beers, smoking cigarettes and joints, and just hanging out. Deadmau5 was as white as white could be, with colored tattoos all over his body, and as skinny as skinny could be. Must have been 5'9", 115 pounds. Tops. He was wearing cut-up jeans, a white T-shirt that had a giant Donkey Kong on it, and a black trucker hat bent into a complete semicircle. He was on the couch tapping away on his laptop, smoking a cigarette next to some chick who was equally tatted up and equally pale. Very punk-rock-looking couple. If I didn't know better, I would have thought Deadmau5 was a computer hacker or some IT nerd.

I walked up to big Mo and said what's up before grabbing a beer from the fridge. I recognized a few of Mo's friends, but couldn't figure out which guy was Porter Robinson. I'd Googled what he looked like on the pledge ride over, but still couldn't tell. Finally, one of Mo's friends took a picture with a guy standing in the kitchen. He was wearing a dark-green shirt with a frat pocket in the front and normal slim-fit jeans. Average haircut, average height, average weight—this guy was the most normal-looking white man on the planet. Honestly, if you combined every high school punter across America, that would be Porter Robinson. It was bizarre hearing a normal American accent from a DJ too. I'd assumed they were all European. He was also young as fuck. Looked about my age. Another Google search later, and I found out he was born in 1992, so was actually a year younger than me. I walked up and said hi and stood and talked to him for a while. He wasn't that popular a DJ so I wasn't surprised he was down-to-earth, but I'd imagined a little more of an aura than your local high school punter. Like have a bodyguard, or an entourage, or at least a manager by his side or something. Nope, it was just a dude who looked like your high school Driver's Ed partner drinking out of a Solo cup in Mo's apartment.

Mo introduced Bo and me to Deadmau5 and the chick sitting next to him. She said her name was Sofi. I'd heard of the song "Sofi Needs a Ladder," so assumed that was her, but really had no clue. She was friendly though. Bo went into the kitchen, and I sat on the chair closest to Sofi and chatted for a little. Apparently they were on a huge tour across America and had been living in that bus outside for the past couple months. Deadmau5 would chime in every now and again during our conversation, but overall he was very standoffish. Not in a rude way, it was more his personality. You could tell he was a massive cynic and viewed the world in a very negative light. Statements like "But these fucking colleges and their sound systems. It's pathetic" or "Let me guess, you're a huge Avicii fan too." Wasn't rude, wasn't offensive to anyone, just, well, a prick.

Porter was the opposite. He was super chill, and hearing the two talk to each other was fascinating. Two opposite personalities bonding over the same craft. Porter smoking a joint while Deadmau5 ripped a cig. They weren't on tour together; their tours just happened to meet in Bloomington, IN, and Porter was completely fine opening for him. Deadmau5 seemed to be way friendlier to Porter than he was with anyone else. I think it was a DJ thing. Like some sort of cool kids' club. They were talking about what systems they used when they were on stage, and Porter said he preferred to have a keyboard and drums on stage but had mentioned this one system he was going to use at the concert. Deadmau5 rolled his eyes at the system he referenced and suggested another one before commending Porter for playing live instruments on stage. It was cool being in that apartment building listening to the two of them talk shop.

We all took a picture together and did a shot of tequila before heading out. Porter and Mo hitched a ride in Deadmau5's bus, then Bo and I took an APES pledge ride to the show. It was about six o'clock, and Porter was supposed to start right at six. *Now I know what these artists are doing when they start late. Literally nothing.*

We pulled up behind the stage. Bo and I looked at each other and were thinking the same thing. *Do we stay backstage?* We didn't have VIP passes, but had showed up with the people setting up the show, so clearly it wasn't going to matter. It sounded crazy, but I almost didn't want to be backstage for Deadmau5. I wanted to be in the crowd watching the show. Porter was a different story. I wanted to see what it was like to be backstage for a concert, and didn't really care too much about his set anyway. He went directly from the bus to the stage and Mo, Bo, and I followed him up the stairs and stood next to the curtain facing the crowd. It was one of the coolest sights I had ever seen. Thousands of people with their hands up and the glow of the lights from the stage illuminating them. I couldn't make out any individual faces or individual arms, it was a single army of people. It must have been the coolest feeling, seeing that crowd and knowing it was for you. In a weird way, that image made me want to be famous or do something important with my life. It was something I'll never forget.

After a couple of minutes, security escorted us off the stage so they could take their places on both ends of the stage. Bo and I said thanks to Mo and walked around the stage into the crowd. It was nuts that Mo and I weren't even close friends, but he let me do this cool shit with him. We had bonded because of selling drugs and partying. But I guess that's what college friends do, minus the drug dealing part, bond over partying.

The entire show was mind-blowing. I recognized a lot more Porter songs than I thought, but that easily could have been other DJs' songs. Nevertheless, no one cared, it was still awesome. There was no other way to describe Deadmau5's show but mesmerizing. His bass shook your entire body and had this massive 40-foot monitor on stage that was showing trippy, Tron-like images the whole time. He was also DJing from a gigantic 20-foot cube, which had LED lights on the outside that changed with the beat. The amount of money Mo and his promoting company minions must have put into it was inconceivable. Speakers, lights, fence wrapping around, paying the people that owned the field, everything. Since it was off campus, the place could sell alcohol, though, which must have helped—having Natty Light sponsoring the event. The organization of everything was impressive.

Unlike Pretty Lights, everyone had energy after the show. I couldn't really place why, but it was like the show inspired everyone to party harder. Maybe it was the drugs. Actually, I'm about 99 percent sure it was the drugs, but regardless, everyone was a lot more animated this time around.

We all went to Acacia with the Third Street houses: Acacia, ATO, Tri Delt, Pi Phi, and Alpha Phi. No one really knew the party was going to happen and there wasn't much organization, but we told Acacia we would have our pledges help out, and then everything started to fall into place. The now seniors in both houses hated each other, but no one liked them anyway, so it didn't matter. It was all six houses' sophomores and juniors, and everyone was in the basement. Lights dimmed, strobe lights on, some Acacia kid DJing in the corner, it was a nightclub. I wasn't rolling, neither was Bo, but we were both liquored up pretty good. I ran into Sara and Jess, and Sara and I hung out for a while in the middle of the party. It was like Pi Kapps basement freshman year all over again, flirty dancing together, but this time, we were both single. After 20 minutes of dancing together, we started making out. It was brief, because, well, we were in public and didn't need to be making out in front of everyone, but it was enough. She looked better than ever, as in, more and more like Eva Mendes. But the kiss was like a release of tension that had been building for years.

After a couple hours at the party, Sara came up and asked if I wanted to leave. The night was a success: got to meet Deadmau5 and Porter Robinson, apparently sold everyone great molly, got drunk and partied all night, and was about to bring back a girl I'd had a mini-crush on since freshman year. Sara and I walked to a practically empty ATO. The vibe throughout the whole school was noticeable. I had no clue what time it was, but it felt late. We walked up into my room and immediately started making out again and eventually made our way to my bed. I had heard that having sex on molly was supposed to be incredible, so, luckily for me, I must have seemed incredible to Sara. After about 15 minutes, we were both still wide awake, so we put our clothes back on and went to the couch to smoke. It was funny how casual it all felt. There was no awkwardness at all, not even when Bo, Kyle, Cutty, Garcia, and Joe came stumbling in to smoke about an hour later. It was like we had gone straight to girlfriend/boyfriend status in one night. It was odd, yet comforting.

After an hour of talking about the night with Sara and the idiots, Sara said she had to go to Acacia to walk home with one of her friends. I walked her outside, where her friends were waiting for her on the front porch of

ATO. I looked at Sara and she looked back at me, not really sure whether or not to hug or embrace in any way. We both laughed as we gave each other a high five, then an eventual hug good-bye. It was another comforting encounter. Something I hadn't felt since Em and I had broken up. I walked upstairs with a smile on my face and went straight to bed.

In the morning I woke up to Kyle running into our sleeper.

"Kyle, I swear to Christ I will murder you if you don't turn around and leave immediately," Bo said from the bottom bunk.

"Dude, you guys hear about that freshman?" Kyle cried out, panting like he had run a mile to deliver the news.

"Dude. Fuck! You!" Bo yelled as he threw his shoe at Kyle standing in the sleeper doorway.

"Bro, a freshman was found dead in her dorm room last night. Apparently people are saying she was either at Acacia or Kappa Sig, they're not really sure yet."

"Wait, what?" Wolf shouted from the hallway.

Kyle turned around and walked into the hallway to talk to Wolf. At the same time Kyle walked out, Bo leaned out of the bottom bunk and looked up at me. As we looked at each other, we had the exact same thought.

*Oh fuck!*

# TWENTY-TWO

**A STUDENT AT INDIANA UNIVERSITY HAS BEEN FOUND DEAD** in her dormitory on the Bloomington campus, authorities said.

Elizabeth Marie Madison, 19, was found unconscious in her Briscoe Residence Center dorm room early Saturday morning, and was later rushed to the emergency room where she was pronounced dead according to the Monroe County medical examiner's office. Bloomington authorities found no signs of foul play. An autopsy is scheduled for Saturday afternoon.

Kappa Sig. That's what everyone was saying. Lizzy Madison was from the same high school as Garcia's girlfriend, who had told a few people she was at Kappa Sig that night. Everyone in the dining room was talking about it. Hearing rumors that she was a big partier, her Facebook pictures showed how tiny she was, apparently she had some sort of heart condition, rumors were flying. It was unbelievable how much information there was about this chick just from word of mouth and pictures. The information spread wildly throughout the school. As I sat in the dining room listening to everyone, I was ashamed of myself that my initial reaction to the news that a freshman had died, a human being had passed away, was that I really hoped she wasn't at Acacia or with ATO guys that night. I was disappointed with myself for thinking so selfishly as soon as I heard the news, but in reality, that was the part that affected me. If the rumors were true, Kappa Sig was going to be put on suspension immediately and, depending on their ethics-board meeting, most likely kicked off campus for A: The death of a student. B: A party that got out of hand. And C: Allowing a freshman into their party. I mean, the dean could technically hit them with the entire kitchen sink in order to make a statement to the Madison family and the other fraternities. However, getting kicked off campus wasn't what Kappa Sig should have been scared of. The police sniffing around and getting sued by the family, at least for me, if I were the risk manager who was in charge of the party where a freshman died, that part would fucking terrify me. It was just a messy situation all around.

The rumors continued to come in throughout the day. Kappa Sig saying she wasn't there, some people saying she was but claiming they kicked her out 'cause she was too drunk, people hearing she was with a group of freshman guys that went to the Deadmau5 show, her roommate saying she didn't go to the show but didn't know where she went instead—the story had taken over the school. It was weird not feeling invincible anymore. Being able to take drugs, drink all night, black out, and just wake up in the morning and feeling various levels of hungover. Worst thing that happened in college was losing your dignity. No one ever thought about something like this; it was scary.

"You nervous at all?" Bo said as I got to our room.

"What do you mean?"

"The autopsy or toxicology report. I mean, nervous if it says she was rolling or on drugs or whatever."

"Why would I be nervous?"

"Because you sold them."

"I didn't sell it to any freshman, didn't even sell it to Kappa Sig guys."

"Dude, she still might have gotten them from you or Cam through other people."

I hadn't really thought about what Bo was getting at; theoretically, it could have happened. I sold molly to Mo, who could have sold it to a guy in Kappa Sig, who could have sold it to some girl, who could have sold it to Lizzy Madison. But even then, there was nothing I could have done to stop that besides stopping selling all together, but really, someone else would still be selling it anyway, so that wouldn't eliminate any problem. It would just be someone else's problem.

"But I mean, you could say that about anyone then. The demand of who wants to do drugs doesn't change if I sell them or not. People are still going to roll at concerts, still going to party at frats," I said in a quieter tone so only Bo could hear me.

"True, but that won't stop the cops from poking around. That's what I mean by nervous."

"Oh, well, no, I'm not nervous then. I mean I haven't really thought about it. It would take a lot of digging and people to point fingers to even get to Kappa Sig, let alone Mo, Cam, you, or me."

"Fuck that! I didn't sell a single pill. I bought one, though," Bo said, packing up his one-hitter.

"I thought you didn't roll?"

"I didn't at the show but did at Acacia. Got it from Cam. But I mean, if it takes a lot of digging, that's what the cops do, they dig. I don't know man. I'm just nervous about it."

Bo had me a little worried and on edge with this whole Lizzy Madison story. He was getting paranoid about it. It was a devastating thing that someone died, but saying because a freshman might have died by drinking and doing drugs didn't mean the cops were going to hunt down the person who sold the drugs and continue to climb the ladder until they got to me. It was a college campus—it sounded shitty, but my guess was the Bloomington PD were used to dealing with this, even if it's as tragic as a death. So how much digging would they even do? Whoever sold it directly to her? Who she was with? It would take a lot of finger-pointing to get to Mo or Cam. Then they would have to snitch to get to me.

Everyone took it easy the rest of the weekend. Hard to party after hearing about a freshman dying. Nothing changed with me and Eric, though, I went over to his place on Monday to pick up some more of everything. It was like a seesaw with IU and drugs. If people went out, I sold a lot more hard drugs; when people stayed in, I sold more bud. Eric was interested in what I had heard about Lizzy. I told him what I knew and the rumors I'd heard, but he didn't seem to be worried like Bo was, more curious. From his reaction, it sounded like we shared similar thoughts.

Eric had gotten another two half ounces of molly, thinking I needed it weekly. It was miscommunication, mostly on my part, but I bought it anyway, since it was only a matter of time until the next concert or party that people would want it for. Besides, with Cam and Mo now selling almost exclusively to GDIs, I never knew what they needed. GDIs were such an enigma, and because of them, both Cam and Mo asked if they could buy even more coke. Only issue was Eric only sold a Big 8, a BQ (big quarter), or half kilo. So 125, 250, or 500 grams. I was already selling Cam a 62 a week and Mo a Big 8. Throw in Delts, Sigma Chi, and Beta getting two 8-balls and Pi Kapps with a half ounce, I now, because of Eric's measurements, had to double the usual BQ order to a half kilo for $12,500. It was the first time in a while I had felt any nerves driving to ATO from Eric's. Probably since the first days with Hippy Mike.

Our first tailgate was on Saturday. It was odd being a junior. Past the halfway point, second oldest at the school, having counselor meetings about life after college and getting an internship. It actually kind of sucked, knowing it was all coming to an end. Seeing all my friends at the bars was a nice change of pace though. Granted, we went to the bars almost every night during the summer, but at IU, you really didn't go to the bars as a full grade regularly until you were a junior and a senior. To me, that's how it should be too. Party in the fraternities and live-outs for two years, so by the time you go to the bars, it feels new, and by the time you leave IU, you aren't sick of house parties or bars because you did them both for two years each. Unlike Iowa or Mizzou, where you just party at the bars for all four years with really no change of pace.

The toxicology report was going to take a couple weeks, but the more I heard about this Lizzy Madison girl, the more she seemed like a wild card. The heart condition rumor was confirmed by her parents. The group of freshman guys she was with said they met up with her after the show at Kappa Sig, and one dude said she did in fact get kicked out. It was still confusing where she was before Kappa Sig or where she went after, but by connecting all the dots, everyone assumed she died by drinking too much. Whether there were drugs involved was still unknown, but a tiny 19-year-old girl with a heart problem getting kicked out of a frat party for being too drunk was enough of a conclusion.

I had my Tuesday early-afternoon class with Max. It was some financial modeling class, but I hadn't really paid attention to the syllabus or what the course was really going to entail. I knew it was boring as shit though, so I mostly was on ESPN and checking my fantasy football roster the whole time. When class ended I saw a couple people grab the school paper, the *IDS*, on the way out.

"Plans this weekend?" Max said as we got up to leave the class.

"Not really, honestly. Tailgate Saturday, that's about it."

"Yeah, same here. There're a bunch of the seniors from last year coming into town for the tailgate, so our house will probably be a zoo."

We walked out and Max grabbed an *IDS* on the table outside the door. *Wait, this is a thing people do? Didn't know anyone read the* IDS. I had a break between classes so was going to stop in the computer lab on the first floor and get organized for the year.

"You see this?" Max said as he lifted up the *IDS* to me.

IU STRIVES FOR CONSISTENCY: 2011 FOOTBALL PREVIEW

"Striving for consistency. Real positive way to say they are hoping to be less shitty this year."

"No, at the bottom." Max said as he handed me the newspaper.

NEW AGE COLLEGE AND THE INTRODUCTION OF PARTY DRUGS

"You read it?" I asked, trying to remain cool.

"No, not yet."

We walked down the hall and down the stairs toward the computer lab. I grabbed a copy off the little newspaper holder in the hallway and kept walking into the computer lab. The place was packed, but I had my mind on something else now, so I found an open seat in the silent area. Max sat down at an open table with some Sigma Chi guys. I sat down and opened up the *IDS* and started reading the article.

Gone are the days of drinking games and a beer pong table in every college apartment. Gone are the days where the keg is the most prized possession for fraternities. Gone are the days when the word "tailgate" implied drinking out of the trunk of a car before eventually attending the game afterward. College traditions change over time, whether it is academic excellence, athletic success, or even the school mascot, but what always remains constant is the parties. From the days way before Animal House through the turn of the century, it was always men, women, loud music, and beer. Music trends would come and go, but the true makeup of every college party remained the same; men, women, loud music, and beer. Until now. Substitute a DJ for the rock band, a handle for the keg, black lights for incandescent lights, and ecstasy for the beer. The average 2011 party is more a nightclub than a bar . . .

I started skimming through to find any real reporting, but it was just an observation piece. *Phew.* Some of it made sense, but the article didn't mention other eras like the seventies when disco made cocaine something to be handed out like gift baskets at parties. Disco and EDM were like the same cultural movement anyway, so this was more click-bait journalism than anything.

I kept speed-reading until I got to one part. I stopped and reread it a couple more times, hoping I was misreading it.

". . . the rest of the force and I would be naïve to think party drugs are new to universities across America, but we have not seen anything like this. Our team is focused on finding the new source of this epidemic and putting a stop to the mass distribution of party drugs in Bloomington."

# TWENTY-THREE

**"DUDE, FUCK THIS, I'M OUT,"** Bo said as I walked in the room.

"What do you mean, you're out?" I replied.

"This Detective Campbell or Officer Campbell or whatever, man. It's too sketchy now, I'm out. I'm done."

"Dude, every cop alive says, 'We are determined to stop crime.' I mean, reading that quote made me nervous too. That's why I texted you. I reread it like four times, but the more I thought about it, the more I realized, no shit he fucking said that. What is he supposed to say, 'You know, this is a pretty big school, so it's going to be hard to track down who has drugs and where they come from'?"

"Whatever, Cory, justify it however you want. I have made way more money than I ever would have thought. I made enough to pay for all of my college expenses besides tuition. I have no idea how much you've made with the coke and molly thing you got going on with Cam, but I don't want any part of it anymore. I'm out."

"So what about your deliveries, are they just mine now?"

"No, Hamilton is going to deliver to my houses from now on."

Hamilton was a sophomore in the house, and actually a pretty normal guy. He was in the Kelley School of Business with me, but I didn't know him that well, to be honest.

"What the fuck? Just not going to tell me?"

"I'm telling you now."

We both paused for a second. I put my backpack down and walked to sit on the couch as the silence grew longer.

"Well, it seems like your mind has already been made."

"That it has, you should do the same."

"Because of this? It's a cop saying he will try and stop crime. Come on Bo. You think we started an 'epidemic' . . . ? Please."

"We? Fuck that, I haven't done shit."

"You know what I mean. Besides, I'll probably stop at the end of the year anyway. Have a chill senior year. But for now, everything is going well, and I'm making way too much easy money. So you're just going to be the sportsbook guy now?"

"Giving up the book too. Giving it to Adam in full."

"What the fuck!"

"Dude, come on. I know it's half yours, but I don't think you need the book money anymore and haven't done a thing with it all year."

"But I think a pretty normal thing to do would be to ask someone if he wanted to stop getting thousands of dollars a semester before you make that decision for him."

"Well, if you want to split it with Adam, talk to him. He has no right to say no. It's half yours."

A few more seconds of silence went by. We both sat on the couch looking at the TV.

"Well, fuck, man," I complained with a smile.

"I know I know. I'm being paranoid. I don't know, I just wanted to stop."

"Look at you. Clean man now."

"Clean indeed. It was a hell of a run, bro," Bo said as he stood up for a hug.

I was hesitant to stand up and return the hug. He flat-out bailed on me with this whole dealing and bookieing thing, but really, besides the deliveries, he hadn't done anything in a while anyway. After a split-second hesitation, I stood up and we had a funny corny moment hugging each other. Nothing was going to change anyway, so it wasn't even that big of a deal, but in the grand scheme of things, he was right, we really did have a great run. He asked me if I wanted to start the sportsbook when we were freshmen, and that made us a little over $8,000. I asked him if he wanted to sell pot when we were sophomores, and that had made us about

$98,000. The money was going to continue to grow exponentially anyway. Majority of my money was now coming from blow and from Mo and Cam's connections. Bo had been delivering to about six or seven houses, but was easily replaced by a sophomore. Which was actually a great idea, giving the deliveries to a sophomore.

We had our second risk manager meeting a couple weeks later on Thursday afternoon, and like last time, everyone knew what the agenda was going to be. Coincidentally, the *IDS* article was written before Lizzy Madison's death, so had come out at the right/wrong time, depending how you looked at it. *IDS*'s party drugs and EDM arguments along with the Lizzy Madison story had been the main headlines over the past couple weeks in Bloomington and even Indianapolis.

The meeting was at Phi Delt. I walked into their dining room and saw two cops sitting up front with the dean and IFC. I knew they were just going to ask questions about Lizzy Madison and reiterate the dean's rules, but still intimidating to walk into given the severity of the issue. I walked to the back and sat down next to a group I didn't know. The dean started by giving a quick speech about Lizzy Madison and her family, and how the IU community needed to stay united across all areas of the school, Greek and non-Greek. I looked around and realized that the Kappa Sig risk manager wasn't there. IFC took a quick roll call before introducing the two officers. Officer Hendricks and Detective Campbell.

"Hey guys, I'm going to make this pretty quick. As you are aware, there has been some sort of a drug problem at IU the past couple of years. This isn't just because of Ms. Madison— trust me, we've been documenting this trend for some time now. But there is now more pressure than ever to really get on top of this problem and figure out how to fix it. Myself along with Officer Hendricks here, want to be your point of contact, and really, be here to help you guys keep your houses safe. So what we've done is set up an anonymous tip line for you guys to call in to if you have any information about any drug-related issues going on in the Greek community . . ."

It was a very surreal feeling, staring at a man who you knew was looking for you. Detective Campbell was trying to find Eric and me, and I was sitting 20 feet in front of him.

" . . . I'm not talking about a sophomore in the house smoking pot in his room or individual use of any kind. I'm talking about a problem. If you hear of anything, like a transaction or even rumors involving mass quantities of drugs, you can call this number on the card my partner is passing around to each of you, and leave an anonymous tip. Guys, let's face it, drugs are in each and every one of your houses, no need to sit there and deny it, but putting an end, or even a dent in the party drug problem helps everyone here. Less drugs means less police and dean involvement. The less you see our faces, the better it is for your fraternities and your social lives. And I can promise you, until we figure out the problem, you will be seeing our faces often."

Detective Campbell was a very military-looking man. He was about 6'2", 215 pounds, with a very wide chest but narrow waist. His high and tight blond buzz cut made him look like he was pretending to be a marine or playing one in a movie. Officer Hendricks walked by our table and handed me a stack of cards to bring to ATO. They were all the same, black cards with white lettering. They had both officers' names and direct lines, and the anonymous tip line with tiny print underneath stating it was in fact anonymous and could not and would not be traced. I saw the kid from Beta with a red stack and Delts with a green stack. I poked my head around and saw that every frat had different-color business cards, but all the cards had the same info.

I was nervous being in the room, especially after Campbell's D.A.R.E.-esque speech, but realistically I knew it was pointless. My bet was that most of the frats would throw the cards out when they got home, and some would use them as joint or blunt filters. The odds of someone picking up the card, let alone calling that number, were the same as Cutty graduating in four years. Zero.

Sitting in the room with the police officers in charge of stopping drug distribution was exhilarating, to tell you the truth. A part of me felt powerful sitting in that room. To everyone else, I was some normal risk manager from a house that partied a lot, but in reality, I was the guy Campbell was after. My heart wasn't racing, I didn't feel nervous, I was calm. I felt like I was undercover and untouchable; it was feeling of supremacy. Now, granted,

I knew I wasn't the only drug dealer at IU, but I was going through two pounds of weed, a half kilo of coke, and about an ounce of molly every week or week and a half. That's close to $16,000 worth of drugs a week, and I bought it cheap as shit, too. I mean fuck, spread that out, and that's $64,000 worth of drugs a month. As much as I tried to ignore it, I knew I was the guy Campbell was after. Eric would obviously be ideal, but to get to him they had to go through me, and to get to me they had to swim through a lot of different people.

When I got back to the house, I put the stack of cards in my underwear drawer and got ready to go out. It was Thursday, so all the juniors and seniors were going to Sports. Bo and I had gotten VIP status there, which was laughable to even say out loud, but honestly, it was pretty sweet. The VIP cards all depended on how much money you had spent at Sports or Kilroy's, and on Bo's bday, we had put two tables in our name and split it—well, sort of split it—with our friends. But since it was under our name, Sports just gave us VIP cards. We got to skip the line every night, not pay covers, bring in two guests who didn't have to pay cover, and snag a table upstairs whenever we wanted. Still, at the end of the day, it was still a college bar in a college town, so apart from skipping the long line getting in, having a "table" upstairs meant next to nothing.

No one really organized a pregame or anything, so we drank in Joe and Barr's room until about 11 o'clock then got rides over. The place was already packed, so our friends walked to the same little area around the circle-bar we always met at. Bo had found an open bar stool and sat down, and I stood behind him grabbing his shoulders and shaking him to piss him off. I realized no one else looked at it this way, because no one really knew, but to Bo and me, the night was a celebration. He ordered 20 Vegas bombs for everyone. About 17 people grabbed one, and Bo and I took the remaining three.

"You're paying, by the way," Bo said as he took the shot.

"So you bail and make me pay?"

"Sucks to suck."

"Well, if it ain't Bonny and Clyde."

"What's good Cam."

"Chillin C. So Big B, how does it feel to be retired?" Cam said as he held a fake microphone in front of Bo.

"You know, I first have to thank my lord and savior Jesus Christ for an incredible career," Bo announced, already slurring his words through the joke.

Cam laughed as he walked a couple feet down to grab an empty spot at the bar, and I followed him over.

"How you feeling?" Cam asked as we stood in the empty nook of the bar between two groups of friends.

"About Bo? Good I guess, nothing really. Honestly, won't be a big loss."

"Nah, about the cops?"

"Oh, feeling great my man," I replied as I put my arm around Cam.

"That's what I like to hear. I'm not surprised the Teddy Bear over there is running."

We laughed as we stood at the bar. Couple minutes of bar talk went by until we saw Bennett's roommate Dave walk past.

"Oh fuck, man, I forgot to tell you. That kid Dave, you know, your freshman-year boy's roommate. He told me last week that your boy Ben is in rehab?"

*Bennett? What the fuck!*

"Rehab? For what?"

"Wouldn't say. Dave laughed it off like it was a complete joke, though."

"Damn dude, that sucks. I saw the kid here at Sports this summer, but not since. Jesus Christ."

"Yeah, never met him, but that Dave kid is crazy, bro. He introduced me to this dude who lives in Smallwood that wants a bunch of pow. Like CC, I mean a *bunch*," Cam said, making it a point to make eye contact with me.

My mind still couldn't comprehend the whole Bennett thing.

"Uh . . . Aight, sorry, yeah, sounds good. We'll chat tomorrow, cool?" I replied as I stuck my hand out.

We did the slap-and-hold handshake, and Cam handed me a gin and tonic before walking toward his buddies on the other side of the bar. *Bennett Schwartz is in rehab?* In a weird way, my first thought was to text Em and tell her. We spent so much time freshman year talking about him and how we both knew he would eventually give in to peer pressure. His mom was so uptight and had wound him so tight, it was only a matter of time until he realized everything he was missing. But Em and I were talking about peer pressure to drink beer or go to a party, not do enough drugs to go to rehab. It was insane, but knowing the mom, I bet it was a "complete joke." His mom could have caught him smoking or found coke residue in his room as she moved him in and could have just gone ballistic.

I took a sip of my drink, forgetting my drink was now Cam's leftover gin and tonic. I never understood why gin and tonics were a thing. Neither gin nor tonic was good individually— actually, they were both horrendous—but somehow so many people loved them together. Like there was not another gin drink that was popular besides gin and tonic, and anyone who drank straight tonic water was a complete thumb. I stayed in the same spot at the bar to order myself a whisky ginger.

"Excuse me," some girl said as she tried creating enough space to get to the bar.

The bar was crowded but not squeezing-for-bar-space crowded yet, so I was puzzled by this chick's move.

"Yeah, no problem. Just have to pay, then I'll be out of here," I said, half looking back.

I took out a $10 bill and waited for the bartender to come around. I realized the chick was still standing behind me trying to get my spot, so I left the $10 on the bar and turned around to leave. As I turned around, I flinched as I realized it was the stunningly beautiful blonde that had been with that group of girls my friends tried hitting on during the summer. I was going to walk away, but that was before the 10 out of 10 decided to make her appearance. I backed up and made a little space for her at the bar and gave her a little head nod.

"Oh, yes! Thank you," she said, nudging her way next to me at the bar.

"Here you go. For your troubles," I said as I handed her Cam's gin and tonic.

"Whoa, did you buy this for me?" she replied, tilting her head.

"Well, if we are being honest here, my buddy ordered me a drink and I didn't want to be rude, so I took it. But when he left I ordered one for myself, so now have an extra . . . just for you," I said, sliding the drink in front of her.

"Appreciate the honesty. What is it?" she said with a grin.

"Gin and tonic."

"Oh, my favorite! Well, thank you to the friend of . . ."

"Cory."

"I'm Brittney."

She took the gin and tonic and I took my whisky and we clinked glasses and both took a sip. *I'm talking to a unicorn AND I avoided the dreadful shake hands with a girl. Attaboy Cory, now don't blow this.*

"Saying I bought it would have worked, wouldn't it?"

"I don't know about worked, but you definitely would have gotten away with it."

The bartender walked by and grabbed my $10 and waited for one of us to order a drink. I turned toward Brittney to see if she wanted anything.

"Well, it was nice meeting you, Cory," she said as she raised her glass and turned around.

*Yup, you blew it.*

The rest of the night was same old same old. Run into people you saw two weeks ago and act like you haven't seen them in years, drink a painful variation of alcohol, lose all grasp of time, get a pledge ride home, smoke pot, eat food that somehow appeared in your room, and pass out.

I woke up in the morning to a text from Cam asking if we could chat. I gave him a call, but I already knew what he wanted. He asked if he could start selling a BQ every other week to the kid in Smallwood and stop selling to Bennett's now former roommate, Dave. I told him I'd talk to Eric, but couldn't see why it would be an issue, and also yes to cutting ties with Dave ASAP.

"Hey Cory, there's a cop here asking for you," a pledge said as he ran into my room.

*For me?*

I walked out of my sleeper to see Cutty and Garcia frantically cleaning up their weed as the pledge stood there staring at me.

"For what?"

"Not sure. He came to the back door asking if you were home."

I looked over at Cutty and Garcia, but neither of them seemed to be too worried about me. I always forgot no one in the house truly knew how deep my drug roots went. *It can't be that hotline, can it?*

"Tell him I'll be down in a second."

# TWENTY-FOUR

MY HEART WAS POUNDING AS I WENT THROUGH EVERYTHING I did the night before. *Talked to Cam. The blonde chick. Bennett in rehab. Could it be about Bennett in rehab? Ran into Max, Jimmy, Mo, fuck, everyone was there. The fight Wolf got in?* I had no idea what the cop could want.

The pledge was by the back door and motioned that he was outside. I walked outside to see Detective Campbell standing by his car parked in the lot. His car wasn't a standard police car; it was one of those undercover cars that everyone on the planet knew was a police car.

"Hey, Cory, right? Detective Campbell, sorry to drop in on you like this."

"Yeah, Cory Carter. Nice to meet you," I said as I shook his hand.

"Late night?" he asked, looking at me with a smirk.

As he smirked, I realized the jeans and shirt I had on were the same as the night before. Throw in the no shoes and probably some A+ bed head, and I must have looked like a real gem of a risk manager.

"You know, I've felt better."

"I know the feeling—well, I'll make this quick then. I'm trying to go around to each house before the tailgate tomorrow. As you know, it's the first one and there will be a lot of excitement and adrenaline from everyone, especially in the Greek lot, you got me?"

"Hmm hm," I replied, nodding my head.

"You're going to set it up in the morning, right?"

"Am I supposed to? Sorry, I wasn't risk manager last year."

"Oh, no, you don't have to. I assumed you would because most risk managers do. Well, regardless, one thing we're implementing this year is a small fence around the Greek lot. We understand there's going to be drinking, and we won't be able to stop underage drinking—we're not stupid like some might believe. But the best we can do is contain it. So tomorrow we're going to make sure there is only one entrance in and out of the lot, and there will be police officers at the entrance. We won't be carding because it's public property, but if anyone tries coming into the lot from any other way but the main entrance, or someone is clearly too intoxicated, they will be pulled aside by an officer. You got me?"

"OK, yeah, that makes sense. Is there anything I have to do?"

"Nothing really, Cory. Relay this to your house and tell whoever is setting up the tailgate to be there by eight in the morning. Is that alright?"

"Works for me."

"Alright, go drink some water. Going to be an early one tomorrow."

"Will do. Thanks, sir," I said as I shook his hand and walked back inside.

My first reaction, apart from confusion as to why the dean didn't just send an email, was that Detective Campbell was a real normal dude. Not what he said, but it was his mannerisms and how he talked to me. Seemed almost like a big brother looking out for us, but could play the authoritative figure if need be. As opposed to the douchebag meatstick cop that existed in most college towns. My second, or I guess third reaction, though, was thank God that was only about the tailgate!

After the encounter I went straight to Hamilton's room and asked if he wanted to do the deliveries for all of the houses, or if he wanted to recruit someone to help him. I knew I was being overly cautious, but I didn't care. Hamilton told me his roommate Dylan was going to help him out anyway, so adding a couple more houses would be awesome. At the end of the day it was 10 houses. Cam and Mo had the other five and all the apartments. I needed to keep distancing myself more and more, and now hopefully to other fraternities it would seem like Bo and I passed down this so-called delivery guy to sophomores in the house and were no longer involved. The only people that could really fuck me over would be someone within ATO, Cam, or Mo. And I guess Eric, but that would make no sense for him to rat on the people he sold to. Cops didn't care about getting the smaller guy if they already had the big guy. Once you got the source, it all stopped anyway.

I wanted Mo or Cam to be more cautious too, so I told them they should probably get delivery people. Mo and Cam could afford $100 a week for a little more security. Especially with Cam asking for an additional $7,500 of coke every two weeks. When I texted Cam and Mo, they both laughed at me like I was an idiot. Mo said he was having pledges deliver his bud since day one, and Cam was having a couple buddies deliver for him in exchange for free shit. I didn't want to tell Mo what he should or shouldn't do with pledges, but then remembered dropping off a backpack to the NYC kid in Smallwood during pledging, so realized I had probably delivered for JR too.

The Saturday tailgate was a success, and so were the deliveries the next couple of weeks. Adding the sophomore delivery guys added to the amount we sold because they had buddies in other houses and knew more GDIs. I liked being the higher-up middleman. It seemed less stressful, and ultimately I was making even more money. Now I understood why Hippy Mike was annoyed I bailed on him.

Homecoming was coming up, so I knew that whole lack of stress thing would change, but for the time being everything was great. Homecoming was going to be the same as Little 5 the year before. I was already getting texts from Mo asking for a bunch of molly, so I texted Eric and gave him a heads-up on the order. This time I refused to buy molly in powder form and individually stuff each pill, so I told Eric I would only buy pills. I understood how important I was to Eric, so I finally grew some balls and threw a little power his way. He responded with "I'll see what I can do," but it still felt good to flash some nuts.

Everything had seemed to settle down a bit since Lizzy Madison. The toxicology report came back with cocaine, amphetamines, and benzodiazepine. She was prescribed Adderall and some heart medicine, and after hearing from her friends and the dudes she was with that night, everyone figured that was the cocktail that did it. Alcohol, cocaine/Adderall, and heart medicine. Or maybe she didn't even take the heart medicine, and had Xanax as the benzodiazepine or something. Regardless, it was two uppers and two downers, combined with someone with a heart condition who either didn't take her medicine or did while on drugs. Both literally deadly combinations. Her parents weren't pressing charges either, so everything kinda fizzled out after the report.

The week of homecoming had come, and everyone was asking for molly. From Mo to Dylan. Hell, even Wolf and Sara were asking too. On top of that, Cam's BQ buddy in Smallwood wanted another BQ for that week alone, and Dylan wanted to sell some coke to his Fort Wayne guys in the Villas. It was crazy. I got my laptop out the Sunday before homecoming and counted up everything I needed. My jaw dropped at what I had said yes to. 1,288 grams of weed, 899 grams of coke, and about 980 pills of molly. *I have to buy a fucking kilo of cocaine!*

Twenty-five grand of drugs, *without* counting the 1,000 pills of molly. I asked Eric about the molly cost and he said he would let me know, he didn't have an answer for me yet. Since he was only buying half ounces before, I wasn't sure how he was going to do it. During Little 5, I turned the first 30 grams into 182 pills. Then another 22 or so ounces into the remaining 143 pills. So about 50 grams got me 325 pills. So if I did the same math, I would be buying 153 grams of molly. If it was $10 a pill, it would be 10 grand, so a grand total of $35,000 worth of drugs for one homecoming week.

The adrenaline rush was unexplainable. I was past the point of nervousness—that train had left the station. I knew I had positioned myself nicely where I called all the shots. Everyone was working under me, and no one could fuck with that. That wasn't the feeling, but it was a weird uncontrollable sense of authority. Authority to affect so many people.

Buying such high volume meant the price was going to be the lowest yet. Kilo was selling for $20 a gram, then I would sell it to Cam for $32 a gram, then he would sell it for $54, $57, or even $80 a gram. I would be making $12,000 profit just on cocaine. Molly was probably another $5,000 if I bought $10 pills, sold them for $15, then other people sold them for $20. Bud, I was buying $3.50 grams and selling them for $11 to people who would sell them for $14, then eventually $20 at the gram level. So I would make another $7.5 a gram on 1,288 grams. Thus, another $9,600. If everything went according to plan, all I had to do was pick up from the same guy I had been picking up from all year and sell to four people—Mo,

Cam, Hamilton, Dylan—and I would make roughly $27,000 in one week. All cash, all profit, splitting with no one.

That's $27,000 for being a middleman for the college drug life. As I drove to Eric's, I thought about the cycle I was in. A crop of new students would come in every year, but nothing would change. It honestly was like a company, and everyone kept retiring while others got promoted. JR replaced Jason when he retired, I replaced JR when he retired, then I got promoted to replace Hippy Mike when he retired, now Eric was getting promoted and I was essentially promoted to Eric's old job. My new job consisted of selling to people and letting them distribute around campus. I was as close to the pinnacle as I possibly could be. I was IU's number-one drug dealer. I was Detective Campbell's man, and he had no clue.

I had created a business and had absolute power over it.

# TWENTY-FIVE

**EVERYTHING WENT ACCORDING TO PLAN.** I didn't do any of the molly because that room of Pretty Lights tweakers still haunted me, but according to everyone who did, it was amazing. But really, that just meant no one tweaked. Which I guess was the only thing that mattered. After homecoming, we had no tailgates for two weeks. Midterms were during that time too, so everything was pretty tame. I texted Eric and told him I would come the following Monday to pick up. He didn't respond, but that was par for the course. I would still show up and he would always be ready.

When Monday came, I skipped class, since we had just had midterms and were essentially in another syllabus week.

"How's life without me?" Bo said as he walked into our room.

"Found out you're pretty replaceable. The sophomores are pretty damn good at doing nothing and smoking free pot too."

"Wait, you're not selling herb anymore?" Cutty interjected as he paused his Xbox game.

"Don't worry Snorlax, I'm still selling. Bo's not."

"Got a sophomore helping you out now?" Kyle said from the other side of the couch.

"Yeah, Hamilton and Dylan."

"Oh, the great Hambino and Fort Weezy's finest?" Cutty replied as he resumed playing Xbox.

We laughed and all shook our heads while he sat there stoned, drafting players in franchise mode in *NBA 2K12*.

"Speaking of Fort Wayne, did you guys see that group of chicks that was at the bar Saturday?" Bo asked as he sat down.

"Yeah dude, the group from Sports? With that blonde?" Kyle responded quickly.

"Yeah, with that blonde chick. Dude, who the fuck are they?" Bo replied.

"I have no clue. I was talking to a kid in Sigma Chi about that on Saturday. They just appear out of God's thin air at the bars at random times."

"Bo, what does that have anything to do with Fort Wayne?" I asked.

"It doesn't, just reminded me."

"Chick's name is Brittney, met her at Sports a couple weeks ago," I said confidently.

"Wait, what? Who the fuck is she?" Bo replied, shocked I knew her.

"No clue honestly, she was trying to buy a drink, and I talked to her for maybe five seconds. Enough to get her name."

"I heard she fucked Hambino," Cutty claimed, chewing the breadsticks that had been on the table for a couple days.

"Honestly I ignore everything you say," Kyle said as Cutty chuckled to himself.

"I have to know who they are. Like are they in a house, do they even go to school here? Where do they live?" Bo said as he also grabbed a breadstick.

Kyle looked over at me and then at Bo and Cutty both eating breadsticks and shrugged his shoulders. I laughed as I stood up.

"Well, they are for sure not in a house, we would have known that by now."

"And I doubt they are even our age, because we would also know that by now," Kyle added.

"But if they are all at the bars every time we see them, then they can't be freshmen or sophomores. I mean they could have fakes, but they don't look that young. Are they seniors?"

"Probably, I don't know many senior girls," I said as I grabbed my backpack.

"Where you going?"

"Class," I said, winking at Bo.

"Oh, for sure . . ."

"I know, I'm going to pick up bud."

"Oooo how about a 5-sack for your boy," Cutty shouted as I walked out the door.

*12:21 p.m.: Leaving now. Be there in 5*

I walked out of the room and went to get in my car. Eric's was only about five or 10 minutes away. Down Atwater, merge onto Third Street, take Third about two miles past College Mall, turn onto some side street I didn't even know the name of, and follow that around about four blocks, and you're there. I never understood who lived in college towns though. I always thought it would be the strangest thing to grow up, as a 10-to-18-year-old, in a college town. Like, were the parents teachers or faculty at the school? Did they go to school and never leave? I never understood how townies were created.

As I passed College Mall, I saw a cop turn out of the Target parking lot and pull right behind me. I slowed down and started to focus on my driving. I was doing that thing where as soon as a cop pulls behind you, you stop driving well and start driving like an 80-year-old grandmother. Going 34 mph in a 35, hands at 10 and 2, trying so hard to drive perfectly that you in fact drive worse than you were.

All of a sudden the cop's lights went on. *Fuck! Wait, I have nothing in the car besides money. I'm fine. Was I speeding? I don't care; I'll take a speeding ticket.* I pulled over to the right as the cop went zooming past me and down Third Street. My heart was still in my balls, but all I could do was smile and laugh at myself. I turned back onto Third Street and kept driving until I got to the turnoff. I turned into the little community Eric lived in and followed the winding street around. The area was a nicer part of town. All two- or three-story brick homes with basketball hoops outside, real tall trees filling each front lawn. It seemed like a nice neighborhood. *Must be where the professors live. And Eric. Why does he live here?*

I was about two or three blocks away from Eric's when I saw the flashing police lights in the distance. I kept driving another 100 yards when I realized they were all at Eric's house.

*OH FUCK!*

My heart sank again into my stomach as I slowed down. There wasn't another cross street between where I was and Eric's, so I decided to turn into a random driveway and wait 30 seconds before pulling back out and leaving out the other way. As I picked out the driveway, I saw another car coming behind me about a half block down. *A U-turn or pulling into a random driveway now would look really sketchy only a couple blocks from all these cops!* I looked into my rearview mirror at the car behind me and could tell it was an undercover cop car. I stared toward Eric's house trying to think of a plan for how to get away when it dawned on me. *Undercover cop car! It's Detective Campbell!* I checked my rearview mirror again and saw the undercover gaining ground on me. I was only about a block away from Eric's and about 80 yards in front of the undercover car, so I couldn't pull over. I knew I was going to have to pass Eric's house. *I can't let Campbell see me. I don't care about any of the other cops, but he can't!*

I sped up as I approached Eric's house. There were three cop cars pulled into the U-driveway with their lights still on, one cop van parked out front, and about four or five neighbors standing outside their houses observing the scene. I only saw two police officers talking out front, but didn't see Eric at all. I kept my speed of about 35 mph and blew right by Eric's house. I bet it looked strange to the cops to see a car drive that fast by them, but I didn't care about how the cops felt—I only cared about Campbell not seeing me. As I passed the house, I checked my rearview mirror and prayed Campbell wouldn't follow me. *Come on! Please stop!* On cue, Campbell slowed down and pulled in right behind the van. I immediately made the first right-hand turn onto the next street.

*Thank God!*

I could barely breathe and was light-headed, like I had vertigo. I drove another three blocks until I saw another main street and took a left without thinking. *Get me as far away as possible!* I passed two or three green lights as I kept checking my mirrors. *No cops, please no cops, please no cops!* I pulled over into a random church parking lot and parked the car. My heart was pounding so violently I had to put my hand on my chest and eventually get out of the car. I had no clue where I was, but I stood outside bent over with one hand on the car as I tried to catch my breath and compose myself.

It wasn't that exciting rush you have in middle school when you run away from the cops and feel alive. It was a terrifying feeling, like when you're waiting for the second shoe to drop. Everything in my life was up for grabs now. I felt genuine fear. *I can get expelled from school, parents could kick me out of the house, I mean fuck, I could go to prison!* Through all of the driving and wondering if Campbell saw me, I hadn't even thought about Eric yet and how or what had happened.

*Why the fuck are the police at Eric's? And so many. There wouldn't be that many officers for a small offense. And why is Campbell there? It has to be because of the drugs. Campbell would only be there if it's because of drugs. Right? How did they catch Eric? Had Campbell leapfrogged me and found the source? How was this possible? Did I do something to get him caught? Did Campbell see me driving? Fuck, what do I do now? Does he know my car? Wait, can I still get caught? I don't have any drugs; they have no proof. If Campbell caught Eric, then he doesn't care about me. He knows I'll be done selling drugs. I mean, I am 100 percent done selling drugs. He didn't put a kink in the hose—he went straight to the faucet and just turned it off. Wait, is this why Eric didn't text me back? Has he been arrested for a while? I feel like I would have heard something in the news about this big of a drug arrest in Bloomington, IN. Why would cops be there today right as I'm . . . Wait! Oh fuck. No! No! No! Please God, no! FUCK! FUCK! FUCK! FUCK!*

I stood outside the car feeling nauseated as I realized I'd texted Eric 10 minutes ago saying I was coming over.

# TWENTY-SIX

"BUT DID HE SEE YOU?"

"I mean, he saw the car, he was right fucking behind me. But I don't think he saw me specifically, no."

"How do you even know it was him?"

"Bo, I literally just told you how. The detective came over a couple months ago before the first tailgate. He drives the black undercover cop car."

"No dude, how do you even know it was the same undercover cop car?"

"I mean, come on, what are the odds? He's a detective who made it his mission to catch the IU drug dealer and drives the same car I saw out front of the IU drug dealer's house. It was him!"

"Dude, just trying to help."

"I know. Sorry. Fuck! What the fuck do I do?"

"Do nothing. There is nothing you can do. Have Hamilton and Dylan tell everyone the delivery guy got arrested. Tell Cam and Mo to tell the other people the same thing. If college kids hear 'arrested,' they won't make a fuss about anything and shut up real quick."

"I want to get out of IU. Just leave town for a little while."

"Thanksgiving break is in like three weeks. No wait, two weeks. We're done with school Friday the 18th."

"No, I mean like get out of IU now. Like this weekend."

"Where do you want to go?"

"Anywhere."

"Yo, you guys in here?"

"Yeah, come in."

"What's good boys. CC what happened?"

"What's up Cam. Dude, my hookup got arrested."

"That's what Bo said. How do you know?"

"I was there."

"Wait, what?"

"He was driving to pick up and saw a bunch of cops out front of his house," Bo said as Cam sat down in our room.

"And one of the cops was that detective from the *IDS* article."

"Fuck man. He see you?"

"I don't think so. Or, at least he didn't stop me. He was driving behind me for a block or so, and I just passed Eric's house and kept driving."

"Hold up. Eric what? What's his last name?" Cam replied.

"I have no idea. Why, you know him?"

"No I don't. Have you guys not seen the news?"

"What do you mean?"

"Never mind, of course you didn't see it. Neither of you have boys in Indy. Fuck man, Google it. Or check Facebook."

"Bo, toss me my phone."

"I'm already looking it up. Cam, what is it?"

"My boy who lives out on 14th who I deal to sometimes texted me about this dude who got arrested."

"It's already in the news?"

"Bro, it was like three days ago. He didn't get arrested for drugs. He was arrested for murder."

"Murder?"

"Yeah, Cory, I just pulled it up. *Indianapolis Star* from November 4th, so, yeah, that was Friday. But it says the Marion County Sheriff's Office arrested a man Friday in connection with a homicide that police said occurred south of Indianapolis late Thursday night. Eric Thompson, 29, is facing the charge of first-degree murder of an Indianapolis resident, according to the Marion County Sheriff's Office. He is being held at the detention center without bond."

"Dude, that has to be him. I thought he was in his late twenties, so that fits the description. Where is Marion County, though?"

"That's Indy. That's why my boy told me. He lives blocks away from where it happened."

"But Cory, haven't you talked to him since Friday?"

"No. Well, yeah, I mean, I texted him on Wednesday, but he never responded. Then I texted him today saying I was coming over."

"You texted him today?" Bo blurted out.

"Yeah, I know dude. That's why I am freaking out."

"Fuck."

"Shit CC."

"That's why I want to get out of town."

"Fuck it man, I'm in. Where you want to go?" Cam said, holding out his fist for a pound.

"Alright guys, chill out for a second. What I don't get is, Cory, didn't you say a cop pulled up behind you passing Target? So like, cops were just getting to his house today? Why today if he's been arrested since Friday?" Bo asked curiously.

"Well, I don't think that cop was going to Eric's. I think he was pulling over another car, but as for the detective, that's what I can't figure out. Unless it's because I texted him saying I was coming over in five minutes."

"No dude, because then they would have had a blockade and like a trap. Not two cars with the lights on in the driveway and a van parked out front ignoring anyone who drove by," Bo replied.

"Yeah, I guess you're right. It honestly looked like they were searching his house."

"I mean, that is for sure what they were doing. They could have found the drugs in his place."

"Yeah, I don't know. Fuck, dude, murder?"

"I mean, guys, think about it. Guy gets arrested in Indy on Friday for murder. They are going to search his house eventually. Probably search it on Sunday or even today. Then find a bunch of drugs while they were looking for the weapon or whatever they were looking for in the murder case, so call more cops down and the K9 van or whatever that van was."

"Yeah, CC, I got to go with Bo here. And that would explain why yo' detective friend was there. 'Cause they found the shit so called him, 'cause it his case. I think you good, bro."

"Good? My drug dealer got arrested for murder the day after I texted him asking him for drugs. Then the day they found drugs, I texted him saying I was coming over."

"Yeah, I don't know man," Cam mumbled, shaking his head.

"I'm no police officer but just thinking about movies. If they catch the main guy, it's over, right? It's not like in *Scarface*—they caught Tony Montana and then proceeded to arrest his little minions."

"Bo, Scarface didn't get arrested. Motherfucker got popped a million times in the chest," Cam replied laughing, breaking the tension a little.

"You know what I mean. Like in *Blow*, when they caught Johnny Depp, they didn't then look for his gay friends or the flight attendants. They got the source, it was over."

"My lord, just listen to you two. You're comparing this situation to the fucking movies about drug kingpins. How the fuck did I get myself in this situation? And Bo, don't even say 'I told you so.' I know you did, I should have listened."

"Boys, fuck it, let's go somewhere this weekend. Flights to Vegas are like $120. My boys check every week, telling me we should go. Almost went for Labor Day."

"Only $120. Are you kidding?" Bo said, looking at me and waiting for my reaction.

"Swear," Cam said, holding his phone out, insinuating he could show us the text for proof.

"Guys, I don't care about the price. I'll pay. If we get 10 people to go to Vegas, I'll leave tomorrow."

"Yeah, Cory, Cam's right. It's right here. Leave Friday morning return Sunday afternoon. It's $137 on Southwest."

"Leave from Indy?"

"Yeah."

"Tell Kyle, Cutty, Garcia, Joe, Wolf, fuck, tell whoever. Cam, you too. Say I won some promotion thing with Starwood because of our Puerto

Vallarta suite, so got another suite paid for. If people pay $130 for the flight, the rest is on me."

"I mean Cory, Cam, and I have made plenty of money because of you. We'll split it."

"Truth. I can afford a hotel room for two nights."

"I'm booking the flight for tomorrow, though. I'm not even kidding. I'll be there for three days hanging out, waiting for you guys."

"I'll go with you," Bo said, grabbing his laptop.

"Aight, hell yeah! We doing Vegas! I'll hit up my crew today. Get chicks too?"

"Doesn't matter, honestly. They won't come, but why not ask a few. Regardless, it's Vegas. As long as we get like 10 people to at least have a crew to hang with, we'll find some chicks. Bo, what time could you leave tomorrow?"

"Should probably go to class, so any time after 4:30. Well, 6:00, really, to have time to get to the airport."

"There's no Southwest flight that late. There's a 4:15, though."

"Fuck it, that works. Do that one then. I'll go to two of my classes and have a pledge take notes in the third."

"Aight, boys, I'm bouncing. Me and my boys won't leave till Friday. But hey man, CC, it was fun doing work with you. Let's celebrate the good times."

"Hopefully it's a celebration, my man. I'll let you know what hotel we pick. Let me know how many guys you're bringing from Acacia."

"Heard it. I'll get Acacia, you get the bros, and we good."

"Alright, sounds good," I said, giving Cam the slap-and-hug handshake.

"Aight brothas. See you in Vegas."

"See you in Vegas."

# TWENTY-SEVEN

"THEY WANT US TO KEEP DEALING? Who is 'they'? You? Who are you?" I said, pointing to the grey sport-coat guy.

I knew this was the guy Eric was getting the drugs from, but I wanted to hear him say it first before I incriminated myself.

"Well, Cory, let me explain this to you. This thing, you and I, it's all like a game of chess really ...," the guy said, walking toward me.

I looked at Brittney again, but she refused to acknowledge me.

"...Pawns do the dirty work, bishops and rooks make the moves...."

He stopped walking toward me and turned toward Brittney.

"...and then knights hop around from time to time..."

He turned back around and took another two steps, so he was now standing next to me.

"...but essentially the queen is the most important part, and that is, to protect the king. The queen can do everything. Makes the game operate efficiently, effectively, and smoothly. Keeps everything in check. A king can't survive without the queen, but that doesn't mean the game stops when you lose your queen—the game continues. But in order to win the game, well, then the king will need another queen...Enter, the pawn...," the guy said, putting his forearm on my shoulder.

I looked over at Bo, who was terrified, still sitting in the chair next to the two bouncers. A part of me felt guilty bringing him into this. Especially because he had quit dealing close to two months ago, but whatever, I knew he would be fine. This guy was here for me.

"A pawn can turn into a queen once it reaches its potential. Changing a pawn into a queen restores order in the game. Keeps the king alive. You see, Cory, the queen in our little scenario had to make a move for the king, but unfortunately, the queen wasn't careful when he made his move. A sacrifice that eliminated him from the game forever. So now, the king needs a pawn to be the new queen."

I was sick of this guy's dumbass chess metaphor, but his point was clear as day. He had Eric as his bitch, doing everything for him. Without Eric, he was exposed. *But why did he look at Brittney when he said "knight?" And is he saying Eric killed a guy for him?*

"With all due respect, sir, I don't think I could replace Eric. Can't you just find someone else?"

"I've been following you for a while, Cory. Ever since Eric's little festival friend passed you along to him, I have been watching you. You are perfect for this job. According to our lovely mutual friend here, it seems like you have already been doing a good job delegating and spreading the wealth around campus. Sounds like you have stepped into this role already."

*Our lovely mutual friend? What is Brittney, this guy's ear to the ground or something?* I glanced at Bo then back to the guy. I knew what I wanted to say next but didn't know how to say it. I didn't want this guy thinking I was the one who got Eric arrested, but I also wanted him thinking the cops were on me.

"I'll be honest with you, sir, I don't think you want me to keep going. I think the cops are closing in on me too."

"Cory, the police didn't 'close in' on Eric. He wasn't arrested for working with you. From my understanding, the police didn't even find anything at his house. It was a total separate incident that Eric made a mistake doing."

*What? They didn't find the drugs?*

"Well, when I was going to Eric's last week to pick up, I saw cops at his place. And I can't tell if one of the officers saw me or not. And I was texting Eric throughout the week, so that's why I assumed . . ."

"Assumed they were after you? Are you talking about Donald Campbell? He was the one you are worried about, right?"

"Yeah, how do you know him?"

"Don't worry about that. Let me assure you, that man has no clue what is going on."

"Well, sir, I really don't want to keep dealing. I appreciate you thinking of me to replace Eric, but I was planning on stopping at the end of the year anyway."

The guy let out a deep sigh and started to shake his head while he walked away from me toward Bo. Once he got about five feet from Bo, he turned toward me.

"You know, Cory, I think we got off on the wrong foot," the guy said as he opened the right side of his sport coat.

*Is that a fucking gun?*

"This isn't really an offer, but more a solution. One of you will help me. That part is not up for debate. Both of you are juniors, so one of you will help me for another year and a half until I find someone else. The reason I am here is to find out who. So, who will it be?"

It was a gun. No question about it. He had a gun tucked in his waist, just like in the movies. My whole body was frozen. I wasn't nervous, or anxious, or even scared. I was nothing. I was frozen. I had never seen a gun before. Never went hunting, never went to a gun range, nothing. But now there was a drug dealer threatening me with a gun, trying to make me sell drugs for him while my best friend was sitting with two henchmen behind him. I couldn't move, couldn't think, nothing.

"Cory, answer the guy!" Bo yelped from the chair.

"Uh, sorry. Yeah, I will help you. What do I need to do?"

"That's the spirit, gentlemen! Well, Cory, we can talk details when you get to campus. But for the time being, let's just say you will keep doing what you were doing, then add in a couple more drop-offs. That's all it is."

"Drop-offs to who?"

The guy motioned to the two bouncers, and they started following him toward the door.

"Details will come another time. We'll have one drop next week. Then to make things easier for you, we'll do one more after Thanksgiving, then you're done until after winter break. We good?" he said holding his hand out for me to shake it.

*No, we're not good! You are holding me hostage to sell drugs for you!*

"Uh, yeah, do you want me to call you, or . . . ," I asked, shaking his hand.

"I have your number. We'll be in touch," the guy replied as one of the bouncers opened the door and they started walking out.

"Oh, and Cory. I know you have friends in town, let's keep this a little secret. For everyone's sake," he added, patting his waist.

The guy walked out and the door shut behind him. I stood there staring at the door. No one moved. Bo was in the chair in the same clothes as last night, I was shirtless with an ecstasy hangover, and Brittney was in yoga pants and my shirt. I finally turned around and looked over at Bo. He was rubbing his eyes, wiping away tears that were welling.

I turned to glare at Brittney. She was completely dejected.

"Cory, I can explain."

"Oh, you can? Can you explain in chess metaphors, please? Because I would fucking love to hear it!"

"Cory, I'm sorry, that wasn't supposed to happen. I really am sorry, please believe me," she said as she started walking toward me.

I took a step back and she stopped. I stared right into her eyes as she stood there in front of me. Her eyes that had illuminated the whole club the night before were now soulless. She was completely distraught. I was furious, but for some reason I felt bad for her. Clearly there was more to the story, but I didn't want to hear it.

"Believe you? You're working with the guy! Why the fuck would I believe you?"

"I don't work with him! Well, not technically, I mean, not in this way. I work at his bar in Indianapolis, that's it."

"Then why the fuck are you even here? What was supposed to happen?"

"Dante wanted me to talk to you and set up a meeting with you two because I was the only one he knew you had met before. Clearly he didn't trust that I would be able to talk to you, so he flew here himself."

"How the fuck did he know we would be in Vegas?" Bo asked as he got off the chair.

"Well, I went over to the ATO house on Wednesday to talk to you and set up the meeting, but you weren't home, and one of the guys there said you were going to Vegas this weekend. So Dante flew me out here to talk to you."

"But like, why the fuck would he fly out a bartender from his bar to do this for him? Like why you?"

"I told you, because I was the only other person besides Eric you had met before."

"Am I missing something?" Bo shouted, quickly morphing from afraid to pissed off. "So he flew a random bartender out to Vegas to talk to a guy about something she has no idea about? And we're supposed to believe that?"

"Random bartender? Something I have no idea about?" Brittney said, looking toward me for backup.

"Why the fuck are you looking at *me*?" I replied.

I looked at Bo and back at Brittney.

"Wait, you have no idea, do you? Eric never told you? I'm his little sister. I thought you knew this whole time. So I'm not a random bartender—I know all about you, Cory, and your relationship with E the past year or so. . ."

*What?*

". . . And I have known Dante my entire life, so has Eric. Dante has been like an older brother to us our whole lives. When our parents died, Dante was a family friend in the neighborhood and took us under his wing. Eric started working for him years and years ago," Brittney said, starting to tear up.

I was speechless. I was so frightened from what had just happened with this Dante guy and so angry at Brittney for lying to me that it didn't all click right away, but then I realized the moment and the weight of the situation. *Her brother was arrested for murder a week ago!*

Brittney's crying got progressively harder until she finally broke down. She dropped to her knees and started sobbing. I made eye contact with Bo, and he looked the way I felt: flustered.

"Dante used to be so nice, so nice!" she cried out as she tried to force away her tears.

"He helped us through some tough times when I was growing up. He paid for everything my whole life, and for that, Eric was always too loyal to him. I fucking kept telling him!"

She stopped talking and went silent. This wasn't an act; she was truly miserable. Those eyes weren't lying. I couldn't relate to the feeling at all. I just stood there with a blank face not knowing what to think. I mean, I appreciate and love my parents, but they chose to have me, so kind of had to pay for my shit. I couldn't imagine losing them and having to rely on someone else in order to survive. She was in debt to this guy. And Eric was too.

She lifted her head up as I took a few steps closer.

"Cory, I really am sorry. When Eric was arrested, I didn't know what to do. I didn't know who to turn to. Dante was the only one who was close to us that could help. I knew he could help. When he asked me to talk to you I first said no, but then when I heard you were in Vegas, it was like perfect for me. I wanted to leave Indiana, I'm guessing just like you did. I wanted to get away from it all. Seeing my brother being talked about on the news, in the newspapers, I wanted to run and hide, Cory. I swear to God I was going to tell you all of this this morning."

She gazed into my eyes defeated as I leaned down and helped her stand up.

"I'm sorry about your brother, I really am."

We stood there for a second not talking. It wasn't an awkward silence; it was a needed silence. We all just stood there. Everyone needed a little time to soak in what had happened. When I came to Vegas it was to get away from cops and drug dealing forever. Wipe the slate clean and come back as a new man who had made a lot of money. A shit ton of money, actually.

I rubbed my face in my hands a couple times as I looked around and digested everything. I was in a suite in Vegas with 15-foot ceilings and a glass spiral staircase going up to a loft, there was a sister in front of me sobbing because her brother went away for murder, and her next-closest father figure threatened me with a gun to deal drugs for him. Oh, and my temples were pulsing from doing molly for the first time.

I made eye contact with Bo. I took a deep breath and for some reason, everything started to feel clearer. Not in the everything-is-OK way but more in the I-understand-the-situation-now way. After the initial confusion and shock, it was all starting to play out in my head.

*At the end of the day, taking away the kidnapping of Bo and the gun, all I have to do is drug deal like I was before. Sure I'll have to add to the order, but when has that ever been an issue? That was it. I'm not going to be doing anything else for this guy. Just do what I was doing before Vegas and be more conscious about the police . . . Jesus Christ, Cory, listen to yourself!*

It was depressing how I immediately started to internally justify the situation as a nonissue. I was trying to brainwash myself, but it wasn't going to work. I was horrified and had a terrible feeling about it all.

"So now what do we do?" Bo asked, breaking the silence.

"Brittney?" I replied.

"Do what Dante says. No matter what. He's really smart. I know he's a complete dick, and like, a bad guy, but if you do what he says, you'll be fine. And, Cory, whatever you do, don't piss him off or go behind his back. You will not be safe."

I didn't have a response. I wanted to bring up Eric because if he'd followed Dante, then clearly that negated her whole "you'll be fine" point, but this wasn't the right time. And really, it didn't even matter because I wasn't going to go behind this guy's back—I couldn't. I had no power, no control, and no authority. This guy controlled Eric, controlled Brittney, and now controlled me.

# TWENTY-EIGHT

BLOOMINGTON FELT EERIE AFTER VEGAS. Nothing about it had changed, but knowing what was to come was unnerving. I got a call from some guy telling me to meet at a bar in Indianapolis Tuesday night to talk with Dante about the details. Apart from Bo, I wasn't going to tell anyone else about this new little dilemma. I left town in such a hurry that I didn't even have time to tell the houses I was quitting. So to everyone else, I missed one delivery 'cause I went to Vegas, but it was going to be business as usual going forward.

After class on Tuesday, I went to my room to change clothes before heading up to Indy. I really wanted someone to talk to about this, but Bo was at class, so couldn't. Before I left, I reached into my safe and grabbed a stack of cash. About three or four grand worth. I didn't have a reason why; I just thought having money on me could help me in any situation I got in. I didn't have the balls to do anything drastic if shit hit the fan, so figured I could pay someone off if I had to.

I got into my car and started to drive. I still couldn't shake what had happened in Vegas. It wasn't settling in—something wasn't clicking for me. *If Brittney assumed I knew Eric was her brother, wouldn't she think I would have said something?* My mind was questioning if there was anything I could have done to avoid this situation I was in: driving to a bar owned by a drug dealer in order to supply all of Indiana University with drugs for the remainder of my time in college. I didn't even know if Dante would let me stop when I graduated. I tried to avoid negative thoughts and rationalize it as a homecoming order every week or something, but the harder I tried, the more anxiety I felt. Pushing the feelings down wasn't going to work this time.

As I pulled up to the address, there was nothing there. There were a couple empty buildings and a parking garage on the street. I tried replaying what the guy said to me, but I couldn't remember if he'd said, "I'll see you when you get there" or "Call me when you get there." *Did I plug the address in wrong? Fuck!* I started to panic. I didn't have his number so was a sitting duck waiting for more instructions.

"Park your car," some guy yelled out from a car parked on the opposite side of the street.

I turned and saw one of Dante's henchmen from Vegas. He was a black dude, about 6'4", who must have been close to 275 pounds. You could tell he used to be muscular or at least in shape, but he had this gut now. The sight of this guy was surprisingly reassuring. I parked the car on the street and the guy signaled to get in his black Suburban.

"First rule, always park here. We'll explain more, but you never drive straight to the bar. Got it?"

"Got it," I said as I got in and shut the door.

He drove us another four blocks and pulled into a parking lot on the right of the bar and then drove around back to a smaller parking area behind the bar. It was about six o'clock, and there were only a handful of cars in the lot. We walked around the bar to the front. I couldn't find the name of the place anywhere—there wasn't a single sign out front—but it was a relatively big two-story bar. We walked in the front door and through the second door inside. The place was empty. Even the bar stools were on the countertop. The place was a new-age sports bar. One of those bars you could tell was more a club scene at night, but there were still big TVs on the wall behind the bar. There was a huge circle bar in the middle with half booths on the right wall and standing tables on the left. There were lofted walkways overhead, sharing the same ceiling as the first floor. It was actually a cool-looking bar.

We kept walking past the circle bar toward the back. The back had another bar in the right corner, a kitchen in the left corner, and a hallway splitting the two. I followed the guy up the back stairs as he turned right down a hallway. We went down about four steps, down the hallway, and eventually turned into the bathroom. The guy turned around as he opened the bathroom door.

"If you ever come here again, you wait downstairs until someone tells you to come up into this bathroom," he said as we walked in the door.

"There will be a guy working in the bathroom. He'll know you're coming, but to double-check, walk straight up to him and say, 'Hey Tim, we're out of soap downstairs.'"

I was staring dumbfounded.

"The guy will open the door for you. Make sure you walk all the way in the door and shut it behind you before you . . ."

As he was talking, he walked into the utility closet. The closet was just a normal walk-in closet with a few plungers on the right wall, toilet paper and paper towel rolls on a cabinet along the back wall, a couple bottles of soap on the left cabinet wall. The guy reached to his left to move a couple bottles of soap and pushed a black button on the wall. After he hit the button, you could see the toilet paper on the back wall shake. The guy took a step forward and pushed the cabinet, and the wall moved open like a door.

"Pretty easy. 'Hey Tim, we're out of soap downstairs.' Walk in, shut the door behind you, press the button, push the back door. Make sure you shut the door when you walk through."

*We have very different definitions of "easy" when it comes to walking in a room.*

We both walked through the hidden door and up the four or so stairs into the secret room. The room was small with only about seven-foot ceilings or so. There was a bar on the right, a circular table on the left, and a desk straight ahead. Dante was sitting at the desk with the bald henchman sitting at the circle table having a drink.

"Cory. Welcome, how was the drive?"

"Uh, it was alright."

"Good good," he said, standing up from his chair.

"Please take a seat. We won't normally do business here, but thought it would be good to show you the place. Need a drink?"

"No I'm alright," I said as I took a seat at the round table.

There were chairs in front of the desk Dante was standing behind, but I wasn't in the principal's office so didn't want to sit on the opposite side of his desk. Really, I just felt awkward so wanted to sit as far away from him as possible.

"Oh, bullshit—Terry, get him a drink."

*Sure bro, your world, I'm just living in it.*

Terry was the other henchman from Vegas. He was also big, but not as muscular as the other dude. About 6'2", 190 pounds, and a huge bald head.

"Alright, I won't keep you here long. But before we get started . . . ," Dante said, signaling the guy who walked me in.

The big black dude came over and motioned for me to stand up. I stood up and he lifted my arms and patted me down. The guy gave Dante a little head nod then walked toward the bar on the right.

"Can never be too safe, right?"

*Fuck you.*

"So here is the deal, Cory. Everything should stay relatively the same as it was before we met; there will be a couple of changes. Number one, no more weekly deliveries. I don't know how you got away with that or how you convinced Eric into doing that nonsense, but that's just irresponsible and unnecessary. The riskiest part is the drop itself. Having the material at your house or apartment is much safer than continuously completing a drop."

The Terry guy handed me a glass with some brown liquor and one big ice cube in the cup.

"Thanks," I said as I grabbed the drink.

"The drops will be closer to once a month, so you'll have a surplus at your house in case any one of your pals needs more. You don't have to ask us for more; you'll have it already. Number two, after this, my guys will show you where the drop spot will be. It will be closer to Bloomington to make it easier on you, but you'll still have to drive about 15 minutes or so."

The difference in professionalism between Dante and Eric was noticeable, let alone Hippy Mike.

"OK, so I have a couple questions. Do I give you my order each month, or will it be a set amount?"

"We'll start with a set amount. I'll give you what I was giving Eric. Should suffice. If you ever need more, we'll give you a number to call or instructions."

"OK, what will that set amount be, because I was . . ."

"Yes, Cory, I know how much you were getting from Eric, it was impressive. And now without doing weekly it will be four times that much. Plus there will be a couple more people Terry will put you in touch with."

"Who are the other people? Like, students at IU?"

"Let me bring you in on a few things, Cory. Indiana University, or Bloomington in general, brings in anywhere from $2 to $2.5 million a year in drugs. I am responsible for about 80 percent of that. College campuses are cash cows. Got a few of them around here. Thirty-some thousand kids looking to party, the population of students always changing, but the ages staying the same. But what really makes it work are the connections in college campuses. Look at you, for an example—you live under the same roof with what, 50 or 75 other friends? Try being 30 years old and finding 75 guys, period, let alone friends. When you get older, that many friends simply do not exist. The little network you have created is responsible for around half of what I supply to Bloomington. Now, that is not to say you personally will be making that amount, but all together, your relationships are responsible for a quite a bit."

*I'm responsible for making this fucker like a million fucking dollars a year?*

"So, to answer your question. Yes, the other people will be a combination of students and other connections I know. With Eric gone, you'll be helping me finish that other half of the relationships."

*I'm doubling my orders? And they are now monthly!*

"Uh, Dante . . ."

*Wait, he knows I know his name, right?*

"It's Dante, right?"

Dante let out a laugh.

"Brittney explained to you, I see. Yes, go on."

"Uh, yeah, well, I, um, never mind. Yeah, that works."

I didn't know what to say. He was so intimidating. I took a sip of the drink and the brown liquor burned slowly down my throat. Dante stood up and walked toward the round table I was sitting at.

"When we do the first drop, there's no need to bring any money. We'll supply the material and tell you where to meet the others, then one of my guys will pick up the money at the next drop and leave you a cut of it. Got it?"

I wanted to ask what the cut was, but it was useless. My anxiety was making me so uncomfortable I wanted to leave the bar as fast as fucking possible. This guy had his system and was going to run it the way he wanted to. I had no control or buying power. He was going to give me what he wanted and I had to accept it. He was using me for my network.

"Cory?" he said, holding out his hand.

*Shit, how long has his hand been out?*

"Oh, sorry, yeah, sounds good. Got it. These guys will show me where the drop is and who to give half of it to. Then the rest is just mine for a month," I responded as I shook his hand.

"Exactly. Not too hard, right?"

*Fuck. You.*

"Alright," Dante said, giving Bald Terry a head nod.

"My guys are going to drive with you to the drop spot and give you the names and numbers of the other people. Do you have any questions?"

"No, I don't think so," I answered as I stood up.

"Great then," Dante said, squeezing my shoulder.

"If you ever hear anything from the police or that detective you seem so fond of, you tell us right away, OK?"

"OK."

"This is a great opening for you, Cory. You will make more money than you ever could have imagined. Let's consider this a signing bonus," he said, putting a wrapped stack of money on the table.

I had put about three grand in the car before I left, but this stack was like three times that size. It was a literal brick. *This must be $10,000!* I was so jumpy at this point, I just stared at Dante, nodded my head and forced a fake smirk, then followed Bald Terry and the big black dude. They walked the opposite way from the bathroom to a door at the back corner. Terry opened the door, and I followed the other guy down the black metal staircase. The back stairwell led to a tiny concrete area with a door on either side. One of them clearly led to the kitchen, but the other door was just a blank black door.

"This way," Terry said as he opened the black door.

We walked outside and the door shut loudly behind us. I turned around at the noise and saw there was no handle from the outside. *These guys have a legit secret room.*

The two guys drove me back to my car, and I followed them onto 465 then to 37 and toward IU. About five minutes after we passed Martinsville, I got a call on my cell phone from an unknown number.

"Get in the left lane. Turning left in about a mile. Follow us."

The black Chevy Suburban pulled off the highway at a side street—not an exit ramp, but a side street that looked like it led to a farmhouse. We drove for another five minutes down the long road, which turned into a winding road that led into the woods. There were no cross streets, no houses—the street seemed to just go deeper into a forest. I pulled out my phone to see where we were. Morgan-Monroe State Forest, 24 minutes from ATO. *Well, I guess it's only once a month.*

The Suburban followed the road around a couple minutes and turned into a mini-driveway on the right. It was a driveway to nothing: 20 feet of extra road that led directly into more trees and hills. They parked the car and got out, so I followed.

"So this is where the drops will be. It may seem confusing, but coming from Bloomington you turn right on 37 and continue onto Forest Road, and it will lead you right here."

"Why do you guys do it here?"

Both the guys looked at each other and then back at me. Terry nodded his bald head up into the trees. I followed his eyes up toward the trees. It took me a second, but then I saw what he was referencing: a camera. There was a camera in the tree pointing right down on us.

"Alright, so here is a new cell phone for you. It's a burner phone that has the numbers you need in it. Numbers 1 to 5. They are who you have to call to set up your other deals. We already called them and told them you would be calling them later this week, so you are good there. Just call them and plan to meet wherever. I don't give a fuck where you do it. You can come here if you want, but it's not needed. Do what you have been doing with your normal drops."

"And if they don't answer, or like something happens, do I call you?"

"There are three more numbers saved. B, T, and L. T is me, Terry."

"L is me, Lamar. And then the third you already met, E's little sister, Brittney. She's down in Bloomington a lot so will help from time to time."

*I knew she was a part of this fucking crew!*

"Soo, call any of the three?"

"Call me," Terry stated firmly.

"OK," I replied, looking around.

I didn't really know what to do now. The place was in a legit jungle. There was nothing around.

"Alright, well I think I got it. When will we do the first drop?"

Terry gave out a little chuckle.

"This is the first drop, hotshot," Lamar said as he opened the trunk of their Suburban.

Both of them grabbed the two big duffel bags I always saw at Eric's and started walking to my car.

"Pop the trunk."

*Oh fuck, we're doing this now?* I opened the trunk of my Cherokee, and they loaded the bags.

"Don't open the bags until you get to your place. And as for the other five people you're dropping off to, I'll text that phone the details so you can remember, but then I want you to delete that text immediately after the drop, alright?"

"OK. How much is here though. Like overall? Or I guess, how much will be left over for me."

Lamar looked at Terry for clarification. Terry shut my trunk and started to walk toward his car.

"Dante said half. Delete the text when you get it, and don't open the bags until you are in your room. OK?" Terry answered forcefully, like he was getting annoyed now.

"OK," I whimpered timidly.

They got into their car and I got back into mine. I pulled out onto the main street and kept backing up to let the other guys go out first. The Suburban followed my queue and pulled out. Everything seemed so professional, yet there wasn't much communication back and forth. I mean, Hippy Mike and I talked longer than this our first time. These guys pretty much handed me two duffel bags of drugs, I gave them no money, they told me to sell to people I don't know, then drove away. *Is Dante watching this whole thing on camera?* Dante knew I didn't have the balls to cross him, so I guess the less they told me, the better.

The whole Brittney thing still stuck with me. *Down in Bloomington so helps from time to time? What does she do?*

The burner phone let out an obnoxiously loud *ting* noise, so I reached into my pocket. It was weird hearing any other phone that wasn't an iPhone or a Droid. It was your basic flip phone.

Message from T: 10:03 p.m.: #1 – 3 pounds = $4k . . . #2 – 1 pound and half key = $14k . . . #3 – key = $20k . . . #4 –pills = $5k . . . #5 – 3 pounds and half key = $16k . . . Rest you.

*Holy fuck! That's what, three, four, seven, seven pounds, one and a half, no, two kilos, and 5K of pills? And that's* half *of it?*

I understood I was pretty much multiplying my usual order by four since it was monthly now and then doubling that to do the other half, but I hadn't really put it all together yet. I pulled onto 37 south to head to Bloomington. My legs were shaking, heart was fluttering, and hands started to grip the wheel harder as I did the math in my head.

*I am driving with 14 pounds of weed, 4 kilos of cocaine, and 1,000 pills of something . . .*

# TWENTY-NINE

**I TEXTED THE FIVE NUMBERS SAYING I WAS GOING TO DRIVE TO THEM AND DELIVER THEIR SHIT.** I felt more comfortable driving to them rather than meeting them somewhere or having them come to ATO. Had more control that way. All five drops went surprisingly smoothly; they all seemed like normal students. One of the guys was awkwardly older, but could have been a grad student. I didn't care at this point. My guess was some of the drugs were actually going to townies or high school kids. The fact I might have sold coke to high school students was sickening, but I tried not to think about it. There was nothing I could do but continue to stay ignorant to everything. None of the other guys seemed to know what had happened to Eric; they just carried on with me as their guy the way I carried on when Eric became mine.

Cam, Mo, Hamilton, and Dylan didn't want to switch to monthly deals. They all said they liked not having it on them all the time. I didn't want to tell them I had a new guy and that things had changed, so I broke out the remainder into four weekly baggies and dropped off the normal amounts to them and held on to the rest. Cam asked a bunch of questions about the cops and the murder trial, but I just told him I went back to the hippy to get everything. He didn't bat an eye and kept on dealing through the sophomores just like I was. I didn't mind holding on to everything after all. Nothing smelled because it was all in vacuum-sealed bags, but the sheer volume of drugs and the random duffel bags were annoying. It took up so much damn room that I left the bags in my car and hid the rest under Bo's bed.

Bo and I hadn't really talked about anything yet. Honestly, I didn't think we ever would. I would make eye contact with him and take a deep breath, insinuating it was going on, and he would nod his head. I think I had become so immune to dealing with drug dealers that Vegas hadn't fucked with me as much as it did with Bo. He was really shaken up. I guess he had never technically met any of the drug dealers before, so it was probably terrifying for him. I mean, it was terrifying, but it seemed like Bo was a legit changed man after it happened. It really got to him. It also may have been because I wasn't kidnapped. *Shit, how was he kidnapped?*

Not doing any of the deliveries or even the gram-level dealing was still refreshing, but knowing the amount of drugs that was under Bo's bed kept me on edge. The two weeks before Thanksgiving came and went. School was an afterthought now. Some of my friends were interviewing for summer internships, but I had no more willpower to do that. It wasn't because I didn't need the money, that wasn't even it. I knew I was more or less taken in terms of employment for the next year and a half, and that probably included summer, so it was pointless.

After Thanksgiving break, a week went by without another phone call. I remembered Dante saying I was going to do one more drop after Thanksgiving break, so I knew it was coming. I kept up with the whole Eric saga online. Dante was right; there wasn't a single mention of drugs anywhere, but it didn't look good for Eric. The *Indianapolis Star* was reporting that there was surveillance footage of Eric putting something that looked like a body into his trunk at some abandoned lot in the south side of Indy. I didn't know all of the details, but a video of a body in a trunk? Pretty self-explanatory. Which would explain why the police were searching his house too. Probably doing forensics on the car. But I still couldn't figure out why Campbell was one of the cops there.

I got the call on Monday, December 5, saying the drop would be the next night at 10 o'clock. I didn't want to hold on to everything overnight like I did the first night, so I texted the Numbers 1 to 5 saying I would drop off the drugs around 11. I was going to keep calling them Numbers 1 to 5 because I didn't want to know their names. I grabbed all the money I'd received from everyone and put it in one of the duffel bags in the trunk. I counted and triple-counted the money what seemed like 15 times: 4K from Number 1, 14K from Number 2, 20K from Number 3, 5K from Number 4, 16K from Number 5, then about $53,000 from my end. A total of $112,000. *What am I doing?* I still had some leftover bud and a shit ton of capsules, too.

I drove to the drop, but it wasn't as easy as they made it seem. I had to plug it into my Google maps, and it probably took 25 minutes to get there. The Suburban was already in the spot, parked and ready. I got out and handed them the duffel bag with all the money and then the other empty one. Terry and Lamar both came again, but only Lamar got out of the van.

"All here?"

"It's all there. I probably have about 200 pills and a QP left over, though, so it'll be short about . . . well like two grand and may. . ."

"We'll count it. Smaller order this time, anyway. Winter break. T will text you again," Lamar said as he walked back to the Suburban.

"Hey, so do I get a cut, or was I supposed to take some from that bag?"

"It's in the new bag, hotshot. You'll get the text from T. Make the other drops, the rest is yours."

I didn't understand why they were being so short and secretive, but it made me so much more uncomfortable and nervous. Their downplaying the situation was actually magnifying it for me. I was so in my own head. Then again, it was 112,000 fucking dollars, so maybe not talking was best.

I looked up at the camera before looking around the woods. Past the street there was a pretty substantial drop-off, almost like a cliff down a hill into what was either a creek or more trees; it was too dark to tell. I got in the car and pulled out, letting the other car go out first. I drove back to campus and went straight to each of the five dude's places and dropped off the orders. Everyone's orders were almost cut in half, or cut by about a third or so, besides Number 5. His order stayed the same, which was strange because that was the awkwardly older-looking guy, but he must have been the one dealing to townies and high school kids, since winter break didn't matter to them.

I got back to ATO and could hear yelling coming from the basement. It was the pledges getting hazed for something. I walked straight to the stairs and up into my room. I opened the door and saw Bo, Kyle, and Joe smoking and watching TV.

"The fuck, you playing hockey or something?" Joe said at the two duffel bags I was carrying.

"No, just got them. It's, uh, to pack up my shit for winter break. I didn't bring a suitcase home, so needed to get a couple bags," I explained, scrabbling to figure out what to say.

I glanced over at Bo, but he just sat there stoic. He saw right through the lie. The face he was making was that of concern. He looked sincerely worried for me. I think all three of them saw through the lie, but none of them knew what was really happening besides Bo.

I went into the sleeper and put one of the duffel bags under Bo's bed and opened the other one. There was a stuffed manila envelope in it. I opened the envelope and quickly shut it again. I looked behind me to make sure no one was walking in and reopened the envelope. There were five of those stacks of hundreds, but this time, they were wrapped in a blue label. I had counted the other brick, so I already knew how much was in each. *This is $50,000!* I had made $10,000 for introducing myself to Dante, then $50,000 for one drop. I get that it was monthly now, but still, that was double the homecoming money where I made $27,000, and with that I was delivering, selling grams, finding new people to sell to, etc. This time I was simply replacing Eric on a normal non-IU party month. I was now every college student's drug dealer's drug dealer's drug dealer. It was a dark, dark feeling. The word unbelievable gets overused, but the feeling of seeing $50,000 of cash and knowing it was yours was truly something I could not believe. I thought being on top of the food chain would be better, more organized and simpler, but that organization was what made it such a dark feeling. It felt so nonchalant, dropping these bags off to other people, that the actuality of the situation was lost. *I might be giving cocaine to fucking high school kids!*

The next day I gave Cam, Mo, and Hamilton their bags and said I had extras if they needed any before winter break. Finals week went by and only Dylan's buddies wanted more. After my last final, I hid the other bags in my room and locked up the sleeper and left town. A lot of my friends were staying the weekend to party before heading home Sunday or Monday, but I wanted to leave ASAP. I was not in a good place mentally. I needed to leave more than anything. Honestly, all I wanted was to hang with my family. Family and friends. I needed relaxation and to feel safe again.

At home I went over to Ricky's to hang out in his backyard and grab a couple beers. As much as I tried to relax and enjoy myself, the inevitable return to school wouldn't leave my mind. It was the same shit in Vegas. It felt amazing to party and gamble, but in the back of my mind, there was still anxiety, knowing what was waiting for me at IU. As I talked to Ricky and Steve about random sports topics, I couldn't escape it. I could tell I was being awkward in conversations. It's like that feeling when you notice someone with shit in their teeth, you can listen to what they say and maybe have a mini-conversation with them, but the conversation will never feel right and normal until you say something. That was me. Just never felt right.

"Sports, sports, sports," a girl said from behind me.

I didn't even need to turn around to know who had walked in. It was Em's best friend, and Em and she were inseparable. *Em has to be here.* I looked around to see who could have invited them, but all the guys were standing up to give the group of girls a hug hello. I saw Em walk in through the screen door. I could tell she was avoiding eye contact. She gave a hug to Ricky while she was facing me, but wouldn't move her eyes up to look at me.

Seeing her face surprised me. I mean, she was beautiful and always was beautiful, but seeing her gave me a calming feeling. Like a peaceful feeling, really. It was bizarre.

"Hey Cory," Em said, giving me a hug.

"Hey Em, how have you been?"

She looked up at me with her eyebrows raised, implying, "Oh, now you want to talk?" Oblivious, my friends started to walk toward the bonfire, which left Em and I as the last ones standing on the patio. She turned toward her friends then back at me, almost like she was settling in to talk for a little.

"Uh, good. Real good. And yourself?"

"Yeah, good. I don't know, just pretty stressed at school."

"Yeah, I've heard."

*Heard what?*

"What do you mean?"

"Vegas is a really stressful place. Must be tough."

"No, it wasn't really like a Vegas trip. Well, I mean it kinda was, but . . . well, it's a long story."

"I bet it is."

I could see the disdain in Em's eyes. We had broken up mutually, and I had moved on like it was nothing, but for some reason, the look in her eyes crushed me. I hadn't even thought about her in months, not even a little bit, but the disgust she had for me hit me right in the heart. I didn't know what to say to her. I didn't want to get her involved with my state of affairs; she didn't deserve to get caught up in that bullshit. She was too nice and innocent, but another part of me wanted to tell her everything. To explain to her and show her I wasn't a bad person, and that Vegas wasn't really just a guy's trip, but I was in real danger. *I am in real danger! But what can she even do about it?*

"Are you OK?" she asked, leaning closer to me.

"What? Yeah, why?" I said, caught off guard.

"I don't know, you don't seem right."

"What do you mean?"

"I mean, don't take this the wrong way, but it doesn't look like you've slept in weeks. You have huge bags under your eyes."

*Don't say it, Cory. Don't say anything!*

"You look great too, Em," I replied, faking a smile.

"I didn't mean it in a mean way. I'm sorry."

"No, I was joking—well, not about the you-looking-good part, I mean . . ."

Em cracked a smile as I fumbled my words.

"How awkward could this get? Let's start this one over," I said, sticking out my hand. "Hi Emily, good to see you."

"Shaking a girl's hand? Guess you have changed. But good to see you too," Em said, shaking my hand.

We both walked down the stairs to the bonfire. It was cold but not terribly cold. Probably about mid-forties. We all sat around the bonfire talking about school and old stories from high school. Every once in a while I could feel myself looking Em's way. The more we drank and talked about old stories, the more comfortable I felt. I couldn't get a grip on it, but it was some sort of reassuring feeling that didn't exist when I was with the guys. Em made me feel this way. She made me feel ordinary, and that was exactly what I needed.

People started to leave Ricky's relatively early. We all wanted to see each other and hang out briefly, but ultimately winter break was still more a detox period.

"Anyone need a ride?" Em announced to a few of us guys.

I made eye contact with Steve. We had been friends forever, so he knew exactly what I was thinking.

"No, Emily, I'm good thanks," he replied.

"Cory?" Em responded firmly.

You could tell she purposely said my name firmly, as if to prove there was nothing going on between us. Like she was being the better person for asking and not making a big deal of it. But I didn't care what she was implying, I wanted to talk to her more. I wanted the comfort and wanted to lose the anxiety for a little longer.

"If you don't mind, yeah, that would be great." I replied, standing up.

We walked to her car, which was parked out front.

"You couldn't walk home, huh?"

"Hey, you offered."

"Using me like always. What else is new?" she said, half kidding.

"I will walk if you want, I really will. I thought we could talk more."

"Talk more? About what, Cory?"

"I don't know."

"What is wrong with you? You don't talk to me for months, didn't see you over summer break, didn't see you over Thanksgiving break, nothing, and now you want to talk more?"

"I don't know what to tell you. I haven't been myself recently."

"I know, and that's why I asked what was wrong. You look and seem hollow."

*Hollow? Jesus, do I look that bad?*

"There's a lot of stuff going on, I don't know . . ."

"Is everything OK?" Em said, cutting me off.

"Yeah, I mean I think so."

"Cory, we dated for almost a year and a half, I can tell when you are lying. If you don't want to tell me, then that's fine, you don't have to tell me. It's none of my business anymore, but don't say you want to talk and then don't."

*Seriously, Cory, don't say anything! She deserves better than getting involved in this. It will only hurt her.*

"I do want to talk, Em, that's the thing. I want to talk, I just don't know what to say. I don't know, it's hard to explain. I'm not doing too hot these days."

"I don't know what that means, but I'm sorry. I'm always here if you want to talk, Cor. I hope you know that."

We both sat in the car not saying anything. There was nothing more I could say. I wasn't going to pretend like all my troubles were gone and have a fake conversation with her. I had lied to her for too long. Sitting in the car with her made me feel even shittier about my situation than I already felt. It wasn't her fault, though; her innocence was captivating. Her presence alone made you want to be a better person because she was naturally kind and compassionate. Her sincerity was contagious. I never knew how much I missed that feeling. The feeling of being loved, the feeling of being around someone who made you comfortable, the feeling of being with someone so down-to-earth and genuine that you didn't ever have to think about what to say and when to say it. That was it, genuine. Nothing fake about it—good or bad, you knew she was going to be herself. No need to lie, no need to cover anything up, no anxiety, just 100 percent genuine.

That feeling was gone now, and there was nothing I could do about it. Em had been right all along. I had surrounded myself with such horrible influences that I not only had become immune to them, but also had become fully submerged in them. And because of that, Dante now controlled me. Whether I liked it or not, it was true. And as long as I was working with him, I could never even entertain the thought of being with Em or someone like her. I wasn't going to bring anyone else into my situation. I got into it myself, and wasn't going to drag anyone down with me. The college train had swept me off my feet, and I had missed the last stop to get off— the last opportunity to get off the train and get back to some sort of normality. But instead, I stayed on and was now locked in. Bo got out, but I was too selfish. I wanted more, knew I could have more, and so I went for it, and it all backfired. I had no more control over my life again. I was a puppet, and it was depressing. *I really am depressed.*

I got out of the car and walked toward my house. I turned around to wave good-bye, but Em had already started to pull away. I never knew that Em was the stability I coveted, but she was. I could feel it. Almost like I was looking at a former life. The hollowness she saw in my eyes—she was the reason for it. I wanted that life back, but could never have it again. *I ruined it. I ruined my life.*

# THIRTY

I HAD ALWAYS QUESTIONED PEOPLE WHO SAID THEY WERE DEPRESSED. Like is it an actual illness, or is it just people who are super super bummed out about something? I never really had sympathy for people who were depressed because I thought life was too short to be that sad about something. But driving back to school was the first time I really understood it. It wasn't necessarily sadness, that wasn't the right word. It was more this deeply rooted issue that no matter what happened, the issue was never going away. It was not having any hope. It was a general gloom view on life.

Everything about returning to school seemed miserable. I didn't want to go to class, I didn't want to go out and party, and I sure as hell didn't want to go buy four kilos of cocaine. But above all, I didn't want to get caught, and that's what kept me going. That's why my feeling wasn't a feeling of sadness or true depression; it was misery mixed with fear. A fear of ending my life at age 21. Not only ruining my life but also ruining the lives of my family. But as dark a place as I was mentally, whether it was possibly supplying high school kids or contributing to Lizzy Madison's death, I still couldn't give up. I had to keep some sort of hope in order to make it out of college.

It sounds terrible, but there is no other way to say it: I knew I was good at dealing. I really was. I could read people well and had enough self-awareness in order to make it in the criminal world. I knew I just had to gut it out for another year, keep my ear to the ground, and position myself the way I always had, and at the end of senior year, walk away with more money than I ever could have imagined. There was no other option.

Everything was business as usual. I did a drop the first Wednesday I got back. Since I got paid for the previous drop, there was another manila envelope, this time with 20 grand inside. The new drop was for 16 pounds, 5 kilos, 750 pills, and this small pink bag of coke I had to give the awkwardly older guy. Everything felt routine but never felt informal. Clearly Lamar and Terry were told to make it a point to keep me on my toes. It was all business to them, which I could at least respect. The next drop was exactly four weeks later. I had made 35 grand from the previous drop and picked up another 17 pounds, 5 kilos, and 1,000 pills. The percentages of how much money I was making per drop weren't adding up. The first one I didn't have to pay for but still made roughly 50 percent of the revenue. The next two I made roughly 30 percent of the revenue. So following that pattern, I was expecting another 40 grand from the drop I had just picked up. That was 145 grand in four months, plus the 10-grand handshake to start, so $155,000 profit since Vegas.

Another four weeks went by without a call. That was the only positive thing about this new gig; going four weeks without having to deliver anything. Well, not the only positive. At the end of the day, I was still making $20,000 to $50,000 a month. I had racked up more money in the first four months of my new gig than my dad or mom made a year. It was honestly crazy to see the amount of drugs IU soaked up. Sixteen pounds of pot was a pain in the ass because it took up two full duffel bags and weighed, well, 16 pounds. But really, it was a plant. It was weed. It was harmless. It could be going to a professor for all I knew, so whatever. But five kilos of cocaine! That's 5,000 grams of coke! Gone! In four weeks! Granted, there were 40,000 students at the school, plus faculty, bartenders, staff, high school students, townies, parents, businessmen, etc., but regardless, that was a preposterous amount of drugs.

The next drop was scheduled for Tuesday, March 6. On Monday we had another one of those risk manager meetings. It was the second of the year, but the first one for all intents and purposes was a waste of time. The meeting was in Beta's basement, so I drove over there myself. When I pulled into the parking lot, I saw Campbell's car. It was the first time I'd seen it since the drive-by at Eric's. I hadn't seen any other person in town drive that car but him. The moment I saw it, I was 100 percent positive it was the same car.

I walked into the basement and sat next to my risk manager buddies in Acacia and Pi Kapps toward the middle of the room. I looked around but couldn't see Campbell anywhere. The meeting started, and there was nothing major on the agenda. IFC talked about new freshman sorority girls, some new rule about outdoor speakers, and something about four-way pairs with another frat and two sororities. The whole time they talked, my eyes kept surveying the room for Campbell. *Where is he?* After about 20 minutes of IFC talking to us about nonsense, the risk manager of Beta stood up and turned toward everyone else.

"Well, unless there are any other questions, I think we're good."

*Yeah, I have a question, why the fuck is Detective Campbell's car here?*

"Nope? Alright thanks guys, and next month, Monday the 2nd, it will be at ATO. Is that right, Cory?"

*Huh?*

"News to me, but sounds good," I responded as everyone in the room laughed and stood up to leave.

*Wait, why the fuck is Detective Campbell's car here?* I got up and grabbed the sheet of paper at the front that had a recap of the meeting. It was the same thing every week.

"Hey Cory."

*Campbell!*

"Hey officer, how's it going."

"Hey you mind if I grab you for a second?"

"Yeah sure, what's up?"

"I wanted to ask you a few questions about some things."

"Yeah, that's fine, here?"

"Yeah, it shouldn't take long. Here, let's go take a seat," he said, pointing toward the back of the basement, which was empty.

*Where the fuck did he come from? Has he been waiting for me?* Beta's basement wasn't a party room like ATO's or Acacia's or Pi Kapps's; it was more a study with tables and booths. They partied in another room on the opposite side of the house. Campbell and I walked toward the back and sat down. I glanced around the room before I sat down to see if anyone else was staying in the room. *Nope. But if he's here about the Eric drive-by, he would have arrested me already, right? It's been four months.*

"Hey Cory, so I'll cut to the chase here."

*Please do.*

"So as you know, I'm heading this investigation to help get drugs out of IU . . ."

*Oh fuck.*

". . . And as a part of that investigation we have that anonymous hotline anyone can call in to leave tips or get more information about the investigation. We gave you guys cards about that hotline, do you remember?"

"Yeah, I got the cards."

"Right. So the other day I got a call from a mother who called in to ask questions. As we talked at length about the investigation itself, she raised some concerns about her son and the people her son hung around with. As you can probably connect the dots, you were one of the names . . ."

*Who the fuck snitched on me? Who of my friends' moms even knows me that well?* I stared, not knowing what to say.

"OK, so first I want you to know you are not in trouble in any way and certainly not under arrest. We understand a mother telling us she is worried about her son is in no way evidence for any wrongdoing. But I wanted to at least talk to the people she mentioned and see if they had any ideas why she would give them up. So, do you know of anything or why your name would get brought up?"

"Are you allowed to tell me who the mom is?"

"Why should that matter?"

"I have no idea what you are talking about, but maybe if I knew who it was, then maybe I'll have an explanation or something."

"No, I'm not allowed to say who."

"Honestly, sir, I have no idea."

"Do you know anything about drugs being delivered around the school?"

"No, not at all."

"Neither you nor your friends do any drugs?"

"Um, excuse me, sir, do I need a lawyer here? Sorry, I really don't know the protocol of how this goes, thought I'd ask."

"If you're innocent, you don't need a lawyer."

*So everyone who has a lawyer is guilty? That's moronic.*

". . . So none of your friends do drugs?"

"Not that I've seen, no."

"Cory, every fraternity has drugs in the house, I'm not an idiot."

"I don't know what to tell you, sir. I don't see anything or get involved in any of that stuff."

"But 'that stuff' goes on in your house? See, Cory, reason I'm asking you is because we already spoke with one of the kids, and after we searched his apartment, we found a considerable amount of cocaine, marijuana, and heroin."

"Heroin? Jesus."

"So what, cocaine and marijuana aren't a big deal to you?"

*Yeah, you fucker.*

"No, I meant like I haven't even heard of anyone doing heroin before. Only in like movies and stuff."

"But cocaine and weed you have?"

"Officer, I don't know what else to tell you. Yes, I have heard of people who have done cocaine and pot before, like a kid in my high school went to rehab because of coke and prescription pills, and I know people who smoke pot occasionally. I just don't associate myself with those people."

"Then why was your name on this list?"

"I have no idea. I don't even know of anyone who was arrested recently or had their apartment searched, so I can't even think of what group of people this would even be."

"Define *recently*?"

"No, I mean like at school. Ever. Like none of my friends have been arrested, and no one I hang out with or know of has been arrested, so I don't even know who the mutual friend you arrested could be."

"So if we went to your house, we wouldn't find anything?"

"No sir."

Detective Campbell sat there nodding his head as he tried to read if I was lying or not. He knew he had me, but he needed proof.

"Well, that's really all I needed, Cory. Thanks for your time, and sorry to keep you here late. We really are trying to tackle this case and have made some pretty substantial strides in it. If you know anything or see anything, feel free to call me, OK?" Campbell said as he handed me his business card.

It wasn't the hotline card; it was his own personal number.

"No problem. Sorry I couldn't help," I stated as I stood up and stuck my hand out to shake his hand.

"We'll be in touch soon, Cory," Campbell said with a smirk as he squeezed my hand.

# THIRTY-ONE

I DROVE TO THE HOUSE AND WENT STRAIGHT INTO MY SLEEPER AND TOOK OUT THE DUFFEL BAGS. They were almost empty but I didn't care. I still put the bags in Wolf's room and gave Hamilton the rest of the bud and coke. He said he didn't have enough money for it, but I said it was a gift from the dealer. It was only about an ounce of pot and like a half O of coke. I didn't give a fuck if it was a kilo, I just needed it out of my room.

I walked up to my room, and Bo was sitting in there with Kyle and one of his buddies from Acacia.

"Hey, can you guys leave the room for a second? I got to talk to Bo about something."

Everyone looked at me confused, but I didn't give a shit. Kyle clearly got the hint and stood up right away. The other dude looked at Bo and back at me and slowly stood up.

"Alright Bo, I'm going to bounce, thanks for the herb. I'll hit you up tomorrow."

"No problem Greeny, peace," Bo said.

I followed them out, shut the door, and locked it behind them.

"Sorry dude, I need to talk. I'm fucked!"

"Bro, I don't want to get involved, I really don't."

"You're not, just fucking listen, please. I met with that detective again tonight."

"The guy who followed you?"

"Yeah. Well, not followed me, but yeah, that guy. He was at the RM meeting tonight and pulled me aside. Said a mom called that hotline and gave up a couple names of potential drug dealers. He said he already arrested one of the kids because he searched his apartment."

"Wait, hold up. He already searched some kid's apartment because a mom called in? What mom?"

"I have no fucking clue, dude."

"What kid got arrested, though?"

"I don't know that either."

"How can they search an apartment so fast, did they have a warrant?"

"I mean, I doubt it. If that's the case he would have already searched this place."

"Wait, why here? I'm confused."

"Sorry, yeah, because the mom said my name too."

"What? What mom? Never mind. Do you have drugs here?"

"No, but a fuck ton of money."

"Well, get rid of it."

"I will. I also gave Hamilton the rest of the bud."

"What fucking mom would snitch on you? Like did you try looking online to see who got arrested?"

"No, I didn't even think about that. But dude, no, I have no idea! What fucking mom could it be?"

I took out my phone and started Googling drug arrests in Bloomington. A bunch of results popped up, but all from months and even years ago. I then searched the Bloomington, IN, police beat and found a bunch of different jail listings by subject and date. I scrolled through all of the jail bookings that consisted of burglaries, intoxications, theft, you name it, until I stumbled on one: "Police Beat: Drugs/Alcohol Jail Booking." I opened up the link and started reading.

400 block North College Avenue, 8:17 p.m. Sunday, a 22-year-old man was arrested on possession charges following a police investigation.

"That's all it says?" Bo said as I read it out loud.

"Yeah, not like a newspaper, it's the actual police report. That was yesterday, which would explain the meeting today. That has to be it."

"What's 400 North College, Smallwood?"

I took out my phone and Googled Smallwood.

Smallwood Plaza, 455 N College Ave, Bloomington, IN 47404 (812) 331-8500

"Yeah, Smallwood," I confirmed.

*So what mom ratted on her son's friend in Smallwood that sells drugs? And how would that mom know me?* It took me all of one second to figure out who it was.

"Dude, it's my freshman roommate. It's his mom. I'm positive."

"How?"

"Fuck! It makes so much sense. A: She's a psychopath and for sure would call an anonymous hotline. And B: Her son went to rehab for drugs, so she has a clear motive."

"And C: Smallwood would mean GDI, which would eliminate our frat friends. And even D: That would explain how they searched the place. It's her son's apartment. He lives in Smallwood, right? Or lived? She must have given the permission. Honestly, I bet her name is on the lease. Meaning, she could actually give permission."

*Fuck, does that mean Dave got arrested? Wait, I thought Cam wasn't selling to Dave anymore.*

"But dude, they found heroin. I don't sell heroin."

"Heroin? Fuck. Well, that would explain the rehab."

"I know. That's exactly what I was just thinking."

"But I mean, Cory, this is for sure your roommate's mom, right? That would explain why she gave your name. She named all her son's former or current roommates. I mean, if someone goes to rehab, it's more than plausible that one of the former roommates also did drugs or at least knew about it."

"Yeah dude, it was for sure her. Fuck, now what do I do?"

"I mean, stop fucking selling. Tell that guy from Vegas this whole story. He doesn't want to get caught just as much as you."

"Dude, you were in that room, you think that guy cares about us?"

"I don't know what to tell you, Cory. You have to do something. The guy got a list of names, one of them got arrested. It's only a matter of time until he gets a warrant for this place. That cunt from Vegas won't want to risk another one of his guys getting arrested."

He was right. I had to do something. A mom giving up her son's room-mates was one thing, but having the first name investigated be a drug dealer is another. The mom was now credible. *Fucking Mrs. Schwartz. Wait, oh fuck! Tomorrow is the next drop!*

My anxiety was at an all-time high. I couldn't stand still, let alone sit down. *I can't do the drop tomorrow. I'll have kilos and pounds of drugs in my room!* I took out the burner flip phone and looked at through the contacts. B, L, N1, N2, N3, N4, N5, T.

*Message to T: 9:57 p.m.: Hey T, I can't meet tomorrow. The guy I was talking about who is "on to me" is really on to me now. Don't want to talk over the phone, but I can't do it.*

I tried to be as cryptic as possible. The phone wasn't linked to me in any way, but I was panicking.

Message from T: 10:01 p.m.: Still on for tomorrow.

*Still on for tomorrow? I can't do it, I can't!* I didn't know who else to talk to. *Brittney!* I opened up the contacts and clicked on *B*.

"Hello?"

"Brittney?"

"Cory? Why are you calling me?"

"I don't want to explain over the phone. Can we meet somewhere?"

"I'm in Indy, what's wrong?"

"Are you at the bar?"

There was a silence on the phone.

"Cory, what is it?"

"The detective I was talking about, the guy who followed me when I drove to your brother's, he met with me again. He already arrested a guy I sell to and asked if he could search my place. He knows, Brittney. Tell Dante I can't keep doing this."

"Did you talk to Dante?"

"No, I texted Terry."

"Cory, I'm sorry, I don't want to get involved."

"Get involved? You helped drag me into this bullshit, Brittney. Tell Dante I won't be there tomorrow."

"What about tomorrow? Sorry, hold up, let me go outside."

I could hear Brittney walking through the bar. My time period of feeling bad for her had passed. I was being selfish now. *Fuck this guy and fuck this whole thing. I'm out. It sucks that she's in debt to this scumbag, but if she's going to work for him, then do your job and go talk to him.*

"Hello," a guy's voice said, annoyed.

I paused and didn't know what to say, so stayed silent.

"Cory, you will go to the drop tomorrow, 10:00 p.m. Please don't make this any more difficult than it needs to be."

"Who . . . ," I started to say, but there was no one on the line.

He hung up on me. I couldn't tell if that was Dante or Terry, but the message was clear. Show up or cause trouble. But I really didn't care about the message—I wasn't going to the drop. I wasn't showing up. I would rather deal with them being pissed at me than picking up all of those drugs and getting arrested and put in jail for years. *Fuck Brittney for putting him on the phone! She always sounds so innocent, though—is she really this programmed to do whatever he says?*

Bo was right; it was only a matter of time until cops searched my room. I couldn't keep hiding a combined 30 pounds of drugs. It was all or nothing, and so my only option was to do nothing and hope. *I can't give up, have to keep hope.*

# THIRTY-TWO

**IT WAS 10:07 P.M. AND I HADN'T HEARD ANYTHING.** 10:30, 11:00, 11:30. Sitting in my room rocking back and forth, I kept looking at my phone. I was scared for my life. Midnight, 12:30, 1:00. Still nothing. Not even a text from Brittney. It was silent. 1:30, 2:00, 2:30. Sleep wasn't even an option; I was too paranoid. My head started to hurt, and I started to get real light-headed. I tried smoking around 2:45 a.m., but it didn't help, only made it worse. Eventually around 3:15 a.m. I didn't know what else to do, so went down to a sophomore's room and grabbed a half a Xanax and went back up to my room. The headache turned into exhaustion real quick, and I passed out.

When I got up in the morning, I checked my phone. Nothing. It was like that all day. No word from anyone. *Had I called their bluff?* The anxiety remained, though. I didn't go to class or leave the house. I felt safer inside ATO.

Wednesday night, Thursday morning, Thursday night, Friday morning. Not a single call or single text. Absolute radio silence. I started Googling and checking police reports. Still nothing. Dante had let it go, but I refused to believe it. I had missed the drop, the drop I was threatened at gunpoint to do, and nothing had happened. A week went by like this. Slowly I started going to class. Tuesday I went to two but missed Wednesday just in case. I was so in my head. *If Dante really is the guy not to fuck with, then why has nothing happened?*

Thursday night was Bo's birthday, so we all planned on going to the bars around midnight. I had gone to class all day and had finally accepted my freedom. Well, my freedom from Dante, but I knew Campbell was still an issue. A random assortment of sorority girls came over to pregame. It wasn't a pair or anything, it was pretty much the girls Bo was closest with. It felt weird not having drugs in my apartment when people were in there. I had never noticed the minor apprehension that had given me, but not having them anymore was like a weight being lifted off my shoulders. If Campbell showed up, I would be good for the first time since freshman year. I had put my safe in Kyle's room. He didn't ask any questions. He was like that. No need to explain anything to him, he was loyal, almost to a fault. And besides, if Campbell came to search my room, he would have a warrant for my room and my car. Not a whole frat house. That would be a bomb threat or terrorist status. Not mom-worried-that-her-son's-freshman-year-roommate-might-have-contributed-to-her-son's-drug-addiction status.

We stayed in our room until about 11:30 p.m. then walked to Kilroy's. The place was pretty packed, but we knew mostly everyone inside. I couldn't tell if it was a week and a half of anxiety had gone away or just the booze, but it felt great not looking over my shoulder anymore.

After about an hour, I went up to the bar to order another round of shots. I always had a cash tab going at bars instead of using my card. I did this because I had thousands and thousands of dollars in cash, but also because I realized bartenders were idiots with cash tabs. For some reason with credit cards, they took your card and wrote down your order as you went, but for cash tabs, a lot of bartenders tried to remember what you ordered or had a separate sheet behind the bar but would forget to write an order or two. I must have gotten at least a free drink a night because of bartenders forgetting my order. I would always leave a tip covering the difference, but then the bartenders would give me another free drink for the nice tip. It was a remarkable system.

"Hey hey Cory, it's your chick," Joe said, nodding upward.

I looked up and saw Sara off to the right. I started to shake my head as I grabbed the shots and drinks in front of me.

"Dude, what are you doing? Go talk to her!" Garcia urged.

"You guys big fans of Sara? Since when?"

"Sara? I thought her name . . . ," Joe replied before getting interrupted by Bo.

"No! Cory!" Bo shouted over the music, elbowing me in the side.

He was absolutely bombed, so I put my arm around his sweaty shoulders, but then looked into his eyes. It was like looking into the eyes of a little kid after he'd woken up from a nightmare. *I've seen that face before.* I followed his eyes. It was Brittney.

*Why is she here?* My heart dropped into my stomach and I felt my jaw stiffen up. We made eye contact, but it wasn't even necessary, she was already making a beeline toward me. She was here for me.

"Cory, don't walk away, we need to talk!" Brittney pleaded as she made her way toward me.

"What do you want?"

"Cory, why the fuck would you do this? I told you not to fuck with him!"

I could see Garcia and Joe watching Brittney, confused why she was yelling at me. Almost like a wait-does-he-really-know-her-this-well look. Brittney didn't care. I nodded toward the patio, insinuating we should walk over there. We were still surrounded by people, but at least it wasn't my friends listening.

"Brittney, I didn't have a choice. There is a detective who knows it's me! I couldn't pick up!"

"Cory, you have to call Dante and do the drop tomorrow. You have to."

"I'm not going to. Like I'm done, it's over."

"Cory, please! I'm begging you, you have to," Brittney pleaded again.

She had that same look as before. Like she was going to gradually start crying before breaking down.

"Why does this matter so much to you?"

"It's too long of a story, Cory, but believe me! Dante pays me, Dante pays my rent! Cory, I have to do what he says! He told me I had to get you to do this. That's all I know. Please, Cory, please!"

"Or what?"

"Or your life is ruined. My life is ruined. You don't know him like I do. I've been working for him my whole life. I can't do any other job, Cory! I haven't exactly been the best good girl my whole life," Brittney said as the tears started to well.

"Dante knows too much about me, he has too much on me. Cory, please, just do this one drop for me! It'll be a big one, then you will be done for a while. I swear!"

"Brittney, one big one is worse, that means more at my house."

I was curious what Dante knew about her, but it wasn't the place to ask. She was an emotional wreck and was held hostage by this lunatic. I wanted to help her but just couldn't. I wasn't doing another drop.

"Please . . . ," she said as a tear started to roll down her face.

"I'm sorry, Brittney, I can't. End of conversation."

I walked a couple steps to the bar, handed the bartender $60 for my tab, and walked back to Brittney.

"Tell Dante he can find someone else. I can't do it."

"Cory, wait!"

"I'm sorry, Brittney, I really am. I can't help you. I'm done."

I started to walk toward the side door when I heard Brittney yell something at me. I turned as she tried to fight through the crowd. Crying and running through a crowd of people, and somehow she still looked gorgeous. She was honestly so stunning regardless of what she did. I felt bad for her that her life was so shitty, and the only person to protect her was going to jail for life, but in order to save my ass I had to stay strong and be selfish.

I walked out the side door and turned left toward the ATO house. It was still relatively early, but I wanted to get home. The anxiety was back. The thought of another Xanax bar crossed my mind, but I quickly shook it off to try and keep a sliver of pride and dignity.

Straight ahead on the small side street before Third Street was a black Mercedes. My whole body almost collapsed as both side doors opened and two guys got out. *Terry and Lamar!* I froze and looked in all directions. *Run Cory, fucking run! FUCK, there are too many people to run! And what would running do; they would just drive to ATO and wait for me. I'm trapped!* Terry stood by the front of the car and opened his jacket. The same move Dante had done in Vegas about five months back. Lamar opened up the door, and they both stood there waiting.

I had nowhere to go. I had to get in the car. I walked another 30 feet or so, avoiding eye contact with them, and got right in. Dante was sitting in the back as Lamar got in shotgun and Terry walked around the car and started driving.

"You made this more difficult for yourself, Cory. You know that, right? You made things difficult for everyone."

I didn't say anything. I was fucked and I knew it. I tried to think of an out, but there was nothing. We drove another couple of miles with no one saying a word. We parked in some tiny parking lot off campus and sat there. I wasn't going to speak until they said something to me. Dante's head was in his phone while Terry and Lamar sat in the parked car staring straight ahead. It was complete silence.

About 10 minutes later another car pulled up. It was the black Suburban. Terry and Lamar got out of the Mercedes and opened both doors. Dante got out first and I followed. The driver of the Suburban got out of the car and walked around to the trunk and started to unload the duffel bags. *They are doing the drop here!* Terry got in the driver's seat of the Suburban and Lamar got in the back.

"Get in," Dante said as he held the door of the Suburban for me to follow Lamar in.

I climbed in and Dante shut the door and started to walk around the front to sit shotgun. As I got in, I saw Brittney in the third row next to another random guy. Her face was really red and she was wiping away tears. *Did they hit her?* Next thing I knew, Lamar sucker punched me on the right side of my face. My head went flying back and hit the window. I saw Lamar ready for another punch, but before I could defend myself, the dude behind me grabbed my shoulders and Lamar punched me right in the gut. The face punch felt like a brick had been thrown at me, and the back of my head felt like it was bleeding from bashing into the window, but I had never felt something like the stomach punch. My organs and entire insides felt injured. Whatever the sensation past pain is, it was that. Not like my face, which was just an instant pain—no, this was unbearable. Something felt severely damaged.

I sat there leaning forward, holding my stomach as the guy behind me grabbed my shoulders again and pulled me back and put me in a chokehold. Not a chokehold where I couldn't breathe, but more a grab so I couldn't move. Lamar took out a gun and pressed it hard against my right cheek he had just punched. My insides were in shambles and my head was throbbing, but the gun against my skin made all of that pale in comparison. I stopped grabbing my stomach, stopped trying to get out of the chokehold, my whole body went stiff. The feeling of a gun pressed against your face was nothing I thought it would be. Frozen wasn't the right word; it was still. Everything went still. Everything I had done in my life, every accomplishment, hope, dream, relationship I had made, all of it was now in another person's hands. I couldn't afford to lose my composure, and I was surprised how quickly my body and mind understood that. Staying calm was the only defense I had. I knew he wouldn't shoot a calm person who agreed with him. *Right?*

"I thought I made myself clear when we spoke in Vegas, Cory, but evidently that was not the case. This isn't a request; this is a job. There is no quitting this job. Bloomington is one of my biggest moneymaking networks, and you will *not* impede the process! Bills need to be paid, Cory, and now debts need to be repaid. You got me?"

"Got it," I said without moving my head.

"Your little police difficulties are not material problems, Cory. Officers demand answers every day, but they never know what the real questions are. They probe, examine, request all this information, but they don't even know what they're looking for. An essential part of all investigations is a slipup. Culprit criminalizes himself during the nonsensical line of questioning or makes a fundamental, routine mistake. So, Cory, unless you have told this officer something you should not have, he has given up on you already. He can't inquire if he doesn't know the inquiry. So, have you told him anything?"

Lamar moved the gun back a couple inches, implying I should speak. But with the gun still pointing at me, every word I said had to be the truth. Lying was too risky, and this was not the time to take a risk.

"No. The officer got a call from a mom asking questions about the IU drug investigation. The mom named me and a couple other people. The, uh, the officer searched the apartment of one of the guys the mom named, and it's someone I sell to. Well, not sell to directly, but like, through another person. Regardless, the officer asked me if I knew anything, and if they searched my house would they find anything."

"And did . . ."

"No . . . ," I said, cutting Dante off. "Sorry, no, I didn't say anything. I swear to God. I think the mom was my freshman-year random room- mate's mom. He was a momma's boy who never drank or anything and is now in rehab, or, at least was in rehab. I'm not really sure, I'm not friends with him. But that would explain why the mom panicked and called the officer. And the guy who was searched and arrested was my old roommate's current roommate. So that would also explain how the cops could search his place."

Dante let out a little chuckle and looked at Terry, who was still facing forward. Terry shook his head with a smirk as he looked through the rearview mirror at me.

"Seems like you have already solved the puzzle, huh, Cory."

Dante gave a little head nod, and Lamar put his gun back at his side and the guy behind me let go of my shoulders. I felt my shoulders relax and my stomach and head pain came back instantaneously. I started feeling really light-headed and sick to my stomach. *I think he broke my lowest rib.*

Terry got out of the car and opened my door. When the lights inside the car came on, I turned around to look at Brittney. Someone had hit her. It was obvious. The right side of her face was red, and her eye wouldn't open all the way. On top of that, as soon as I made eye contact with her, she moved her head toward the window to hide her face.

"Come on," Terry said, standing outside the door.

I got out and Terry shut the door behind me. He got back in, reversed the Suburban, and drove to the other side of me, so I was now standing on the passenger side of the car. The window started to go down, and Dante tossed a set of keys to me.

"That's you from now on," Dante said, nodding toward the Mercedes. "It has a few more, let's say, capabilities, which will help us keep an eye on you. So this little adventure doesn't have to happen again. Use that car for all drops from now on. Got it?"

*He's giving me a black Mercedes? What, does it have a fucking tracker on it?*

". . . Oh, and this month's drop is in the trunk already. You OK to drive home?"

"Yeah."

"Great. And Cory, let's not do this again. Got it?"

*Fuck you.*

"Got it."

# THIRTY-THREE

**I GOT IN THE MERCEDES, PUT MY FOREHEAD ON THE STEERING WHEEL, AND STARTED SOBBING.** My stomach hurt, my cheek hurt, back of my head was fucking throbbing, and I had now been threatened at gunpoint twice to keep drug dealing by a guy who seemed to have arranged a murder. My life seemed to be over. It was as low as low could be. No amount of money could make this feeling any better. No amount.

I was ashamed to go back to ATO. *And what the fuck do I do with a new Benz?* It was clear someone had punched me in the face, and I didn't know what to tell people. I had just disappeared from the bar, so I guess I could make up anything. *Fuck it, who cares. I have bigger issues to worry about.* I got back to ATO and mostly everyone was bombed. I went into some shy sophomore's room and gave him $40 for a couple Xanax bars. He seemed intimidated by me, but I really couldn't care less what the hell he thought. I needed something to forget everything. All I wanted was to go to sleep. I knew I was going to do the drops in the morning, I knew everything would be back to fucked-up normal in the morning, but for now, I wanted to pretend there was no more anxiety.

I lay in bed the next morning replaying the night in my head. The full Xanax bar knocked me out cold, and I must have slept 14 hours. In the morning, my face hurt to touch, but wasn't too bad. But my stomach still didn't feel right. You never realize how often you use your abs until you crack a rib. Standing up, sitting down, breathing, any sort of movement in general. It hurt constantly. I couldn't really move around so lay on my back thinking what I was going to tell everyone.

*"That chick Brittney punched me, that's why I left." No, that won't work because then if people see her they'll think I punched her back. "I got jumped." Yeah, but who the fuck jumps people in Bloomington, Indiana? The hell with it, I'm going with sucker punched at the bar and so got kicked out. That'll explain why I left, too.*

I felt so disconnected from everyone and everything. Like I was living in a different world. I texted Numbers 1 to 5 in the morning saying I was going to drop off the shit later. I hadn't checked the flip phone in a while, but Terry had texted me everyone's orders.

Message from T: 1:52 a.m.: #1 – 6 pounds = $8k . . . #2 – 3 pounds and key = $24k . . . #3 – key = $20k . . . #4 – pills = $15k . . . #5 – 4 pounds 2 keys and pink bags= $51k . . . Rest you.

The size of the orders didn't even overwhelm me anymore. I mean, granted, it fucking sucked carrying around 40 pounds worth of drugs, but once you reached a certain limit, it really didn't matter. I was a goner if I got caught, regardless. It was crazy how each person was asking for more and more each time. It was like everyone was similar to me and Bo back in the day. Expanding to more and more people each passing month. Keep dealing to people who know more people who deal to more people. It was an endless cycle that kept growing. The little pink bags I was dropping off to the awkwardly old guy scared me a little bit, though. Four pounds and two keys would be about $45K. Pretty much a little less than double Number 2's order. So those three pink bags that had been included in the order were about $6K worth of white powder. But what was confusing was why it wouldn't be included with the two kilos. *Why separate those into pink . . . Wait! Fuck me, is that the heroin? Am I selling fucking heroin?*

After I made the drops I sat in the Mercedes and started punching the armrest until my knuckles started to bleed. I sat in a random apartment-building parking lot crying. The thought of dealing heroin to a creepy 30-year-old who might be selling to high school kids officially made me a piece of shit. I'd thought I couldn't get any lower than before, but I had. I was a degenerate, menace to society, true drug dealer. There was no justifying this one. I was officially a bad person.

The thought of my parents, my grandparents, and my siblings crossed my mind. The hope I had that differentiated me from depressed people was gone. I was hopeless. Detective Campbell still freaked me out, though, and that fear kept me going. I didn't give a shit what Dante said; he didn't see the look in Campbell's eyes when we shook hands at Beta. He knew he had me. I mean yeah, Dante can say detectives don't know what they are looking for because, sure, I bet Detective Campbell didn't know I bought over $100K of drugs a month, but he knew I was a part of it or at least knew something about it.

All of IFC and the risk managers were coming to ATO the first week of April, and I knew Campbell would be there. I had to think of something and something fast. After about a week it dawned on me that money wasn't an issue anymore. In fact, it could be the solution. Every decision I made, I still made with money as a leading influence for or against it. It was a tough habit to kick, but once I kicked it, I realized I could just rent another apartment and put my shit there. And so that's exactly what I did.

I decided to rent a furnished one-bedroom on Walnut to put all my shit. I told the lady I was going to start up school in the summer and was going to work in the meantime, but it didn't matter. She saw dollar signs. To her, it was a rich white kid with a Mercedes renting a one-bedroom for 12 months. I was still going to stay at ATO, but the more I thought about it, the more perfect it was. I could park my Mercedes there, bring over the two safes of money I had, and leave all the on-the-shelf drugs at the apartment. I went to the hardware store and bought an insanely expensive padlock and had a guy come and install it on the front door of the apartment. I was creating a legitimate stash house, but honestly, it gave me a little peace of mind, and there really wasn't a price on that feeling. Well, actually, the price was $650 a month, and that even included the utilities I was never going to use. I was netting about $40K a month, so $650 of that for a fraction of serenity seemed reasonable. It didn't fix everything, though. It was like having a Band-Aid when I needed stitches. Or like taking Xanax when you have anxiety issues. The problems still existed, but for the time being, it felt a little better.

After I set up the apartment, I heard my phone go off on the round glass kitchen table.

3:34 p.m.: Hey man not sure if you still have my number but it's Phil. Was wondering if you had any herb? Give me a call man.

*Hippy Mike asking me for pot?* It was a super strange text, especially because he called himself Phil, which was strange in itself and ultimately just a really funny name, the more I thought about it. But really it was strange because my old drug dealer was now asking me for weed. I texted him back, saying I was in the car and would drive by and bring some over. I didn't know how much he wanted, but knew he'd probably lost his connection when Eric was arrested. I was already in the apartment, so grabbed about an ounce and headed over to his place.

It felt weird driving to Hippy Mike's. Instinctively I called him as I pulled in the driveway, but he was already on the porch waiting for me.

"Damn, you got a new car?"

"Oh, it's not mine," I replied quickly.

"Rents' whip?"

"Uh, no, buddy in ATO's."

"Damn, nice friends you got there. Here, come on in man, how you been?"

"You know, hanging in there. You?"

"Yeah man, same here. Not sure how much you know or what, but did you hear about Eric?" he said as we walked into his house.

"I just read some stuff online. Pretty crazy."

"Yeah, some scary shit. Feel bad for the guy, man. He was never a bad dude, just hung around the wrong crew."

I wasn't planning on staying at Hippy Mike's long, but as soon as he said "wrong crew," something inside me told me to stay. I wanted to pry as much information as I could out of him.

"What do you mean?" I said as we sat down in his family room area.

"Eric's a local kid like me. I used to hang around his older cousin back in the day. His rents died in a car crash or some shit when I was in middle school, so he must have been in second grade or something."

"Oh shit, I didn't know that."

"Yeah, his rents' place was out behind College Mall, where my mom used to live."

*That explains Eric's part-time house in Bloomington.*

"What happened to Eric then?" I replied in a concerned tone.

"Eric? Well, when his rents passed away, his aunt and uncle didn't want to take full responsibility for him and his little sister. I got the scoop from my friend, but apparently they could barely afford raising my buddy, let alone two more kids. Shit got a little messy in the court system, and then when my friend and his rents moved up north, near South Bend, Eric and his little sis left town. Moved in with some family friend up in Indy."

"Sorry for asking so many questions, but the whole Eric thing kinda shocked me. I realized I knew nothing about him. So how did you and Eric get back together?"

"Fast forward a couple years, and Eric's cousin reintroduces me to Eric so I could buy some herb. He was growing, so it was a perfect match. So yeah, now with Eric out of the picture, I need to start getting my greens elsewhere. Where you getting yours from these days?" he asked as I took an ounce out of my backpack.

"Just this other guy now."

"This other guy now . . . ," Hippy Mike said, mimicking me. "Sounds like Eric rubbed off on you. Damn, this looks like the same shit I used to get. I'm not a big enthusiast or anything, but after about a decade of the same stuff every day, you start picking up a couple things, you know what I mean?"

*Shit.*

"Haven't really looked at it to be honest, but yeah, I think it's pretty good. I'm not the biggest smoker so can never tell."

"Am I right, though? Damn man, yeah, this is for sure the same shit."

I didn't know what to say. I hadn't told anyone about anything, really. Bo was the only one who knew about Dante. Hell, Bo was the only one who knew about Eric and Hippy Mike, but even then, he didn't know the half of it. I looked at Hippy Mike as he stared down at the bud and smelled it. It was clear he was positive it was the same stuff. *I mean, fuck, Cory, the guy has lived here his whole life. Realistically, how many different strains of weed circulate around Bloomington, Indiana?*

I wanted to keep everything to myself, it was safer that way, but I needed to know more about Eric, about Dante, about this "wrong crew" he mentioned earlier. I knew it would be easy to lie and say I pick up from some dude in ATO and let Hippy Mike wonder, but I needed more information. I needed to get some sort of hope back. I wanted a way out.

"Yeah, I'm actually getting it from the dude Eric was getting it from."

"*What?*"

"Yeah, I guess Eric wasn't growing after all."

"Do you know the guy's name?"

*Dante!*

"No, I get it from some guys who work for another guy, I think."

"Fuck me, man. You got to be careful. That's not a crew you want to fuck around with."

"What do you mean by crew?"

"Well, this is from Eric's cousin so could be a little biased, but when Eric and his sis moved, they moved in with this guy up in Indy. My cousin used to know him, grew up here in B-town. But I guess that guy's family is deep in the mob or some shit. Own a couple bars up in Indy. Could be rumors, man, but my friend said he's notorious—all the cops know him, just can never catch him. Shitty for Eric and that sister he has. Pretty much raised by the mafia. I get that Eric didn't really have a choice, just shitty how things turned out, you know?"

"Do you know the guy's name?"

"No, I can't remember. Something Mariano. Or maybe Marino. Never met him. I just know that's not the group you want to be around, man. You should try and find a different connect."

*Trust me. I know.*

"Yeah, will do. Hey thanks for the heads-up, Phil," I said as I stood up off the couch.

"Yeah man, no problem. Hey, I'll let you know if I find another connect too. We can rekindle the old flame," he said, holding out his hand.

We did the signature Hippy Mike slap-and-pound handshake before I walked out the front door. I didn't get as much information as I wanted out of Hippy Mike, but it was still, for lack of a better word, good to hear someone else validate the full story. The cops knowing about Dante was terrifying, though. He seemed like such a mystery man, but I guess that would explain his cockiness and invincible attitude.

I got in the car and started to drive toward ATO when I realized I had to go park the Mercedes at the apartment. Turning west onto Third Street, I saw a bunch of cop cars out in front of the gas station. I started to panic, but then realized I had nothing on me, was doing nothing illegal, and wasn't speeding. I was just being a tweak. As I kept driving, I saw another cop on Walnut, and even though I already knew better, it was still the same feeling. My anxiety was uncontrollable at this point. *Wait!* My nerves stopped immediately when the words of Hippy Mike replayed in my head over and over again. *"Cops know him but can never catch him."* *The police want to catch Dante, but don't know how. I want out from under Dante, but don't know how. The police knowing Dante isn't terrifying—it's actually a* good *thing! Dante getting caught is my only hope, and if cops already know him, it makes things easier. This is it!*

My mind was scrambled, but I could feel a plan in there. I tried to figure out some master plot, but nothing was coming to mind. I tried to think and think and think, but all I could come up with was just telling Campbell the truth and hoping he would let me off. I knew that wouldn't work. I was selling too much for him to let me go. I mean, maybe I could get a plea deal, but my life would still be ruined after spending a couple years in prison. Let alone what would happen if I told Campbell and he didn't catch Dante. Then I would be royally screwed, not to mention the ditch Dante would leave me in if he found out. As I got to the apartment I started thinking about what Dante had said to me.

"An essential part of all investigations is a slipup. Culprit criminalizes himself or a fundamental, routine mistake. Can't inquire if he doesn't know the inquiry."

I put away some shit in the apartment and locked the bedroom door. As I walked out the front door, it all started to click. Everything. Campbell, Dante, Eric, Eric's house, the conversation at Beta, all of it.

*Campbell does know what he is looking for! He does know the inquiry! He's just waiting for someone to speak up or slip up! Dante is responsible; Campbell has to know that. That's why he was at Eric's house. If all the cops know Dante, then they sure as shit know the kid he adopted and the kid who works for him. Campbell might have even found drugs at Eric's but kept it secret to keep Dante from running off. Fuck. This is way bigger than me. I'm not the guy Campbell is going after. He's been one step ahead of me this entire time but hasn't done anything about it. That's not because he doesn't know what he's looking for, but because he's using me to get what he's looking for. I am his best chance at getting Dante. With Eric gone, I'm the last pillar to the system before the whole thing collapses.*

*"The pawn can restore order and become the queen, but the king can't survive without the queen." Motherfucker! Dante doesn't realize the implications of his own metaphor, but Campbell does! Without me, Dante may be out of Bloomington for a while. What other college student is going to push over $150,000 of drugs a month? No one. And without me, Dante may be out of Campbell's reach forever. That's why Campbell is pressuring me to talk but not arresting me. If I don't talk, he has nothing, because if I make a mistake, it all collapses anyway. Either I talk or Campbell catches Dante in the act. If neither happens, Campbell has to arrest me. He just has to. He can't keep letting a dealer continue to deal. The clock is ticking for Campbell to make a move. I have to give him his slipup before the clock runs out. I have to give him a "fundamental, routine mistake." That's my only hope.*

# THIRTY-FOUR

I HAD GOTTEN A TEXT FROM TERRY ABOUT ANOTHER DROP the first week of April, but I still couldn't come up with a plan. I had nothing. Another week and a half went by, and all I could think of was leaving an anonymous tip. But that tip wouldn't be enough to catch Dante. The guy seemed invincible. There had to be some sort of credibility. Like the mom of a kid in rehab accusing his roommate. But what I couldn't figure out was how to show credibility without giving up my name. Campbell already knew it was me, so the only one credible would be me. *Or I guess my mom, if we're using that same ridiculous comparison. I'm still baffled that Bennett's mom said my name. What a bitch.*

The IFC meeting was Monday, and I had warned the whole house about the meeting to get everyone to stop smoking in their rooms for at least a couple hours. No one had to clean anything; that was the pledges' responsibility. It was a little ironic having pledges clean a house for a meeting with the fraternity police and the actual police, but I had become immune to double standards.

All the risk managers started showing up right around 7:00 p.m. and filtered into the dining room. It was funny to see everyone look around the house on their way to the dining room. It was funny because I did the same thing at every house we had meetings at. I had only been inside a handful of fraternities and knew nothing about most of them. So it was always interesting to see the setup of the houses and how they compared to the ones I had seen, and ultimately compared to ATO.

"Cory," I head Campbell's voice coming from outside.

"Good evening, officer," I said as I continued to hold the door open.

"Hey sorry, quick question—does everyone in your house park out back? I think I may have taken someone's spot," Campbell said, pointing to the parking lot.

"Yeah, everyone parks out in the lot. Don't worry, though, I think we have extra spots this semester."

"Oh, OK. Was just wondering. I didn't know if there was another lot you guys parked in because I didn't see your car out there. The black Mercedes, right?"

*How the . . .*

Detective Campbell looked at me as he walked by and into the dining room. I stood by the back door as the last of the RMs trickled in. I tried my hardest not to turn around and look to see if Campbell was waiting for me, but I could feel my face blushing. *He tricked me. He flat-out fucking tricked me. How does he know about the Mercedes? Does he know about the apartment too?*

I walked into the dining room like a robot. I couldn't think of anything but that comment. *How the fuck does he know?* The IFC president started talking as I stood by the dining room doors letting everyone else take a seat. Campbell was sitting up front, but I refused to look at him. *Has he run the plates? Whose name is even registered to the car? Is it Dante? Oh shit, is it Eric's old Mercedes? Dante can't be that stupid, right?*

The meeting was a short one. Only about 15 minutes. We had another meeting in two weeks because Little 500 was in three. I held the agenda sheets for everyone as they walked out into the parking lot. Campbell started to walk toward me, but I had nothing to say. *Maybe the clock ran out faster than I thought!*

"You know, Cory, not everything is adding up with you. Is there something you want to tell me?"

"Tell you? Sorry, officer, I don't know what you mean."

"It's alright. I think we will be seeing each other pretty soon. We can talk then," Campbell said as he walked past me.

I couldn't tell if that meant I'll-see-you-at-the-meeting-in-two-weeks soon, or the-time-has-run-out-and-I'm-going-to-arrest-you soon. Either way, I knew I was fucked, soon. The look on his face was like when my mom used to know I didn't clean my room and started to walk upstairs, calling my bluff. It was like a cocky confidence, and he was giving me one last chance to speak up before he was going to prove I was lying.

After Campbell left, I walked up into my room and sat there thinking some more. I had to think of a plan and think of one quickly. I had another drop in 24 hours. My anxiety was debilitating, so I went down and grabbed another couple of Xanax bars from that sophomore. I still didn't know his full name, only called him Toon because that's what everyone else seemed to call him, but had no clue if that was last name, nickname, short for something, no idea.

As the Xanax started to kick in, I sat in the room with Bo and Cutty as they were smoking and binge-watching *Homeland* episodes. Xanax helped me more than smoking did. Smoking did the opposite of what most people say it does. I didn't get all relaxed and couch potato when I smoked. I mean, yeah, I lay on the couch and didn't move, so I guess that was the couch potato part, but never really felt relaxed. When I smoked, I turned into the dude from *Beautiful Mind*. I overthought everything, overanalyzed everything, and sat and created these connections and ideas in my head. Seriously, like imagine Russell Crowe stringing pictures together in a room, that's what my brain did when I smoked. But Xanax helped more in situations like this. It almost gave me a "who cares" attitude. Like that trigger in your brain that gave a shit basically turned off. The fight-or-flight response became fight-or-fuck-it. But really when I say fight-or-fuck-it, I mean that in all aspects of my life, so inevitably when I took a bar, I ended up just falling asleep.

When I woke up on Tuesday the anxiety had returned in full force. I went to class to try and take my mind off the upcoming drop, but it didn't help. Especially because we were learning about supply chain management in my business operations class.

The drop was at 10:00 p.m. like it always was. I drove the Cherokee to the apartment to pick up the duffel bag of money and the Mercedes. I drove to the spot but was the first one there. I almost missed the pull-in because it blended in with the road and the rest of the forest so easily. I checked my phone. 9:51 p.m. I was a few minutes early, but had never been the first one there before. Each time I went there, the Suburban was waiting for me. I stayed in the car and waited. I really didn't know what else to do. At 9:57 p.m., I saw a pair of headlights and froze for a second before I realized it was the Suburban rolling up. I got out of the car and started walking toward the Suburban.

"Don't ever come early, OK?" Lamar said aggressively as he got out of the passenger seat.

"Uh, OK," I responded, confused.

"Pop the trunk."

After getting punched in the face and held at gunpoint by Lamar, we weren't very talkative at the drop-offs. Not like we were very good at small talk before, but I didn't want to say a damn thing anymore. As Lamar was loading the car, Terry rolled down the driver's-side window.

"Come here."

"Yeah?"

"Give me the phone," he said, holding his hand out.

I handed him the flip phone, and he immediately snapped it in half.

"Here is a new one. You are going to have a few more drops next time. Numbers are already in there."

"Wait, what? What do you mean by next time?"

"Friday before Little 500 week. So in two weeks. Going to be a bigger than normal drop. So we added a couple of people to the list. Is that going to be a problem?"

*Little 500! Fuck!* I hadn't even thought about the Little 500 drop. When Eric was the dealer, I bought almost double the drugs. *Was everyone going to double their orders?* I couldn't even imagine what it was going to be, but couldn't do or say anything to Terry, so I had to go with it.

"Uh, no. Not a problem. So this time it's the same five?"

"Same five. I'll text that phone like always."

Lamar got into the car and Terry rolled up the window, backed up, and pulled away. I looked down at the phone, which seemed identical to the previous one, and opened up the contacts list. B, L, N1, N2, N3, N4, N5, N6, N7, N8, N9, T.

*Fuck this! They added four people?* I headed back to the apartment and dropped off the duffel bags and triple-locked the door. I wasn't doing the other drops until tomorrow, so the bags were going to have to sleep over for the night. *This is legitimately the definition of a trap house now.* I left the Mercedes in the lot and hopped in the Cherokee to head to ATO.

Bo and Cutty were in my room, again, smoking, again, and binge-watching *Homeland*, again. I sat down full of self-doubt, but tried to think of anything from the drop that could at least spark some sort of plan. I couldn't muster up anything worth attempting. It was such a risky move, trying to fuck up a drug deal, but only fuck it up enough to where the seller gets caught. *Wait, why was Lamar pissed I was there early?*

I sat down and started to watch *Homeland* with Bo and Cutty. I refused to take another Xanax because I wanted to keep some sort of self-control. It was a shitty feeling knowing how badly I wanted one, but I had let myself get a little too dependent, and needed a reminder that I had control of something. Well, control of my drug intake, that is, not my life. That was out of my control at the moment. But I did grab the still-burning blunt off the table and take a couple hits. Again, smoking to me was like drinking alcohol. It seemed legal compared with everything I was dealing with. It almost felt like a child's drug at this point.

I couldn't tell if my stoned brain had taken over, but *Homeland* was just a ridiculous show. I had already watched this season, so knew what was going to happen, and maybe that's why I had a different opinion about the show, but essentially it was like one CIA lady against an entire army of terrorists. That was the premise. It was almost like no one else at the CIA mattered. I mean, yeah, there were other CIA agents involved, but none of them really did anything significant except spy on people and help Carrie with whatever she needed.

*The basic idea of the show is a good one, because there really has never been a show about terrorists on TV, especially terrorists within America, but at the end of the day the concept of one whack-job CIA lady doing everything herself is too unrealistic. Ignoring the entire CIA team and just having Carrie . . .* I paused for a second as I started to have my *Beautiful Mind* moment and recognized the similarities in the show and my life.

*Carrie does everything herself. That's it! It's unrealistic to think it's just her doing everything by herself. Same with Campbell! That's how Campbell knows I have a Mercedes! There's an entire fucking team on this investigation! He's just the only one I know of. Like Carrie in the show. Everyone else is spying and doing the behind-the-scenes shit to give him all his information. Everything that Campbell knows, every cop in Bloomington also knows!*

My mind had cleared out any other thought as I started to piece everything together. *I drove past the cops at the gas staion in the Mercedes. They must have noticed me and told Campbell I have a Mercedes. I mean, Cory, if people think you are a drug dealer and then you start driving a Mercedes, it's not really a good look. Of course the cops told him! So if all the cops know, then, fuck! Then I don't have any time left! I mean, Campbell by himself might be able to hide me being the IU drug dealer in order to keep me as a stepping-stone to get to Dante, but with the pressure of the entire police force knowing? No chance they were going to let me keep doing this. And with me slapping them in the face, driving a Mercedes? The police chief won't ignore a freshman girl dying, a mom calling about her son going into rehab, the drugs being on the news, the head guy's sidekick going away for murder—it's coming to an end. Quickly. They're going to arrest me sooner rather than later.*

That was the most important part. I had to find a flaw in Terry's and Lamar's or Dante's way of doing things in order to get them arrested. *Think, Cory, think!*

*The new phone, I understand. They have new numbers to give me, so it's easier to give me a new phone rather than plug the new numbers into my old phone. But why would they be pissed I was there first? Why would being there first matter? Do they scope out the scene first? I mean, fuck, I feel like you would want the . . . the opposite . . . You would want the opposite!*

"Hey, Cutty, you mind leaving the room after this?"

"Huh?"

"Sorry bro, this episode ends in like 30 seconds. I need to talk to Bo."

# THIRTY-FIVE

"YOU HAVE A FUCKING MERCEDES?"

"It's not mine. But wait, that is what stood out from what I just said?"

"I mean, once you said 'my Mercedes,' I had to cut you off. How much are you fucking selling these days?"

"Alright, I guess I should go back a little further then. Dude, please listen, this isn't a joke. So your bday night, when I got punched, I wasn't sucker punched at Kilroy's. I was basically kidnapped by that Italian dude from Vegas and was held up at gunpoint by his two henchmen. The big black guy was the one who beat the shit out of me while the bald guy drove. That night, they gave me the Mercedes so they could track me. The Mercedes has a tracker on it, and I'm supposed to use it every time I go to pick up. So whatever, that's where the car comes from. But then that detective, the one I talked to you about, remember? My freshman-year roommate called him and said my name?"

"Yeah. No, I got that part, I didn't get the Mercedes part. So then what?"

"OK, so then I drove the Mercedes yesterday to go pick up the stuff, and I got there first. Oh, remember the two dudes in Vegas? I've been getting it from them each month or couple weeks, whatever. So I waited like 10 minutes, and then when they showed up, the one dude got all pissed that I got there before he did."

"That's it?"

"No. I'm saying they were pissed I was there first. Meaning, if I show up a little late, it's OK. Which then means, they are just sitting there, like sitting ducks, waiting for me in a driveway in the forest with pounds and kilos of drugs."

"Why would they be upset you got there first?"

"That's what I'm saying! Like, maybe the cops could be with me, or they didn't get to scope out the scene first. That's probably it, they don't get to scope the scene first. I'm not sure, but I am positive if it were me, I would want the opposite. I would show up five minutes late each time to make sure if cops were there, the first dude got busted. Right?"

"Right. But I'm confused—why is this a good thing?"

"I need to find a way to get these guys arrested before I get arrested. The issue is that everything they do is so scripted, it seemed impossible to fuck with their routine without getting myself caught too. But now I know how to get them caught. When I was sitting there and saw their headlights, I had a brief second of panic. Where I felt trapped. I mean, granted, all I had on me was money, but the feeling was that 'oh shit, the cops' feeling. If those lights were cop lights, I had nowhere to go. Meaning, they will have nowhere to go. These guys have a huge Little 5 drop coming up, and they won't risk fucking it up by changing any plans. They won't let it fail. No way."

"So what are you going to do?"

"Bring the cops to them. But I have to make sure the Vegas guys think I'm not in on it. These guys are tracking my car, so it shouldn't be that hard for them to know I'm not with the police or talking to them. I'll show up a little late, because he told me to, and then the cops will beat me there and arrest them."

"And if they don't beat you there."

"I don't know, I haven't gotten that far. This is the best I got right now."

"Jesus Cory. There is no way that is worth it. You'll go to jail if they catch you, dude, like are you kidding me? Why don't you tell the cops?"

"Because it's even worse than you can imagine, Bo."

"How much are you selling? Actually, Cory. Don't fuck with me."

"I have $396,000 sitting in an apartment on Walnut Street with another $125,000 worth of drugs in there too. I'll sell a little more than half of that tomorrow, then the rest I'll sell over the next week to Mo, Cam, Hamilton, and Dylan."

Bo stared at me, speechless.

"Yeah, dude, this isn't a fucking joke. That's not counting what's in my bank account or what I've spent already. This is ending in prison for someone. Me or him. This is my last chance."

"You have an apartment dedicated for your money? Does anyone know about this?"

"No one. Don't say a fucking word to anyone."

"No, I won't. I won't, I swear to God," Bo said fearfully.

It was like Bo hearing about my money and drugs made him instantly afraid of me. I could hear the nerves and the intimidation in his voice.

"I can't believe you are realistically thinking of doing this. You may go to jail, Cory!"

"That's what you're not getting, Bo. Someone is going to jail. Him or me. I don't know what else to tell you. This next Little 5 deal will be $200,000-plus worth of drugs. Think about it. Detective Campbell and his office got a call from some mom saying that my name and four others were dealers. They searched one of the four and found cocaine, heroin, and pot. Then he saw me driving a new Mercedes that is registered to God knows who and told me to my face that not everything was adding up. All signs point to me—you'd have to be an idiot to think otherwise. My name is probably at the top of some whiteboard in the police station, or at least second from the top. If they haven't gotten the top guy yet, then I'm next. The school year ends in less than a month, and this is the biggest party week of the year. This is it, Bo. There really isn't an option. Unless he gets caught on his own in the next two weeks, this is it."

"How are you going to get the cops to go there?"

"That hotline."

"And you think they'll believe you?"

"I don't know how else to do it. I get that they need credibility, but honestly, I think the cops will at least check out that spot. And hopefully the Suburban is waiting there with about 35 pounds of pot, 10 kilos of coke, and quadruple the molly I had for Deadmau5."

Bo sat there, astonished. I realized it was a lot to take in, but I needed someone to bounce my idea off. I'm glad I did, too, because it made me think more about the plan and really lay it all out on the table. Exactly how to lure Campbell or the cops to the drop spot was still hazy, but I didn't really have another option. This was it.

On Wednesday I went and made the five drops and gave Mo, Cam, Hamilton, and Dylan their bags too. Everything seemed to be moving fast. A week went by with no action, no phone calls, nothing. Our RM meeting was on the Wednesday before Little 5, and the big drop was supposed to be that Friday. I couldn't figure out how I was going to tell if the cops had arrested Terry and Lamar, or even worse, how I was going to know if nothing had happened and the cops were just waiting for me to show up.

Thursday. Friday. Saturday. Time was flying by, and I still had no plan B if Terry and Lamar hadn't gotten arrested at the drop while I was on the way there. I was panicking about the whole situation. The plan didn't have an ending to it. The only thing I did know for sure was that Bo was going to make the call for me. I had a pledge go out and buy a pay-as-you-go phone and had convinced Bo to call the hotline on Wednesday. I wanted there to be enough lead time before the drop so the cops could be prepared and actually show up. More importantly, I wanted to do it on the day of the RM meeting, so then Campbell wouldn't arrest me at the meeting and would have to wait till Friday. It would buy a couple more days as Little 5 approached.

Sunday. Monday. Tuesday. I couldn't sleep, couldn't keep food down, I was a mess. I was taking a half bar to go to bed, an Adderall around lunch to focus, and then a quarter bar around dinner to keep calm and control my anxiety. On Wednesday morning, Bo said he had to go to class but would make the call with me around one o'clock. I had written down exactly what I wanted him to say in the voicemail.

Hey, so I'm not sure how this works, but I ride my bike in Morgan-Monroe State Forest almost every night as I train for Little 500. I saw a couple cars parked in some driveway cutout in the road a couple of Fridays ago. So if you take Route 37 and continue onto Forest Road about a mile or so, it is on your right. Anyway, there must have been three or four people, and they seemed to be making some sort of drug deal. The guys were loading bags into the two cars. Then last Friday night I saw the same cars there. I don't think they saw me, since the bike path is further up the hill than the actual road, but each time it was right around 10:10 p.m.

I wanted to say 10:10 p.m. to make sure Terry and Lamar had already done their coast-is-clear sweep before the cops showed up. I was slowly coming up with the rest of the plan. I was going to drive up 37 so the Mercedes showed it was headed to the drop, but not turn onto Forest road. If the plan worked, I would just drive home and hope to read it in the paper. If not, I would tell Terry I saw a cop car so got paranoid and started to drive home.

"Alright, you ready to do this?" Bo said to me as he got back from class.

"Let's do it, bro. I wrote down what you should say."

"Is it an answering machine?"

"Yeah, I think so."

Bo grabbed the sheet and gave it a read as I went and locked the door to our room.

"You got the number?"

"Already dialed it into the phone," I said handing him the phone.

"Alright. No turning back."

*No turning back.*

Bo called the number and put the phone on the table on speaker.

Ring.

Ring.

Ring.

"Hello?"

Bo violently lifted his head up and looked at me bug-eyed, not knowing what to do. I made a forceful head nod toward the piece of paper to start reading the sheet.

"Hey, so I'm not sure how this works..."

"This is an anonymous tip line with the Bloomington, Indiana, police department. Anything you say will be 100 percent confidential," the officer said, cutting off Bo.

Bo stared at me, and I pointed again for him to read the paper. This time more aggressively, as I could tell Bo was having second thoughts.

"Um, OK, so . . . Uh, I ride my bike in Morgan-Monroe State Forest almost every night as I train for the Little 500 race. I saw a couple, um, a couple cars parked in some driveway part of the road a couple of Fridays ago. The, uh, the driveway is if you take 37 and continue to Forest Road about a mile or so. It's on your right. Anyway, there must have been three or four people there, and they seemed to be making some sort of . . . uh . . . some sort of drug deal," Bo stuttered, reading through the sheet. "The, uh, the guys were loading bags into the two cars. Then last Friday night I saw the same cars there. I don't think they saw me. The bike path is further up the hill than the actual road, but each time it was right around 10:05 or 10:10 p.m."

"Did you see the make of the cars at all?" the cop responded firmly.

I was not expecting follow-up questions, but after an excruciating eight seconds of silence, Bo answered.

"No."

"Description of the people?"

Bo glanced at me and I shook my head.

"No."

Bo picked the phone up off the table ready to shut it. He looked at me for confirmation, and I nodded my head yes.

"That is all I wanted to say. I'm sorry."

"Wait! Sir, sorry, one last thing," the officer said before Bo shut the phone.

At that moment I could tell it wasn't Campbell. At first I was unsure, since his tone of voice was way deeper, but when the cop said, "Wait," I could tell it wasn't him.

". . . Where did you get this number?"

"Some sort of business card–looking thing I found on campus," Bo responded quickly.

*Good response, Bo. But why is he asking that?*

"What color is the card?"

*What color is the card?* Bo looked around the room for the card and lifted up the pillow he was sitting on. *Why does he want to know the color? Are there different numbers depending on the reasoning? Like a drug investigation hotline, a sexual assault hotline. What could the* . . . I stopped my thought as soon as Bo and I both saw the card on the ground. It was black. *I got black cards at the RM meeting that night. Every frat got a different color! He wants to know what fraternity this call is coming from! This isn't anonymous! Those fucking liars! Wait, Bo!*

"Black," Bo replied.

*FUCK!*

"Black. OK, great, thank you, sir, for your contributions to this investigation. Is there anything else you would like to share?"

Seeing how distraught I was, Bo slammed the flip phone shut.

"What is it? What did I do?"

"The card. ATO got black cards. Other houses got different color cards. He was asking to see where the card came from."

"Fuck, Cory, I didn't know. I'm. I'm. . . ," Bo said agitatedly.

"It's not your fault. I should have thought about that quicker. Fuck! Fuck!" I yelled as I stood up and started to pace around the room.

"Bro, what do we do?" Bo said, putting his hands on his head.

"I have no idea, dude, that's such bullshit. I mean, I guess there is nothing we can do. The guy will undoubtedly document that someone from ATO said this, and hopefully the cops go check it out Friday night, and everything else stays the same. I mean the ATO part doesn't matter that much in this instance, right? It's supposed to be a Little 5 biker saying he saw a sketchy drop spot. They know it's me anyway. That's not the point of the call."

"I guess," Bo replied hesitantly.

Bo didn't believe my optimism for one second, but there was nothing I could do. The plan was in motion already. My best friend had just told the cops where and when my $200,000 drug deal was on Friday night. Last time I missed the drop, I was beaten up and had a gun pressed against my face. There was only one option I had, and that was to stick with the plan. Whether it had an ending or not, it was still my only way out.

# THIRTY-SIX

**THERE WAS NO CHANCE I WAS GOING TO THE RM MEETING AT FIJI.** No shot. There were zero positives of going and a whole bunch of negatives if I went. I walked down to the sophomore VP's room and asked if he could make it to the meeting, and he said he could. Fiji was across the street, so not a tough ask to go there for 30 minutes on a Wednesday night.

The rest of the night I tried to take my mind off everything. It was an impossible task, but at least that's what I tried to do. Cutty and I drafted a team in *NBA 2K* and played what must have been 20 seasons with that team over a four-hour period. Every time Cutty had control of the game, I would hop on my iPhone and check any police reports or arrests. I feared that the cops would go to the spot early and ruin the plan, but I was hopeful Campbell was smart enough to connect the dots.

The more I thought about the hotline call, the more I thought saying 10:10 p.m. seemed sketchy. If it were an actual tip, the biker who saw and reported this would have just said "around 10:00 p.m. or so on Friday." But really at this point, being sketchy didn't matter. If anything, you could argue saying 10:10 p.m. and making it sketchier was a good thing. Make Campbell think this was an inside job. Gave it more credibility.

I was so in my own head and so paranoid that I switched from Xanax to melatonin and went into my room to watch *SportsCenter*, waiting for my body to shut off. It was that weird period in sports after March Madness, after the Masters, but before the NFL Draft and the NBA/NHL playoffs started. *SportsCenter* had begun going game-by-game through the newly released NFL schedule and predicting its Super Bowl picks. After about

35 minutes, I felt my head start to spin so lay down on the couch and passed out.

In the morning I felt a lot better. Almost felt excited in a way. Like this nightmare was all coming to an end, one way or another. Almost like I had a trick-play up my sleeve that the other team didn't know about.

I had a quiz in my 1:00 p.m. accounting class that I had to take. I hadn't studied at all, but you got a zero if you missed it. That class was 50 percent tests, 30 percent quizzes, 10 percent homework, and 10 percent on some group project we did. So while each quiz was only five questions, all the quizzes combined counted for 30 percent of my grade. Six quizzes might only be 30 questions total, but that was one percent of your final grade per question. You skip a quiz and you're screwed.

While I was in class, my phone vibrated in my pocket. Thirty seconds later, my phone vibrated again. Another minute, another vibration. *What the fuck!* I hurried finishing the quiz and walked it down the steps to turn it in. I made my way to the hallway in the back so I could check my phone, but before I got to the door, my phone rang again.

"Bo, what? I'm in class!"

"Dude, the fucking cops are here! They searched our entire fucking room!"

"What? Who let them in?" I whisper-yelled into the phone.

"Dennis. They had a warrant, Cory. A fucking warrant. Dennis had to let them in and walk them up to the room."

*Holy fuck, this is really happening!*

The hallway was empty, but I instinctively turned and leaned up against the wall, trying to hide my face.

"What did the warrant say?" I asked, practically out of breath.

"How the fuck am I supposed to know? They found my safe, but it only had four grand in cash, my passport, and my old fake ID."

*Goddamnit!*

"What did they say?"

"Took the fake and snapped it, then asked me about the money. I said it was a just-in-case fund my dad gave me before I went to college. Said my dad told me if nothing happens to me all four years, I get to keep it.

If something does happen, I use that money and can't ever ask him for money ever again."

"Jesus. How did you think of that?"

"Because it's true. But my dad gave me $500, not $4,000. Where the fuck are you?"

"I'm at class, or, I mean, outside of class. Did they search the whole house? Like did they find anything?"

"No, they only searched our room. It was just me and Dennis upstairs. He made everyone else go into the dining room. I think the warrant was for your room only. I can't see them being able to come back upstairs and search the whole house."

"Oh, wait, they left already?"

"They're in Dennis's office talking. I don't know, they might have left. I'm in our room. The place is a fucking mess. They ripped down the bunk beds, broke open our bar, flipped over the couches. It's like a tornado hit."

"And they actually found nothing? Like no pot, no coke, nothing?"

"No. Luckily we smoked in Cutty's room last night, so all our shit was in there. And the pledges vacuumed and cleaned this morning. All your shit isn't here, right?"

"Right."

"I don't think you should come here, bro. The cops seemed furious they didn't find you or anything, and everyone is pissed at you, too, for bringing cops to the house. Some detective guy. Tall blond military dude kept asking where you were. I said I had no clue, but probably class or studying somewhere. He didn't buy it. What are you going to do?"

"I don't know, dude. I got to go, though."

"Alright, call . . ."

I hung up the phone before Bo could finish and ran back into the class-room, grabbed my backpack, and ran out. I looked both ways down the relatively empty hallway and started to power walk through the business school. *Fuck, fuck, fuck! My time ran out!* I walked out the door of the business school and saw one of the IU buses pulling up, heading west on 10th Street. I looked for any sign of cops, then ran out the door and jumped on the bus. It wasn't even the right bus, but it took me away from campus, so good enough. I sat down and started looking out the window. *Are they following me? Are they trying to arrest me or just search the room?* I knew the apartment was now the only place I could go safely. If they knew about the apartment, there would be no reason to even search ATO.

I got off the bus and walked about seven or eight blocks to the apartment, ran up the stairs, and hurried inside. I shut the door and went into the bedroom and made sure all the money was there. One safe had exactly $275,000 in it, and the other had $121,685 and a manila envelope of $119,000, then about an ounce of blow, a couple ounces of pot, and a big bag of about 300 to 500 pills. So $515,685 was all there, plus about $6,000 or $7,000 worth of spillover drugs.

I looked out the bedroom window overlooking the parking lot, but didn't see anyone. I was so fearful, I didn't know what to do. I checked my phone and went on Facebook and saw a bunch of the younger guys in the house bitching about me in our ATO Facebook group, saying I should move out and demanding our president to kick me out of the house. I wasn't going to respond. I had nothing to say. They were probably right anyway. I wouldn't want someone living in who had the cops come raid his room. I was moving out in less than a month anyway, so it didn't matter to me.

After about 35 minutes of flipping through my phone, I finally calmed down a little. Even though the apartment was a stash house, it was comforting. No one knew where I was, the TV wasn't set up, I didn't know if the building had Internet—it was my own little getaway from the world. It was a hideout. I put my phone down and lay down on the beige couch that came with the place.

All along, Campbell was two steps ahead of me. His anti–poker face was downright forceful, but there was always a part of me that thought maybe he didn't know everything. That maybe Dante was right, and Campbell only had a feeling that I knew about drugs on campus. But that comforting thought had sailed away. He knew everything. It was surreal knowing that the police were actually looking for me.

I sat in the apartment wondering what to do next.

*Does this even change anything? Yeah, there was a chance Campbell didn't know, but the drop is still tomorrow, and everything I've done up to this point was with the thought of Campbell knowing. I'll still leave for the drop, I'll still drive toward it, and I'll still pull off the highway and go back to the apartment and hope the cops arrested Terry and Lamar. Nothing changes. I just can't leave the apartment until tomorrow night.*

I was surprised no one had tried to call or text me. Bo, Cutty, Kyle, even Mo, Cam, or Hamilton. No one—but I guess if cops were investigating my friend, I would stay as far away as possible. Let the dust settle a little. I had no one to talk to, nothing to eat, and nothing to do, and it was three o'clock on a Thursday. I looked outside and still didn't see anyone, so I ran about a block to the market to pick up a couple things. The place wasn't a grocery store; it was more like a 7-Eleven. I grabbed some bread, peanut butter, pasta, pasta sauce, chips, couple drinks, apple, lighter, and some Nyquil. Nyquil was for bedtime, apple and lighter were for smoking, and the food was to hold me over till Friday night.

I got back to the apartment and made some pasta and attempted to watch ESPN highlights on my phone. After about an hour or so, I started to get really bored and really lonely. I was literally in solitary confinement. It was like house arrest. *Is this really what my life has come down to? A fugitive on the run, staying at a trap house, hoping to frame a drug dealer to get out of it?* I carved the apple into a bowl and packed it as I lay on the couch smoking. Lying there, I started to think about my entire college experience and how everything came to be.

*Freshman year dating Em, my mom fake crying as they moved me in, rushing Pi Kapps and ATO. Getting hazed, the sportsbook with Bo, dealing with JR, dealing with Hippy Mike, who became Phil. It's crazy that it's already been three years! Scared to ask Hippy Mike for two ounces of pot, meeting and working with some Chris Pine–looking dude who ended up being a murderer, Puerto Vallarta, that random night I woke up in the Zeta cold dorm, meeting Deadmau5, meeting Chris Pine's absolutely beautiful sister, Brittney. I wonder what she will do if this all goes down. Will she be let free? Do the cops know about her too?*

I lay there stoned, having a mini-rerun of my college experience as I started to tear up. Everything was coming to an end, and I knew it. A part of me still believed I would make it out unscathed, but I knew deep down I was going to jail. A police force had already gotten a warrant from a judge to search my room. You couldn't really rebound from that. But it wasn't so much my current situation that was making me tear up; it was the thought of what could have been. It was the thought of the choices I'd made in the past three years. The one tipping point that kept circling my head was the bottle caps night. I was brainwashed that night, and there was no other way to explain it. I let a bunch of blacked-out seniors convince me to put all my weight on bottle caps and bleed as I tried to keep balance, all because they didn't get a six-block ride home quick enough. Allowing myself to submit so easily had never sat well with me, and that unsettling feeling was the catalyst of my mistakes. Everything I had done since that night had been to gain back the control I had lost. I never wanted to surrender my life to anyone ever again, but that ironically ended up costing me my own life.

The tears began to grow as the mistakes since that night cycled through my head. *Would I have told Jason and JR no? Would I have listened to Hippy Mike when he said no? Hell, would I have even listened to Bo when he said no? Would I still have had the urge to go from bud to blow? Would I have kept dating Em? Would I have continued to drug deal if I stayed with Em? Em. I really do miss Em. Em! That's it! That's who I can talk to! Em.*

I wiped my face, picked up my phone, and went to my favorites. Em was still saved in my favorites, right below my mom, dad, and house phone number. I never used that favorites tab in my phone, but also never seemed to change it either. Every time I opened my contacts list it would pop up. House, Mom, Dad, Emily. Maybe it was a comforting feeling seeing Em's name, maybe it was a subconscious motivation to be a better person; regardless, for some reason I never changed it. And clearly the "become a better person" motivational tactic hadn't worked. But I had the urge to talk to someone. To vent, to unwind, whatever you want to call it. The burning feeling in my heart was insufferable. I couldn't hold it in anymore.

"Cory?"

"Hey Em, can you talk for a second?"

"Uh, yeah, hold on, let me go into my room. Is everything OK?"

"Um, yeah, well, no. Sorry, yeah, everything is OK."

"Are you drunk?"

"No, not at all. I'm just at the apartment by myself."

"Apartment?"

*Shit.*

"Sorry, I meant house. Like my room of the house, by myself."

Em didn't say anything. I didn't know why, but whenever I talked to her post breakup, I was always so disoriented and flustered. When I was with her, it was the opposite. I never felt more comfortable in my own skin than when I was with her. I could do and say anything and knew I wouldn't be judged, but now, everything felt different. It probably didn't help that I was stoned, but regardless, I had this weird desire to unload and finally tell her what I felt. I knew this might be one of the last times I could have a meaningful conversation with her, let alone anyone, so there was no need to sugarcoat anything.

"Well, can I help you with something?"

"No, I don't need any help, really. Just wanted to talk for a little. I'm not really doing that well, Em. I'm not really in a good place."

"What do you mean, what's wrong?"

I wanted to tell her everything, but again, I knew it would only hurt her and could fuck things up. So all I could do was tell her the truth about everything except my current situation with Dante, Campbell, the apartment, any of it.

"Honestly Em, I haven't been right since we stopped dating. I've made a lot of mistakes since then—a lot of mistakes. And plenty of mistakes while we dated. After we talked over winter break, it kinda all hit me how big of an asshole I was to you."

"Cory, are you really doing this now?" Emily said, cutting me off.

"I'm not doing anything. I promise. There are just a couple things I need to get off my chest. A couple things I think you deserve to hear. Like for one, it was all my fault. Everything. From lying to you, to putting you in uncomfortable situations and not trying to help you, for not sticking up for you, and for trying to defend my friends and my school all the time. I hope you know you couldn't have done anything, our breakup was inevitable, and it's because it was my fault."

"Yeah, no shit."

There was silence on the phone for a couple seconds.

"Cory, I was kidding. I'm sorry, I shouldn't have said that."

"No you are right. It was obvious Emily. And it was unfair to you."

"Why are you saying all this? What is wrong?"

"A lot of things are wrong Em. When I was with you, everything seemed OK. Like, we fought a bunch, but it was about dumb shit. Everything else in my life was on the straight and narrow, and I was a good person when I was with you. I can't really say the same anymore. The things that are wrong with me now aren't dumb, childish problems, they are serious. They are actual problems."

*Like selling heroin and living in a trap house with a half million in cash.*

"I mean like why now? Why are you saying it now? What problems do you have, Cory. You're making me worried."

"Why now? Because I have waited too long to say it. I don't know when I'll see you next, if I'll have to stay this summer, I don't know Em."

"I don't know what you want me to say Cor."

"I don't want you to say anything. I . . ."

"Cory, I do appreciate everything, everything you said, I don't know. I just wasn't prepared for this phone call."

"I'm sorry. It was selfish of me. I wanted to get this shit off my chest and thought what better time than now."

"What, 6:30 on a Thursday night?" Emily said jokingly.

*Actually, a Thursday night before a legitimate sting operation. But, semantics.*

"Cory, you were an asshole, and you did change a lot when you went to school, but it wasn't just you. It was me, too. I couldn't see past all the things going on at that school. I grouped you in with it all. I put you together with all those bitchy girls, douchebag guys, all the partying, the drugs, all of it. I took a lot of my anger and frustration out on you. But you got so impossible to talk to. It was like everything you said, you said because you thought that was what you wanted me to hear. Like, like not telling me what you actually did, or what you actually thought, but whatever you thought would please me. I loved you for who you were, not whoever you thought I wanted you to be."

"I know, I sucked. I wanted to make things better, that's why I lied a lot. I just didn't want you to get mad Em."

"But I would get even more mad when I found out you lied! You are really bad at hiding things."

*You'd be surprised.*

"I know. I know. I just wanted to be a better boyfriend."

"I know that now. It was kind of hard to tell when you were lying to me."

"It's impossible to date long-distance."

"I wouldn't say impossible. But you have to be pretty damn strong to do it. I'm not strong enough, I know that now."

There was a pause in the conversation. A healthy pause, though. Sort of like the pause in Vegas. Not like we had nothing else to say, but like we needed a moment. Neither of us thought the conversation was going in this direction. By direction I mean forward. I more or less selfishly wanted to vent and wasn't expecting a reply. There was so much to chat about, but truthfully it felt good to hear her smartass yet respectful comebacks. The way she always seemed to understand and know what was going on. Almost like she was letting me figure it out on my own. *Did she have to wait two years for me to figure it out?*

We talked on the phone for another 15 minutes or so. I didn't bring up anything to do with drugs or any of that. She sort of just ignored me saying I had serious problems. We talked about us, about our friends and families. She wasn't seeing anyone and neither was I, and I think we both knew that based on how much we wanted to talk. When you date someone, you vent everything freely at any point in the day, and the other person will listen. They have to; it's their job. But when you're single, it's just you. You can vent to your friends, but they won't listen to you like a boyfriend/girlfriend would, because they don't have to. It was a lonely feeling being single after dating for a long time.

After I hung up, I didn't even check what time it was. It was dark out, and that seemed good enough for me. I went into the bedroom and put both safes under the bed. I picked up the Nyquil but decided against it. I had accepted that tomorrow was going to be the end of it all anyway. There was no alternative, so there was nothing to be nervous about. It wasn't in my hands anymore. I was on the run, the cops were looking for me, and they knew exactly where I would be. I had hope for the first time in months. Tomorrow brought hope. Hope the cops showed up to arrest Terry and Lamar. Hope Campbell could connect the dots. Hope this was the ending to the college life that had taken control of my life.

# THIRTY-SEVEN

**FRIDAY MORNING I WOKE UP AND MADE MYSELF A PB SANDWICH.** I still had no missed texts or calls from anyone. Luckily I had my phone charger with me, because for the next two hours, all I did was Google search my name, Dante's, Campbell's, read local newspapers, police blotters, anything I could get my hands on. There was nothing. No news of anything. Everything was set and ready to go.

I didn't have a change of clothes or anything, so took a shower and hung the same pair of jeans and quarter-sleeve grey shirt in the bathroom to at least steam them and make it seem like they were clean. The rest of the day went by agonizingly slow. Once seven o'clock came around, everything started to clear up in my head. No nerves, no panic, nothing. I had convinced myself the plan was bulletproof. I had done seven drops with these guys, and apart from the *Fight Club* drop, each time was the same. I pull up, they were there, drop happens, done. They wouldn't expect anything different to happen and wouldn't panic when I didn't show up on time. Lamar told me to my face not to beat them there, so I was expected to be 5 or 10 minutes late this time.

Place was about 20 minutes away. I waited a little longer than normal before I left. At 9:45 p.m., I grabbed the manila envelope with the $119,000 in it and put it in one of the duffel bags. *Wait, if I'm not going to do the drop regardless, why even bring the money?* I thought about it for a second, and ended up just leaving the bag in the apartment and walking out the front door. I double-checked the parking lot, across Walnut Street, down the alley. There were no police or police-looking cars in sight. I hopped in the Mercedes and pulled onto Walnut, turned left onto 45/46, and then jumped onto 37 north toward the drop. My phone said I would be there around 10:07 p.m. All that mattered was that I was on the way so Dante could see I was on the way. How fast I drove didn't matter, so I stayed in the right lane and set my cruise control at 60. Highway was relatively empty, but still a car every 100 feet or so. I kept checking my mirrors, but the coast was clear. My heart was pounding, but I was unexpectedly more excited than afraid. It was like those butterflies in your stomach you get before a big sporting event or a surprise party. This was the big moment that was going to determine my future. Saying that sentence by itself sounded dramatic, but it was true. If everything went smoothly, Dante could be in jail, and I could be free forever.

A couple miles behind me, I saw a car pull quickly onto the highway. My body stiffened up for a second until I accepted it was almost certainly a random car. Another mile or so down the highway I saw the car was staying the exact same distance away from me. It was about a football field away, but at this time in the night, in the right lane, it was the only car behind me. I knew I was overreacting, but to be sure, I slowed down to about 45 miles per hour pretending to turn off the highway. When I hit the brakes, the car got within about 75 to 100 feet of me. I checked the rearview mirror and caught a better glimpse of the car before it had time to slow down as well. *No! No! No! It's Campbell! He's following me!*

I had passed an exit ramp about 15 seconds prior, so had nowhere to pull over. My left leg started shaking as I clenched the steering wheel, looking back at the car. *It's 100 percent him.* The day I drove by Eric's house was a day I would never forget, and the sight of Campbell's car was a sight I would never forget. This was the same car. There was no question about it. *How did he find me? Was he waiting for a Mercedes to drive by? Fuck! Wait, can I get arrested if I just turn around? I have nothing on me.* I tried to think of anything I could do to fix the situation, but then I remembered he might have a warrant out for my arrest, so turning around wasn't an option either.

The flip phone started to ring and I looked at the clock. *It's Terry! It's only 9:55! No! It's not time yet! He's not arrested! This can't be happening!*

"Hello?" I answered, trying to sound composed.

"Have a little issue. Don't go to the drop spot. Do, not, go to the drop spot! Where are you?"

"Uh, driving on 37 about 10 minutes out. Why?"

"Hold tight. I'll call back to let you know the new spot. Make sure you answer!" Terry barked out quickly as he hung up the phone.

*The entire plan is ruined. Not only that, but Campbell is now following me, while Terry and Lamar seem to be fine! Everything has blown up in my face in a matter of minutes! I'm fucked. My only chance is leading Campbell to Terry and Lamar, but even then, I don't know where they will be and I'll have nowhere to run. I would just get arrested with them, or the camera would see . . . The camera! That's how they saw the cops! They have a fucking camera in the forest! Fuck, how could I forget?*

My excitement had taken a complete tailspin toward depression. Any hope I had created was gone. I started to tear up as I looked back and saw Campbell still behind me. I was trapped. If I went to the new drop, I would get arrested; if I turned around, I would get pulled over, then arrested. I always knew this would end in an arrest, but didn't think *both* options would involve me getting arrested. *Once again, I am a step behind everyone.*

I kept driving north on 37. I looked out the window and saw a state police officer between the median posted up trying to catch speeders going south on 37. Instinctively, I slowed down, but quickly realized I wasn't speeding or even going south. I let out a desperate chuckle and shook my head as I realized how dumb it was to slow down trying not to get a speeding ticket, while I was about to get arrested for being involved in a multimillion-dollar drug ring. The sight of a cop car was just ingrained in my head forever, and regardless of the situation, I was always going to avoid them.

I kept driving, but saw an exit two miles up. I decided I was going to get off and just take my chances with Campbell interrogating me. I had nothing on me, and he had nothing of substance on me. He needed this bust as much as I did. Pulling over a random guy with nothing on him was a bad look, especially after you already searched his place and found nothing. I was about to take the exit when I thought about that state trooper for a second. *Everyone is afraid of cops, everyone. So if*

*Terry and Lamar saw cops at the drop, why the fuck aren't they avoiding them or afraid? Why are they still trying to do the drop tonight?*

A little bit of curiosity entered my already surrendered brain for a second as I thought about Terry telling me to hold tight. *If I were in their shoes, and cops had found out about my drop spot, I would A: Assume it was the guy I was selling to who snitched and sure as shit wouldn't tell him to "hold tight" as I thought of a new plan. Or B: Make the drop another night once I had a bulletproof plan. Are they this desperate? Sure, I have $119,000 for them and another $5,000 in drugs at the apartment, but, like, just pick it up later. Why tonight? I'm not fleeing the country or anything.*

I stayed on the highway and passed the exit. I thought about where the new drop could or would even be. Regardless of where it was, I wasn't going to it. As soon as I showed up, I would get arrested. The alternative besides turning around and hoping Campbell didn't know a lot about me was calling him and telling him that I would lead him to Dante.

*There is no way he would believe me or let that happen. Once I admit to him I'm involved, he will pull me over right away and take his chances in court with my testimony, Eric's murder case, and the anonymous hotline. Besides, I'm not even going to meet Dante right now, I'm going to meet . . .*

I passed the drop turnoff and looked in the rearview mirror and saw Campbell's car following me. *He's following me the whole way! He won't let me out of his sight! I can't bring him to a random drop spot with two random guys he doesn't know; he'll arrest me before I even get out of the car. But if I bring him to Dante, maybe he'll let it play out and not arrest me right away. This is my shot! This is my plan B! I have to bring Campbell directly to Dante, not Terry and Lamar!*

I knew Dante probably thought I was the reason the police found his drop, and even though his eagerness to continue the drop tonight was telling, I still had to have him think of the plan. I was going to have to trick him like Campbell tricked me about parking the Mercedes. I picked up the flip phone and started to call Terry.

"What is it?" Terry said in an annoyed tone.

His annoyance confirmed it. I knew what to do. This was possible. They weren't afraid of the cops. It wasn't necessarily desperation; it was blatant cockiness. They felt as if their infrastructure was so sound and their system was set up so flawlessly that there was nothing for them to ever worry about. *I have to feed into their egos. Let them believe that I think their routine and ideas are as good as they think they are. If they come up with the plan, as long as Dante will be there, I'm good. Stay relaxed and act like I have no idea what the problem is.*

"You tell me? I'm driving up 37 still, should I just go home or what?"

"I said hold tight. Where are you?"

*Coming to you, jackass.*

"You guys got the tracker, you tell me. I would guess about 20 minutes from the bar."

There was a pause on the other end of the phone. I wanted the word "bar" to stick in Terry's head. I knew he was on the other line or with Dante. That bar of theirs was like a fortress. Hidden rooms, hidden stairs, secret code words. It was the epitome of their arrogance. It was the perfect place for them to feel confident the drop would go smoothly, but also the perfect place to bring Campbell to Dante. *Campbell must know about the bar. He won't arrest me as soon as I get out of the car.*

"Anyone following you?"

"Following me? The hell are you talking about? No, I'm looking behind me and besides a semi truck I can't see another car for like a mile. Why, something wrong?"

"I don't know, is there?"

"Don't know what that means, but no. Everything is the same on my end. You guys are the ones acting weird."

It was the first time I was assertive with these guys, but the more self-confidence I showed, the more their eagerness would take over any doubt they had. I wanted them to think I could do this. All they had to do was sit in their hidden room, hand me a couple bags, and get paid $119,000.

"Drive to the bar. Park in the normal spot and wait for the call. You remember where it is?"

"Yeah. Sounds good. Be there in about 20 minutes."

I looked back and saw Campbell's car still following me. It was almost double the distance away as before. But he was there. He wasn't letting me out of his sight. That was all that mattered. Needed him to follow, needed him to call in backup. This was the Plan B. This was my last chance.

*But what even is Plan B? Now what do I do?*

# THIRTY-EIGHT

**I PULLED OFF THE HIGHWAY ABOUT THREE MILES BEFORE THE BAR.** I made a real slow right so Campbell could follow me easily, but my guess was he didn't need me to go slowly. He knew where I was going. I still couldn't figure out what I was going to do, since I had to park on that off-street.

I tried to put myself in Campbell's shoes. He was following a college kid to pick up drugs. Wait, no, even further. He had been chasing this infamous IU drug dealer for a little over a year. He had gotten a tip and acted on it and found it to be true. The information also led to this college kid. He questioned the kid a few times, but his story didn't seem to add up. Then he saw that college kid got a Mercedes, and got an anonymous tip from that kid's fraternity about a big drug deal. He took all this information to a judge, and it was strong enough to get a warrant. With the warrant, he searched the fraternity, but didn't find anything. So now he starts following this college kid to a drop spot where he thinks a deal is going down, but the kid passed the spot and was now driving toward a bar in Indianapolis. The bar owned by an alleged mafia family. The family who adopted a kid just charged with murder a couple months ago. So what would you do? Pull the college kid over you already searched? Or let everything play out? If he let everything play out, then what? Call in backup or do it yourself? Keep the kid in your sight or forget about the kid and go for the mafia guy who might be the infamous IU drug dealer? Those were the questions I was asking myself as I made a left and was now only about a mile from the parking spot.

*If I'm Campbell, I'm not letting the college kid out of my sight. I call in backup to make the arrests, but in terms of actually making the arrests, I'm following the kid. I would even try and work with the kid. The mafia guy is the big fish, and if I already baited the big fish with the smaller fish, there would be no need to go after both when you got the big one in sight.*

Time was running out, so I had to go with my best judgment. I had to assume Campbell would follow me and backup was going to be called. Which meant I'd have to lose Campbell on top of avoiding the backup before the arrests. *Campbell following me is out of my control, but how do I avoid the backup?*

I was a couple blocks away and cringed when I saw the Suburban parked on the opposite side of the street from where I was going to park. It was the same setup as last time. Which meant that as soon as I parked, they would drive me to the bar and park around back. I started to mentally document things as I tried to think on the go. *The Suburban is their getaway car, and they will park it out back. From a timing standpoint, that Suburban will still have the drugs in it. Meaning, the drugs are going to be parked out back, unless they brought them inside. So if they brought them inside, they will bring them to the secret room that you can only get to from the bathroom or, again, out back. The getaway car, entrance to the secret room, all the drugs, they are all going to be out back!*

I knew their entire plan. I had done the drug game long enough to know the ins and outs. It wasn't that hard to think like Dante because we were in, pathetically, similar situations. We both dealt drugs for years, both had our right-hand man stop helping, and both had cops knowing everything but unable to do anything about it. Except now the cops could do something about it, and I was the one who had control of that. I was going to have to be the one calling the shots.

I pulled up to the street and parked the car. I looked over and saw Terry sitting in the driver's seat, but he wasn't looking at me. I couldn't see Campbell's car, but I could almost feel him watching me. *He's going to search the Mercedes. Or at least someone will.* I had to make a decision right then and there. *Do I try and work with the cops or just hope they figure it out?* They had figured it out up until this point, but it took a couple pushes from me. I couldn't afford for them not to figure it out this time.

I quickly flipped open the phone and opened up a new text message and started to type.

Message to : 10:43 p.m.: Go through the back door of the bar and y

All of a sudden a knock on the glass came from outside. I flinched as I dropped the phone into my lap. It was Lamar nodding for me to get out of the car. He opened the door as I turned off the car and stalled, acting like I was trying to find my phone.

"Who the fuck's that?" Lamar said holding his hand out.

"Jesus Christ, you scared the shit out of me. It's the burner phone. I was about to text Terry, he told me to wait for the call."

"We've been here for five minutes."

"My bad, I was waiting for a call."

I faked like I'd found the phone and shoved my empty hand into my right pocket. Lamar turned his back and started walking toward the Suburban. I made sure the door was unlocked as I got out of the car. Before I shut the door, I leaned inside and turned off the headlights and put the open flip phone on the driver's seat facing up toward the window. Before I shut the door, I realized turning off the headlights also turned the lights off inside the car. Meaning while the door was open, the lights were still off. *If I keep the door cracked open, then I don't have to hope they'll peep through the window to read the phone; they'll just open the door and grab it!*

I left the door slightly cracked as I turned around. Lamar was already getting in the passenger seat, and Terry was saying something to him. *No one saw it.* I walked over and got in the Suburban, and Terry did a U-turn past the Mercedes and down the street toward the bar. I started to turn around to see if I could see Campbell, but didn't want to be obvious, so pretended like I was reaching to put my seat belt on. Neither Terry nor Lamar said anything to me the short four-to-five-block drive to the bar. We pulled into the parking lot, went around the bar, and parked out back. Everything felt the same planning-wise from the first time I was at the bar, except when we got out of the car, I could hear music blaring from inside.

"Walk in like you are coming to the bar, and wait for the signal. You remember, right?"

*I can't just walk in with you?*

"Uh, yeah, the bathroom thing, got it."

We walked around front and there was a small line of five to six people taking their IDs out and showing them to the bouncer to get in. They were all upper twenties and dressed like they were going clubbing. Girls were in short, tight skirts, and the guys were wearing either button-downs or a sport coat. Terry gave the bouncer a fist pound as they moved inside.

After about two minutes, I got inside. The place was packed. Like Friday-or-Saturday-night-in-Bloomington packed, which I was not expecting. I looked around for Terry and Lamar but couldn't see either of them. I walked around and made my way through what seemed to be a big birthday group along the wall. I felt awkward walking around aimlessly, so I went up to the bar to grab a water. Brittney was at the other end of the bar pouring a group of guys their drinks. As she moved to plug in their order, she looked up and saw me. Immediately, she looked around, almost for a reason why I was there. She motioned for me to leave the bar as she walked over.

"What are you doing here?" she yelled over the music.

"Terry and Lamar brought me."

"You shouldn't be here. Just leave!"

"No, Brittney, you should leave!"

"What?"

I looked around to see if anyone was watching. I felt terrible that she was trapped bartending for a psychopath while the police were hopefully closed in. I knew I couldn't explain everything to her, so it was a lost cause, but this was her chance to get out too.

"Can't explain, but trust me, Brittney!"

"What are you talking about! Why should I leave?"

"Just trust me!" I snapped back, staring right into her eyes.

"I'm not leaving, Cory."

The other bartender passed by and gave Brittney a tap on the butt, asking for help. Brittney did a double take at the bartender then back to me. She stared right into my eyes as only she could. There was this emptiness in her stare. The same hollowness Em saw in my eyes. She had accepted not having hope, without knowing I was her only hope. Looking into her eyes brought everything into reality. This wasn't some game of hide-and-go-seek. This was my life on the line and hers as well.

Brittney walked away, and I grabbed a glass of water from the other bartender. About a minute later, I made eye contact with some security guard and he nodded upstairs and gave me a thumbs-up. *Pretty blatant signal.*

I started making my way through the crowd, but the place was so loud that people couldn't hear me saying "excuse me" trying to get by. I turned back to see if Brittney was watching me, and out of the corner of my eye, I noticed Campbell walking into the bar. *Yes! He followed me! Shit, but has he seen me? I can't let him see me. Wait, can I?* I looked at Brittney, trying to make eye contact with her one last time before taking a quick peek at Campbell. The security guard was still standing by the stairs, waiting for me. Once I made my way through the crowd I walked up to him, and without saying anything, he switched places with me and started to walk through the crowd toward the front. As he walked by me, I couldn't help but turn around and see if there were any other cops or exit strategies I could find. I gave one last glance over at Brittney, but as I did, I made eye contact with Campbell, who had made his way halfway toward me. *Fuck! Is it over? Wait, is this a good thing? I want him to think it's a good thing, right? Fuck it, I've already made it this far, we're in it together now.*

I glanced to my right briefly to see if I could see Terry or Lamar. Before turning my back to Campbell, I gave him a subtle head nod up toward the stairs. Without missing a beat, he nodded his head down indicating he understood. *He must have seen the phone! Shit, this could work!* Excitement took control of me as I turned around to walk up the steps and eventually took the right down the hallway toward the bathroom. *Now what? How the fuck do I escape this?* The bathroom had one guy washing his hands, three guys pissing, and an older black man sitting by the door holding out mints and paper towels. *Shit, what was the line I say again?*

"Hey, we are out of toilet paper downstairs."

"Sorry, son, didn't hear you. You say soap?"

He turned toward me and I saw his name tag. *Tim, right.*

"Hey Tim, sorry, I said we are out of soap downstairs, can I grab some?"

Tim nodded his head down, ironically like Campbell did moments earlier, and got up to unlock the closet door. The closet door opened, and suddenly I realized Campbell wouldn't have any clue where to look if he even found his way into the bathroom. *Do I even want him to find the hidden room?* I gave the guy a pat on the shoulder and turned on the light in the closet. I saw the broom against the wall on the right, and without really weighing the pros and cons, moved the broom so part of it stuck in the door to keep it partially open. But as I pulled on the doorknob, I heard the click of the door shutting and locking completely. *Shit*!

I noticed that parts of the bristles of the broom were sticking out the other end, but couldn't do anything about it anymore. I turned around and moved the soap bottles on the left and pressed the black button. The toilet paper on the back wall shook a bit as I pushed the wall open. I started to shut the door behind me, but stopped to leave it cracked open in case I needed to get out or I wanted Campbell to come in.

"Cory, welcome back. Can I get you a drink?" Dante asked as I walked up the steps.

"Uh, yeah, sure, I'll take a whisky ginger," I said confidently, signifying nothing was wrong.

"Lamar, whisky ginger," Dante stated as he stood up from the round table to shake my hand.

"Sorry you had to come up here. Had some difficulties with our normal spot."

"Yeah, that's what Terry said. What happened?"

Dante looked at me for a second, trying to read my face.

*Uh-oh.*

"Nothing new, really. You know, Cory, when we talked about a month ago, one thing I remember saying was to not make things more difficult. You know that, right?" Dante said as he walked toward the bar to grab my drink.

"Um, yeah, I remember that pretty well too. But what do you mean?"

Dante grabbed my drink and walked toward me. I could see the four duffel bags next to Lamar's feet by the bar. I was still standing at the top of the stairs leading down into the bathroom closet as Dante went to hand me the whisky ginger. I stuck my hand out to grab the drink, but before I could grab it, Dante swung his arm forward to smash the glass across my head. I tried to duck, but that only stopped the momentum briefly as the glass shattered over the top of my head. I took a step back, but almost fell down the steps into the closet. I caught myself on the railing, but as soon as I regained balance, Dante pulled me toward him and pushed a gun into my forehead. I slowly started to stand up, making sure not to make any sudden movements. My head didn't hurt that badly from the glass of whisky, but I knew the last time a gun was in my face all the pain I had went away briefly, only to come back later.

"Well, then why the fuck do you make things more difficult for us!" Dante screamed, raising his voice to another level.

The look in his eyes wasn't that of a composed, arrogant man. He seemed desperate and borderline insane. He always had this poised business feel to him, like there was nothing he hadn't seen before, and he knew exactly what to do at all times. But not now. He was furious. *Fuck, he might actually shoot me!*

"Dante, I don't know what you're talking about!"

"You know exactly what I'm fucking talking about, Cory!" Dante shouted. He pressed the gun harder against my forehead before pulling it back and motioning it toward the left wall.

I turned toward Terry and looked over his bald head and saw four TV monitors. First one was showing what looked to be a live feed of the bar parking lot, second one of the inside of the bar, the third one was the inside of the bathroom, and the last one was paused.

"Far right screen, Cory. Can you explain this?"

*What the fuck does he have recorded?*

He hit play, and it was the video footage of the drop spot. The time stamp at the bottom said 9:45:25 p.m. The video ran for about 15 seconds of nothing. All I could see was the driveway with leaves blowing across the street. Suddenly, you see two cop cars drive by. The second car slams on the brakes, reverses, stops, then turns right into the drop spot. The cop gets out of the car and starts searching for something. He radios to someone about something and then starts to walk up the hill and out of the picture. Another cop walks up from the street, gets in the parked car, and pulls it away, leaving the one officer in the forest.

"So you know nothing about this?"

"No, why would I know anything about it?"

"Well, because we've been using that spot since long before you even came to Indiana, Cory. And then what? Coincidentally, the day after a couple of Bloomington's finest stop by your little house is the day one of our spots gets paid a visit?"

*Fuck, he knows about the search! How?*

# THIRTY-NINE

**I STARED AT DANTE, SPEECHLESS.** I didn't know whether to confess or lie. When Lamar had the gun in my face, I was motionless, but could tell he wouldn't shoot me. Dante didn't have that look. This wasn't a scare tactic.

"So I'm going to ask you one more time, Cory. And please, for your own sake, don't make this more difficult than it needs to be," Dante said, crossing his arms and holding the gun across his chest, waiting for me to talk.

"I can see how it looks, I really can. But remember when I told you about my freshman-year roommate's mom calling in? Well, that's why they searched my place. Because two of the other five names that mom gave, the cops searched their apartments and found drugs. So I guess a judge must have thought that was credible enough to search the remaining three places."

"A judge?"

"No, not a judge! Well, I mean, yes, a judge—don't judges create warrants? I have no clue, I'm just guessing. I don't know anything, I swear. That's only my prediction."

"What did they find?"

"Nothing. Well, my roommate's fake ID and a couple thousand in cash. But they took the fake and . . ."

"I don't give a fuck about your fucking roommate! You're saying they didn't find a single drug, the money you owe us tonight, nothing?" Dante said, cutting me off.

"Nothing, I swear to God. You think I would be here now if they did?"

"Yes! That's exactly why I think you are here, Cory! And that's why I think they were fucking *there*!" he barked out, pointing the gun at the TV monitor.

"I didn't say anything, I swear to God! I wasn't even there—I was at class! I can prove it. We took a quiz."

"A fucking quiz? A quiz will prove to me you didn't talk to the cops?"

"Dante, I swear to God. My roommate called me while I was in class, I can show you my phone."

"So you weren't there, and they still didn't find anything. Then where is everything? Where is my money, Cory?"

"Well, right now it's in the car parked a couple blocks away. You told me to keep it in the car. But like the drugs and my own money, I keep it stored in an apartment building I rented off campus."

Dante turned around and took a couple steps away before turning back to me.

"You weren't home, so told them nothing . . . ," he stated as he glanced over at Terry, almost for validation that he was hearing everything correctly.

"You brought all of the money and material to an apartment building, so they found nothing . . . ," he added as he looked at me.

"Yet, here we are, Cory. Police officers," he said, pointing to the video recording, "at our drop spot. The drop spot that has never had a single sniff of a pig in over 10 years. And I'm supposed to believe you because you took a quiz and your roommate called you?"

"I don't know what to tell you. If I was there and they found something, I would be arrested and wouldn't be here. If I wasn't there and they found something, they would have found me and arrested me already. If I had told them something, they wouldn't go scope out some random street in the woods, they would have gone to your house or wherever and arrested you. I don't even know your full name. I don't even know if Dante is your real name. I didn't say anything to them—I swear to God, I didn't!" I pleaded out of desperation.

It was all true. I hadn't said anything. *Bo did.* I wasn't arrested. *Yet.* I didn't have to act at all; I was being sincere. Dante looked over at the TV monitors one more time as the video of a now empty drop spot kept playing. My hands and legs were shaking as I wondered whether or not Dante was going to accept that answer. I turned toward the video monitor and noticed the third screen. I looked closer and glanced over to Dante to see if he had noticed too. *Campbell is in the bathroom! Right down these steps! And the drugs are right there by the bar!* I looked at Dante then at the monitor to see Campbell walking to a urinal.

"It just doesn't add up, Cory. But the thing is, I believe you. You're a smart kid, you really are, but I don't like when things don't add up. That's not how I do business. If things don't add up, I make changes, and I fix them."

Dante took a couple steps toward me and pointed the gun directly at my chest. My body went stiff like it did the first time. *Oh my God, he's going to shoot me! Should I scream for Campbell? Fuck, should I tell him about Campbell?*

"Let's fix it, then! I'll do whatever you want! The cops got information from a fucking mom because other people fucked up. The police saw a chance to try and catch me, but they missed! Now they have nothing! It's, it's like you said, right? Cops don't know what they are looking for. They just look until someone messes up! I haven't messed up! You haven't messed up! We just need to find a new spot! That's all we need! A new spot and to not overreact or tell the cops anything."

Dante looked at me and started to smile.

"Overreact? You know, Cory. We could have been friends, you and I. We are very similar people at very different stages in our lives. Your innocence is respectable. It will take you a very long way in this life."

Dante lowered his gun and put it on the table. I let out a sigh and reached back to grab my head. I felt a little wetness and pulled my hand down. *I'm bleeding?* I softly rubbed the back of my head and felt shards of glass in my hair. As I pulled my left hand down to see how much glass was on my hand, I looked up at the TV monitors and saw Campbell pulling his gun out on the bathroom attendant down the steps. *Holy shit, it's happening now!*

I took a couple steps toward the bar to prevent Dante from looking at the monitors.

"Do you have a towel up here? Sorry, my head is bleeding pretty badly, and I'm getting a little light-headed."

Dante turned his head around toward me as he bit his upper lip and took a step toward the bar.

"These are for you, Cory. It's a bigger order. Terry, you told him, right?" Dante said, softly kicking the duffel bags as he stepped over them and walked around the bar.

"Yup. He's got the new phone. All set," Terry replied from his place at the round table.

I looked above Terry and saw the bathroom guy standing with one arm raised and the other shuffling for his keys or something in his pocket.

"Here's for your boo-boo," Dante said, tossing a towel to me as he rolled his eyes.

Lamar let out a forced laugh. As soon as I grabbed the towel, I put it on my head and turned toward the TV monitor to see the bathroom guy opening the closet door for Campbell. With my hands shaking, I turned around and glanced at the door leading to the back stairwell past Dante. *Run, Cory! Run!*

"What, you don't believe me? You fucking broke a glass over my head," I said to Dante, taking a couple swift steps toward him.

I lowered my head so Dante could see the bleeding. Dante let out an irritated sigh, and right as he took a step to look at my head, I kicked one of the duffel bags at his legs and bolted toward the back door. Dante fell on top of the bags as I heard Terry and Lamar make sudden moves. I crashed into the back door and my momentum flung it open. I started to run down the black metal stairs, but heard a gunshot followed by a piercingly loud *ting* noise inside the stairwell. I lost my footing and stumbled down the first couple steps. I instinctively covered the back of my head, trying to protect myself from the gunshots as my body smashed into the wall of the first landing. Right before the upstairs door shut behind me, another gunshot ricocheted off the ceiling, illuminating the stairwell with sparks. The flash caused my body to tighten up as I grabbed the railing and pulled myself down the next set of steps.

"Nobody move!" I heard Campbell yell as he kicked open the bathroom wall-door upstairs.

The top stairwell door opened as another round of gunshots sounded, but this time, it didn't echo inside the stairwell. I could hear pounding footsteps above me as I practically jumped down the last eight steps, but right as I kicked open the outside door, I remembered the text message I'd left. *If Campbell saw the phone, then, shit, Campbell's backup is outside!* The outside door flew open, but without looking, I bolted the opposite way toward the kitchen.

"Stop right there!" came a voice from outside.

I yanked open the kitchen door and made a run for it. Before the kitchen door shut behind me, I heard another gunshot from inside the stairwell. My body collapsed onto the ground, but when I looked behind me to see who was shooting at me, I saw one of the cops pointing his gun up the stairs. I bear-crawled a couple feet before I regained my balance and continued to weave through the virtually empty kitchen. I threw open the kitchen door and nearly decapitated some bartender walking down the hallway. The music must have been loud enough, because no one had moved or reacted to what was going on. I collided into a group of girls as I ripped through the crowd. I turned my head around but didn't see anyone chasing me, so I cut through the opening of the circle bar.

"Come with me! Now!" I screamed, running past Brittney.

Without even waiting for a response, I grabbed her arm and kept running behind the bar. I looked back one more time, but still didn't see anyone following me. *They must have caught whoever was coming down the stairs!* Brittney resisted a little, but I yanked her forward as we picked up speed. We ran out the other opening of the bar then out the front door. Brittney smashed into the security guy, but before he could react, I shoved him over the black rope he was holding. We both looked around to see if the cops were out front.

"This way!" Brittney yelled as she pointed right down the street.

I let go of her arm and we both went sprinting away from the parking lot, down the sidewalk, and turned on the first street. I saw a taxi a couple buildings down driving away from us.

"Taxi!" I yelled, sprinting ahead of Brittney.

The taxi stopped, and once I caught up, I opened the door. Two seconds later, Brittney hopped in and I jumped in after.

"Just drive that way!" I shouted at the cab driver.

I turned to look out the window. As soon as we passed the alley, you could see the parking lot of the bar.

"What the fuck, Cory!"

"Look!" I interrupted, pointing out the window at the bar.

We both watched as two cop cars went flying into the parking lot with their lights on. The back door of the bar was still wide open with what looked like another two or three cop cars surrounding it. About three seconds later, the taxi passed a warehouse, and we couldn't see anything anymore. I looked out the rear window. *No one is following us!*

"What the fuck happened, Cory?"

"It's all over, Brittney. It's. All over," I said, trying to catch my breath.

"What do you mean? What did you just do?"

"Cops were on to me. They searched my house yesterday but didn't find anything. They were tailing me tonight, so I brought them straight to Dante, but right before they came into that hidden room, I ran."

"What happened to your head?"

"Dante hit me with a glass. But Brittney, listen! This is our chance. Everyone in there is getting arrested. Everyone. Dante, Lamar, Terry, that other guy you ran into. They all are. Dante had the drugs there, Brittney!"

Brittney was rattled. Her eyes wide open, she was unsure what to think.

"All his money is there too, Cory . . ."

"Exactly! Money and drugs. He's done! Finished! We're free, Brittney! We have to get as far away from here as possible."

"Cory, my money is there! My life is there! All the money Eric saved for me! It's all at that bar!"

"Fuck. Well, what would you rather have? A new start or that money? You can make more money. We can't go back! It's over!"

"How can I make more money, Cory? I'm a 24-year-old with no high school degree! You don't know me! My brother is in jail for murder, and my former boss and practical father is getting arrested for drug dealing! I have *nothing!*"

"Shut the fuck up, Brittney! Jesus Christ, you *had* nothing! You were a prisoner to those guys! You even said it yourself. Stop thinking so short term. We both get second chances!"

Brittney was breathing heavily as she unwrapped her bartending earpiece and tossed it out the cab.

"They can't hurt you anymore. They can't hurt me anymore. I'm done dealing, and you are done working for that monster."

The cab driver kept his head facing forward, too frightened to look at us. I turned around again but still didn't see any sign of cars or people following us. I had no clue where we were, but the cab driver had driven straight through three green lights before making a left onto some busy street. We must have been two miles away already.

"How do you know we're free? How do you know they won't catch us?"

"I don't know. For your sake, you're free. They have nothing on you and in all honesty probably don't care, since they already have Dante, and Terry, and Lamar, and, well—and Eric too."

"And you?"

"Don't worry about me. I'm hoping I'm OK, too. It's a long story, but in the end, they don't have anything on me. No drugs, no money, didn't catch me in the act. They have no proof."

I looked down to see Brittney's hands rubbing her legs out of nervousness. We drove another five minutes or so not saying anything to each other. I couldn't catch my breath, but kept trying to take deep breaths anyway. The cab driver didn't seem to mind driving us around. He was getting paid to go wherever he wanted.

"Now what?"

"I don't know. Act like nothing happened, I guess. I'll go to Bloomington; you go back to your apartment."

"I can't go home. It's one of Dante's places. I don't want the police finding me there."

I looked at Brittney and she looked up at me. It was outrageous how many times we were both in this situation. Lost, confused, not sure what to do, staring into each other's eyes. But this time was different. This time our uncertainty wasn't because someone else was controlling us; it was because we didn't know what to do. We had our own choices to make, and neither one of us was used to that.

I reached out my left hand and put it palm up on the middle seat. Without hesitation, Brittney moved her right hand on top of mine and squeezed.

"You can come to Bloomington. Another long story, but I have an apartment there. You can stay there for a little."

Brittney tilted her head and raised her eyebrows, questioning what I had suggested. I let out a well-overdue laugh and let go of her hand.

"Don't worry, I'm not asking you to live with me. I still live at the fraternity; the apartment is for you."

Brittney looked at me even more confused than before, but then back down at the ground and slowly started to nod her head.

"Excuse me, sir. Can you take us to Bloomington?"

"Yes. Yes, sure," the cab driver responded in broken English.

We hopped on the highway and started driving to Bloomington. It still hadn't sunk in that plan B had worked. Or at least, for the moment. I was leaving the Mercedes and the burner phone in Indy, but Brittney was leaving everything. Her job, her money, her clothes, her home, her so-called family. She had nothing now. She stared out the window with a tear going down her face. I decided against trying to talk to her, and I just let her decompress from what had happened. *Shit, I need to decompress from what's happened.*

I reached down and pulled out my phone and saw a text from Emily.

11:41 p.m.: I'm glad we got to talk yesterday. It was good to hear you sound like you again.

11:42 p.m.: Have a good weekend Cor!

Neither Brittney nor I spoke the rest of the cab ride home. We got to my apartment and walked up the front steps. I walked around and cleaned up a little while Brittney went to the bathroom.

"Do you need anything?" I asked, handing her a cup of water.

"No, I'm OK. Thanks."

"OK, unless you need anything else, I think I'm going to walk to ATO."

"And then what?"

"I haven't really thought that far. You can stay here as long as you want."

"I don't know what to do," Brittney said bleakly.

I took a couple steps toward her and put my arm on her shoulder.

"You are a stunningly beautiful, smart, witty girl. You carry yourself so effortlessly and when you are in a good mood," I said, lifting her chin up so she was looking at me, "you have this soft confidence that can't be taught. You'll be fine. I think you'll be able to figure out what you want to do. Take a couple days, weeks, however long you want. This place is yours for as long as you need it. OK?"

"You're so cheesy, you know that?" Brittney replied with a smirk on her face as she wiped a tear away.

"Works, doesn't it?"

"Somehow."

Brittney grabbed my arm and we gave each other a big hug.

"Thank you, Cory. I really mean it, thank you."

We held the hug for a while before I walked into the kitchen and got the spare set of keys the landlord gave me.

"These are for you. There is literally nothing in here, so enjoy."

"Perfect. Thanks."

"I'll come back tomorrow morning, alright?"

"Alright."

I gave her one last quick hug and kiss on the forehead and walked out the front door. I knew I was leaving Brittney with all the money in the safes under the bed, but I knew she wasn't going to take anything. She had nowhere to go, no car to get there, and wasn't going to be able to open the safes anyway.

I walked down the steps and started heading south down Walnut. I reached into my pocket to grab my phone to call for a ride, but stopped at the thought of talking to anyone. It was a beautiful 65-degree clear night, and all I wanted to do was be by myself. No explanations, no one yelling at me for ATO getting searched, not being followed, not being traced, no gunshots, no running, nothing. I wanted peace. I was at peace. For the first time in a long, long time, I was at peace. I knew there was a good chance a police officer would question me in the future, but they had nothing on me. Dante wasn't going to rat on people he sold down to. That would make him look even worse and wouldn't help him in any way. Also, Dante knew that I knew about Eric. If he ratted about me, I could just say Dante orchestrated the murder Eric committed.

I kept walking down Walnut and took a left on Third. Walking home didn't even feel real. It felt like I was coming back to school as an alumnus. Looking around, everything felt like a memory. Almost like a dream. My whole night felt like a dream. Staging a sting operation, involved in a shootout, running from the cops, it all seemed fake. It was going to be hard to walk away from this like nothing had ever happened. Because it did happen—it wasn't fake, it was just over now. Nothing else would change or even did change. The whole time, I was the only one who was changing. It was a strange feeling, not having to hope for something. I had my life back. I had Em as a friend back. I had helped Brittney get her life back. There wasn't any need to hope for something, because it had all come true. It wasn't a dream—it was a nightmare, and I was just waking up.

I laughed to myself as I walked up the steps of ATO. *Well, that nightmare fucking sucked.*

# FORTY

**OFFICER WOUNDED DURING A DRUG BUST AT INDIANAPOLIS NIGHTCLUB:**
Three men were arrested and charged with various drug offenses at Legacy's Nightclub late Friday night after a yearlong investigation uncovered that narcotics distribution was taking place at the establishment, police said. For more than a year, members of the Bloomington Police Department, Monroe County Prosecutor's Office, Marion County Prosecutor's Office, and Indianapolis Metropolitan Police Department investigated activity taking place at Legacy's Nightclub in downtown Indianapolis, Lt. Mark Andreesen said.

According to police, Officer Donald Campbell took fire while uncovering a private room on the second floor of the downtown nightclub. As a result, one individual, Terry Justice, 39, was arrested for aggregated assault, and all three individuals, Justice, Dante Marino, 36, and Lamar Graham, 27, were arrested and charged with possession of marijuana, cocaine, heroin, and MDMA with intent to distribute. During the bust, over four million dollars, three vehicles, 27 kilos of cocaine, 42 pounds of marijuana, and "various quantities" of heroin and MDMA were seized, Andreesen said.

No other employees of the business were arrested or accused of drug activity, but Legacy's is now being investigated by the Department of Criminal Justice for the "blatant dealing of narcotics in their establishment," Andreesen said. In addition, the bar is being charged for having "less than premium alcohol in bottles that were labeled premium alcohol," Andreesen said.

As if getting four million seized by the cops along with a gazillion felonies worth of drugs wasn't bad enough, the "less than premium alcohol in bottles that were labeled premium alcohol" has to be a dagger. *Hahaha! Suckers!* In all honesty, that could be one of the funnier additions to a police beat I had ever read and would ever read. Just such a fuck you from the cops. *How did they even find that out? But whoa! Campbell got shot! If it was serious they would have said something; it just said* wounded.

I drove over to the apartment in the morning and found a note in the kitchen from Brittney.

You weren't kidding, you literally have nothing here. Realized I don't have your real phone number so went to a friend's apartment. 317 684 1865 – B

I grabbed the note, put it in my pocket, and went into the bedroom to make sure the safes were there. I grabbed the first one and walked down to put it in my car. I went back up and grabbed the second one but first, opened it and pulled out the manila envelope I was supposed to give to Dante. *An extra $119,000, all mine!* I started to laugh to myself as I put it back into the safe. I walked down the stairs toward my car, but stopped halfway. *Wait, extra money. This is the extra money! This can be Brittney's extra money!*

I walked back up into the apartment and took out the envelope and put it on the kitchen counter before walking the safe out to the car. Then I remembered I forgot my backpack in the apartment the night before, so went up a third time to grab it. As I walked down the steps I heard a deep voice coming from the parking lot.

"Moving in?"

I flinched out of fear as I saw Campbell standing by the Cherokee with his left arm in a sling.

"Nah, just at a friend's place," I said, walking down the rest of the steps.

"Friend's place. Sure." Campbell replied, smiling.

"What happened there?" I asked, pointing to the sling.

"Yeah, it's nothing. Luckily the guy was chasing someone else when I got there."

"Oh, luckily," I replied, trying not to smile.

"Look, kid. I don't know how long you've been hiding this little plan of yours, but it's over now. Got it?"

"Got it. Don't have to worry about me."

Campbell looked down at the backpack in my hand and then at the car and then right at me. *Shit, I forgot there are drugs in one of the safes!* I tried to stay cool, but I had gone too far and was too close to the end to have this be the way I got busted. Campbell must have seen right through me.

"I'm not here to search you, kid. Already tried that song and dance."

I stood still trying not to ruin the mood.

"You made things pretty difficult for us, but I got to say, without you, I don't think we ever would have caught those pricks," Campbell admitted, sticking his right hand out to shake hands.

"Thank you," he said as we firmly shook hands.

"No, thank you, officer."

"Definitely not your plan the whole time, was it?"

"A plan B never hurt, right?" I replied.

"I guess not."

We stood there looking at each other for a second.

"Well, Cory. Hopefully we don't cross paths ever again."

"I can promise you we won't."

"And don't do shit like this anyway. What the hell were you even thinking? You're a little kid. Get your college degree. Don't be dumb next time. Got it?"

"Got it."

He nodded his head and slapped my shoulder.

"Friend's place, huh?" he said, leaning forward to look up at the apartment. "Well, take care, Cory."

He turned around and started walking to his car parked at the end of the lot. It was over. I had done it. No more Dante, no more Campbell. Seeing a police officer walk away and not being worried was once a normality but was now an unforgettable feeling. A feeling that the average person felt every day. A feeling of freedom.

I got into my car and went back to ATO. I gave Bo the couple ounces of pot as a gift and then walked into the bathroom. *My last drug deal*, I thought as I flushed the ounce or so of coke and pills down the toilet. I grabbed my phone to see what time it was: 1:22 p.m., Saturday, April

13, 2012. I walked into Cutty's room to see Bo and Cutty smoking and gambling on their game of *Madden*. I couldn't help but laugh, thinking about the irony of the situation. *Drugs and gambling.* I grabbed a beer from their mini-fridge then took a seat on the chair and put my feet up on the table. Neither of the two even reacted to me walking into the room. I looked down at my phone again, but still, no one had texted me. *No one is going to text you, Cory, it's over.* I took a long sip of the beer, smiling, looking up at the ceiling. *Thank you.*

*1:23 p.m.: It was good to talk to you too, Em. I'll be coming home over summer break. Let me know what your plan is. I owe you a dinner.*

# Acknowledgments

For helping me from start to finish and spending a lot of hours answering my naïve and ignorant questions, I owe many thanks to Bethany Brown and everyone at the Cadence Group.

For listening to my stupid and vague ideas, thank you to Gwyn Snider for turning the cover and overall layout into a creative and artistic success.

For helping a kid who legitimately doesn't know how to spell write a book without errors, I would like to thank Melissa Stein, Melanie Zimmerman, and Microsoft Word's auto-correct.

For reading this manuscript in its early stages and sharing thoughts and ideas to make it the finished product you hold in your hands, I owe a beer to Kevin Brinkman, Lindsey Arenberg, Pat Thomas, Keegan Tiernan, Brett Tomfohrde, Tommy Chase, David Kiyosaki, Max Messina, Tom Owens, Jimmy Vondrasek, Luke Verdin and my two brothers Danny and Matt Connor (just kidding on the beers, but serious on the thank yous).

To all publishing professionals who didn't respond to my emails, told me it wasn't the right time, said it wasn't a fit for you, and said my platform wasn't big enough to waste your time, thanks for driving me to finish this in spite of you. If you're reading this, you know who you are.

To my entire family, Mom, Dad, Laura, Danny, and Buzz, thanks for inspiring me over the years and being the greatest family I could ever ask for.

And finally, to the coolest person I've ever met, the person who continued to motivate me even when the hate started pouring in, I owe the greatest debt—a debt I can never repay—to you Brigid. Thanks for being you.

CPSIA information can be obtained
at www.ICGtesting.com
Printed in the USA
FFOW03n1725160417
34603FF

9 780998 476100